MAP OF THE
MARVELOUS LAND OF OZ
Drawn by Prof. Wogglebug T.E.

L. Frank Baum (1856–1919), poster published by the
George M. Hill Company, 1900.
Courtesy the Alexander Mitchell Library, Aberdeen, South Dakota.

W. W. NORTON & COMPANY

NEW YORK • LONDON

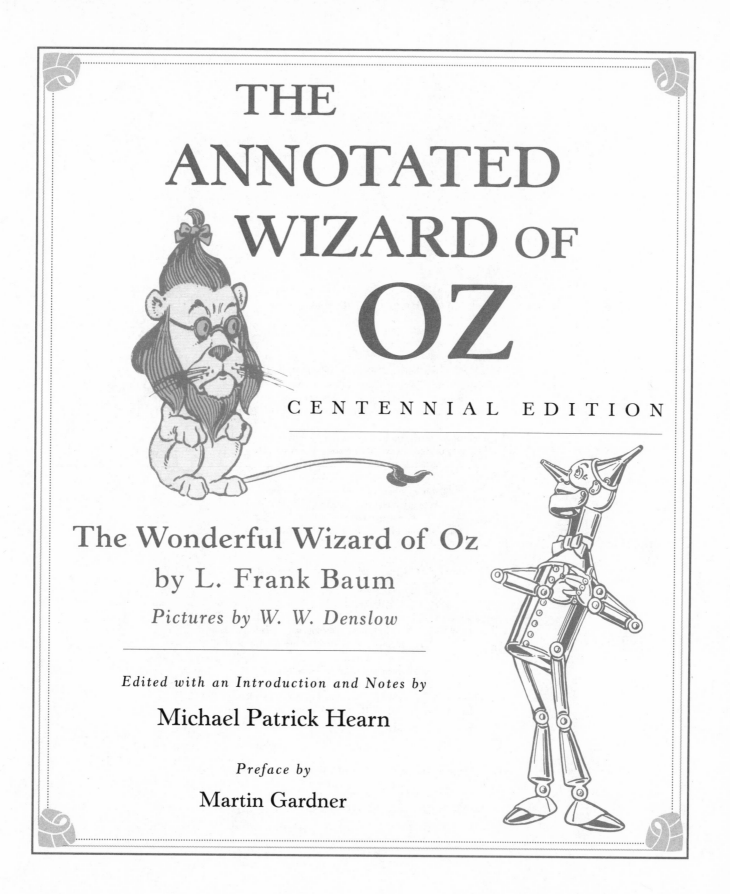

THE ANNOTATED WIZARD OF OZ

CENTENNIAL EDITION

The Wonderful Wizard of Oz
by L. Frank Baum

Pictures by W. W. Denslow

Edited with an Introduction and Notes by

Michael Patrick Hearn

Preface by

Martin Gardner

Unless otherwise indicated, all of the full-color photographs have been
provided by Zindman/Fremont, Fine Art Photography, New York. They are
also responsible for the black-and-white illustrations on pp. xxvii, xxxxi,
xxxvi, li, lxxviii, lxxxvi, lxxxvii, 64, 114, 135, 146, 235, and 360 (top).

For information about permission to reproduce selections from this book,
write to Permissions, W. W. Norton & Company, Inc.,
500 Fifth Avenue, New York, NY 10110

The text of ths book is composed in Granjon
with the display set in Horley Old Style
Composition by Sue Carlson
Manufacturing by R. R. Donnelley & Sons Company
Book design by JAM Design

Library of Congress Cataloging-in-Publication Data

Baum, L. Frank (Lyman Frank), 1856–1919.
[Wizard of Oz]
The annotated Wizard of Oz : the wonderful Wizard of Oz / by L. Frank Baum ;
pictures by W.W. Denslow ; with an introduction, notes, and bibliography
by Michael Patrick Hearn ; preface by Martin Gardner.—Centennial ed.
p. cm.
Includes bibliographical references (p.).
ISBN 0-393-04992-2
1. Oz (Imaginary place)—Fiction. 2. Wizards—Fiction. I. Denslow, W. W.
(William Wallace), 1856–1915. II. Hearn, Michael Patrick. III. Title.

PS3503.A723 W59 2000
813'.4—dc21   00-031867

W. W. Norton & Company, Inc., 500 Fifth Avenue, New York, N.Y. 10110
www.wwnorton.com

W. W. Norton & Company Ltd., 15 Carlisle Street, London WID 3BS

FOR CYNTHIA, COLLEEN, AND CHRISTOPHER

Acknowledgments

HANKS are due to everyone who contributed in one way or another to the original and the present editions of *The Annotated Wizard of Oz*: Philadelphia Andrews, Josh and Betty Baum, Robert A. Baum, Robert A. Baum, Jr., Ruth S. Britton, Willard Carroll, Bruce and Gail Crockett, Gregory K. Dreicer, Joan Farnsworth, Doris Frohnsdorff, John Fricke, Matilda Jewell Gage, Michael Gessel, David L. Greene, Douglas G. Greene, James E. Haff, Margaret Hamilton, Peter E. Hanff, Edith and C. Warren Hollister, David Kirschner, Nancy Tystad Koupal, Bernhard Larsen, Russell P. MacFall, Daniel P. Mannix, Ozma Baum Mantele, Patrick Maund, Dick Martin, Dorothy Curtiss Maryott, Natalie Mather, David Maxine, Fred M. Meyer, Brian Nielsen, Gita Dorothy Morena, Annrea Neill, Grace and Hank Niles, Jay Scarfone, Justin G. Schiller, Betsy Shirley, Lynne and Dan Smith, William Stillman, Mark Swartz, Raymond Terry Tatum, Brenda Baum Turner, Sally Roesch Wagner, Pauline and Robert Walker, and Joseph Yranski. I am also indebted to the following institutions for their generous aid in the research and illustration of these books: Special Collections, Syracuse University Library; Brandywine River Museum, Chadds Ford, Pennsylvania; Chicago Historical Society; Columbia University Libraries; Dakotah Prairie Museum, Aberdeen, South Dakota; George Eastman House; Houghton Library, Harvard University; Albert R. Mann Library at Cornell University; Metro-Goldwyn-Mayer, Inc.; History Department, Minneapolis Public Library; Alexander Mitchell Library, Aberdeen, South Dakota; Museum of the City of New York; Arents Tobacco Collection, Donnell Central Children's Room, Prints and

Drawings Division, and Billy Rose Theatre Collection of the New York Public Library; the William Allan Neilson Library, Smith College; South Dakota State Historical Society; Time Inc.; United States Military Academy Library, West Point, New York; Library of Congress; and Copyright Office. I am also thankful to everyone at W. W. Norton who in some way contributed to this beautiful volume. And as always, I am especially grateful to Martin Gardner, who has kindly provided a new preface and was responsible not only for the 1973 edition but for the current one as well.

M. P. H.

Contents

Preface

 **LMOST** every great nation has its immortal work of juvenile fantasy. In England it is Lewis Carroll's *Alice* books. Germany has Grimm's fairy tales, France has the stories by Perrault, Denmark has its Andersen. Italy's classic is *Pinocchio*. In America the classic fantasy is, of course, L. Frank Baum's *The Wizard of Oz*.

When *The Wizard* was first published, exactly one hundred years ago, children loved it, though more than half a century would pass before critics, educators, and librarians would finally recognize its merits. You might suppose that Judy Garland made the novel famous, but it was the other way around. It was Baum's imagination that made Judy famous. Today there is a flourishing Oz society, the International Wizard of Oz Club, with its whimsical annual conventions, its handsome periodical *The Baum Bugle,* and its raft of young members who are as enthusiastic about Oz as children have always been.

It was 1970 when publisher Clarkson N. Potter decided to follow my *Annotated Alice* with an *Annotated Wizard of Oz*. Would I be interested? No, I said at once. I did not feel I knew enough about Baum and Oz. Then a summer or so later came in an unsolicited pro-

L. Frank Baum, 1905.
Courtesy Fred M. Meyer.

posal for an *Annotated Wizard* by someone named Michael Patrick Hearn. He was then an English major at Bard College. Potter sent it to me for my opinion, and I suggested he sign him up. After he turned in the manuscript in person, Potter phoned to ask me if I knew that Michael was only twenty!

For many years Hearn has been working on a definitive biography of Baum. Meanwhile he has annotated Dickens's *Christmas Carol* and Twain's *Huckleberry Finn,* edited a collection of scholarly essays about Baum and a collection of Victorian fairy tales, coauthored a biography of William Wallace Denslow, *The Wizard*'s original illustrator, and written *The Porcelain Cat,* a charming fantasy of his own.

Hearn's notes, in the beautiful volume you now hold, add enormously to one's understanding of the novel's many subtleties and philosophical depths. Enhanced by *The Annotated Wizard of Oz,* we continue the journey, traveling with friends down a Yellow Brick Road, through a fantastic world of endless wonders and surprises.

—MARTIN GARDNER

Introduction to
The Annotated Wizard of Oz

FRANK BAUM knew at once he had written something special when he completed *The Wonderful Wizard of Oz* one hundred years ago, but even he could not have predicted the extraordinary history of his American fairy tale. He set out to change children's books and made a lasting contribution to American literature. The deceptively simple story of Dorothy's adventures in the marvelous Land of Oz has resonated for young and old ever since it was first published in 1900. *The Wizard of Oz* has entered American folklore. It reflected and has altered the American character. The book had sold five million copies by the time it went into the public domain in 1956, the year of its author's centenary. No one has dared estimate how many more millions have been sold since. It has been estimated that the 1939 musical based on Baum's story has been seen by more people more times than any other movie ever made. It is probably the most widely quoted film in Hollywood history (usually lines not written by L. Frank Baum). Even one who has neither read the original book nor seen the picture, if there could possibly be such a person today, is familiar with the little Kansas girl and her three remarkable companions, the Scarecrow, the Tin Woodman, and the Cowardly Lion. When the Children's Literature Association took a poll of its members in 1976 to determine the most important American children's books of the last two hundred years, *The Wizard of Oz* easily made the top ten. Its fame has not been limited to the country in which it was written. *The Wizard of Oz* today is probably the most frequently translated American children's book. Many people believe that it was the now famous movie that made *The Wizard of Oz*. They are mistaken. The picture did not even make back its initial $3 million investment during its original run, and no one at the time suspected that it would become the classic it is considered today. It was television that made the movie. Metro-Goldwyn-Mayer bought the property in the first place because *The Wizard of Oz* was already the most beloved American children's book of the twentieth century. It has also been the most reviled. It has been considered a millstone as much as a milestone in American culture.

This paradox is not surprising, for historically Americans have been notoriously careless in recognizing their own visionaries. Arguably there have been three great classic quests in American literature, Herman Melville's *Moby-Dick; or The Whale* (1851), Mark Twain's *Adventures of Huckleberry Finn* (1883), and L. Frank Baum's *The Wonderful Wizard of Oz* (1900). Each says something different about America. And each has been controversial in its own unique way. All great literature is. *Moby-Dick* was rejected by reader and critic alike when it first came out. Over seventy years had to pass before it could be recognized not as an atypical adventure story but as a cornerstone of American literature. Nearly from the date of publication, *Huckleberry Finn* was banned from its nation's libraries. At first it was called trash that was only suitable for the slums. Today it is attacked for being racist.

Caricature of L. Frank Baum by W. W. Denslow, *Father Goose, His Book, 1899.* *Courtesy Michael Gessel.*

The journey down the Yellow Brick Road has been a long and rocky one the last one hundred years. No other American children's book of the twentieth century has proved to be as popular or as controversial as *The Wizard of Oz*. When Bobbs-Merrill issued its first edition in 1903, a reviewer remarked, "Mr. L. Frank Baum's last delicious bit of nonsense is amusing to the little people, and even more so to their elders. It is no small gift to write a juvenile which is not inane, and this gift Mr. Baum possesses to a degree which is almost monopoly." Nearly sixty years later when the first paperback editions of the Oz series were being published, another reviewer, noting "the genius of this American author," said, "Frank Baum had a flow of imagination, a depth of humor, a sense of character and a narrative control rare in writers of fantasy."[1] The first book of the long Oz series is

1. Reviews in *The Bookseller, Newsdealer and Stationer*, November 15, 1903; and *The Times Literary Supplement* (London), March 4, 1969.

today one of the best-selling books of the twentieth century and remains as popular with children today as when it was first published. Yet, for decades librarians and critics refused to recognize Baum's Oz books as important juvenile literature.[2] Only in the last quarter of the last century have Baum and Oz been the subject of serious literary and scholarly studies. Such writers as Ray Bradbury, Angela Carter, Arthur C. Clarke, F. Scott Fitzgerald, Shirley Jackson, Ken Kesey, Salman Rushdie, James Thurber, William Styron, John Updike, Gore Vidal, and Eudora Welty have all expressed their affection for Oz. Although there still remains some resistance on the part of educators and librarians to admit it, *The Wizard of Oz* is a major work of juvenile and American literature.

DESPITE the long popularity and growing critical interest in the Oz books, their author is not widely known. Baum pursued many other interests besides writing children's books, ranging from the editing of a Western newspaper to the production of musical extravaganzas and motion pictures. His cultural importance must be determined by the work, not the life, but Baum the man was nearly as fascinating as anything he ever wrote.

Lyman Frank Baum was born in Chittenango, a quiet village in Central New York, on May 15, 1856.[3] His father, Benjamin Ward Baum, followed nearly as many careers as his son would. He was building a barrel factory in Chittenango when the boy was born, but made a fortune in the infant Pennsylvania oil industry only a few years later. He relocated the family in

2. The prejudice that *The Wizard of Oz* is poorly written and not worthy of serious critical consideration persists in such recent studies as Humphrey Carpenter and Mari Prichard's *The Oxford Companion to Children's Literature* (Oxford: Oxford University Press, 1984), Gillian Avery's *Behold the Child* (London: Bodley Head, 1994), Perry Nodelman's *Touchstones: Reflections on the Best in Children's Literature,* Vol. 1 (West Lafayette, Ind.: Purdue University, 1985), Peter Hunt's *Children's Literature: An Illustrated History* (New York: Oxford University Press, 1995), and Anita Sylvie's *Children's Books and Their Creators* (Boston: Houghton Mifflin, 1995). British children's novelist and critic John Rowe Townsend addressed this issue in *Writing for Children* (London: Penguin Books, 1974): "But I do not hesitate to say that L. Frank Baum . . . has been shockingly underrated by American authorities on children's literature. . . . I cannot help wondering whether some unconscious snobbery was involved. . . . Yet to an outsider it seems that the unabashed Americanness of the Oz books makes them all the more original and attractive" (p. 109).

3. Named for his uncle Lyman Spalding Baum, he never liked "Lyman" and was always known as "Frank" to his family and friends. He went by several professional names: "Louis F. Baum," actor and playwright; "L. F. Baum," newspaper editor; and "L. Frank Baum," children's book writer.

nearby Syracuse and built for his wife, Cynthia Stanton Baum, a country estate she named Rose Lawn. Many years later, in the children's story *Dot and Tot of Merryland* (1901), Baum recalled his childhood home:

> The cool but sun-kissed mansion seemed delightful after the formal city house. It was built in a quaint but pretty fashion, and with many wings and gables and broad verandas on every side. Before it were acres and acres of velvety green lawns, sprinkled with shrubbery and dotted with beds of bright flowers. In every direction were winding paths covered with white gravel, which led to all parts of the grounds, looking for all the world like a map.

Cadet L. Frank Baum, 1868.

Courtesy Ozma Baum Mantele.

Here Baum and his siblings lived a sheltered childhood, and he was left much of the time to amuse himself. On the great estate he could escape to one of the many rooms of the mansion to read or to the fields to daydream.

He was a sensitive and imaginative child, said to have been born sickly; and his doting parents, having lost four of their nine children, denied him nothing. Like many children of wealthy parents of that time, he and his sisters and brothers were educated at home by English tutors. Harriet and Mary Louise were the oldest children and went on to finishing school. Frank was only the second son, so older brother Benjamin William was the child groomed to succeed their father in business. Frank was closer to young Henry Clay, who shared his literary taste and penchant for puns. Fearful that the boy might become a hopeless daydreamer, the Baums sent Frank off to Peekskill Military School overlooking the Hudson. But unaccustomed to the spartan, often brutish masculine world of the boarding school, he lasted only two years. He then joined his brother Harry at the Syracuse Classical School, but there is no record of his having graduated. He did not go on to college. His lifelong distaste for schoolteachers and the military found expression in his children's stories.

It was at Rose Lawn that young Frank got his first taste of printer's ink. Amateur journalism was all the rage and the children's magazines were full of advertisements for cheap printing presses, so Frank got his father to buy him the best one manufactured. With brother Harry he issued a short-lived four-page literary paper of his own, *The Rose Lawn Home Journal*. Much of the contents was written by its fifteen-year-old proprietor. With a school chum, Thomas G. Alvord, Jr., he proposed *The Empire*, said to be "a first class amateur monthly newspaper, containing poetry, literature, postage stamp news, amateur items, etc." But since no copies are known to have survived, it may have been more a dream than a reality. Baum briefly issued another amateur journal, *The Stamp Collector*, catering to another childhood fad of the day. He also produced his first book in 1873, a little pamphlet titled *Baum's Complete Stamp Dealers Directory*.

But it was soon time to put aside childish things and go into business. Frank earned some practical trade experience by spending a year in his brother-in-law's prosperous wholesale dry goods store, Neal, Baum & Company. While his brother Benjamin oversaw the family's oil and real estate interests, Frank returned to the farm to establish B. W. Baum & Sons, breeders of fancy thoroughbred fowls. He quickly built the business into one of the largest of its kind in the state. Frank Baum seemed to be literally everywhere. He helped found the Empire State Poultry Association and served as its first elected secretary. He did most of the work on the successful poultry shows this organization sponsored in Syracuse. The young man won prizes for his birds all over the country and was immediately elected to the executive committee of the American Poultry Association. He also oversaw the publication of B. W. Baum & Sons' handsome circulars, wrote a monthly poultry column for *New York Farmer and Dairyman*, and edited the short-lived journal *The Poultry Record*. His specialty was Hamburgs, a predominantly black strain known for its fine subtleties in secondary color. He quickly became one of the country's leading experts on the breed, so

Cover of *Baum's Complete Stamp Dealers Directory*, 1873. Courtesy Robert A. Baum, Jr.

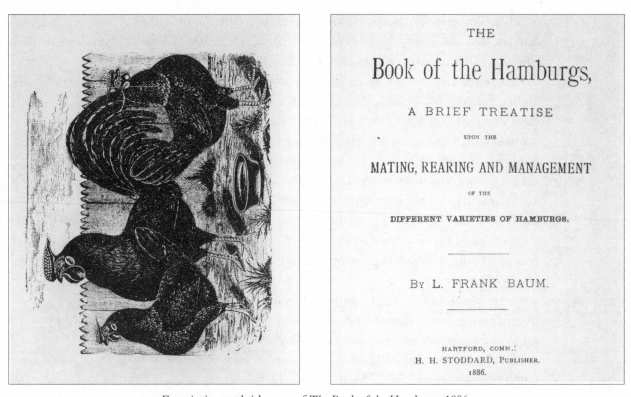

Frontispiece and title page of *The Book of the Hamburgs*, 1886.
Courtesy the Rice Poultry Collection at the Albert R. Mann Library, Cornell University.

Poultry World had him write a lengthy learned article on the subject. It was the basis for his first commercial book, *The Book of the Hamburgs*, published by H. H. Stoddard of Connecticut in 1886.

By 1881, Baum had long abandoned the chicken trade. He was now stagestruck. His uncle Adam Clarke Baum was one of the leading figures in Syracuse's amateur theatricals, and the nephew no doubt performed in some of these plays. When his aunt Katherine Gray returned to Syracuse to teach elocution, Baum became one of her prize pupils. He ran off to New York to study acting, and got a job as a "juvenile" under the name George Brooks in a second-rate repertory company then touring in Pennsylvania coal country. Confident in his thespian ability, he got his father to build him his own opera house in Richburg, New York, a recent oil boom town where the Baums had some investments. It would serve not only as a showplace for his histrionic talents but also as a home for various plays of his own composition. But his luck was against him: Baum's Opera House opened on December 29, 1881, and burned down on March 8, 1882.

Undaunted, Baum made other plans for his theatrical career. He already had three plays completed, and, with his uncle John Wesley Baum as company manager, he opened *The Maid of Arran* in Syracuse on his twenty-sixth birthday, May 15, 1882. Not only did "Louis F. Baum" write the play and all the songs, both lyrics and music, but he also took the male lead. Aunt Kate played two roles in the production, and cousin Genevieve Roberts took another. The play was a typical Irish melodrama of the period, based on William Black's popular Scottish novel *A Princess of Thule* (1877). It was so well received in Syracuse Baum took it on the road, traveling north into Canada and as far west as Kansas, as well as spending a profitable week in New York City. Baum's comedy *Matches* played in repertory with *The Maid of Arran*, but it was quickly withdrawn after a fire in Richburg on the very spot where Baum's Opera House had burned down. Remembering fondly his experiences with *The Maid of Arran*, Baum wrote many other plays over the years, but most were never produced. Only once more did he repeat the excitement of *The Maid of Arran*, with the 1902 musical extravaganza of *The Wizard of Oz*.

"Louis F. Baum" in *The Maid of Arran*, 1882.
Courtesy Matilda Jewell Gage.

During a brief break from the show, Baum married twenty-year-old Maud Gage of Fayetteville on November 9, 1882. He had met her just the Christmas before at a party given by his sister Harriet Neal. She was his cousin Josie's roommate at Cornell, and was visiting the Baums in Syracuse. When his aunt introduced them, she said she was sure he would just love her. "Consider yourself loved, Miss Gage," he told her.[4] By the end of the

4. Quoted in " 'Wizard of Oz' Author Enigma to His Wife," San Francisco *Examiner*, November 5, 1939.

Maud Gage Baum's wedding picture, 1882.
Courtesy Robert A. Baum Jr.

Matilda Joslyn Gage.
Courtesy Ozma Baum Mantele.

evening he did. However, her mother opposed the match. She was the prominent feminist Matilda Joslyn Gage, who helped draft the Woman's Bill of Rights and, with Elizabeth Cady Stanton and Susan B. Anthony, produced the first three volumes of the *History of Woman Suffrage* (1881–1886). Having just married off her two older daughters Helen Leslie and Julia, she did not want Maud to leave Cornell to wed an actor. But Maud Gage was as strong-willed as her mother and threatened to elope if she did not get her mother's approval. Gage gave in and said they could be married in her parlor. Baum and his mother-in-law grew to admire each other and shared many of the same liberal ideas. But that did not prevent him from frequently satirizing the "new woman" in his writings, notably in the character of General Jinjur and her Army of Revolt in *The Marvelous Land of Oz* (1904).

Maud went on the road with her husband, but when she became pregnant with their first child, he left the theater and returned to Syracuse to go into the family oil business. He and his uncle Adam Clarke Baum established Baum's Castorine Company, which marketed an axle grease invented by his brother Benjamin, then a chemist in Buffalo. They did fairly good business, and the grease is still being manufactured in Rome, New York. But when Maud's sisters and brother all settled in Dakota Territory, she just could not bear their living so far away. While on a selling trip for Baum's Castorine in the West, Frank stopped in Aberdeen, South Dakota, to see Maud's brother Thomas

Clarkson Gage and sister Helen Leslie Gage and to check on business opportunities there. He had become a gifted photographer, and the Aberdeen *Daily News* (June 1888) reported on his visit there:

> L. Frank Baum of Syracuse, New York, who has been visiting his in-laws here finds recreation from the cares of extensive business in the fascinating pursuit, amateur photography. Mr. Baum was proficient in the art and during his stay in the city secured a number of fine negatives of Dakota and cloud scapes. One picture taken by the glorious twilight of Dakota will when finished up prove of special interest as an example of advanced photography.

This was a hobby he retained all his life; he developed his negatives and prepared the prints, in later years with the help of his children. The bleak, treeless Dakota landscape fascinated him, and *The Wizard of Oz* opens with his recollections of his early days on the prairie.

Aberdeen, South Dakota, at twilight, photographed by L. Frank Baum, 1888.
Courtesy Matilda Jewell Gage.

The site of Baum's Bazaar, photographed by L. Frank Baum, 1888.
Courtesy Matilda Jewell Gage.

One thing Aberdeen lacked was a novelty store, so Baum and his family went West to open Baum's Bazaar on October 1, 1888. But Aberdeen had already reached the crest of its boom, and depression set in in 1889 when drought ruined the crops. The Baums, however, were caught up in the town's active social life and did not expect the economic downturn to last long. They attended card parties and dances, and Frank performed in local amateur theatricals. He also served as secretary of the local baseball team, which won the territorial championship in 1889. But the economy did not pick up by Christmas, and Baum's Bazaar closed on New Year's Day, 1890.

Former Syracusean John H. Drake was trying to unload his weekly newspaper, the *Dakota Pioneer*, just one of nine local Aberdeen papers, and Baum readily took it over and rechristened it the Aberdeen *Saturday Pioneer*. On January 25, 1890, the first issue appeared with "L. F. Baum, Editor" on the masthead. Most of the paper was "boilerplate," prepared mate-

rial from one of the news services, such as a column by humorist Bill Nye with illustrations by Walt McDougall, or national and fashion news. Baum wrote most of the rest of the copy. The highlight of the paper was the "Our Landlady" column, which reported the opinions of the fictional Mrs. Bilkins on current affairs. Aberdonians eagerly read it each week to find out who was being lampooned. Baum filled the column with local gossip and named names. Mrs. Bilkins commented on the tastes and aspirations of the time while providing a place for Baum to explore his fancy. She discussed the possibilities of lighter-than-air craft, horseless carriages, and the potential of electrical inventions. One of the best columns is a parody of Edward Bellamy's best-selling futuristic novel *Looking Backward,* which, when published in 1888, influenced a generation of Americans. Among the things the landlady mentions in a letter to be read in the far future is *Baum's Hourly Newspaper,* which contains all the events of the world just as they happen, like Glinda's Great Book of Records in the Oz series.

Baum wrote most of the editorials, and his topics varied from spiritualism to woman suffrage. He and Maud were then exploring Theosophy and other occult sciences, and Baum challenged the teachings of the local established churches. His position on women's rights reflected the arguments of his mother-in law, an occasional contributor to the *Saturday Pioneer*. His editorials urged his readers to vote for equal suffrage in South Dakota. There were also reports on the recent activities of Susan B. Anthony and Gage, as well as reviews of the latter's articles for *The Arena* and other publications.

Many of Baum's editorials spoke about the hard times on the vast Dakota prairie. There was always the hope that the next crop would be good, but prosperity never returned. The year 1890 proved to be so disastrous for the farmers that seed had to be brought in from neighboring states. Conditions seemed to be improving by the time of the South Dakota State Fair, and Baum got the commission to publish its official program. He also founded *The Western Investor*, a financial magazine, but it folded after a few issues. There was always the fear of another Indian uprising like the New Ulm massacre of 1862, and xenophobia was rife with the appearance of the Ghost Dancers in Dakota. While belonging to a religious movement, they called for the spirits of dead warriors to rise and drive the settlers off the prairies. Because the government had cut down on its allotments, the Lakota were starving, and many deserted the reservations to hunt for food elsewhere. When Sitting Bull, who had helped wipe out General Custer and the 7th Infantry at the Little Bighorn, joined the Ghost Dancers, the army murdered him. Then Custer's former regiment slaughtered Chief Big Foot and his people at Wounded Knee. Fearful of reprisals, Baum in his editorials called for the extermination of the Indians as the only way to ensure peace in South Dakota. Such intolerance and racism were not typical of his thought and his paper, and the massacre at Wounded Knee proved to be the very last major armed conflict between the North American Indians and the United States Army.

The new year proved disastrous for a variety of reasons, and Baum's subscription and advertising revenues fell drastically. In February 1891, he had to undergo a series of operations to remove a tumor beneath his tongue. Then, with so many people deserting South Dakota, Baum too thought it was time to move on. He joined the staff of the Chicago *Evening Post* and returned the Aberdeen *Saturday Pioneer* to Drake in April 1891. With the World's Columbian Exposition set to open in 1893, Baum knew Chicago was the place to be. But he was so miserable working for the *Post* that he quit after a month, and he took a job as traveling salesman for Pitkin & Brooks, a big Chicago wholesale china and glassware firm. His family soon joined him in Chicago.

The Baums had four sons now, Frank Joslyn, Robert Stanton, Harry Neal, and Kenneth Gage. With Frank away so much, Maud had to raise these boys largely on her own. She, rather than their father, had to discipline them, and she did not think twice about taking a hairbrush to one of them when he misbehaved. She had inherited the Gage temper from her mother: quick to explode and quick to forget. Rob described one particular punishment when he was little:

> We had a cat and due to some childish perversity I took it upstairs one day and threw it out the second story window. Fortunately, the cat wasn't hurt, but my mother saw me do it and to teach me a lesson, caught me up and held me out the window pretending that she was going to drop me. But it was quite real to me and I screamed so loudly that the neighbors all rushed out and were quite horrified by the spectacle of my mother dangling me out of the window, not sure but that she would let me drop. Needless to say, I was quite cured of throwing cats out of windows but I did heave one into a barrel one day and was promptly chucked in myself to see how I liked it.[5]

His father was incapable of such behavior. Harry recalled the time Ken had been naughty and Maud insisted that Frank spank him. He reluctantly did

5. Robert Stanton Baum, "The Autobiography of Robert Stanton Baum, Part One," *The Baum Bugle*, Spring 1970, p. 17.

Maud Gage Baum and her four sons, Robert, Harry, Kenneth, and Frank, 1900.
Courtesy Ozma Baum Mantele.

as he was told, and the little boy cried himself to sleep. The incident so disturbed his father that he could not eat his dinner, so he went upstairs and woke him up. "Kenneth," he said, "I apologize for spanking you, and I'll never spank any of you children again." And he never did.[6]

Maud was the practical one in the family, and more than once she had to take over the family's finances when one of Frank's wild schemes failed. She somehow found time to give embroidery lessons to bring in a little needed cash during the family's early lean years in Chicago. Despite their differences in temperament, it was clear Frank loved Maud and she him. "He told me many times I was the only one he had ever loved," she reported to her family about the night he died. "He hated to die, did not want to leave me, said he was never happy without me, but it was better he should go first, if it had to be, for I doubt if he could have got along without me." And it was as hard for her as it was for him. "It is all so sad," she said, "and I am so forlorn and alone. For nearly thirty-seven years we had been every-

6. Harry Neal Baum, "My Father Was 'the Wizard of Oz,' " *The Baum Bugle*, Autumn 1985, p. 9.

L. Frank Baum in his home with his four sons, Robert, Frank, Kenneth and Harry.
Courtesy Matilda Jewell Gage.

thing to each other, we were happy, and now I am alone, to face the world alone."[7] As an expression of his deep love for her, he dedicated his most important book, *The Wizard of Oz*, "to my good friend and comrade, My Wife."

Baum was first of all a family man, and the job with Pitkin & Brooks took him out on the road far away from Chicago for weeks at a time. Maud hired a "girl" to help her with the housework, but that was not enough. Her mother spent a good part of every year with the Baums to help her daughter look after the household and raise four rambunctious boys. Baum treasured his days home in Chicago with Maud and their sons. Their favorite time together was the family hour, when he read to them or told them stories of his own invention. The younger boys were just learning their Moth-

7. Letter to Helen Leslie and Leslie Gage, May 16, 1919, quoted in Sally Roesch Wagner, "Dorothy Gage and Dorothy Gale," *The Baum Bugle*, Autumn 1984, pp. 5–6.

er Goose rhymes and had so many questions about this and that mentioned in the nursery songs that their doting father began inventing little tales around them to help explain the strange events. He also created a child's land of Cockaigne called Phunniland where candy grew on bushes, the rivers flowed with milk and cream, and it rained lemonade and thundered in a chorus from Wagner's *Tannhäuser*. Gage happened to overhear him one night and urged Frank to write his stories down and sell them. She thought they would make his reputation and might be as successful as *Alice in Wonderland*. He followed her sage advice, and on June 17, 1896, he applied for copyright of the titles for two collections of children's stories, "Tales from Mother Goose" and "Adventures in Phun[n]iland."

"The Wond'rous Wise Man," illustration by Maxfield Parrish in *Mother Goose in Prose*, 1897. *Private collection.*

Like so many novice authors, he submitted his manuscripts in vain to various publishers in the East. None of them was interested in his new fairy tales. He also dropped them off at a small, prestigious Chicago publishing house, Way & Williams. Chauncey L. Williams was one of the most inventive, and impractical, of the city's publishers. His home was one of the first houses designed by Frank Lloyd Wright and a haven for writers of the Midwest such as Hamlin Garland, George Barr McCutcheon, Kate Chopin, and William Allen White and artists John T. McCutcheon and Will H. Bradley. Although the company published few children's books, Chauncey L. Williams wanted to commission the up-and-coming young Philadelphia illustrator Maxfield Parrish to do a new edition of the old nursery rhymes; but when he read Baum's tales of Mother Goose, he decided to publish that instead. He promised to do the "Phunniland" stories next. *Mother Goose in Prose* (1897) was not only the first children's book by Baum, it was also the very first book ever illustrated by Parrish. Baum was proud of what he had done and wrote in the copy he gave his sister Mary Louise Brewster:

When I was young I longed to write a great novel that should win me fame. Now that I am getting old my first book is written to amuse chil-

dren. For, aside from my evident inability to do anything "great," I have learned to regard fame as a will-o-the-wisp which, when caught, is not worth the possession; but to please a child is a sweet and lovely thing that warms one's heart and brings its own reward. I hope my book will succeed in that way—that the children will like it. You and I have inherited much the same temperament and literary taste and I know you will not despise these simple tales, but will understand me and accord me your full sympathy.

But the response to the book was not exactly what he hoped. Baum admitted years later, in a letter to Frank K. Reilly of December 16, 1916, that "the book was not appealing to children, although adults went wild over the beautiful drawings."[8] Williams put out a magnificent volume a bit too late to take full advantage of the Christmas trade, and numerous poor financial judgments forced him to go out of business in early 1898. He sold the firm with all its stock to Herbert S. Stone, who let *Mother Goose in Prose* go out of print.

Tired of the hard life on the road, Baum came up with a new idea for earning his living. He had noticed on his travels from town to town the need for a practical guide to designing storefront windows. So with Williams as publisher, he founded *The Show Window*, a periodical for window trimmers, in 1897. The trade quickly adopted it as its official organ and formed the National Association of Window Trimmers at Baum's urging. He was elected the association's secretary at its first annual convention in Chicago. Baum insisted that he was putting out an *art* magazine and filled it with photographs of many of the most important department stores in the country, many of which he must have taken himself. It was an expensive journal to produce, and Baum provided most of the copy, even some of the advertisements. He pulled together and expanded on various articles he had published in *The Show Window* during its first two years to produce *The Art of Decorating Dry Goods Windows and Interiors* (1900), a well-illustrated treatise sold only by subscription.

Baum and Williams joined the Chicago Press Club in 1898, and here they congregated with many of the city's most important writers and artists.

---

8. Baum and Parrish almost collaborated on another project. In 1915, the producer Walter Wanger approached Reilly & Britton to see if Baum would be willing to write the libretto for a production of *Snow White* for which Parrish was already designing the costumes, sets, and properties. Baum eagerly agreed to the proposal, and Reilly & Britton offered to publish a book based on it, written by Baum and illustrated by Parrish. But World War I intervened, and nothing came of the project.

Among them was William Wallace Denslow. Born in Philadelphia in 1856, he was the same age as Baum, but vastly different in experience and personality. He was bohemian by nature and wandered about the country for years in search of work. Except for some semesters spent at the Cooper Institute and the National Academy of Design in New York, "Den" was self-taught and self-made. His first job was office boy with *Hearth and Home* and *American Agriculturist*, for which he designed some of his earliest illustrations. He went on to county atlases, theater posters, costume designs, trade cards, and all sorts of other advertisements. He was also one

William Wallace Denslow, 1900.
Private collection.

of the many illustrators who contributed to Mark Twain's *A Tramp Abroad* (1880). He went into newspaper work that sent him to Chicago for the *Herald*. He got laid off for drinking and drifted out West, first to Denver and then on to San Francisco, where he worked for William Randolph Hearst. But when the newspaper publisher refused to sponsor a trip to the Columbian Exposition in Chicago in 1893, Denslow went anyway and got rehired by the *Herald*. Denslow's first international reputation came during the art poster craze of the 1890s for his advertisements for Rand McNally and other publishers. He designed cloth and paperback covers and drew decorations for Montgomery Ward catalogues. He was the first artist whom Art and Crafts entrepreneur Elbert Hubbard invited to come to East Aurora, New York, to work for the Roycroft Press. He designed *The Rime of the Ancient Mariner* (1899) and *The Rubáiyát of Omar Khayyám* (1899) as well as bookplates and cartoons for *The Philistine* and *The Fra*. Denslow was indeed a remarkably versatile illustrator, but as yet he had not done a children's book. Since he was better known in the Chicago publishing trade than Baum was, Baum naturally thought of him as a contributor to his book of verse *By the Candelabra's Glare* (1898).

As a break from editing *The Show Window*, Baum picked up a foot-powered printing press and some fonts of type to run off the limited edition of a modest collection of poems. He called it "one of my greatest treasures—a book I set in type out of my head without writing it, and which I personally printed and bound."[9] Actually many of the verses came from published sources, like the Aberdeen *Saturday Pioneer* and Chicago *Sunday Times-Herald*. "Unassisted I have set the type and turned the press and accomplished the binding," he bragged in the preface to *By the Candelabra's Glare*. "Such as it is, the book is 'my very own.'" When friends heard what he was doing, they gave him the paper, ink, and binding materials; Williams provided the endpapers. Several artists, including Denslow, drew the pictures. All of this was free of charge. The author's only cost was his labor, and he provided each of the contributors with one of the limited edition of ninety-nine copies.

Baum had another project for Denslow. He had concluded *By the Candelabra's Glare* with a selection of children's verse and now wanted to expand it into a picture book, and Denslow seemed the perfect artist for it. For years Baum had been scribbling poems on old envelopes and other odd bits of paper while traveling on the road selling crockery and glassware. He

9. In a letter to Isidore Witmark, April 19, 1903, Special Collections, Butler Library, Columbia University Libraries.

68 Humboldt Boulevard, Chicago, where *The Wonderful Wizard of Oz* was written.
Courtesy Fred M. Meyer.

had collected enough of these nursery rhymes for children to fill a book, and the two men began in earnest on preparing it for the press. Artist and author often met in the evening to work on the project in the Baum home at 68 Humboldt Boulevard. "I recall that 'Den,' as we called him, had a striking red vest of which he was inordinately fond," reported Harry Baum in *The American Book Collector* (December 1962). "And whenever he came to our house, he would always complain of the heat as an excuse to take off his coat and spend the evening displaying his beautiful red vest. The family used to joke about it among ourselves, but it was a touchy subject with Denslow, and we were all careful not to say anything about this vanity during his visit." The vest was hardly the most striking thing about the eccentric artist. He had a large walrus mustache, and (as Elbert Hubbard's son explained in a letter of August 11, 1958) he "was a pretty gruff old fellow." When not smoking his corncob pipe, he chewed tobacco. Another contemporary, Felix Shay, in his *Elbert Hubbard of East Aurora* (1926), said that Denslow had "the voice of a second mate in a storm—a fog horn voice," a twisted sense of humor, "always grumbling about nothing, always carping, always censorious, and laughing uproariously when he had secured an effect" (p. 149). In contrast to this temperament was that of his young wife, Ann Waters. She was a gracious hostess and good cook, and one of the reasons why people were always stopping by Denslow's studio over in the Fine Arts Building. She was the daughter of Martha Holden, a Chicago newspaperwoman who wrote under the name Amber after her lovely eyes. Ann was also a gifted writer, and Baum in the new children's book wrote a verse about "little Annie Waters" in her honor.

The George M. Hill Company, Chicago, the publishers of *The Wonderful Wizard of Oz*. *Private Collection*.

At first Baum and Denslow thought of publishing the book themselves, since it was a radical departure from the other children's books of the time. They wanted the pictures in color, and no publisher was likely to pay to have it done exactly as they wanted. They went looking for someone to manufacture the book, and because Denslow had done some recent work for the George M. Hill Company, a big jobber, he brought the project over to see if the firm would prepare the sample dummies for Baum and himself. Hill did better than that: He offered to publish the book if Baum and Denslow were willing to pay to have the color plates made. To save the cost of typesetting the text, Denslow hired a friend, Ralph Fletcher Seymour, to hand-letter the verses, so that the pages now looked like miniature art posters. Another artist, Charles J. Costello, assisted him. Since it was along the same lines as a Mother Goose collection and Palmer Cox's *The Brownies, Their Book* (1887), the book was christened *Father Goose, His Book*. Under the guidance of production manager Frank K. Reilly and secretary and head salesman Sumner C. Britton, Hill produced a stunning volume unlike anything else then on the market.

The first printing of 5,700 copies quickly sold out, and several more printings were soon exhausted. Much to the pleasant surprise of Baum, Denslow, and Hill, *Father Goose* became the best-selling picture book of 1900. Reviews compared Baum to Lewis Carroll and Edward Lear. Mark Twain, William Dean Howells, Elbert Hubbard, even Admiral Dewey praised *Father Goose*. A dozen imitations flooded the market, and Hill released *The Songs of Father Goose* (1900), a selection of the pages from the original book in black and white only, but set to music by Albert N. Hall (later Burton). Baum gave his "Phunniland" manuscript to R. H. Russell in New York, and perhaps to avoid confusion with F. Opper's *Frolics in Phunniland,* which Russell was also publishing that year, Baum's book became *A New Wonderland* (1900), delightfully illustrated by Frank Ver Beck. Hill took two more books of verse from Baum, *The Army Alphabet* and *The Navy Alphabet* (both 1900), illustrated by Harry Kennedy and hand-lettered by Costello. *Father Goose* established Baum at forty-three as one of the most exciting American children's book writers of the day, and he began exploring all sorts of other writing for young readers.

Inscription in Maud Gage Baum's copy of
Father Goose, His Book, signed by both
L. Frank Baum and W. W. Denslow, 1899.
Private collection.

The unexpected success of *Father Goose* now provided luxuries that had been denied the Baums earlier. They enjoyed spending summers at Macatawa Park, Michigan, along Lake Michigan, so with earnings from *Father Goose, His Book*, Baum bought a pretty cottage he named the Sign of the Goose. His doctor advised him to take up some light manual labor, so woodworking became his new hobby, and he built all the oak furniture in the house. Some had leather upholstery fastened with decorative brass goose-head nails, provided by his friend and Chauncey Willams's brother-in-law Harrison H. Rountree, head of the Turner Brass Works in Chicago. There was a grandfather clock and a little bookcase, both decorated with characters from Baum's books. He also built a large rocking chair whose sides were outlines of white enameled geese. He commissioned a stained-glass window of a large goose

The Sign of the Goose, Macatawa Park, Michigan.
Courtesy Fred M. Meyer.

L. Frank Baum reading on the porch of the Sign of the Goose, Macatawa Park, Michigan.
Courtesy Matilda Jewell Gage.

The interior of the Sign of the Goose, Macatawa Park, Michigan.
Private collection.

against a green glass background for the living room, and he personally stenciled the walls with a frieze of green geese. Finally he made a large round sign displaying a brightly painted cutout of a goose from Denslow's cover design and the name of the cottage. He hung it up prominently on the front porch, and passersby often pointed out that that was where the famous "Father Goose" lived. It was a gathering place for card parties and other festivities, and Baum wrote an amusing novel about the summer resort and its characters, *Tamawaca Folks* (1907), which he published privately under the name John Estes Cooke to disguise the goose who wrote it. It was at the Sign of the Goose that Baum told the Grand Rapids *Herald* (August 18, 1907) why he preferred writing for children to that for adults:

> To write fairy stories for children, to amuse them, to divert restless children, sick children, to keep them out of mischief on rainy days, seems of greater importance than to write grown-up novels. Few of the popular novels last the year out, responding as they do, to a certain psychological demand, characteristic of the time; whereas, a child's book is, comparatively speaking, the same always, since children are always the same kind of folks with the same needs to be satisfied.

Portraits of W. W. Denslow and L. Frank Baum, drawings by Ike Morgan, 1899.
Private collection.

He wrote one other Father Goose book here, the ephemeral *Father Goose's Year Book* (1907) for adults, illustrated by Walter J. Enright; but the Father Goose craze was long over by then, so Baum thereafter concentrated on other kinds of writing.

Baum was delighted with *Father Goose, His Book*, but he was determined to do something far more ambitious. Just as the book was coming out, he and Denslow were already hard at work on another one, a "modernized" fairy tale. "I was sitting on the hatrack in the hall, telling the kids a story," he explained to his publishers years later, "and suddenly this one moved right in and took possession. I shooed the children away and grabbed a piece of paper that was lying there on the rack and began to write. It really seemed to write itself. Then I couldn't find any regular paper, so I took anything at all, even a bunch of old envelopes."[10] In a letter to Sumner C. Britton, January 23, 1916, Baum described his general procedure in writing his children's books:

> A lot of thought is required on one of these fairy tales. The odd characters are a sort of inspiration, liable to strike at any time, but the plot and

10. Quoted by Jeanne O. Potter, "The Man Who Invented Oz," *Los Angeles Times Sunday Magazine*, August 13, 1939, p. 12.

plan of adventures takes me considerable time to develop. When I get at a thing of that sort I live with it day by day, jotting down on odd slips of paper the various ideas that occur and in this way getting my material together. The new Oz book is in this stage. I've got it all—all the hard work has been done. . . . But . . . it's a long way from being ready for the printer yet. I must rewrite it, stringing the incidents into consecutive order, elaborating the characters, etc.

Sometime in 1899, either late summer or early fall, Baum signed a contract with Denslow for their next children's book, tentatively titled "The City of Oz." As with *Father Goose, His Book*, Baum and Denslow agreed to share equally the cost of making the plates as well as their ownership. They further agreed that Baum would copyright the text in his name and Denslow the illustrations in his. There was one unusual clause: If fewer than 10,000 copies of the book were sold within two years of the book's publication, "then this contract may be declared null and void by either Baum or Denslow, in which case said Baum shall be declared sole owner of the text and said Denslow sole owner of the illustrations, to be used independently of the other."[11] Baum agreed to provide Denslow with the manuscript by November 1; the pictures were to be completed no later than May 1, 1900. If the two failed to find a publisher who could bring out the book by September 1, 1900, the contract would be either canceled or modified.

Baum did better than expected. He completed the manuscript of approximately 40,000 words on October 9, 1899. He knew the new story was special, because he took another piece of paper, inscribed it, "With this pencil I wrote the manuscript of 'The Emerald City,' " and then dated it. He attached the stub of the pencil to the paper, framed it, and hung it over his writing desk. Baum was left-handed and wrote in an elegant backhand which was clear enough for the printer to set the book directly from this manuscript of assorted odds and ends. Baum and Denslow may have thought they could get it out in 1899, the date Denslow wrote on the pictorial copyright page. With *Father Goose* a hit, Hill was eager to publish anything by Baum and Denslow. But he was not willing to pay for the elaborate color pictures himself. He offered them terms much like those for *Father Goose, His Book*, and they signed a contract for "The Emerald City" on November 16. Baum and Denslow agreed to supply Hill with "complete plates from which to print the book; also cover dies to be used in binding"

11. Quoted in David L. Greene and Peter E. Hanff, "Baum and Denslow: Their Books, Part One," *The Baum Bugle*, Spring 1975, p. 10. Additional information provided by Robert A. Baum.

by March 1, 1900. Evidently they turned the book in earlier than expected, for the Chicago *Journal* reported on January 19, 1900, that Hill was planning to publish it in April or soon after. The publisher still had his doubts about Baum's "modernized" fairy tale, for, after the usual professional readers went over the story, he gave it to two children as well as a kindergarten teacher for their opinion. They liked it. Since author and illustrator were entirely responsible for this material, the publisher likely had no hand in editing the text or preparing the pictures. But he did agree "to print, publish and circulate the said book, and . . . to perform every service which it is usual to perform in respect to the sale and distribution of his books, and to bear all expenses of circulation, advertisement and other work incidental to the placing of said book on the market; and . . . to use all ordinary methods known to the trade to push the sale of the said book." The royalty was set at nine cents for each of them for every copy sold at list price of $1.50. Hill also offered to pay on January 15, 1900, a $1,000 advance to be shared equally by Baum and Denslow, with the understanding that they were granting Hill "the exclusive right of publication of any books or literary works which they may jointly produce, write or illustrate, during a period of five years from the date of this agreement." Hill did pay them $500 each on the agreed date.[12] But the clause was later canceled by mutual agreement. The George M. Hill Company neglected to follow through on another term of the contract: The firm promised "to procure the publication of said book in England and have the said book duly entered at Stationer's Hall." That, as Baum noted, "never was done." It did, however, arrange to distribute copies in Canada through George J. McLeod of Toronto.

The very next day, Baum considered an entirely new title for the book. In drawing up a contract to transfer all rights of his latest literary efforts to Maud, he listed these properties as *Mother Goose in Prose; Father Goose, His Book;* "The King of Phunniland" (published as *A New Wonderland*); and "From Kansas to Fairyland." Denslow and Ann Waters witnessed the agreement on November 17, and Maud paid her husband $1,000 for all claim to these works. "From Kansas to Fairyland" did not last long. The Syracuse *Sunday Herald* (November 19) referred to still another title, "The City of the Great Oz"; and on January 2, 1900, Maud wrote Helen Leslie that it was going to be called " 'The Great Oz' or some such title." James J. O'Donnell Bennett mentioned "The Fairyland of Oz" in his Chicago *Journal* column of January 19; likewise, Hill announced publication under this

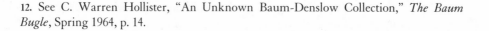

12. See C. Warren Hollister, "An Unknown Baum-Denslow Collection," *The Baum Bugle*, Spring 1964, p. 14.

name in *The Bookseller, Newsdealer and Stationer* (February 1). But when Denslow prepared the book's pictorial title page, he shortened it to "The Land of Oz." That was the title he used in his account book on January 15, and Baum registered "The Land of Oz" with the Copyright Office on January 18. It was still called that when Baum registered copyright of *A New Wonderland* on January 26; the very next day Bennett mentioned it in his column. But it was just not colorful enough. Days later, Denslow pasted a paper label with Baum's new title for the book on his drawing for the title page. It went to press as *The Wonderful Wizard of Oz*.

Baum dated his introduction "April 1900," and the original publication date was to be May 15, 1900, Baum's forty-fourth birthday. On April 8, he wrote his brother Harry about this turning point in his career:

> The financial success of my books is yet undetermined, and will only be positively settled after the forthcoming fall season. We only had three months sale of *Father Goose*, and though it made a hit and sold plenteously we cannot tell what its future might be. . . . I have been grateful for its success. The money has been a pleasure to me and my work is sought by publishers who once scorned my contributions. Harper Bros. sent a man here last week to try to make a contract for a book next year. Scribner's write offering a cash advance for a manuscript. Appletons, Lothrops, and the Century have asked for a book—no matter what it is. This makes me proud, especially as my work in *Father Goose* was not good work, and I know I can do better. But I shall make no contracts with anyone till next January. If my book succeed this year I can dictate terms and choose my publishers. If they fall down I shall try to discover the fault and to turn out some better work.
>
> A lady here, Mrs. Alberta N. Hall, has written some charming music to the *Father Goose* verses. *The Songs of Father Goose* was the result and is now in preparation, being announced for publication June 1st. *The Army Alphabet*, wonderfully illustrated by Harry Kennedy, will be issued May 15th. The book surely *ought* to catch on. *The Navy Alphabet*, also illustrated by Kennedy, will appear August 1st. I have received some proofs of the illustrations Frank Ver Beck has made for my Phunniland book, which appears July 1st from R. H. Russell's, New York. The work is splendid. This is the same man who illustrated Kipling's new book of animal stories, having been selected from over all the other American artists to do that work later collected.[13] The title of the book will be *A New Wonder-*

13. Baum must be referring to Ver Beck's pictures for several pieces then appearing in *The Ladies' Home Journal*, later collected in Kipling's *Just So Stories* (1902). The book was illustrated by the author.

land. Then there is the other book, the best thing I ever have written, they tell me, *The Wonderful Wizard of Oz*. It is now in the press and will be ready soon after May 1st. Denslow has made profuse illustrations for it and it will glow with bright colors. Mr. Hill, the publisher, says he expects a sale of at least a quarter of a million copies on it. If he is right, that book alone solves my problem. But the queer, unreliable Public has not yet spoken. I only need one hit this year to make my position secure, and three of these books seem fitted for public approval. But there—who know anything! I'm working at my trade, earning a salary to keep my family and holding fast to a certainty until the fiat has gone forth.[14]

Hill advertised in the April *Bookseller and Latest Literature* that *The Wonderful Wizard of Oz* would be available about June. The first copy Baum had in his hands was sewn but not bound, and he presented it to his sister Mary Louise Brewster on May 17, when he and Maud were in Syracuse. "This 'dummy,' " he wrote on the flyleaf, "was made from sheets I gathered from the press as fast as printed and bound up by hand. It is really the very first book ever made of this story." He wrote in the first completed copy he received, "This, the first copy of *The Wonderful Wizard of Oz* that left the hands of the publisher, is presented to my dear brother Harry C. Baum by the Author. May 28th, 1900."[15] *The Bookseller* noted in June, "Although the book has been offered but a fortnight over 5,000 have already been ordered. A second edition of 5,000 is in the press." Baum gave copies to his mother and sister Mary Louise on June 20. Hill postponed the official publication of the book until August, but *The Bookseller* reported that the trade got its first glimpse of the new book at the Chicago Book Fair, held at the Palmer House from July 5 to 20. Orders came flying in, and Hill could not fill them until September. The official copyright date was August, but the Library of Congress did not receive a copy until December 12, 1900.[16] Hill advertised

14. Quoted by Frank Joslyn Baum and Russell P. MacFall, *To Please a Child* (Chicago: Reilly & Lee, 1961), pp. 118–19.

15. See Dick Martin, "The First Edition of the Wonderful Wizard of Oz," *The American Book Collector,* December 1962, p. 27. Justin G. Schiller located an even earlier copy, inscribed "Richard Adlai Watson from his Godfather, R. J. Street, May 23, 1900." Schiller suggested in his catalogue *Chapbook Miscellany* (Summer 1970) that Street was somehow involved with the publication of the book and took a copy fresh from the press just days before Baum had a chance to give his brother one.

16. The Copyright Office recorded receiving only one copy, but Baum insisted that he personally sent two in September 1900 as required by law. Apparently the second was lost in the mail. The Library of Congress copy was a third one the publisher sent, a second printing with the corrected text. The copyright was not officially completed until 1903 when Bobbs-Merrill sent two copies of its edition, *The New Wizard of Oz*.

in October that the first printing of 10,000 copies was gone within two weeks of publication, and because the second of 15,000 was nearly exhausted, a third of 10,000 was soon to be run off. Another 30,000 were said to be produced in November, and the last Hill printing of 25,000 was completed in January 1901. *The Wonderful Wizard of Oz* became the best-selling children's book of the 1900 Christmas season, and it continued to sell into the new year. Hill said that in all the company printed nearly 90,000 copies.[17]

The publisher produced a beautiful volume. With twenty-four color plates and over one hundred textual illustrations in varying colors, it is one of the most lavishly illustrated American children's books of the twentieth century. The handsome binding was light green, stamped in dark green and red, and the whole book was wrapped in a pale green dust jacket stamped in emerald green only. The colophon gave the following history of its production:

Copyright registration for *The Wonderful Wizard of Oz* and *The Navy Alphabet,* July 28, 1900. *Courtesy the Library of Congress.*

> Here ends *The Wonderful Wizard of Oz*, which was written by L. Frank Baum and illustrated by William Wallace Denslow. The engravings were made by the Illinois Engraving Company, the paper was supplied by Dwight Bros. Paper Company, and Messrs. A. R. Barnes & Company printed the book for the publishers, the George M. Hill Company, completing it on the fifteenth day of May, in the year nineteen hundred.

When *Life* magazine reprinted a selection of the original Denslow pictures in its Christmas 1953 issue, art director Charles Tudor reported (in a brief printed letter answering inquiries about the article) that the color plates required four plates: zinc etching or "black plate," which was printed in dark blue, and three separate wood engravings for red, yellow, and pale blue. But Arthur Bernhard, who was an apprentice engraver with the Illi-

17. Greene and Hanff estimated that according to royalties listed in Denslow's account book and Hill's bankruptcy records, the number could not have been more than 35,000 copies. See "Baum and Denslow: Their Books, Part Two," *The Baum Bugle*, Autumn 1975, p. 14.

nois Engraving Company when the book was published, said that the text illustrations were reproduced by zinc etchings or zinc plates, not wood engravings, and the gradations of color were applied by the Benday process, patented by Benjamin Day of New York in 1879. Although there are several states of the binding, Hill seems to have printed the book only twice; the second one included minor corrections in text and illustration. Many scrambled copies of different elements of these two printings survive. All printings of the book, including the subsequent Bobbs-Merrill and M. A. Donohue editions, used these plates until the 1920s, when they wore out and the book was entirely reset.

Portrait of L. Frank Baum by the Illinois Engraving Company, Chicago, which made the plates for *The Wonderful Wizard of Oz*, 1900.
Courtesy the Library of Congress.

Because Baum and Denslow were paying for them, the publisher spared no expense in printing the pictures. What exactly Baum thought of Denslow's contribution to the book is not known. Although he praised the illustrations for *Dot and Tot of Merryland* (1901) in his introduction, Baum may not have been as admiring of those for *The Wonderful Wizard of Oz*. "I have always disliked Mr. Denslow's Dorothy," Maud Baum confessed in a letter of May 4, 1940, now in the Lilly Library, Indiana University. "She is so terribly plain and not childlike." Her husband may have agreed. Baum noted in his own copy of *A New Wonderland*, "I like the illustrations more than any of my other books up to now."[18] Perhaps he resented the disproportionate attention the critics gave the pictures over his verses in *Father Goose*. He tended to prefer comic to more graceful and decorative illustrations. When *Queen Zixi of Ix* (1905) was in preparation, he advised the publisher, "If however [Frederick Richardson] could be induced to make the small pictures broadly humorous—even to the verge of burlesque—it would be a good thing all around."[19] At another time, he

18. Quoted by Dick Martin in "Bibliographia Baumiana: *A New Wonderland*," *The Baum Bugle*, Spring 1967, p. 19.

19. Letter to W. W. Ellsworth, September 9, 1904, L. Frank Baum Manuscripts, Butler Library, Columbia University Libraries.

wrote Reilly & Britton in regard to John R. Neill's drawings, September 11, 1915, "What we need is more *humorous* pictures." He once considered replacing Neill with Winsor McCay, who drew the "Little Nemo in Slumberland" and "Dreams of the Rarebit Fiend" Sunday comic strips, or another cartoonist. This demand for the burlesque went to the extreme in Walt McDougall's slapstick pictures for the "Queer Visitors from the Marvelous Land of Oz" comic page; the drawing is coarse and the jokes are dated. They lack the beauty and true wit that Denslow, Neill, and most of Baum's other artists brought to his fairy tales. In the end, Baum admitted to his publishers on October 25, 1915, that "perhaps no author is satisfied with his illustrator, and I see my characters and incidents so differently from the artist that I fail to appreciate his talent." He may not have been mad for Denslow's work; but if his readers were happy, Baum was happy. He grudgingly acknowledged in the letter of September 11, 1915, "I used to receive many compliments on Denslow's pictures when he was illustrating my books, from children and others."

The critical response to the story and illustrations was on the whole favorable. Naturally some reviewers compared *The Wonderful Wizard of Oz* to *Alice's Adventures in Wonderland*. Lewis Carroll's death in 1898 inspired a subgenre in American juvenile literature as the trade fed the market imitations of the famous English fantasy. *The Bookseller and Latest Literature* in July said that the new Baum-Denslow book "is penned with the wild extravagance of fancy that is noticeable in that children's classic, *Alice in Wonderland*." *The Dial* (December 1, 1900), in reviewing *A New Wonderland*, complained that Carroll "had a real distinction of style which is wholly lacking here, though to be found in a chapter or two of Mr. Baum's other book, *The Wonderful Wizard of Oz*." Baum must have been flattered to have his first full-length effort compared with the most famous of modern fairy stories. Of course the similarities between the stories are superficial, and no one attempted any detailed discussion of the two works.

Reviewers could not decide who deserved more credit for the wonderful book, Baum or Denslow. *The Dial* thought it "remarkably illustrated by W. W. Denslow, who possesses all the originality of method which is denied his collaborator." Although the Chicago *Evening Post* (September 21, 1900) complained that Denslow did not know how to draw a "child-like" child, it conceded that if the book was a success it would be due more to the illustrator than to the author. Another review said that while "Mr. Baum has given us a clever and original story that deserves a good reception," "the illustrations are uncommon, suggesting the upset ink-bottle." But most people tended to agree with the October *Kindergarten Magazine*:

Impossible as are the little girl's odd companions, the magic pen of the writer, ably assisted by the artist's brush, has made them seem very real, and no child but will have a warm corner in his heart for the really thoughtful Scarecrow, the truly tender Tin Woodman, the fearless Cowardly Lion. Delightful humor and rare philosophy are found on every page. The artist, whose fertile invention has so seconded the author's imagination, is W. W. Denslow, who illustrated *Father Goose*.

Many critics considered *The Wonderful Wizard of Oz* far superior to the usual fare for children. "Little folks will go wild over it," predicted *The Bookseller and Latest Literature*, "and older people will read it to them with pleasure, since it will form a pleasing interlude with more serious fiction." Even *The Dial* had to admit that Baum's book "is really notable among the innumerable publications of the young, making an appeal which is fairly irresistible to a certain standard of tastes." *Book News* in October quoted a Philadelphia paper that said, "It is not lacking in philosophy and satire which will furnish amusement to the adult and cause the juvenile to think some new and healthy thoughts. At the same time it is not objectionable in being too knowing and cannot be fairly charged with unduly encouraging precocity." The Minneapolis *Journal* (November 18, 1900) declared that *The Wonderful Wizard of Oz* was simply "the best children's story-book of the century." Perhaps the New York *Times* provided the most perceptive and prophetic analysis of *The Wonderful Wizard of Oz* on September 8:

It is impossible to conceive of a greater contrast than exists between the children's books of antiquity that were new publications during the sixteenth century and modern children's books of which *The Wonderful Wizard of Oz* is typical. The crudeness that was characteristic of the old-time publications that were intended for the delectation and amusement of ancestral children would now be enough to cause the modern child to yell with rage and vigor and to instantly reject the offending volume, if not to throw it out of the window. The time when anything was good enough for children has long since passed, and the volumes devoted to our youth are based upon the fact that they are the future citizens: that they are the country's hope, and are thus worthy of the best, not the worst, that art can give. Kate Greenaway has forever driven out the lottery book and the horn book. In *The Wonderful Wizard of Oz* the fact is clearly recognized that the young as well as their elders love novelty. They are pleased with dashes of color and something new in the place of the old, familiar, and winged fairies of Grimm and Andersen.

Neither the tales of Aesop and other fabulists, nor the stories such as "The Three Bears" will ever pass entirely away, but a welcome place

L. Frank Baum writing on his back porch, 1899.
Courtesy Fred M. Meyer.

remains and will easily be found for such stories as *Father Goose, His Book*, *The Songs of Father Goose*, and now *The Wonderful Wizard of Oz*, that all come from the hands of Baum and Denslow.

This last story of *The Wizard* is ingeniously woven out of commonplace material. It is of course an extravaganza, but will surely be found to appeal strongly to child readers as well as to the younger children to whom it will be read by mothers or those having charge of the entertaining of children. There seems to be an inborn love of stories in child minds, and one of the most familiar and pleading requests of children is to be told another story.

The drawing as well as the introduced color work vies with the texts drawn, and the result has been a book that rises far above the average children's book of today, high as is the present standard. Dorothy, the little girl, and her strangely assorted companions, whose adventures are many and whose dangers are often very great, have experiences that seem in some respects like a leaf out of one of the old English fairy tales that Andrew Lang or Joseph Jacobs has rescued for us. A difference there is, however, and Baum has done with mere words what Denslow has done with his delightful draughtsmanship. The story has humor and here and there stray bits of philosophy that will be a moving power on the child mind and will furnish fields of study and investigation for the future students and professors of psychology. Several new features and ideals of fairy life have been introduced into the "Wonderful Wizard," who turns out in the end to be only a wonderful humbug after all. A scarecrow stuffed with straw, a tin woodman, and a cowardly lion do not, at first blush, promise well as moving heroes in a tale when merely mentioned, but in actual practice they take on something of the living and breathing quality that is gloriously exemplified in "The Story of the Three Bears," that has become a classic.

The book has a bright and joyous atmosphere, and does not dwell upon killing and deeds of violence. Enough stirring adventure enters into it, however, to flavor it with zest, and it will indeed be strange if there be a normal child who will not enjoy the story.

But the reviews offer only a slight indication why *The Wizard of Oz* so appealed to the hearts and imaginations of turn-of-the century youngsters. There was nothing on the market quite like it. Baum and Denslow learned from Alice's lament "What is the use of a book without pictures or conversations?" And Denslow embellished the book with many of his most engaging designs. As *Book News* noted, "Mr. Denslow has managed to maintain the reputation for originality that he earned in his former pictures. Besides originality, the illustrations have live action, and humor." He combined the clarity of a Japanese print with the decorative elegance and control of Art Nouveau. His bold lines and flat solid colors must have been a relief after the usual overly sketchy black-and-white drawings that marred much contemporary juvenile literature. In "Children's Books for Children" (*Brush and Pencil*, September 1903), art critic J. M. Bowles tried to express how Denslow's work appealed to a child:

> Den's panels, circles, and spots, and his solid pages of gorgeous hues with perhaps one tiny figure or object in a lower corner are simply baits to catch my attention through the eye, which as yet gets only general impressions. In other words, my friend W. W. Denslow is an impressionist for babies. He omits all but fundamentals and essentials. He leaves out of his books everything except things that exist in our own little world of fact.

Besides the novelty of style, the book was unique in Denslow's use of color. Few children's books at the time so experimented with its possibilities. There were, of course, some picture books, particularly the elegant ones printed by Edmund Evans in England as well as gaudy chromolithographed collections of old nursery lore designed for the very young. But tipped-in color plates were rare for a children's book, and no others had the elaborate textual scheme which changes from locale to locale described in the story.

The extensive colorwork in *The Wonderful Wizard of Oz* revolutionized the design of American children's books. They would never be so wan and boring again. Baum and Denslow proved that novelty could sell. Thereafter Baum sought new and unusual uses of color in his fairy tales. *Queen Zixi of Ix* (1905) imitated the lavish use of color in *The Wizard of Oz* even to its binding, but it was a pale shadow of the original. Many had color plates, others had color pages, and *The Road to Oz* (1909) had signatures of varying colored paper. But none of these was quite as dynamic as *The Wonderful Wizard of Oz*. And none of the others had the built-in integrity of this first one which fully integrated art with text.

Baum, like Denslow, knew what a child liked. He filled his chapters with casual and comic conversations, quite different from the usually stilted language spoken in most contemporary juveniles. He defined character by action and reaction rather than through elaborate description. Baum despised the overtly didactic, so his tales are generally free of the cloying sentimentality and moralizing which lard the now forgotten but once admired children's literature of the last century. Those books that survive often describe the lives of children of other times and other places. *Little Women* and *The Adventures of Tom Sawyer* still interest young readers because they *are* old-fashioned. There were few fairy tales of any consequence by American writers. There were, of course, the wonder stories by Nathaniel Hawthorne, Howard Pyle, and Frank Stockton, but they did not draw as much on American locales or situations as Baum did. They owed much to the flowering of the Victorian fairy tale. American children found more to engage them in Great Britain than at home. They could look to George MacDonald, Lewis Carroll, John Ruskin, Charles Kingsley, Oscar Wilde, and E. Nesbit for their fanciful literature. But children's book publishing in the United States was still saddled with the putrid Puritan morality of the Sunday schools and the American Tract Society. Rarely were little ones given anything to read "just for fun." Baum, however, believed that the pursuit of happiness in their books was their God-given right as American boys and girls.

There were other little nuisances in contemporary juvenile lore which Baum had no use for. The horrors so common to the Grimm and Andersen fairy tales disturbed him as a boy, and he tried to keep them out of his books. He thought romance between princes and princesses tiresome, so love and marriage had no real place in his stories. He also avoided the long-winded descriptive passages that adults adore, but bore young readers. Hans Christian Andersen, he explained in "Modern Fairy Tales" (*The Advance*, August 19, 1909), "had not only a marvelous imagination but he was a poet as well, and surrounded his tales with some of the most beautiful descriptive passages known to our literature. As children you skipped those passages—I can guess that, because as a child I skipped them myself." In the tradition of Noah Webster, Baum generally employed good, solid, unadorned, almost formal American prose. With simple use of detail and emphasis, Baum was able to vividly describe a locale, both atmospherically and physically, whether actual or imaginary. The first few paragraphs of *The Wizard of Oz* alone demonstrate his unique power to create a concrete reality through the barest means. He rarely wasted a word.

Baum was interested first and foremost in telling a compelling story. He criticized Carroll's books for being "rambling and incoherent," but he admired Alice's ability to be "doing something every moment, and doing something strange and marvelous, too; so the child follows her with rapturous delight." Rapturous delight was what Baum sought in his fairy tales. He was not interested in writing for its own sake. He wanted to be understood. He sought clarity in expression despite some clumsiness in sentence structure and syntax. Writing seemed so effortless for him that he rarely revised his work, and some passages could have used more polish. His clarity of imagery sometimes belies his casual manner. Baum wrote for children, but never down to them. He also wrote to please himself, that child within whom he remembered so well. He wanted to entertain. That purpose did not mean he was unwilling to insert a little lesson here and there. In the preface to *Baum's American Fairy Tales* (1908), he explained his intentions in writing "modern tales about modern fairies": "They are not too serious in purpose, but aim to amuse and entertain, yet I trust the more thoughtful of my readers will find a wholesome lesson hidden beneath each extravagant notion and humorous incident." The same could be said of *The Wizard of Oz*. Perhaps he was being ironic when he noted in the copy he gave music publisher Isadore Witmark (now in Butler Library, Columbia

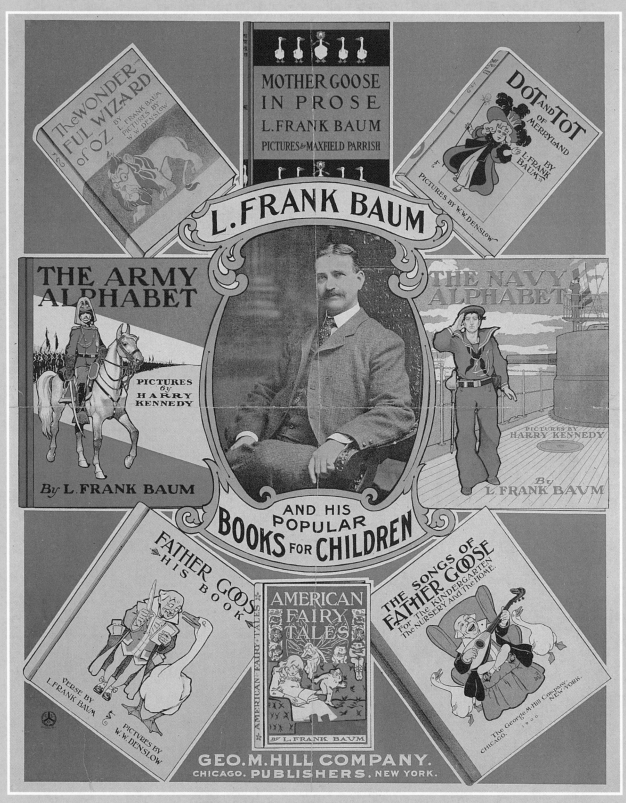

Poster advertising books by L. Frank Baum and published
by the George M. Hill Company, 1901.
Courtesy the Chicago Historical Society.

FATHER GOOSE SHOWS THE CHILDREN HOW TO RUN A DOUBLE-RIPPER---THE AWFUL RESULT. (For Key to the Characters in This Picture See Page 1.)

"Father Goose" comic strip drawn by W. W. Denslow,
New York *World,* January 21, 1900.
Courtesy Michael Gessel Collection.

W. W. Denslow's watercolor for the cover of *The Wonderful Wizard of Oz,* 1900.
*Courtesy C. Warren Hollister Collection; photograph
courtesy the Brandywine River Museum.*

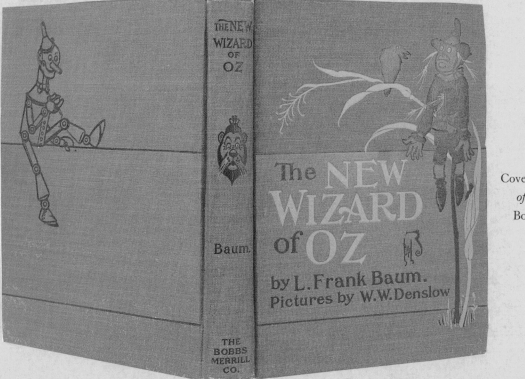

Cover of *The New Wizard
of Oz* (Indianapolis:
Bobbs-Merrill, 1903).
Private collection.

Poster advertising *The Wonderful Wizard of Oz,* issued by the George M. Hill Company, 1900. *Private Collection.*

Poster advertising *The Wonderful Wizard of Oz,* issued by the George M. Hill Company, 1900. *Private collection; photograph courtesy the Brandywine River Museum.*

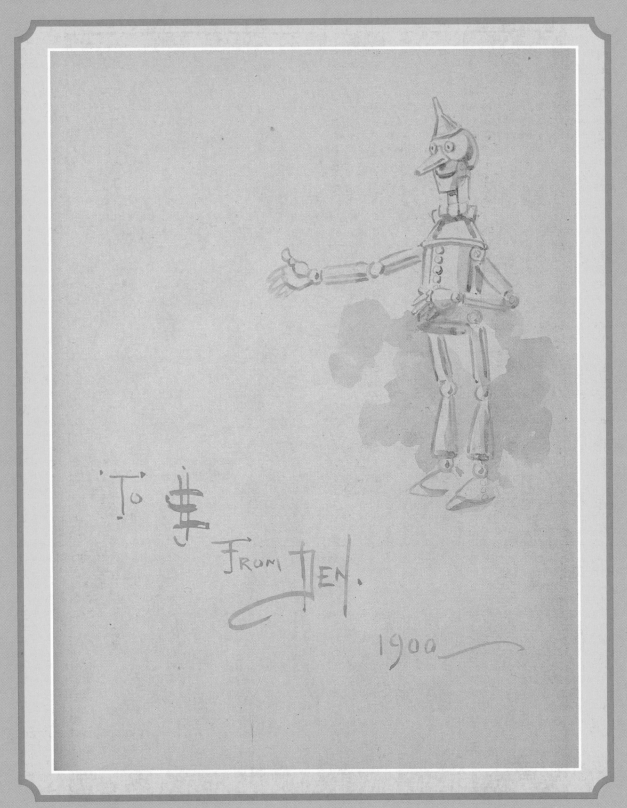

Watercolor of the Tin Woodman by W. W. Denslow in the copy of *The Wonderful Wizard of Oz*
presented to the artist J. C. Leyendecker, 1900.
Private Collection.

Poster advertising the *Wizard of Oz* musical extravaganza, 1902.
Courtesy the Library of Congress.

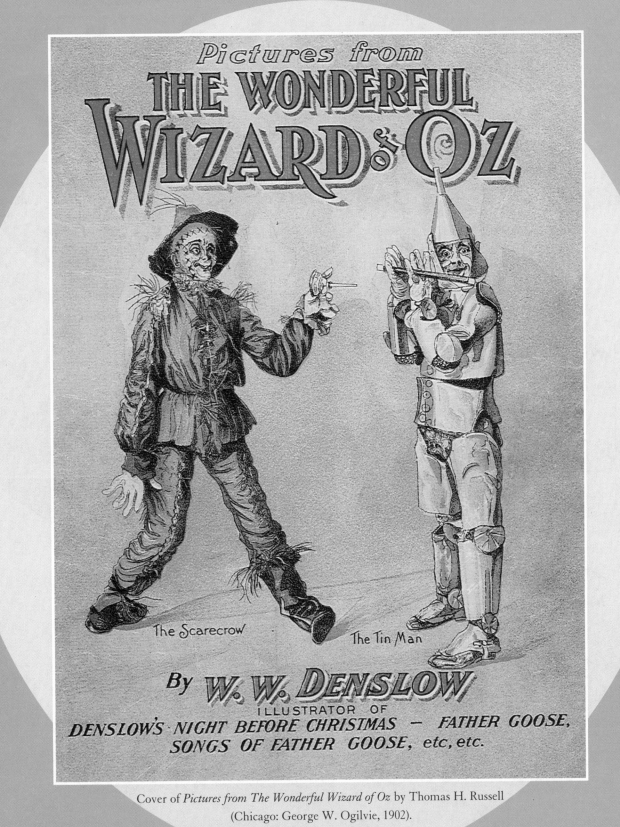

Cover of *Pictures from The Wonderful Wizard of Oz* by Thomas H. Russell
(Chicago: George W. Ogilvie, 1902).

Courtesy Jay Scarfone/William Stillman Collection.

Romola Remus as Dorothy, Frank Burns as
the Scarecrow, George E. Wilson as the
Tin Woodman, Joseph Schrode as the
Cowardly Lion, and Burns Wantling
as the Hungry Tiger in *The Fairylogue
and Radio-Plays,* 1908.
Courtesy Justin G. Schiller.

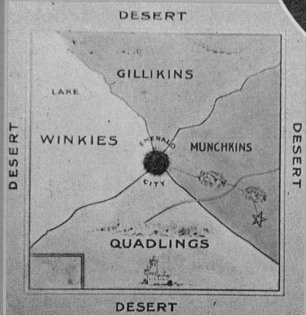

The earliest map of the Land of Oz,
designed by L. Frank Baum for *The
Fairylogue and Radio-Plays,* 1908.
Courtesy Justin G. Schiller.

The Royal Flag of Oz,
issued with *Glinda
of Oz,* 1920.
Private collection.

University) that this was "my most truthful tale." And perhaps not. Many people consider it his most profound work.

Of course, Baum did not intend his story to contain some overriding or underlining moral, as in Aesop's fables or Perrault's fairy tales. He was exploring a personal mythology, in which many truths could be expressed. The characters and incidents in the book may be viewed as symbolic, and symbols can represent many things at the same time. For example, besides possessing courage, intelligence, and kindness, Dorothy's three companions embody the three states of Nature—animal, vegetable, and mineral. Baum contrasts gray Kansas to colorful Oz. Is this to be read as a statement that the real world is far less colorful than the landscape of one's imagination? "But," as W. H. Auden said of George MacDonald's stories, "to hunt for symbols in a fairy tale is absolutely fatal."[20]

One cannot overemphasize Baum's conscious development of the "modernized" fairy tale. There were, of course, earlier attempts at defining America as fairyland. Tales by Washington Irving and Nathaniel Hawthorne reflect this search for an indigenously American mythology. But Baum had no interest in preserving local legends as Irving did or in Hawthorne's disturbing metaphysics. Baum concerned himself with the immediate interests and desires of the child of his own time. He chose not, as Hawthorne did, to return to the Greco-Roman traditions to invent a mythology; he felt no need to imitate the Grimms' wonder tales, as Pyle did. He explained in his introduction to *Baum's American Fairy Tales* that his stories "bear the stamp of our times and depict the progressive fairies of today. He did not look back as did his predecessors. He was a Progressive, not a Romantic. He looked forward and sought new forms. Baum taught children, Edward Wagenknecht pointed out in *Utopia Americana* (Seattle: University of Washington Book Store, 1929), "to look for the element of wonder in the life around them, to realize that even smoke and machinery may be transformed into fairy lore if only we have sufficient energy and vision to penetrate to their significance and transform them to our use" (p. 29).

Baum never succeeded in creating a purely "American" fairy tale. His witches and wizards, magic shoes and enchanted caps, came from Europe to inhabit the same universe as his scarecrows, patchwork girls, and magic dishpans. Not all of the stories in *American Fairy Tales* are either American or fairy tales! And some are rather poor. Several of Baum's finest books are what he called "old-fashioned" fairy tales; Edward Wagenknecht called

20. "Afterword" in MacDonald's *The Light Princess* (New York: Farrar, Straus & Giroux, 1967).

Queen Zixi of Ix one of the best fairy tales ever written. These were "once-upon-a-time" tales, rather than here-and-now storybooks like the Oz series. Only when the children clamored for "more about Oz, Mr. Baum" did he give up these other realms for his most famous and beloved fairyland.

Remarkably, adults embraced *The Wonderful Wizard of Oz* as readily as did the children. Juvenile literature may be written for young readers, but their parents are the ones who buy it. And they were fascinated with the new fairy tale. There was nothing childish about this children's book. Text and art possessed a sophistication that suited turn-of-the-century taste. There was a subtlety to the storytelling that elevated the book above the usual juvenile. Baum slipped little bits of wit and wisdom into his narrative; many of readers do not discover these sly asides until they themselves are grown. As MacFall noted in *To Please a Child*, the most popular American fiction at the time was escapist romance. Adults were reading Anthony Hope's *The Prisoner of Zenda* (1894), Edwin Caskoden's *When Knighthood Was in Flower* (1898), and George Barr McCutcheon's *Graustark* (1901); the latter was the first American best-seller of the new century and for the nearly thirty years inspired countless adventure stories set in fictional European kingdoms. Manifest Destiny had resoundingly manifested itself, and the American West was officially closed as the nation spread from one shore to the other. Now that the American Empire expanded to Hawaii and Puerto Rico and the Philippines as a consequence of the Spanish-American War of 1898, people wanted to read about foreign lands. The naturalism of the nineties eventually gave way to the realists, to the journalists-turned-novelists. The Chicago described by Theodore Dreiser in his scandalous *Sister Carrie* (1900) and Carl Sandburg's "hog butcher for the world" really belonged to a later era. But at the turn of the century, the genteel literary public wanted fanciful stories, and Baum would provide the same for the children. If their parents were heading off to medieval nations and mythical European duchies, why should they not read about a new fairyland?

Despite the immediate success of *The Wonderful Wizard of Oz,* the Baums were still a little short as the holidays approached. The first royalty was not due until January, but Maud insisted that Frank go see Hill and ask for a little money in advance to help pay for Christmas presents. He reluctantly did as he was told, and the publisher instructed the clerk to make out his statement. Baum put it in his pocket without even looking at it and then returned home. Maud was in the kitchen ironing his other shirt when she asked if he had the money. He handed over the check, and expecting $100 at most, Maud was startled to see it was for $3,432.64! In all the excitement, she forgot about the iron and it burned Frank's shirt. Baum later asked Hill to give him the canceled check so he could hang it up in his house as a souvenir of his good fortune.[21] There was good reason to celebrate that holiday, and the Denslows invited the Baums and other friends to join them for New Year's Eve at Rector's, then one of Chicago's most fashionable restaurants. And the guests toasted the new century about a table with a delightful centerpiece of a small replica of the Tin Woodman surrounded by American Beauty roses.[22]

Baum had many more stories to tell, and his new prosperity afforded him the flexibility and luxury to try his hand at all sorts of books for various publishers. He had not yet found his special place in juvenile letters, and the variety of offerings was extraordinary. Just one year after *The Wonderful Wizard of Oz* was published in 1900, he produced "an electrical fairy tale," *The Master Key;* a collection of short whimsical contemporary fantasies, *American Fairy Tales;* and another book-length story along the lines of *The Wizard of Oz*, *Dot and Tot of Merryland*. None of them repeated the phenomenal success of their predecessor. Not even the delightful pictures of *Dot and Tot of Merryland* could save it from relative obscurity.

Cover of brochure advertising L. Frank Baum's books published by the George M. Hill Company, 1901.

Private collection.

Denslow was now riding the crest of the wave of his new reputation as the most exciting American illustrator of children's books. He was being favorably mentioned in the company of

---

21. See "Frank Baum's Manager Tells How Check for $13,700 Awakened Author to Real Merit of His First Published Work," Rock Island (Ill.) *Daily Union,* November 8, 1908; and Harry Neal Baum, "Father was 'The Wizard of Oz,'" *The Baum Bugle,* Autumn 1985, p. 10. The story has been told and retold many times, with the amount of the check varying with each storyteller. Maud Baum said it was $13,000 when she appeared on the Robert L. Ripley's NBC radio program *Believe It Or Not,* September 22, 1939. But according to the account book kept by Denslow, who received payment equal to Baum's, the money owed at that time was $3,432.64.

22. Society column in Chicago *Journal,* January 2, 1901.

Walter Crane, Kate Greenaway, Randolph Caldecott, Maurice Boutet de Monvel. He had other books to illustrate. When readers of the women's magazines wanted to know what they should give their children, the editors often recommended *Father Goose* or anything illustrated by Denslow. He produced an elaborate edition of the old nursery rhymes boldly titled *Denslow's Mother Goose* for McClure, Phillips & Co. of New York and was drawing a weekly Sunday comic page called "Billy Bounce" for the McClure Syndicate. He also spent a summer in East Aurora, New York, designing for Elbert Hubbard's Roycrofters, before opening his studio in New York City. During all this activity, Denslow found time to add some of his finest work to *Dot and Tot of Merryland*.

This book was the last Baum-Denslow collaboration. What actually caused the spilt is not known, but it was likely a number of factors. The first was purely practical: Baum did not need Denslow any more than Denslow needed Baum. Each was now firmly established in the juvenile book trade to go out and prosper on his own without sharing his royalty with the other, and *Dot and Tot of Merryland* had not been a resounding success as their earlier books had been. *The Master Key* was getting such great press that Baum wrote in the copy he gave his son Robert, the dedicatee, "I am sorry, now, I did not end it differently and leave an opening for a sequel." In August 1903, *St. Nicholas* listed it as one of the most popular books chosen by its young readers. Actual sales of the book were disappointing, but *Denslow's Mother Goose* reportedly sold 40,000 copies within the first two months of publication. Neither author nor artist was dependent upon the other now.

Years after their successful collaboration had collapsed, Maud Baum explained simply, "Denslow got a swelled head, hence the change."[23] There had been considerable rivalry between Baum and Denslow ever since the unprecedented response to *Father Goose, His Book*. Who was more responsible for this success, Baum or Denslow? Baum admitted that his work on it had not been good and knew that Denslow's contribution had been more significant than his own, but he did not care for Denslow's attitude. While Denslow may have been better known to the public than Baum was in 1899, there was really no reason why he should at first draw on the cover design of *Father Goose*, which is now housed in the Prints and Drawings Division of the New York Public Library, in large letters "Pictures by W. W. Denslow" and give Baum a smaller credit as author. Denslow also drew two "Father Goose" comic pages for the New York *World* in 1900, neither

23. Letter to Jack Snow, June 21, 1943.

mentioning Baum as co-creator of the book on which they were based. Baum admitted with some bitterness to his publishers, on August 10, 1915, "Denslow was allowed to copyright his pictures conjointly with my claim to authorship," and "having learned my lesson from my unfortunate experiences with Denslow, I will never permit another artist to have an interest in the drawings he makes of my described characters, if I can help it." And he never did. The growing animosity culminated in 1901 during a fractious dispute that went on for weeks over the proposed musical extravaganza of *The Wizard of Oz*. Baum and Paul Tietjens, as librettist and composer of the play, did not feel that Denslow as costume designer deserved a share of the earnings equal to each of theirs. But Denslow, being co-owner of the copyright of the book on which the play was based, demanded the same as the other two, although he was only minimally responsible for the preparation of the story on the stage. To avoid any lawsuit or the possibility that the show would never be produced, Baum and Tietjens finally came to an agreement with Denslow. They always felt that he had cheated them.

Despite their joint contract with Hill, Baum and Denslow were already preparing to go their separate ways by the end of 1901. Baum delivered the manuscript of his new book, *The Life and Adventures of Santa Claus*, to the publisher on Christmas Day, but nowhere in the preliminary advertising is Denslow mentioned as illustrator of the new fairy tale. Then the failure of the George M. Hill Company made it convenient for author and artist to end their previously lucrative collaboration.

Hill was forced into bankruptcy in March 1902, just a few weeks after announcing the construction of a new building and the expansion of the firm. Not even the reputation of the Baum-Denslow line could stall his creditors. On April 26, the court appointed Robert O. Law as temporary receiver and trustee, and he ordered the property sold. *Publishers Weekly* announced on March 29 the sale of "a modern book bindery . . . several hundred sets of plates . . . juvenile books (including a number of the Baum-Denslow copyrighted juveniles) . . . and books in sheets and 'in process.'" Hill tried to regain control of the company, but negotiations to form the George W. Ogilvie Company to handle the holdings were completed on May 8. C. O. Owen & Co. bought Hill's manufacturing plant and then resold it to the newly formed Hill Bindery Company, with George Hill as manager. Frank K. Reilly and Sumner C. Britton quickly founded the Madison Book Company, to take over Hill's technical books and act as sole western distributor of the George W. Ogilvie list. Another new house, Cupples & Leon Co. in New York, became the sole selling agent in the East.

Ogilvie, brother of the New York publisher J. S. Ogilvie, advertised as late as August 1902 that the Baum-Denslow titles would soon be issued under his imprint. They never were.

Baum himself became personally embroiled in Hill's financial problems. *The Bookseller and Latest Literature* reported that on April 4, 1902, at a meeting of the Illinois Women's Press Association, Baum delivered a lecture titled "The Relationship Between the Author and the Publisher." Obviously referring to his experiences with Hill, he advised authors to stick to one house; he spoke of the injustice of deserting a publisher after the publisher had invested heavily in advertising to make a reputation for a writer. Surprisingly he insisted upon a small royalty rate to encourage the publisher to put more money into advertising, which would result in greater sales. He also expressed his disapproval of editorial revision of an author's manuscript, on the grounds that only the writer could make changes fully within the spirit of the original work.

Both Baum and Denslow wanted the book to be reissued in time for the opening of the musical extravaganza *The Wizard of Oz* in June 1902. But debts and other troubles Ogilvie inherited from Hill prevented its happening immediately. *The Bookseller and Latest Literature* reported in August, "In the Baum-Denslow matter the court allowed the claim of Mr. Denslow and ruled that the author and artist were not partner; so the payments to one would not apply to the royalties due both. A large sum is tied up pending the decision of the court on the disputed matters." The trouble arose over the large amount of money Hill was constantly advancing Baum, which Denslow never requested. The artist finally had to sue Ogilvie to recover royalties he said were properly due him. The company argued that Baum and Denslow were a partnership, and it did not have to pay Denslow until Baum's debt was cleared up. The friction between illustrator and publisher grew so ugly that the Madison Book Company refused to sell copies of *The Wizard of Oz* and the other books directly to Denslow, but recommended he buy them at one of the big department stores. The court decided in Denslow's favor, and Ogilvie was obliged to pay what was owed him. And the company sued Baum to recover the debt he owed Hill. Apparently the case was settled out of court.

Baum and Denslow also brought joint suit against Ogilvie to secure the plates for the books, which they claimed were their property. Bobbs-Merrill (named Bowen-Merrill until 1903) of Indianapolis had published *The Master Key* and was eager to issue Baum's backlist as well as his new books. They had already taken over *The Life and Adventures of Santa Claus* from Hill and put it out in plenty of time for the holidays. The Hill company troubles continued into January 1903, and by May one of Ogilvie's backers had backed out. Desperate to make use of the stock he had on hand, Ogilvie hastily put together *Pictures from The Wonderful Wizard of Oz*. (See the Denslow Appendix.) This slim pamphlet was made up of unused sheets of the color plates for the book with an entirely new story by Thomas Russell printed on the versos. It made no mention of Baum or the word "Oz," and Dorothy was only "the Little Girl." While Denslow's name appeared on the cover and title page, he probably had no hand in its publication. It was capitalizing on the musical extravaganza; its cover sported a cover lithograph of its stars, Fred A. Stone and David C. Montgomery, in their roles as the Scarecrow and the Tin Woodman. It may well have been sold in the theater lobbies where the show was playing.

Finally Baum and Denslow got control of the plates and turned them over to Bobbs-Merrill. But not wishing to confuse the children's story with the freely adapted musical extravaganza, the publishers retitled their book *The New Wizard of Oz*.[24] Denslow drew a special new cover, titlepage, and endpapers for the reissue. But the general production of the book was cheapened. Bobbs-Merrill cut down the twenty-four color plates to only sixteen, and the former elaborate color scheme of the textual illustrations was restricted to just bright red-orange and green. Bobbs-Merrill deposited copies in the British Library in London, the Advocates' Library in Edinburgh, and the Bodleian Library in Oxford to protect its British copyright; Hodder & Stoughton published it in England in 1906. Unfortunately, Baum was not happy with how Bobbs-Merrill sold his books, so he went to Reilly and Britton to offer them his new book, a sequel to *The Wizard of Oz*. The

24. The publishers almost immediately dropped "New" from the cover and spine, but retained it on the title page and the running heads. *The New Wizard of Oz* was the official title of all Bobbs-Merrill editions, even after the publisher replaced Denslow's pictures with Evelyn Copelman's and entirely reset and redesigned the book in 1944. In 1921, David L. Chambers of the Bobbs-Merrill Company considered modernizing *The Wizard of Oz* by asking Johnny Gruelle, the creator of Raggedy Ann, to do new pictures for the famous story. Gruelle was all ready to do it when Chambers realized that the company's agreement had been with both Baum and Denslow and he could not see his way around dropping the original illustrations without losing rights to the book. Edward Wagenknecht tried in the 1930s to persuade Chambers to get English artist Arthur Rackham to reillustrate the book, but Chambers finally decided that the public would never accept any other illustrator of the story but Denslow. The release of the 1939 MGM musical changed all that. But it was not until 1944 that Bobbs-Merrill hired a young illustrator, Evelyn Copelman, for an updated edition of *The Wizard of Oz*. Although the title page said that her designs were "adapted from the famous pictures by W. W. Denslow," Copelman used the conceptions in the Judy Garland movie to guide her in drawing the characters. She did a new version of *The Magical Monarch of Mo* in 1947. See William Stillman's "The Lost Illustrator of Oz (and Mo)," *The Baum Bugle,* Winter 1996.

Madison Book Company reformed as the Reilly & Britton Company to publish *The Marvelous Land of Oz* in 1904.

Denslow soon had problems of his own. Not long after he moved to New York, his marriage collapsed. Ann Waters had fallen in love with a young artist, Lawrence Mazzanovich, whom she married in Paris, and she bore him a child. But on Christmas Eve 1904, Denslow himself remarried, to Frances Dolittle, a widow who was said to be wealthy. He continued to illustrate children's books, notably *Denslow's Night Before Christmas* (1902) and his eighteen-volume "Denslow's Picture Book Series" (1903–1904). With royalties from the musical extravaganza *The Wizard of Oz,* he bought an island off the coast of Bermuda and crowned himself King Denslow I of Denslow Island with his native boatman as the admiral of his fleet and his Japanese cook as prime minister. He succeeded in getting his children's book *The Pearl and the Pumpkin* (1904), written with songwriter Paul West, turned into a musical extravaganza, but it was not another *Wizard of Oz*. He began drinking heavily, his third wife divorced him, and he had difficulty securing work. He briefly lived in Buffalo, where he designed charming advertising pamphlets, but his last years were back in New York City, working for a second-rate art agency. He drew sheet music covers and pictures for *John Martin's Magazine,* and his future looked brighter when he sold a full-color cover to the original *Life* magazine, then a comic weekly. Elated with the commission, he went out to celebrate, got drunk, and caught pneumonia.[25] W. W. Denslow died on May 27, 1915, the same year Elbert Hubbard and his wife went down with the *Lusitania*. All this time Baum heard little about his old collaborator; when Denslow died, Baum was erroneously informed that the artist had committed suicide.

Although he lost both his illustrator and his publisher in 1902, Baum was also blessed with the biggest success of his career, the musical extravaganza based on *The Wizard of Oz*. Who came up with the idea of the show is not known. According to Paul Tietjens's diary, the composer had been urging Baum for weeks to consider it, but the author was reluctant to do anything with the story, because Denslow shared the rights and the two of them were then not on good terms. Baum and Tietjens labored on a comic opera, *The Octopus or The Title Trust*, which they could not place, so Baum gave in to Tietjens and Denslow and wrote the libretto for a musical spectacular based on his children's book. Denslow then took it to Fred A. Hamlin, business manager of the Chicago Grand Opera House. Since the family had made

25. In a letter to David L. Greene from Maurice Kursh, who knew Denslow in his last years, May 11, 1968.

Cover of prospectus announcing the production of the musical extravaganza
The Wizard of Oz, 1902. The illustration is an "Inland Gnome," drawn by
W. W. Denslow in 1894 for *The Inland Printer.*
Courtesy the Billy Rose Theatre Collection, The New York Public Library
for the Performing Arts, Astor, Lenox and Tilden Foundations.

its fortune from a cure-all called Wizard Oil, Hamlin thought he had
another winner and agreed to produce it next summer.

Baum presented him with a five-act operetta which stuck closely to the
children's story. But when Hamlin sent it to Julian Mitchell, stage director
of the Weber & Fields musical reviews and later *The Ziegfeld Follies,* he
wrote "NO GOOD" across the front of the manuscript and sent it back. Ham-

lin then mailed him the children's book, which so intrigued Mitchell, particularly the characters of the Scarecrow and the Tin Woodman, that he agreed to direct the show only if the libretto was entirely rewritten. He drew up a scenario himself to guide Baum in his revision. Baum recalled it somewhat differently in the Chicago *Record-Herald* (June 10, 1902):

> But after Julian Mitchell had seen the manuscript he urged my adapting it to a modern extravaganza, on account of the gorgeous scenic effects and absurd situations suggested by the story. This I accomplished after much labor, for I found it necessary to alter materially the story of the book. When I wrote the fairy tale I allowed my imagination full play, so that a great deal of the action is absolutely impossible to adapt to the limitations of the stage. So I selected the most available portions and filled the gaps by introducing several new characters and minor plots which serve to throw the story of Dorothy and her unique companions into stronger relief. The main plot of the book is retained, and its readers will have little difficulty in recognizing the well-known characters as they journey in search of the Emerald City and the wonderful Wizard.

Actually Baum's collaboration with Mitchell and the script doctors was a rocky one, and Hamlin finally informed Baum that either the show would be done Mitchell's way or it would not be done at all. "I was told," Baum explained, "that what constituted fun in a book would be missed by the average audience, which is accustomed to a regular gatling-gun discharge of wit—or what stands for wit. So I secured the assistance of two experts in this line of work, selected by the advice of Manager Hamlin, and they peppered my prosy lines with a multitude of 'laughs.' " The play was written and rewritten, numbers tossed out and replaced by new ones. "The original story was practically ignored," Baum wrote the Chicago *Tribune* (June 26, 1904), "the dialogue rehashed, the situations transposed, my Nebraska wizard made into an Irishman, and several other characters forced to conform to the requirements of the new schedule." Toto was replaced by a cow named Imogene, and other new characters included Sir Dashemoff Daily the Poet Laureate (played by a woman in tights), a Kansas waitress named Tryxie Tryfle, Cynthia Cynch the Lady Lunatic, and Pastoria, a Topeka motorman and Ex-King of the Emerald City. By opening night, few of Baum's original lines remained in the script.

The produced play hardly resembled the children's book on which it was based. It was more a musical revue or vaudeville show, stringing together topical songs and eccentric dances, comic routines and spectacular scenic effects. On opening night, June 16, 1902, *The Wizard of Oz* made theatrical history at Hamlin's Grand Opera House. Mitchell's vast knowledge of what the public wanted turned *The Wizard of Oz* into the most successful show of its day, and its influence on the musical comedy was evident for the next decade. A New York engagement was quickly secured, and it was the very first offering at William Randolph Hearst's new Majestic Theatre on Columbus Circle in January 1903. During this era, perhaps only the revue *Florodora* and the operetta *The Merry Widow* did better on Broadway than *The Wizard of Oz*. No one was more pleased with the triumph of the musical extravaganza than the author himself, as he told the Chicago *Sunday Record-Herald* (June 29, 1902):

> Few people can understand the feelings of an author who for the first time sees his creations depicted by living characters upon the stage. The Scarecrow, the Tin Woodman and the Cowardly Lion were real children of my brain, having no existence in fact or fiction until I placed them in the pages of my book. But to describe them with pen and ink is very different from seeing them actually live. When the Scarecrow came to life on the first night of *The Wizard of Oz* I experienced strange sensations of wonder and awe; the appearance of the Tin Woodman made me catch my breath spasmodically, and when the gorgeous poppy field, with its human flowers, burst on my view—more real than my fondest dreams had ever conceived—a big lump came into my throat and a wave of gratitude swept over me that I had lived to see the sight. I cannot feel shame at these emotions. To me they were as natural as the characters were real. Perhaps all authors have like experiences, and if so, they, at least, can sympathize with me.

Much of the musical's success was due to Mitchell's direction and the cast's performances. The script was little more than serviceable, and today seems dated and lifeless. The music was mediocre, and none has survived the play. Former vaudevillians Montgomery and Stone were the hits of the show as the Tin Woodman and Scarecrow. Overnight, *The Wizard of Oz* made them musical comedy stars, and they went on to success after success in *The Red Mill, Lady of the Slipper,* and other Broadway productions. Anna Laughlin was a lovely Dorothy, and Bessie Wynn and Lotta Faust sang several successful interpolated hit songs. Also popular were the cow Imogene (performed by Fred Stone's brother Edwin) and the Cowardly Lion (English "pantomime" star Arthur Hill). Mitchell provided more for the eye than the ear, beginning with a thrilling cyclone. There were troops of marching chorus girls and all sorts of specialty numbers. The most spectacular scene was the Deadly Poppy Field. Baum had dressed the chorus as blossoms, and Mitchell destroyed them with a snowstorm onstage. "I was filled with amazement, indeed," Baum recalled his initial response to the show in the Chicago *Tribune* (June 26, 1904), "and took occasion to protest against several innovations that I did not like; but Mr. Mitchell listened to the plaudits of the big audiences and turned a deaf ear to my complaints. . . . The people will have what pleases them, and not what the author happens to favor, and I believe that one of the reasons why Julian Mitchell is recognized as a great producer is that he faithfully tries to serve the great mass of playgoers—and usually succeeds." Among the people who affectionately recalled the show were playwright Eugene O'Neill, poet Vachel Lindsay, and essayist E. B. White.

Mitchell was not finished: he added and threw out songs and jokes and characters to keep the show in the black for years on the road. He started up a second company that toured simultaneously with the original production. Even after Montgomery and Stone deserted the show, it played to packed houses across the country.

Fred A. Stone as the Scarecrow and David C. Montgomery as the Tin Woodman in the musical extravaganza *The Wizard of Oz,* 1902.
Courtesy the Billy Rose Theatre Collection, The New York Public Library for the Performing Arts, Astor, Lenox and Tilden Foundations.

Anna Laughlin as Dorothy in the musical extravaganza *The Wizard of Oz,* 1902.
Courtesy the Billy Rose Theatre Collection, The New York Public Library for the Performing Arts, Astor, Lenox and Tilden Foundations.

The cyclone scene in the Broadway production of the musical
extravaganza *The Wizard of Oz*, 1903.
*Courtesy the Billy Rose Theatre Collection, The New York Public Library for the
Performing Arts, Astor, Lenox and Tilden Foundations.*

Hamlin and Mitchell's immediate successor to *The Wizard of Oz* was Victor
Herbert's famous *Babes in Toyland,* with some of the same players in the
cast; it was only one of many musical comedies that tried in vain to capture
the magic of Baum's show. None of these others ran for eight years as *The
Wizard of Oz* did.

Baum had never lost his love for the theater, and the success of the musical extravaganza gave him the confidence to seek other productions. He
now juggled his career between children's books and librettos. Unfortunately, despite the reputation of *The Wizard of Oz* and all the time he devoted to these projects, he just could not interest any producer in putting one
of his plays on the stage. So he wrote a sequel to *The Wizard of Oz* with the
intention of turning it into another musical extravaganza. Originally called
"The Further Adventures of the Scarecrow and Tin Woodman," a title no
one liked, the story was tailored to the talents of Montgomery and Stone.

The snowstorm in the Broadway production of the musical extravaganza
The Wizard of Oz, 1903.
Courtesy the Billy Rose Theatre Collection, The New York Public Library
for the Performing Arts, Astor, Lenox and Tilden Foundations.

LADY LUNATIC   **WIZARD OF OZ**   **TRYXIE TRYFLE**

Characters from the 1902 musical extravaganza of *The Wizard of Oz*,
drawn by W. W. Denslow.
Private collection.

Sketch of Fred Stone in the role of the Scarecrow in the 1902 musical extravaganza of *The Wizard of Oz*, drawn by W. W. Denslow, Lewiston (Me.) *Saturday Journal,* February 21, 1903.
Courtesy the Library of Congress.

William Randolph Hearst caricatured by W. A. Rogers as "The Wizard of Ooze," *Harper's Weekly*, October 1906.
Courtesy Michael Gessel.

Baum even dedicated it to the two actors, and their pictures in costume graced the endpapers. Reilly & Britton brought out *The Marvelous Land of Oz* with illustrations by John R. Neill (1877–1943), a young Philadelphia newspaper artist chosen by the publishers. It was just as successful as *The Wizard of Oz* and established the long line of Oz books. Baum immediately adapted it as *The Woggle-Bug*, with lyrics by Baum and music by Frederic Chapin. He was unable to secure Montgomery and Stone in the end, and it was one of the worst failures of the summer of 1905. Labeled a "kiddies' show," it discouraged adults from coming. Although the score was praised, the libretto and performers were flat. Baum had promised the Chicago *Tribune* (June 26, 1904) that "should I ever attempt another extravaganza, or dramatize another of my books, I mean to profit by the lesson Mr. Mitchell has taught me [with *The Wizard of Oz*], and sacrifice personal preference to the demands of those I shall expect to purchase admission tickets." But he had not learned his lesson from Mitchell, for he failed to refashion his fairy tale to the demands of a sophisticated theater public.

Before the play closed, Baum and his publisher aggressively promoted it and the children's book upon which it was based in all sorts of ways. With the cartoonist Walt McDougall (1858–1938), Baum prepared a Sunday comic page titled "Queer Visitors from the Marvelous Land of Oz," which the Philadelphia *North American* syndicated to other cities around the country from November 1904 to February 1905, just months before the play was ready to open. The early installments carried a Woggle-Bug Contest to familiarize the public with the book and play's most eccentric character. Baum and Tietjens wrote the song "What Did the Woggle-Bug Say?" to promote the contest. Baum also put

John R. Neill.
Courtesy the John R. Neill Estate.

Caricature of W. W. Denslow's Dorothy and Toto by
John R. Neill in *The Road to Oz,* 1909.
Private collection.

Fred Mace as the Woggle Bug in
The Woggle Bug, 1905.
Courtesy the Billy Rose Theatre Collection,
The New York Public Library for the
Performing Arts, Astor, Lenox
and Tilden Foundations.

out a gaudy, oversize picture book, *The Woggle-Bug Book,* illustrated by Ike
Morgan; it was probably the worst children's story Baum ever wrote. None
of these novelties helped the play; it lasted less than a month.

Another consequence of the publication of Baum's sequel to *The Wizard
of Oz* was Denslow's free use of the same characters elsewhere. Unfortunately, since the illustrator co-owned the copyright of the book with the
author, Denslow had as much claim to them as Baum did. And Baum never
thought of hiring Denslow to do *The Marvelous Land of Oz.* Instead, the
illustrator of *The Wizard of Oz* put out a children's book of his own,
Denslow's Scarecrow and the Tin-Man (1904); but rather than basing it directly upon the earlier fairy tale, he wrote a story about the stage characters
running away from the theater one day. He dedicated it to "Little Freddie
Stone." It was issued in a single volume and in an anthology of his picture
books. (See the Denslow Appendix.) He too drew a Sunday comic page,
"Denslow's Scarecrow and the Tin-Man," but it was not as widely circulated as Baum's "Queer Visitors from the Marvelous Land of Oz." Just as
Baum did not mention Denslow in any of his new Oz projects, Denslow
never acknowledged Baum as co-creator of the characters.

Despite the failure of *The Woggle-Bug,* the Baums were now comfortable. The royalties from the *Wizard of Oz* musical extravaganza made its
author both wealthy and famous. His children's books continued to do well,
and Baum increased his income by writing potboilers, both adult and
teenage fiction. The Aunt Jane's Nieces series by "Edith Van Dyne" was
nearly as popular as the Oz books. Besides having a home in Chicago and a
summer cottage in Macatawa, the Baums now spent their winters at the
luxurious Hotel del Coronado in California, where he wrote several of his
Oz books. In 1906, with several manuscripts in his publishers' hands, Baum
and his wife could now afford to go on a six-month tour of Egypt and
Europe. Of course, he was writing all along the route to meet his contracts.
Publishers Weekly (January 6, 1906) reported that Baum was preparing a
new series of fairy tales based upon "The Fairies of the Nile." These were
never published, but some of their ideas may have been incorporated into
other stories. He gathered material along the Nile that was incorporated
into *The Last Egyptian,* an adult novel he published anonymously in 1908.
The Baums tried to see everything they could from the eruption of Vesu-
vius in Italy to the Louvre in Paris. But it was really Maud's trip rather
than Frank's, and she eagerly ascended the Great Pyramid and visited an
Egyptian harem. The following year Frank collected and edited her letters
home as *In Other Lands Than Ours*, and he took the photographs that illustrated it.

While visiting Paris, Baum reportedly looked into the infant motion picture industry. Intrigued by a new Parisian transparent coloring of film, Baum bought from the inventor, Michel Radio, the rights to exploit the method in the United States. His son Frank J. Baum was delivering a series of slide talks of his recent experiences in the Philippines and other parts of Asia, and Baum thought why not do the same thing about the Land of Oz. He conceived of a "fairylogue"—a travelogue that took one to fairyland rather than to China. But what made his tour so novel, in addition to hand-colored slides by E. Pollack taken from pictures in his children's books, was a series of short "Radio-Plays," hand-colored trick movies shot in the Selig Studios in Chicago. Colonel William Nicholas Selig, a largely forgotten movie pioneer, had patented a motion picture camera in 1896. He then opened a studio in Chicago as well as the very first one in Hollywood.

L. Frank and Maud Baum in Egypt, 1906.
Courtesy Robert A. Baum, Jr.

The films were then sent to Paris, where they were colored by hand by Duval Frères. Baum's *Fairylogue and Radio-Plays* was a complex advertising campaign for the Reilly & Britton Oz books and another fairy tale illustrated by John R. Neill, *John Dough and the Cherub* (1906), combining colored lantern slides and brief color motion pictures, but Baum alone paid all the production costs through loans from banks and wealthy friends. These costs included everything from making the slides and shooting the movies to the shoes, wigs, and papier-mâché properties. Since this was the days of the early silent pictures, Baum lectured about the Land of Oz while the slides changed and the films rolled. The whole performance was accompanied by a live orchestra playing a score Nathaniel D. Mann wrote specially for the show. Since he was paying for everything, *The Fairylogue and Radio-Plays* was the first Oz production of which Baum had entire artistic control.

In an interview in the New York *Herald* (September 26, 1909), Baum described how some of these special effects were accomplished:

> One of the simplest of these [tricks] is shown in the introduction of my fairy story entertainment, when my little characters step from the pages of an Oz book preparatory to becoming the moving actors of my little tales. A closed book is first shown, which the fairies open. On the first page is disclosed a black and white picture of little Dorothy. . . . I beckon, and she straightway steps out of its pages, becomes imbued with the colors of life

L. Frank Baum surrounded by the characters in *The Fairylogue and Radio-Plays*, 1908.
Courtesy Robert A. Baum, Jr.

and moves about. The fairies then close the book, which opens again and again till the Tin Man, the Scarecrow and all the others step out of the pages of the book and come, colored, to life. . . .

How is it done? Well, grooves were cut to the exact shape of each character, and each character stood within its groove in the books and so was photographed in black and white. At the signal each steps forth, and the groove in which each stood being backed by white, no grotto can be seen, while at the same time the fairies close the book. Between each character the camera is stopped, the new character is arranged in his grotto till all is ready—then the arrangers move away, the camera starts again, the fairies open the book, and a new character steps into life. . . . We found it necessary to color the figures in this particular movement artificially, as we found a difficulty in changing from black and white to colors on one film, but even this needed great ingenuity. You can imagine that when the figures are enlarged from three-quarters of an inch to eight feet high the coloring of them would have to be exceptionally delicate or great smudges of tint would occur upon the screen. So the films had to be colored under a tremendous magnifying glass and many attempts were made before thoroughly satisfactory results were obtained.

The short moving pictures employed elementary tricks of stop-action animation and double exposure already developed by George Méliès, Edwin S. Porter, and other early screen wizards. They were remarkable by the standards of 1908 when they were filmed; and some were quite simple, like the construction of the flying Gump from *The Marvelous Land of Oz* (1904):

They first drag in two sofas, which are placed with the seats together and bound with a long clothesline. They place a stuffed Gump or deer head at one end and a broom at the other to serve as a tail. Then they run off the stage and fetch some big palm leaves to act as wings. When the characters have all climbed into this queer flying machine and begin to wave the palm leaf wings the machine rises into the air and flies away with them.

The effect . . . is startling, but is easily explained. When the characters leave the stage the camera that is taking the picture is suddenly stopped, and then workmen come on and attach invisible wires to the sofa flying machine. These wires extend into the flies, where they are joined to a runway. When everything is properly prepared the workmen leave the stage, the camera again begins taking the succession of minute pictures and the characters appear with their palm leaves and climb aboard the sofas. Next moment the invisible wires pull them into the sky, and the effect is complete.

Bewitchments were also achieved with just a little cinematic ingenuity, as in another incident from *The Marvelous Land of Oz* in which a boy was transformed into a girl:

> He melts before your eyes, thinner and thinner, till he is almost gone, when, growing out of the mist of him, which is almost gone, appears a little girl, vague and shadowy at first, but stronger and stronger till she at length stands before you solid as she can be. How is the result arrived at? It is a matter of the length of exposure and a little adjustment. You see, the moving picture camera film is prepared from tremendously quick exposures. Should the exposure be made longer—that is, the camera be made to go more slowly—the film becomes over exposed, and in proportion as this occurs the pictured happening becomes more and more shadowy. So when we want to efface the boy we just gradually slow down the action of the camera till it finally stops. . . . Then we take the little boy away and put the little girl in exactly the place he was standing. When everybody else has gone out of range we slowly start the camera again, gradually increasing its speed till it has reached its normal speed again, taking care, however, to make the first slow impression of the little girl overlap the last slow impression of the little boy. The little girl will thus slowly strengthen on the film till the machine is running normally again, when she appears her little solid self. Of course, when the negative is made from this positive strip and it is whirled off upon the screen the intermission in which the exchange is effected is simply eliminated. . . . This is another instance of where one cannot always believe one's eyes—a camera can be made to be a fine liar.

Far more complex than any of these other scenes was one from *Ozma of Oz* (1907):

> Little Dorothy in a chicken coop is seen to be dashed about in the middle of a storm at sea with a fury almost indescribable. The little girl . . . was never at sea in her life. When I proposed this effect to the moving picture manufacturers they laughed at me. . . . In the first place, I took motion pictures of a storm at sea. Then I went to the immense glass studio. . . . In the center is a stage. I draped with dead black cloth a space in which I placed little Dorothy in her chicken coop. The coop was built upon rockers which were fitted with a series of casters, and invisible wires were attached, all being concealed beneath the black cloths except the coop and the child. When this was prepared I projected upon a screen at one side the picture of the sea, and as the waves rolled in we made the chicken coop

follow its curves and float across the black space, at the same time taking another motion picture of it upon a strip of film.

When this strip was developed it showed the girl on the chicken coop plainly, but the dead black surrounding made the film transparent in every other part. We next placed the chicken coop film above the film containing the sea scene and printed them together against the strip of positive film which is now used for projection. The result is that the child appears to be floating upon the sea, since the sea scene is printed through the transparent portion of the film, while the child in her coop is shown upon the surface. To make the chicken coop follow the roll of the waves was quite difficult, and seven trials were required to obtain a satisfactory result.

Baum divided his show into two parts: "The Land of Oz," illustrating incidents with both slides and movies from *The Wizard of Oz*, *The Marvelous Land of Oz*, and *Ozma of Oz*, directed by Francis Boggs; and "John Dough and the Cherub," directed by Otis Turner, plus an introduction to his latest Oz book, *Dorothy and the Wizard in Oz* (1908). During the brief intermission, Baum readily signed copies of his books for the children.

Opening on September 24, 1908, in Grand Rapids, *The Fairylogue and Radio-Plays* played to usually small audiences in the Midwest and East before ending up in New York City for the holidays. Baum charmed the children in his white frock coat with silk-faced lapels and white woolen broadcloth trousers. The papers said he looked like America's best-known humorist, Mark Twain; the St. Paul *News* noted that despite his fierce mustache, Baum, like Eugene Field and James M. Barrie, was the "Eternal Boy." "L. Frank Baum was a character," recalled the poet Eunice Tietjens, wife of composer Paul Tietjens, in her autobiography, *The World at My Shoulder* (1938). "He was tall and rangy, with an imagination and vitality which constantly ran away with him. . . . Constantly exercising his imagination as he did, he had come to the place where he could honestly not tell the difference between what he had done and what he had imagined. Everything he said had to be taken with a half-pound of salt. But he was a fascinating companion." His insouciant innocence must have added to the entertainment of the show. "Mr. Baum reveals himself as a trained public speaker of abilities unusual in a writer," reported a reviewer in the Chicago *Tribune* in October. "His enunciation is clear and incisive, and his ability to hold a large audience's attention during two hours of tenuous entertainment was amply demonstrated." Most critics found his *Fairylogue and Radio-Plays* to be unlike any other show and equally enjoyable for parent and child.

A scene from the silent Selig motion picture *The Wonderful Wizard of Oz*, 1910.
Courtesy George Eastman House.

Baum also proved to be the "Eternal Boy" financially. The production was an enormously expensive undertaking. The costs of moving a big heavy projector and screen and the salaries of the projectionist, his son Frank J. Baum, and the orchestra all cut deeply into the box office, and ticket sales were often poor. He was forced to close just before Christmas during its run at the Hudson Theatre in New York. He told Selig that he was planning to reopen in the new year, but that was just wishful thinking. To pay off part of his debt to the studio, Baum turned over the film rights to several of his books, and Selig released four delightful one-reelers, *The Wonderful Wizard of Oz*, *Dorothy and the Scarecrow in Oz*, *The Land of Oz*, and *John Dough and the Cherub*, all in 1910. He was confident that his debts would be paid out of the profits from several plays he was then working on. Charles Dillingham was interested in a musical extravaganza based on *Ozma of Oz*, and the Shuberts contracted another to be cobbled from the old *Woggle-Bug* and *Queen Zixi of Ix*. He and Edith Ogden Harrison, wife of Chicago's mayor, were behind plans for a children's theater to be erected near Carnegie Hall. Its first production was said to be *Prince Silverwings*, an operetta Baum based on one of Harrison's children's books back in 1903.

The theater was never built and the play never staged. As late as 1915, the two were still trying to get it produced, this time as an extravaganza with music by Dr. Hugo Felix and a motion picture with the Essanay Film Manufacturing Company.

None of these plays saw production, and Baum's financial problems continued to mount. On June 3, 1911, Baum filed for bankruptcy in the Los Angeles District Court. According to "L. Frank Baum Is 'Broke,' He Says" (New York *Morning Telegraph*, June 5), he listed his only assets as some clothing, a worn typewriter, and a reference book. Wisely, he had already transferred all his property, including the rights to his children's books, to his wife. His old friend Harrison Rountree was appointed trustee of the estate, responsible to Baum's many creditors. Baum then turned over to Rountree the publishing rights to *The Wizard of Oz* and the rest of the Bobbs-Merrill line so that the royalties could be used against his debts, with the understanding that these rights would revert to the Baums once everyone had been paid. L. Frank Baum never saw another penny from *The Wizard of Oz*. Not until 1932 was his widow finally able to reel in all rights to the famous children's book.

In 1910, in an economy move that preceded the bankruptcy, the Baums sold their cottage at Macatawa, stopped wintering in Coronado, and moved to Hollywood. The climate in Southern California had always been more congenial to Baum than that in Chicago, and Hollywood was then just a quiet little suburb of Los Angeles. They built a handsome bungalow he christened Ozcot on the corner of Cherokee and Yucca streets, using some money Maud had inherited from her mother and borrowing more from a wealthy friend. The long run of the *Wizard of Oz* extravaganza was winding down, and relinquishing the Bobbs-Merrill books did not entirely solve his financial troubles, but the Oz books were selling well and Baum was sure he would soon get out of debt. With six big books in the series, Baum felt he had written enough about America's favorite fairyland. He had other stories to tell, so he abruptly ended the saga with *The Emerald City of Oz* (1910). It concludes with a letter from Dorothy explaining that there will be no more stories, because Oz is henceforth cut off from the rest of the world by a Barrier of Invisibility to protect it from all outside harm. He then wrote the two "Trot" books, *Sea Fairies* (1911) and *Sky Island* (1912), both excellent fairy tales, illustrated by John R. Neill. But the public was only interested in Oz. Baum even added a few Oz characters to *Sky Island*, but the children were not fooled. He had to return to the Emerald City for financial aid, so he issued *The Patchwork Girl of Oz* and the six "Little Wizard Stories" in 1913. Baum explained in the introduction to the new Oz book that he had contacted Dorothy by "wireless" and could now record all the latest news from fairyland as it came in. He could not disappoint his young readers any longer and was now committed to writing an Oz book a year.

The return to Oz did not solve all his troubles. Because of the onset of World War I and changing economic conditions at home, the later titles did not sell as well as the earlier ones. Reilly & Britton suspected that the decrease was due largely to the flood of cheap Baum books now on the market. Without consulting the author, Rountree and Bobbs-Merrill turned over the plates of *The Wizard of Oz* and the other books to M. A. Donohue of Chicago, a big reprint house, which offered them at a greatly reduced price, as low as a sixth of what Reilly & Britton was asking for its editions. This generated bigger sales for Rountree and Bobbs-Merrill and stiffer

L. Frank Baum telling stories to children at Coronado, California, 1908.
Courtesy Fred M. Meyer.

Ozcot, Hollywood, California, 1911.
Courtesy Fred M. Meyer.

The library at Ozcot, Hollywood, California, 1911.
Courtesy Fred M. Meyer.

L. Frank Baum working in his garden at Ozcot, Hollywood, California, 1911.
Courtesy Fred M. Meyer.

competition for Baum and Reilly & Britton. Baum in effect was competing with himself.

Baum's luck finally seemed to be changing when Oliver Morosco agreed to produce his musical extravaganza based on *Ozma of Oz* in early 1913. Morosco was the wonder boy of the West Coast theater world. He had a hit with *Peg o' My Heart* and later produced the long-running *Abie's Irish Rose*. He spared no expense in staging *The Tik-Tok Man of Oz* at the Majestic Theatre in Los Angeles, on March 31, 1913. It was beautifully mounted with an excellent cast, led by Frank Morton and James Morton as the Shaggy Man and Tik-Tok and Fred Woodward as Hank the Mule, and there were marvelous stage effects. Louis F. Gottschalk provided a lovely score, and Baum's libretto and lyrics were superior to his previous efforts. Unfortunately, although it created a sensation in California, *The Tik-Tok Man of Oz* did not do well on the road. When it hit Chicago, the critics who recalled the 1902 show unfavorably compared it character for character and incident for incident to *The Wizard of Oz*. It was too expensive a show to keep running, and Morosco removed it from the boards while it was still in the black. It never reached Broadway. Baum readily capitalized on the

Poster advertising the musical extravaganza
The Tik-Tok Man of Oz, 1913.
Courtesy the Theatre and Music Collection,
the Museum of the City of New York.

show by basing his 1914 Oz story *Tik-Tok of Oz* in part on the play, and he dedicated the book to Gottschalk.

Not long after the show closed, Baum met with members of the Los Angeles Athletic Club to discuss the possibility of forming a motion picture company to make pictures of his Oz stories. The movie industry was literally growing up around him, and everyone seemed to be making a fortune in it. On December 10, 1913, Baum had helped found the "Lofty and Exalted Order of Uplifters," a private social club within the Los Angeles Athletic Club, and its members readily financed the Oz Film Manufacturing Company. Baum was elected president, Gottschalk vice president, Clarence R. Rundel secretary, and Harry M. Haldeman treasurer. They built one of the best studios in the business, in the Colegrove section of Los Angeles, and got right to work on their first production, *The Patchwork Girl of Oz*. Baum had originally adapted the children's story as a play, but quickly reworked it as a screenplay. Within a month they had a five-reeler ready for screening, but it was far easier to make a movie than to distribute it. The American Motion Pictures Patent Company, led by Thomas A. Edison, went after the Oz company and other independent producers for patent infringement; Baum's company settled out of court. Paramount agreed to release the first of the pictures, but *The Patchwork Girl of Oz* did so poorly at the box office that Paramount dropped its option on any other movies from the company. In all, the Oz Film Manufacturing Company made *The Patchwork Girl of Oz; The Magic Cloak of Oz* (based on *Queen Zixi of Ix*); *His Majesty, the Scare-*

crow of Oz (released as *The New Wizard of Oz*); *The Last Egyptian; The Gray Nun of Belgium* (a World War I drama written by Frank J. Baum); a short slapstick comedy titled *Pies and Poetry;* and four one-reelers released as the "Violet's Dreams" series. *The Scarecrow of Oz*, his book for 1915, was one of the first "novelizations" of a movie script, for he reused episodes and characters of *His Majesty, the Scarecrow of Oz* in the fairy tale. Alliance released *The Last Egyptian* and *The New Wizard of Oz,* but no one was much interested in any of the others. These were big, lavish productions, far above the usual "flickers" of the period, each with an original score composed by Gottschalk. But they were branded "kiddie shows," while the public was demanding Charlie Chaplin, Theda Bara, and *Birth of a Nation*. Some refused any pictures from the Oz studio, so it changed its name to Dramatic Features. It was too late. The company folded and sold the studio to Universal.

Baum had had great plans for the adapting of his stories to the screen, but it was not until 1925, six years after his death, that another movie of *The Wizard of Oz* was released. Unfortunately, it had a dreadful script, written in part by the author's son Frank J. Baum, that bore little resemblance to the fairy tale. Larry Semon, then one of Hollywood's favorite comedians, took

A scene from the silent Oz Film Manufacturing Company motion picture
His Majesty, the Scarecrow of Oz, 1914.
Private collection.

Oliver Hardy as the Tin Woodman, Dorothy Dwan as Dorothy, and
Larry Semon as the Scarecrow in the silent Chadwick motion
picture *The Wizard of Oz,* 1925.
Private collection.

the lead, but he appeared only briefly, dressed as the Scarecrow. His wife,
Dorothy Dwan, played Dorothy as a young lady, and Oliver Hardy, several years before he teamed up with Stan Laurel, was the Tin Woodman. It
was a dreary hodgepodge of chases and slapstick, totally lacking the magic
of Baum's book. It was not a success.

Hollywood waited until 1939 to try again, and this time it made a classic.
The famous MGM musical took considerable liberties with the original
book, but it retained much of the plot and spirit of Baum's fairy tale. The
cast was nearly perfect: Ray Bolger as the Scarecrow, Jack Haley as the Tin
Woodman, Bert Lahr as the Cowardly Lion, Billie Burke as Glinda, Margaret Hamilton as the Wicked Witch, Frank Morgan as the Wizard, and,
of course, Judy Garland as Dorothy. The special effects are still impressive,
and the beautiful score by E. Y. Harburg and Harold Arlen includes "Over

the Rainbow," winner of the Academy Award for Best Song. Herbert Stothart also won an Oscar for Best Original Score, and Garland received a miniature statue for Best Performance of a Juvenile. *The Wizard of Oz* did not show a profit from its original release, but it became a national institution after it began appearing annually on television in 1956. After sixty years, it still remains the major introduction most children have to Baum's Land of Oz.[26]

26. Not all other dramatizations of the book have been so happy. Ted Eshbaugh produced an early Technicolor animated short of *The Wizard of Oz* in 1933, but contractual disputes prevented it from being distributed. There have been two dreadful full-length animated "sequels," Videocraft's *Return to Oz,* which aired on NBC on February 9, 1964, based on a short-run Rankin/Bass cartoon series *Tales of the Wizard of Oz,* and Filmation's *Journey Back to Oz,* featuring the voices of Margaret Hamilton as Aunt Em and Judy Garland's daughter Liza Minnelli as Dorothy, which was released in theaters in 1974. In 1967, NBC briefly ran a weekly anthology series, *Off to See the Wizard,* derived from the 1939 musical, with animated sequences by Chuck Jones. Hyperion Entertainment Inc. issued a series of amusing *The Oz Kids* animated cartoons on video in 1995 similar to Warner Brothers' *Tiny Tunes* series. Shirley Temple produced an admirable adaptation of *The Land of Oz* on her NBC television program *The Shirley Temple Show* on September 18, 1960, but there was also an awful full-length live-action "kiddie matinee" version released as *The Wonderful Land of Oz* by Cinetron Corporation in the fall of 1969, as well as a 1976 modernized rock film of the first book from Australia called *Oz* there and *20th Century Oz* elsewhere.

The story finally returned to Broadway when *The Wiz* opened on January 5, 1975, at the second Majestic Theater. *The Wiz,* with lavish sets and costumes designed by its director, Geoffrey Holder, a lively score by Charlie Smalls, and Stephanie Mills as an ebullient Dorothy, revived the musical extravaganza on the American stage. This funky updating of the children's book was a risky production, but a shrewd advertising campaign on television prevented it from closing on opening night. It went on to become a hit and won the Tony Award for Best Musical of the Year. The 1978 Universal picture failed to capture the magic of the Broadway show. Although miscast, Diana Ross gave an affecting portrayal of Dorothy as a shy twenty-four-year-old kindergarten teacher. Michael Jackson played the Scarecrow, Richard Pryor the Wiz, and Lena Horne Glinda. Unfortunately, *The Wiz* was the first musical directed by Sidney Lumet, and the story, score, and performances were lost in overproduced, confusing musical numbers.

Walt Disney owned the film rights to Baum's remaining thirteen Oz books from 1956, but the studio did little with the property for years. There were plans to make a Technicolor musical tentatively titled "The Rainbow Road to Oz" and starring the Mouseketeers, and two numbers from the projected film were performed on the *Disneyland Fourth Anniversary Show* on September 11, 1957. It was not until 1985 that Disney returned to Oz with *Return to Oz.* This expensive, special-effects-driven adaptation of *The Marvelous Land of Oz* and *Ozma of Oz* was the first and only major motion picture directed by the Oscar-winning film editor Walter Murch. While the production contained some fine elements, particularly Fairuza Balk as Dorothy, the movie was lacking in humor. Unfortunately, *Return to Oz* opened during the major reshaping of the studio, so it was treated as just another mistake of a former regime. Also the public was expecting another fantasy musical like the famous Judy Garland picture, and *Return to Oz* failed at the box office.

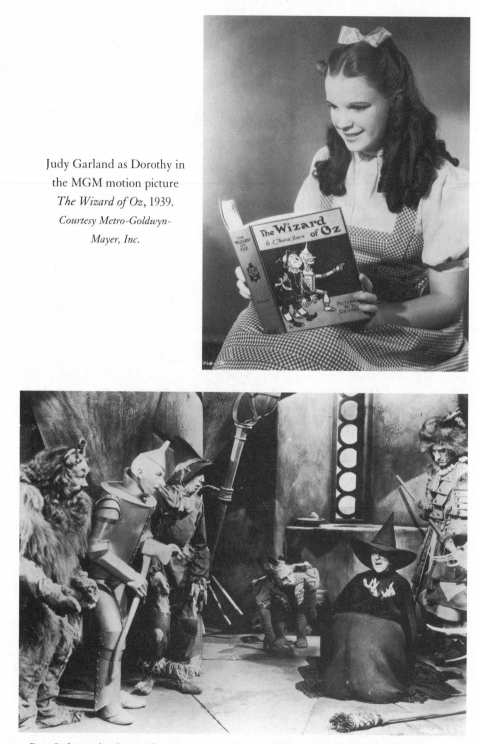

Judy Garland as Dorothy in
the MGM motion picture
The Wizard of Oz, 1939.
*Courtesy Metro-Goldwyn-
Mayer, Inc.*

Bert Lahr as the Cowardly Lion, Jack Haley as the Tin Woodman, Ray Bolger as the
Scarecrow, and Margaret Hamilton as the Wicked Witch of the West in the MGM
motion picture *The Wizard of Oz*, 1939.
Courtesy Metro-Goldwyn-Meyer, Inc.

Judy Garland as Dorothy with Frank Morgan, Charley Grapewin, Ray Bolger,
Jack Haley, Bert Lahr, and Clara Blandick in the MGM motion
picture *The Wizard of Oz*, 1939.
Courtesy Metro-Goldwyn-Mayer, Inc.

Jack Haley, Ray Bolger, Judy Garland,
Frank Morgan, and Bert Lahr in the MGM
motion picture *The Wizard of Oz*, 1939.
Courtesy Metro-Goldwyn-Mayer, Inc.

Hinton Battle as the Scarecrow,
Stephanie Mills as Dorothy, Ted Ross
as the Cowardly Lion, and Tiger Haynes
as the Tin Woodman in the Broadway
musical *The Wiz*, 1975.
Photograph by Martha Swope. © Time Inc.

Fairuza Balk as Dorothy in the Walt Disney motion picture *Return to Oz*, 1985.
© Disney Enterprises, Inc.

After the Oz Film Manufacturing Company failed, Baum was resigned to writing his annual Oz book. He now called himself "The Royal Historian of Oz." Pressures from the studio nearly ruined his health, and the economic restraints caused by World War I hurt the sales of his books. But the Baums lived comfortably, though modestly, at Ozcot. His greatest comfort was his garden, where he would retire to work on one of his stories or answer the hundreds of letters he got from his young admirers. He became famous for his beautiful chrysanthemums and dahlias, which won all the prizes at the local flower shows. He also built an enormous circular bird cage, provided with a constantly running fountain and a large variety of songbirds. "My father wrote all of his books in longhand on a clip board containing plain single sheets of white typewriter paper," wrote his son Harry Neal Baum in *The American Book Collector* (December 1962), "and a great deal of his writing was done in his garden which he loved and cherished. He would make himself comfortable in a garden chair, cross his legs, place the clip board on his knee, and with a cigar in his mouth, begin writing whenever the spirit moved him. This is the picture I have of him in my mind which I most frequently recall. When he finished an episode or adventure, he would get up and work in the garden. He might putter around for two or three hours before returning to his writing; or it might be two or three days or a week before the idea he was seeking came to him. 'My characters just won't do what I want them to,' he would explain." He rarely made a wrong move and did little revision; the few longhand manuscripts which survive are remarkably clean copy. He then went up to a reconverted bedroom that acted as his study. "After a book was completed, Father typed it himself, using the first two fingers of each hand and developing quite a speed. It was during this typing that he made any changes or revisions that seemed necessary."

Dr. Edwin P. Ryland, a Methodist minister and close friend, recalled many years later the gentle resident of

L. Frank Baum, 1915.
Private collection.

Ozcot: "He was a very handsome man, but very modest and reserved. He liked to meet people, mingle with them, talk with them. He was a good listener as well as an easy mixer, and had a keen sense of humor. If he'd not taken to writing children's books he might have been one of the country's best known technical writers for he had a strong leaning towards technical matters."[27] His best friends were the businessmen who made up the Uplifters (to whom he dedicated *The Scarecrow of Oz*), and he greatly enjoyed writing little comedy skits with Gottschalk for their annual outings. Frequently he entertained one or more of his child admirers over lemonade in the garden at Ozcot.

Although there was little to indicate it in his stories, Baum suffered excruciating pain during the last years of his life. These included angina attacks, and he finally went into the hospital in early 1918 to have his gallbladder removed. Complications from an inflamed appendix weakened him further. His smoking, his diet, and the Baums' propensity for consulting quacks took their toll on his precarious health. The pain persisted after he left the hospital, and he finally had to resort to morphine to get some relief. "I want to tell you, for your complete protection," he informed his publishers on February 14, 1918, "that I have finished the writing of the second Oz book—beyond *The Tin Woodman of Oz*—which will give you a manuscript for 1919 and 1920." These were *The Magic of Oz* and *Glinda of Oz*. "Also there is material for another book, so in case anything happens to me the Baum books can be issued until and including 1921. And the two stories which I have here in the safety deposit box I consider as good as anything I have ever done, with the possible exception of *Sky Island*, which will probably be considered to be my best work." What he referred to as "another book" was his "Animal Fairy Tales," which had not yet appeared in book form. The publishers, however, did not follow his wishes, for Reilly & Britton (later Reilly & Lee) never published the book.

Despite his failing health, Baum did his best to remain optimistic and took time to cheer up his son Frank, now a captain fighting somewhere in France. "But do not be too downhearted, my boy," he wrote on September 2, 1918, "for I have lived long enough to learn in life nothing adverse lasts very long. And it is true that as years pass, and we look back on something which, at the time, seemed unbelievably discouraging and unfair, we come to realize that, after all, God was at all times on our side. The eventual outcome was, we discover, by far the best solution for us, and what then we thought should have been to our best advantage, would in reality have been

---

27. Quoted in Jeanne O. Potter, "The Man Who Invented Oz," p. 12.

quite detrimental."[28] On the morning of May 6, 1919, Baum died nine days shy of his sixty-third birthday in his home in Hollywood, with Maud by his side.

The children refused to let the Oz books end with their creator's death. Sales were better than ever when World War I ended, and Reilly & Lee could not afford to drop so lucrative a series. William F. Lee secured from Maud Baum permission to have the stories continued by Ruth Plumly Thompson, the young editor of the Philadelphia *Public Ledger*'s Sunday children's page. She had grown up on the Oz books and readily wrote the first of her nineteen additions, *The Royal Book of Oz* (1921). Although it had Baum's name on the cover and title page, Thompson did *not* base the story on any notes Baum left behind as stated in the introduction. *The Royal Book of Oz* was entirely her own work. Thompson did not slavishly imitate what Baum had done, but instead built on his creation. She did take liberties with his stories from time to time, but she did not violate the integrity of his vision with her own. "In her earlier books," noted Edward Eager in "A Father's Minority Report" (*The Horn Book*, March 1948), "she shows a fine ear for a pun, a real feeling for nonsense, and in lieu of style, a contagious zest and pace that sweep the reader beyond criticism." The series continued to sell handsomely, for Thompson had nearly as many little admirers as Baum did.

Ruth Plumly Thompson surrounded by Oz characters.
Courtesy Dorothy Curtiss Marryot.

28. Quoted in Baum and MacFall, *To Please a Child,* p. 272.

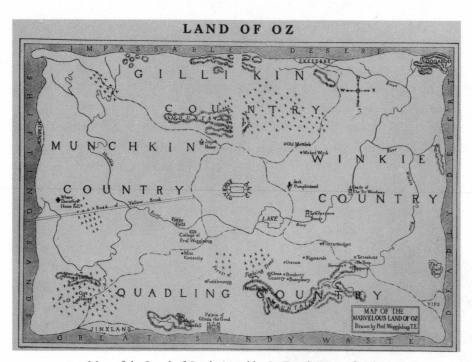

Map of the Land of Oz designed by L. Frank Baum for the
endpapers of *Tik-Tok of Oz*, 1914.
Private collection.

When Thompson retired as "Royal Historian of Oz" in 1939, John R. Neill, illustrator of all the Oz books except the first, briefly continued the series for three titles until his death in 1943. Although he was a fine illustrator, Neill had difficulty pulling all of his discordant ideas together into a coherent narrative. His successor was Jack Snow, a minor science fiction writer who composed two pastiches of Baum's fairy tales, *The Magical Mimics in Oz* (1946) and *The Shaggy Man of Oz* (1949), as well as the heavily edited reference book *Who's Who in Oz* (1954). The other two books of the forty titles of the Oz canon, Rachel Cosgrove's *The Hidden Valley of Oz* (1951) and Eloise Jarvis McGraw and Lauren McGraw Wagner's *Merry Go Round in Oz* (1963), are fine adventure stories, even if they do not add anything significantly new to the saga. As the books were going out of copyright, countless apocryphal Oz stories appeared, most of dubious literary value. The most curious of these unauthorized publications is Frank J. Baum's *The Laughing Dragon of Oz* (1934), one of Whitman's "Big Little Books," illustrated by Milt Youngren. This was an abbreviated version of the unpublished "Rosine in Oz," which the author's son had written about 1930. When Reilly & Lee returned the manuscript unopened, he took out a trademark on the word "Oz" in his own name and had the book published else-

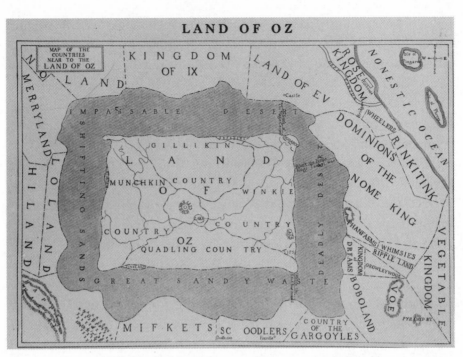

Map of the Land of Oz and surrounding countries designed by
L. Frank Baum for the endpapers of *Tik-Tok of Oz*, 1914.
Private collection.

where. When Reilly & Lee threatened to sue, Whitman withdrew *The Laughing Dragon of Oz* as well as another story then in production, "The Enchanted Princess of Oz." Frank J. Baum then sued Reilly & Lee for trademark infringement. The case finally pitted son against mother, and when the court decided in Maud Baum's favor, Reilly & Lee continued the series as before.[29]

Although the Oz books were the leading juveniles of their day and were often mentioned in the newspapers, little discussion of these stories and their creator can be found in contemporary magazines. Carol Ryrie Brink in "Some Forgotten Children's Books" (*South Dakota Library Bulletin,* April–June 1948) ran down the librarian's litany of complaints against the book: "*The Wizard of Oz* was too popular with children. Presentable copies could never be kept on the shelves because they were worn out by eager hands. *The Wizard of Oz* won itself a bad reputation because it became a musical comedy and a movie, and because it was followed by a shoddy

29. Of late there has grown up a peculiar literary sub-genre of adult novels drawing on the Oz mythology: March Laumer's *The Green Dolphin of Oz* (Belleair, Calif.: Vanitas Press, 1978); Philip José Farmer's *A Barnstormer in Oz* (New York: Berkley Books, 1982); Geoff Ryman's *Was* (New York: Alfred A. Knopf, 1992); Gregory Maguire's *Wicked: The Life and Times of the Wicked Witch of the West* by (Scranton, Pa.: HarperCollins, 1995); and Martin Gardner's *The Visitors from Oz* (New York: St. Martin's Press, 1998).

series of books, mostly written by hack writers who took over the original author's idea and extended it to impossible lengths." In an era when major periodicals noted the best children's books of the year in their Christmas issues, Baum's name was conspicuously absent from recommended lists. Many of these magazines were owned by the leading book publishers and designed to promote their interests by printing short stories and literary comment by and about their authors. The titles reflect this control: *Harper's*, *Scribner's*, *The Century*. The same was true with the trade journals. Scribner's issued *The Book Buyer*, Macmillan *Book Reviews*, and Bobbs-Merrill *The Reader*. Baum did serialize one of his children's books in a major magazine *St. Nicholas*; but, as he reported to Reilly & Britton on February 9, 1912, the Century Company (the owner) paid him "for the serial rights of *Queen Zixi of Ix*, and Mr. [W. W.] Ellsworth [the company's secretary] lately gave me to understand they will not serialize anything in *St. Nicholas* which they do not own the book rights for." These magazines controlled their lists of "suggested reading"; generally the only works mentioned were their own or those of their advertisers. With the exception of the Bobbs-Merrill titles, few of Baum's books were widely reviewed in the periodicals. The George M. Hill Company was concerned primarily with the printing and distributing of books, not the editing and promotion of them; it was a minor house with a small list of new titles and did not invest heavily in advertising. *Father Goose, His Book* was a freak success because of its novelty and was well received by the critics despite modest financial support from the publisher. Hill did not think the other books, including *The Wonderful Wizard of Oz*, required much advertising, and they were generally ignored by the major magazines. "When the Hill company published *Father Goose* and *The Wizard of Oz*," Frank Reilly wrote Baum on New Year's Day 1914, "Mr. Britton and the writer were able to put over a lot of stunts—the best sort of advertising, free publicity in the newspapers—because we had something absolutely new. Now, however, there is nothing novel in presenting—either to the trade or to the public—a new Oz book. The professional buyers do not read such books and merely regard the annual Baum book as one of a thousand other items of general merchandise." The press eventually viewed the new Oz book as no different from the last and generally failed to acknowledge it.

Baum chose his publishers, so the lack of contemporary critical recognition of his work may be in part his own fault. As Gardner recognized in "Why Librarians Dislike Oz" (*The American Book Collector*, December 1962), most of his books were published by Reilly & Britton (later Reilly & Lee), a small Chicago house that specialized in Baum, teenage fiction, and the verse of Edgar A. Guest. Reilly & Britton was actually formed in 1904 to publish the second Oz title, *The Marvelous Land of Oz*. Baum's reputation might have been enhanced if his work had been published alongside that of more prestigious writers on the list of a major Eastern firm. Several leading houses begged Baum for manuscripts, but he generally turned them down out of loyalty to the smaller, more devoted firm. He had better control over the manufacture and promotion of his work than if he had gone with one of the larger publishers. Reilly and Britton became his close personal friends in addition to being business associates. His relationship with Bobbs-Merrill was more complicated. Although Bobbs-Merrill was putting out a steady stream of adult best-sellers, it had trouble with juveniles, even *The Wizard of Oz*. Baum deserted Bobbs-Merrill when Reilly & Britton made *The Marvelous Land of Oz* such an enormous success.

BAUM paid little attention to his critics. So long as the books kept selling and the children liked them, he was content. Also, Baum had a special agreement with Reilly & Britton by which he was paid a monthly salary against royalties, a rare contract between an author and his publisher at the time. Moreover, the Baums were personal friends of the Reillys and the Brittons, and the author received certain courtesies and privileges from his publishers that no other house probably would have granted him. He had faith that their interests were mutual, that the company was as devoted to his work as he was. Baum's books for this firm may not have appeared on the recommended reading lists, but they never failed to make the best-selling juvenile lists.

There have been countless critical studies of Baum and his work of late, but they do not always deal exclusively with *The Wizard of Oz*. Many are more concerned with the movie than with the book. One of the most persistent is Henry M. Littlefield's "The Wizard of Oz: Parable on Populism" (*American Quarterly*, Spring 1964). It theorizes that Baum was thinking allegorically about his own time when he wrote the first of the Oz stories. While some valid points are raised, it too often strains for symbols that the text does not support. For example, Littlefield argued that the Silver Shoes reflect the political preoccupation with silver in 1896, and that the Yellow Brick Road is really a reference to William Jennings Bryan's famous "Cross of Gold" speech. But are the streets of Oz really paved with gold? Because Bryan accepted the Democratic Party's nomination in Omaha, Baum just had to have the Wizard come from that city. But Baum was not so prosaic a writer as this article insists. Littlefield has admitted that his theory evolved from a classroom assignment to teach American history to high school students, and *they* came up with many of the metaphors.[30] Today the reputation of this theory far outweighs its critical value. It has been paraphrased, plagiarized, and argued over by academics with an intensity that would make even Professor Woggle-Bug blush. It is significant that no review nor any other contemporary discussion of the book noted any parallels between the story and the Populist movement. The Boston *Beacon* observed on September 29, 1900, that "under the sweet simplicity of the tale for children is a satiric allegory on modern history for big people. The Scarecrow wears a Russian blouse, the fierce Tin Woodman bears a striking resemblance to Emperor Wilhelm of Germany, the Cowardly Lion with its scarlet beard and tail tip at once suggest Great Britain, and the Flying Monkeys wear a military cap in Spanish colors." These remarks may have been made partly in jest, but there is not one word about Populism.

One of the oddest discussions of the Oz books is Osmond Beckwith's "The Oddness of Oz" (*Kulchur*, Fall 1961). This psychoanalytic interpretation of *The Wizard of Oz* suggests (among other things) that the Wicked Witch of the West is Dorothy's evil mother figure and therefore must be killed, and that the lack of brains, heart, and courage expresses Baum's castration complex. These facile Freudian interpretations are more amusing than enlightening. Other psychoanalytical studies have appeared, but they tend to deal with the 1939 movie rather than with Baum's children's book.

Another curious piece on *The Wizard of Oz* is "The Art of Being," one of the Lecture-Lessons of Marc Edmund Jones, published in 1964 by the Sabian Assembly, a society devoted to the occult sciences. It argues that each chapter of Baum's book suggests a particular virtue which each child must follow toward maturity. Each act is a moral one in accordance with the tenets of this organization. Although not convincing, the argument has some validity in regard to Baum's dalliance with the occult. The author of *The Wizard of Oz* was first drawn to Theosophy through his mother-in-law, Matilda Joslyn Gage, who joined the Rochester Theosophical Society in 1885. She kept up with the latest books on the subject and subscribed to the society's journals, then passed them among the family to read. While living in Aberdeen, the Baums held séances in their home and entertained clair-

---

30. The best discussion of this phenomenon is Michael Gessel's "Tale of a Parable," *The Baum Bugle*, Spring 1992. See also Henry Littlefield's defense, "The Wizard of Allegory," pp. 24–25. The best response to the Populism myth has been David B. Parker's "The Rise and Fall of *The Wonderful Wizard of Oz* as 'Parable on Populism,'" *Journal of the Georgia Association of Historians*, 1994, pp. 49–63.

voyants. When they moved to Chicago, their first home was said to be haunted, and they joined the Ramayana Theosophical Society in 1892.[31]

Interest in the occult was quite common among liberal thinkers at the time. The Spiritualist movement that began in America in 1848 was still widely followed in the latter part of the century. In describing the peculiar powers of the clairvoyant in an article in the Aberdeen *Saturday Pioneer* (April 5, 1890), Baum described the following cosmography:

> Scientists have educated the world to the knowledge that no part of the universe, however infinitesimal, is uninhabited. Every bit of wood, every drop of liquid, every grain of sand or portion of rock has its myriads of inhabitants—creatures deriving their origin from and rendering involuntary allegiance to a common Creator. The creatures of the atmosphere, while admittedly existent, are less widely known in that they are microscopically and otherwise invisible to ordinary humanity. No student of Nature can conceive that the Creator, in peopling every other portion of the universe, neglected to give the atmosphere its quota of living creatures. These invisible and vapory beings are known as Elementals, and play an important part in the lives of humanity. They are soulless, but immortal; frequently possessed of extraordinary intelligence, and again remarkably stupid. Some are exceedingly well disposed toward mankind, but the majority are maliciously inclined and desirous of influencing us to

31. Robert Baum in his autobiography (published in *The Baum Bugle*, Christmas 1970) reported one peculiar psychic occurrence at their first home in Chicago:

> My brother Kenneth was just a baby and Father had rigged up a "jumper" between the door way, a little chair suspended by springs in which he sat and could be jumped up and down to quiet him. A cord was attached to it so Mother could sit in a chair and jump him up and down by pulling the cord while she was doing her sewing or reading. One night when the baby was especially fretful and Mother was tired of pulling the cord, she cried out, "If there is any such thing as spirits I wish they would rock this baby for me." And, according to the story as told by my mother, the jumper immediately began to go up and down for a considerable length of time without anyone touching it. (p. 18)

In an unpublished section of this same autobiography, he discussed his grandmother Gage's fascination with the occult:

> She was more or less interested in Spiritualism and had also made a study of the science of Palmistry. She used to delight in reading our hands and I can remember how she would have us place our palm on an ink pad and then make an impression on a piece of paper so she could study the lines of our hands at her leisure. She was also interested in Astronomy and used to take us children out doors at night and point out to us the various stars and constellations.

evil. The legendary "guardian spirit" which each human being has, is nothing more or less than an Elemental, and happy is he who is influenced hereby for good and not incited to evil.

H. P. Blavatsky, founder of the Theosophical Society, described these "Elementals" or "Elemental Spirits" in *Isis Unveiled* (Vol. 1, 1878, p. xxix) as "the creatures evolved in the four kingdoms of earth, air, fire, and water, and called by the kabalists gnomes, sylphs, salamanders, and undines," and said they "may be termed the forces of Nature." She explained, "Under the general designation of fairies, and fays, these spirits of the elements appear in myth, fable, tradition, or poetry of all nations, ancient and modern. Their names are legion—peris, devs, djinns, sylvans, satyrs, fauns, elves, dwarfs, trolls, norns, nisses, kobolds, brownies, necks, stromkarls, undines, nixies, salamanders, goblins, ponkes, banshees, kelpies, pixies, moss people, good people, good neighbors, wild women, men of peace, white ladies—and many more. They have been seen, feared, blessed, banned, and invoked in every quarter of the globe and in every age."

Of course, this belief goes back to ancient occult teachings. The theory that all things are formed from the four building blocks of Nature, the elements of earth, air, fire, and water, derives from the Aristotelian age. Paracelsus, the sixteenth-century Swiss alchemist and physician, divided them into four categories: sylphs (air), nymphs or undines (water), gnomes (earth), and salamanders (fire). They also parallel the ancient concept of four states of matter—gas, liquid, solid, and energy. The Rosicrucians and other groups adopted Paracelsus's system; and the tradition can be traced through Alexander Pope's *The Rape of the Lock* (1712), Le Motte-Fouqué's *Undine* (1811), and Sir Walter Scott's *The Monastery* (1820). A quick glance at Baum's fairy tales reveals that he wrote about each Paracelsian classification of spirits. His sylphs are the "winged fairies" (Lulea of *Queen Zixi of Ix* and Lurline of *The Tin Woodman of Oz*); the undines are mermaids (Queen Aquareine of *The Sea Fairies* and the water fairies of *The Scarecrow of Oz*); the gnomes are the Nomes (the Nome King of *The Life and Adventures of Santa Claus* and *Ozma of Oz*); and the salamanders are the fairies of energy (the Demon of Electricity in *The Master Key* and the Lovely Lady of Light in *Tik-Tok of Oz*). Baum drew freely on this traditional occult cosmography in inventing his own secondary world.

Baum said that the basic belief of Theosophy was that "God is Nature, and Nature God." Likewise, the Three Adepts of *Glinda of Oz* (1920) explain that their magic comprises "secret arts we have gleaned from Nature" (p. 244). Therefore the goals of science and magic are identical: the unlocking of the mysteries of Nature. An important goal of Theosophy was to reconcile ancient religious beliefs with recent scientific discoveries and theories. "Of all that is inexplicable in our daily lives," Baum argued in the *Saturday Pioneer* (February 22, 1890), "we can only say that they are Nature's secrets, and a sealed book to ignorant mortals; but none the less do we marvel at their source and desire to unravel their mystery." Science and magic therefore have the same ends. One need have only the right tools to solve one's problems. It is no surprise then that Baum described Oz in *The Patchwork Girl of Oz* (1913) as fairyland "where magic is a science" (p. 140).

In an article on Theosophy in the *Saturday Pioneer* (January 25, 1890), Baum described his own era as an "Age of Unfaith," but pointed out that "this is not atheism of the last century. It is rather an eager longing to penetrate the secrets of Nature—an aspiration for knowledge we have thought is forbidden." The Theosophists are "searchers for Truth" and "admit the existence of God—not necessarily a personal God." The growth of Theosophy and spiritualism in general was a direct reaction to the growing power of the sciences as disciplines divorced from religious teachings. The theory of "Elementals," for example, tried to adhere to the principles of physical science while retaining occult properties. The Romantics sought a new "paganism," a return to a religion of Nature in which emotion rather than reason reigned. Many people could not accept the compromise between the Protestant churches and Darwinism. The rebirth of all sorts of secret societies in the nineteenth century confirmed this desperate desire to commune with both God and Nature. Poets such as Arthur Rimbaud and William Butler Yeats sought (in different ways) a new mysticism in a world slouching toward Thomas Huxley's "agnosticism." Central New York was a hotbed of religious activity during this period, known as "the Burned-Over District," and its radical ideas profoundly affected Baum and his work.

Whether he actually believed all of this is debatable. Frank J. Baum admitted that his father was interested in Theosophy, but he could not accept all of its teaching.[32] He firmly believed in reincarnation and in the immortality of the soul, and that he and Maud had been together in many past states and that they would be together again in future transmigrations, but he rejected the possibility of souls passing from human beings to animals or vice versa, as in Hinduism. He agreed with the Theosophical tenet that man on earth was only one step on a great ladder passing through many states of consciousness, through many universes, to a final stage of enlightenment. He did embrace karma, the belief that whatever good or

32. In a letter to Martin Gardner, November 21, 1955.

evil one does in this lifetime returns to him as reward or punishment in future reincarnations. Baum could not fathom the idea of a wrathful godhead, a theme that runs throughout the Oz books. He did not believe in unredeemable villainy and evil. He had no sympathy for the preachings of hellfire and damnation of his Methodist ancestors. His mother was a devout conservative Christian whose faith he often tested, and he rejected early this form of Christianity.[33] Good acts were more important to him than good intentions.

Baum was both curious and skeptical about religion. But he could not accept the concept of the devil, a denial he believed kept him from joining any particular branch of Christianity. In the *Saturday Pioneer* (October 18, 1890), he lambasted the organized church. "When the priests acknowledge their fallibility," he demanded; "when they abolish superstition, intolerance and bigotry; when they establish the true relations between God and Christ and humanity; when they accord justice to Nature and love and mercy to the All-high; when they abhor the thought of a vindictive and revengeful God; when they are able to reconcile reason and religion and fear not to let the people think for themselves, then, and then only will the Church regain its old power and be able to draw to its pulpits the whole people." Believing that all religions derive their inspiration from the same source, a common Creator, he could not accept the petty rivalries among different sects. The few references to religion in his books (particularly *American Fairy Tales*) are unfavorable. "He wasn't what you'd call a religious man," recalled his

---

33. In a letter to Jack Snow, June 7, 1943, Baum's nephew Henry B. Brewster reported:

> Mr. Baum always liked to tell wild stories, with a perfectly straight face, and earnestly, as though he really believed them himself. . . . His mother was very religious . . . and felt she knew her Bible very well. Frank Baum seemed to take particular delight in teasing her and I recall, not once but many times, how he would pretend to quote from the Bible, with which he definitely was not familiar. For example, once she said, "Frank, you are telling a story," and he said, "Well, Mother, as you know, in St. Paul's epistle to the Ephesians he said, 'All men are liars.'" Whereon his mother said, "Why, Frank you are wrong, I do not recall that," and irrespective of the fact that she had been fooled so many times she would look up in her Bible to see if she were wrong, and he right. Frank Baum was one of the most imaginative of men. There was nothing wrong, but he did love to "fairytale," or as you might say, tell "white lies."

His mother could not find the line in the Bible, because Baum was probably playing with Epimenides' statement, "All Cretans are liars." A similar joke occurs in the Aberdeen *Saturday Pioneer* (December 20, 1890): In response to the rector of St. Mark's Episcopal Church who said that there is no such things as psychic phenomena, Baum suggests that the clergyman refer to Acts V: 38, 39; of course, this passage has nothing to do with the minister's point.

friend Dr. Ryland, "that is, he wasn't a denominationalist. When he went to church at all in Hollywood he attended mine, but he wasn't a member of it. He had a gospel of his own and he preached it through his books, although you certainly couldn't call them religious either. I once asked him how he came to write the first Oz book. 'It was pure inspiration,' he said. 'It came to me right out of the blue. I think that sometimes the Great Author has a message to get across and He has to use the instrument at hand. I happened to be that medium, and I believe the magic key was given to me to open the doors to sympathy and understanding, joy, peace and happiness. That is why I've always felt there should never anything except sweetness and happiness in the Oz books, never a hint of tragedy or horror. They were intended to reflect the world as it appears to the eye and imagination of a child.' That was as close as we ever came to a discussion of religion. But he certainly had one, and he lived and wrote by it."

The world of Oz as described in *The Wizard of Oz* differs significantly from that described in the later sequels, for Baum's concept of fairyland evolved as the series progressed. Dr. Edward Wagenknecht was the first to suggest that Baum invented an American utopia.[34] S. J. Sackett further explored the economic, social, and cultural aspects of the Land of Oz in "The Utopia of Oz" (*The Georgia Review*, Fall 1960). In *The Marvelous Land of Oz*, the society and even the very landscape changes after *the Wizard* leaves *Oz* and the throne is restored to its rightful ruler, Princess Ozma.[35] All the flora and fauna of each kingdom of Oz becomes the same color as the favorite one of that region. The great desert that surrounds the country has some mysterious power that threatens to destroy any traveler who dares set foot upon it. Baum most fully defines the utopian nature of his fairyland in *The Emerald City of Oz*:

> No disease of any sort was ever known among the Ozites, and so no one ever died unless he met with an accident that prevented him from living. This happened very seldom, indeed. There were no poor in the Land of Oz, because there was no such thing as money, and all property belonged to the Ruler. The people were her children, and she cared for them. Each person was given freely by his neighbors whatever he required for his use, which is as much as any one may reasonably desire. Some tilled the lands

34. In *Utopia Americana* (Seattle: University of Washington Book Store, 1929).
35. The second syllable of "Ozma" may refer to Maud, Baum's wife. When he rewrote his 1913 musical extravaganza *The Tik-Tok Man of Oz* as *Tik-Tok of Oz* (1914), Baum changed the Rose Princess "Ozma" into "Ozga"; the second syllable of that name may come from Gage, Maud Baum's maiden name.

and raised great crops of grain, which was divided equally among the entire population, so that all had enough. There were many tailors and dressmakers and shoemakers and the like, who made things that any who desired them might wear. Likewise there were jewelers who made ornaments for the person, which pleased and beautified the people, and these ornaments also were free to those who asked for them. Each man and woman, no matter what he or she produced for the good of the community, was supplied by the neighbors with food and clothing and a house and furniture and ornaments and games. If by chance the supply ever ran short, more was taken from the great storehouses of the Ruler, which were afterward filled up again when there was more of any article than the people needed.

Every one worked half the time and played half the time, and the people enjoyed the work as much as they did the play, because it is good to be occupied and to have something to do. There were no cruel overseers set to watch them, and no one to rebuke them or to find fault with them. So each one was proud to do all he could for his friends and neighbors, and was glad when they would accept the things he produced. (pp. 30–31)

Baum wisely added, however, "I do not suppose such an arrangement would be practical with us, but Dorothy assures me that it works finely with the Oz people." Ozma preserves a few minor laws, such as a law forbidding anyone from picking a six-leaf clover in *The Patchwork Girl of Oz*, but the Tin Woodman reveals the most important law of Oz in *The Tin Woodman of Oz* (1918): "Behave Yourself" (p. 38). There are, of course, wild tribes hidden throughout the rough unexplored territory of Oz, far away from the Emerald City, and selfish, discontented magicians and witches try to take over Ozma's happy kingdom. But generally, Oz is a gentle land where the good are rewarded and the bad forgiven. Under the benevolent rule of Ozma of Oz, the united country becomes "The Land of Love." Ozma is like an all-embracing mother. That is a step forward from *The Wizard of Oz* and its classic struggle between Good and Evil. If the Wizard's regime under which death and taxes are inevitable is a dark age in the history of Oz, then Ozma's reign must be viewed as a return to the golden age. Parallels between the social structure of Oz and those described in such contemporary utopian novels as Edward Bellamy's *Looking Backward* (1888) and William Morris's *News from Nowhere* (1891) may be found, but the seemingly "socialist" structure of Baum's fairyland is only superficial. Oz is closer to a benevolent despotism than to either a Marxist or a welfare state.

The niggling suspicion that Oz may be a "socialist" state may explain in part the prejudice against Baum and his work. In "The Red Wizard of Oz" (*New Masses*, October 4, 1938), Stewart Robb said in jest that the reason there were no Oz books except *The Wizard of Oz* on the shelves of the New York Public Library was political; he argued that the seemingly anarchistic structure of Oz approximated the Marxist dream. That *The Daily Worker* (August 18, 1939) "heartily" recommended the Judy Garland musical as "an outstanding film" must have made conservatives squirm. While "regretting that MGM neglected the opportunity to satirize dictators" and admitting that "the social angle is comparatively nil," Howard Rushmore still called the picture "one of the most expensive (and also the most beautiful) examples of film fantasy ever to grace the American scene." After World War II, *Collier's* in an editorial titled "45 Years of 'The Wizard'" defined the book's patriotic message as "Don't believe in the big, bad wolf . . . don't be overawed by people who talk big . . . dig out the facts for yourself . . . don't depend on hearsay and propaganda." It was this philosophy that helped America defeat the Axis powers, the editorial insisted. "Let's just hang onto that realistic, inquiring, skeptical and fearless attitude of mind," it concluded. "It's a priceless national asset."

During the McCarthy years, when even the legend of Robin Hood was viewed as a Marxist tract, Baum's gentle utopia was easily misconstrued as something it was not. Ray Ulveling, director of the Detroit Public Library, caused a wave of protest when he carelessly mentioned in April 1957 that his libraries did not keep the Oz series on the open shelves in the children's rooms. The press quickly interpreted this as a "ban" of Baum. Ulveling declared that these stories were "of no value," for they encouraged "negativism" (whatever that might be) and misled young minds to accept a cowardly approach to life. "There is nothing uplifting or elevating about the Baum series," he sniffed. "They do not compare in quality to fairy tales by Grimm and Andersen."[36] He said that the public preferred do-it-yourself

36. Quoted in Neil Hunter's "Librarian Raps 'Oz' Books," Lansing (Michigan) *State Journal*, April 4, 1957. Ulveling insisted that he had been misquoted: *The Wizard of Oz* had been in the Detroit Public Library since the year it was published, but it was not in the children's room at the Main Library or in the branches. It was stored in the stacks safely away from young readers. "More than thirty years ago," he explained in a letter to the editor of *ALA Bulletin* (October 1957), "the decision was made that with so many better books available for children than was the case when *The Wizard* was first published, the library would simply let the old copies wear out and not replace them. Three copies were held for the record, however, and they are still available to readers. This is not banning; this is selection." But a book that does not circulate might just as well be banned. "Well, as Humpty [Dumpty] said, words can mean whatever we want them to mean," replied Martin Gardner in "A Child's Garden of Bewilderment" (*Saturday Review*, July 17, 1965).

books to mysteries, fairy tales, and other forms of popular fiction. His colleagues came to his defense, insisting that after 1920 there was a new approach to children's literature and *The Wizard of Oz* did not conform to this new attitude. In February 1959, the Florida Department of State sent throughout its system a list of "Books Not Circulated by Standard Libraries." These were series judged to be "poorly written, untrue to life, sensational, foolishly sentimental, and consequently unwholesome for the children in your county." The state instructed that they were "not to be purchased, not to be accepted as gifts, not to be processed, and not to be circulated." L. Frank Baum was the first name on the list. *The Wizard of Oz* was banned from the children's sections of the Washington D.C., public library system until 1966, and even then it was kept out of the city's school libraries. "I know children like it," school library director Olive C. DeBruler told *Library Journal* (November 15, 1966), "but there is so much fantasy of better quality." It was too sentimental, and the anthropomorphism represented by the Cowardly Lion was considered poor. Maxine LaBounty, coordinator of children's services for D.C. public libraries, added that Baum's kind of fantasy "does not have the finesse or the high standard of *Alice in Wonderland*, for example." The press protested this censorship of Oz, but as late as April 1961, the Westwood-Brentwood (California) *Villager* published an article accusing Baum of communist leanings![37] Stubbornly, some libraries still do not circulate the Oz books.

Another common complaint of librarians and critics is that *The Wizard of Oz* is poorly written. But this is more a matter of individual taste than serious criticism. Many people have enjoyed Baum's work and even admired his writing. Baum was not a stylist in the tradition of Hans Christian Andersen, Robert Louis Stevenson, Kenneth Grahame, or James M. Barrie. He was not interested in words for their own sake, in *bons mots*, clever conceits, or learned literary allusions that flatter the intelligence of

"Personally, I find it easier to believe in the Scarecrow than in Mr. Ulveling." Noted Ray Bradbury in "Two Baumy Promenades Along the Yellow Brick Road" (*Los Angeles Times Book Review*, October 9, 1977), "There are all sorts of ways of burning books. One is by pretending they don't exist."

37. C. Warren Hollister in "Baum's Other Villains" (*The Baum Bugle*, Spring 1970) suggested that a passage in *The Magic of Oz* (1919) may be Baum's reflection of the Bolshevik Revolution in 1917. Hollister interpreted the Nome King's speech to the animals of the Forest of Gugu as the Royal Historian's attempt to show how innocent creatures can be talked into war through the effective use of Marxist dialectic, anticipating George Orwell's *Animal Farm* by twenty-seven years. If so, Baum must have worked quickly, for he finished the manuscript of *The Magic of Oz* (as well as that of *Glinda of Oz*, 1920) before February 1918, when he went into the hospital for a gallbladder operation.

the self-consciously and self-congratulatory sophisticated reader. Communication was Baum's first rule. He wrote in a simple, effective manner. He wanted to tell a good story and generally avoided anything that might get in the way of the adventure's path. His writing is also refreshingly free of the sentimentality and class consciousness that mar so much of nineteenth-century juvenile literature. As with all great works of fantasy, the style and mood of *The Wizard of Oz* are timeless; it reads as well today as when it was first written.

The Wizard of Oz is also well structured. Dichotomy is important. The first and last chapters take place in Kansas; the loss of home is reassuringly restored in the end. Two Good Witches befriend Dorothy: The Good Witch of the North presents her with a pair of Silver Shoes in Chapter 2, the Good Witch of the South discloses their power in the second-to-last chapter. She receives one Wicked Witch's Silver Shoes in the first part of the story and another Wicked Witch's Golden Cap in the second. The exact center of the book is the discovery of Oz, the Terrible. He disappoints Dorothy twice: first, after she has killed the Wicked Witch of the East and he appears to her as the great head; second, after she destroys the Wicked Witch of the West and he escapes in his balloon. Far from being prosaically anticlimactic, the second half of the book reflects the first. Intelligence, kindness, and bravery, which are discovered within themselves on the journey to the Emerald City, must be tested on the trip south, once they have been given the outer symbols of brains, heart, and courage. There are conscious rephrasings of conversations of the first part in the second. Dorothy's interview with the Good Witch of the South is reminiscent of that with the Good Witch of the North. Within this durable framework, Baum introduces several of the most memorable characters in all juvenile literature. The Scarecrow, the Tin Woodman, and the Cowardly Lion in their search for a brain, a heart, and courage are today as beloved and as much a part of childhood as any other nursery characters.

Another irrational criticism of the Oz books was that they compose a series. The argument has been that once children get hooked on one particular author's work, they will shun anything else. But with librarians, there have always been series and then there have been *acceptable* series. At the same time they were banning the Oz books, they readily stocked the Peter Rabbit series, the Doctor Dolittle series, the Mary Poppins series, the Narnia series, the Prydain series, the Borrowers series, the Green Knowle series, the Wrinkle in Time series, the Miss Bianca series, and the Little House series. And who can honestly say that the Freddy or the Black Stallion books are *better* written than the Oz books? Of course, fairy tales and

especially *American* fairy tales are not for everyone, for, as E. M. Forster wrote, "Fantasy asks us to pay something extra."[38] When American librarians did buy literary fairy tales, they tended to choose only those by British writers. Their prejudice seems to have been a case of reverse snobbery. The American children's book establishment has long been Anglocentric. The American Library Association named its annual award for the most distinguished contribution to American juvenile literature after English publisher John Newbery and that for the most distinguished picture book after English illustrator Randolph Caldecott. *The Horn Book* and other juvenile literarure journals devoted extensive articles and bibliographies to such minor American figures as Laura E. Richards and Susan Coolidge and scarcely a word to Baum or the Oz books. What they did say was nearly always negative. Despite this decades-long assault, the series remained among the most popular American juveniles ever published. The children liked them even if certain adults did not.

While librarians carried on their battle against the Oz books, prominent writers and scholars on occasion came to their defense. Dr. Edward Wagenknecht became the pioneer in Oz criticism when he published *Utopia Americana* in 1929. His enthusiasm was shared by C. Beecher Hogan, English professor at Yale University, who amassed the first important collection of Baum's books, now in Yale's Beinecke Library. Carol Ryrie Brink, who won the Newbery Medal for *Caddie Woodlawn* (1935), dared to announce at the Young People's and School Librarians' Luncheon of the Upper Midwest Regional Library Conference, Pierre, South Dakota, on October 4, 1947, that *"The Wizard of Oz* is one of the few great American books for children. It tells a good story in a simple, direct style. It has humor, fantasy, and best of all truth and integrity in the interpretation of human nature." Roland Baughman, curator of Special Collections at Columbia University, was responsible for the college's monumental centennial exhibition of L. Frank Baum in 1956. The following year, Martin Gardner and Pulitzer Prize–winning historian Russel B. Nye published the first critical edition of the book, *The Wizard of Oz and Who He Was*, through a university press. Much of this renewed interest in Oz was due to the International Wizard of Oz Club, Inc., founded in 1957 by thirteen-year-old Justin G. Schiller. Its triquarterly, *The Baum Bugle*, still serves as the leading repository for Oz scholarship. The first full-length biography of L. Frank Baum, Frank Joslyn Baum and Russell P. MacFall's *To Please a Child*, appeared in 1961. The original edition of *The Annotated Wizard of Oz* did

---

38. In *Aspects of the Novel* (New York: Harcourt, Brace & World, 1927), p. 109.

much to legitimize Oz as a topic for serious study. Baum and Oz are currently taught in college courses all over America and abroad. Those who grew up watching *The Wizard of Oz* on television now recognize Baum as an American original. Hardly a year goes by today that some journal, scholarly or otherwise, does *not* publish a learned piece on Oz. A selection of these essays appears in the 1983 Schocken Critical Heritage Edition of *The Wizard of Oz*. New editions of the Oz books appear all the time. Several documentaries have explored Baum's life and work, and he was the subject of the December 10, 1990, NBC Movie of the Week, *The Dreamer of Oz*, starring John Ritter as the author of *The Wizard of Oz*. The Oz books may even be found in libraries that once shunned them. To commemorate the book's centennial and its own bicentennial, the Library of Congress, the greatest institution of its kind in the world, mounted an exhibition in honor of L. Frank Baum and *The Wizard of Oz* in 2000.

John Ritter as L. Frank Baum in
The Dreamer of Oz, 1990.
Courtesy David Kirschner.

The magic of Oz has spread far beyond the shores of the United States. Today this quintessential American fairy tale has been translated into nearly every language around the globe and is viewed as an international children's classic along with *Alice in Wonderland*, *Peter Pan*, and *The Wind in the Willows*. Baum and his publishers were cavalier about the foreign distribution of his work. The George M. Hill Company and Bobbs-Merrill haphazardly made some of the early titles available in England to protect their British copyright, and Reilly & Britton sold most of its line in Canada through the Copp Clark Company. Although the St. Paul *Pioneer Press* (October 11, 1908) reported that there were editions of the Oz books in Germany, France, Italy, and even Japan, the earliest authorized translation of *The Wizard of Oz* was in French and was published in 1932. Most that have appeared since were the result of the international popularity of the 1939 MGM picture. *The Wizard of Oz* proved to be so popular in the former Soviet Union that the translator Aleksandr Volkov wrote a long series of original sequels based upon his reworking of Baum's book. Today all of Baum's original Oz books have been translated into Russian. No one knows how many copies of *The Wizard of Oz* have sold or how many different editions have been issued in its first century.

This centennial edition serves as an introduction to Baum's great body of work. It was compiled keeping in mind the note to "Margery Daw" in *Mother Goose's Melody* (1791): "It is a mean and scandalous practice of authors to put notes to things that deserve no notice." (Perhaps the sensitive reader should avoid Robert Benchley's amusing essay "Shakespeare Explained.") The most complete checklist yet compiled of Baum's published and projected work appears at the back to indicate the author's profuse and diverse output and the great wealth of material the annotator has had to consider. All of Denslow's illustrations appear here in their original colors, and this is the only edition currently in print that reproduces them as he drew them. A century has not dimmed the magic of the first edition of *The Wonderful Wizard of Oz*. These pictures have been supplemented by a number of other drawings Denslow did of the famous characters of Oz, several of which have never been published before. The Denslow Appendix explores the illustrator's many independent projects based upon his collaboration with Baum.

The Annotated Wizard of Oz is intended for adults. It should amuse the already avid and often purist Oz enthusiast. Those who know Oz only through Judy Garland may find Baum's story a pleasant surprise. For those who have long been self-exiled from Baum's domain, it may serve as an enlightening reintroduction to Oz. Children have never needed one, for they have known the magic all along.

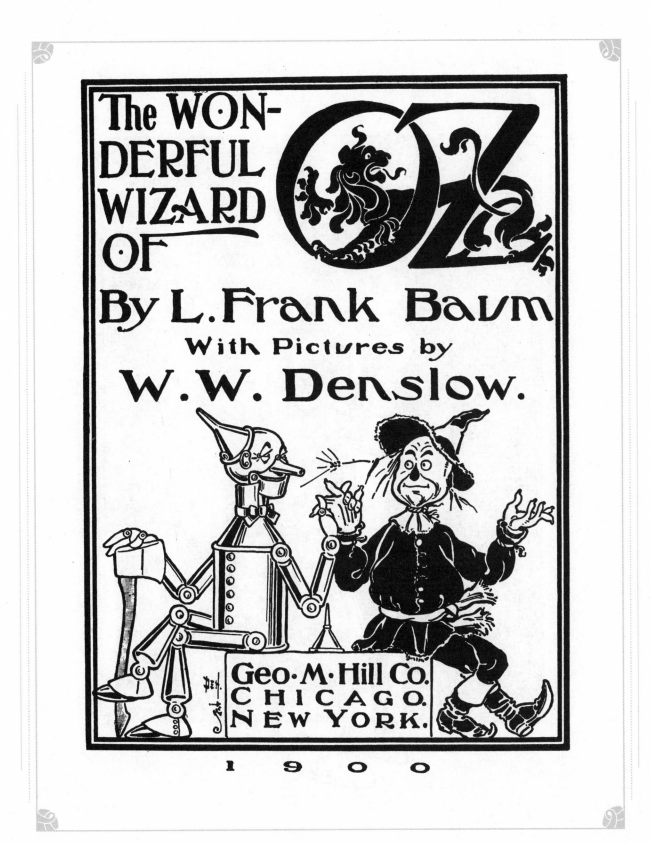

This fine picture of the Tin Woodman appeared on the copyright page of the first edition. While the original drawing reads "Copyright 1899/by L. Frank Baum and W. W. Denslow," there is no evidence in the Copyright Office in Washington, D. C., that Baum, Denslow, or the George M. Hill Company attempted to register the book prior to 1900. They may have intended to publish it by the end of 1899, but Denslow never got around to changing the date when production dragged on into the next year.

The copyright of *The Wonderful Wizard of Oz* was bungled at every step. The notice appeared on page 6 of the finished book rather than on the verso of the title page as required by law. The publishers hastily tried to correct the mistake by rubber-stamping a new copyright notice on the blank versos of the title pages; in the later issue it was printed in the proper place. Consequently most copies of the Hill edition carry two copyright notices. The law also required that two copies of the finished book be delivered to the Copyright Office at the time of publication and then transferred to the Library of Congress. Only one copy, however, was received in 1900. It was not until 1903 that Baum provided a second one. Technically, it could be argued, *The Wizard of Oz* never met the legal requirements of copyright and therefore was always in the public domain. Fortunately, its status was never challenged in the courts.

INTRODUCTION.

Folk lore, legends, myths and fairy tales have followed childhood through the ages, for every healthy youngster has a wholesome and instinctive love for stories fantastic, marvelous and manifestly unreal. The winged fairies of Grimm and Andersen have brought more happiness to childish hearts than all other human creations.

Yet the old-time fairy tale, having served for generations, may now be classed as "historical" in the children's library; for the time has come for a series of newer "wonder tales" in which the stereotyped genie, dwarf and fairy are eliminated, together with all the horrible and blood-curdling incident devised by their authors to point a fearsome moral to each tale. Modern education includes morality; therefore the modern child seeks only entertainment in its wonder-tales and gladly dispenses with all disagreeable incident.

Having this thought in mind, the story of "The Wonderful Wizard of Oz" was written solely to pleasure children of today. It aspires to being a modernized fairy tale, in which the wonderment and joy are retained and the heart-aches and nightmares are left out.

L. FRANK BAUM.

CHICAGO, APRIL, 1900.

1. *Introduction.* This manifesto for the liberation of American children's literature reflects ideas current within Chicago literary circles that rose in part out of discussions at the World's Columbia Exposition of 1893. There was a demand for a new literature, an indigenously American literature, one that rose from the vital, vibrant West rather than from the tired old East. "There is a Chicago literature and a Western literature, limited as yet, but virile and independent," declared the novelist Stanley Waterloo in "Who Reads a Chicago Book?" (*The Dial*, October 1, 1892). "There is a great West, with its great life and its great themes and colorings. Those who have shorn away forests, and built railroads and huge cities, have had their hopes, their aims, their consciences, their passions, their temptations, and their loves; and the story of them is worth the telling. It is a new story, and its relation has just begun. There is nothing reflected or imitative about it." Baum agreed. "The West is rapidly growing as a literary center," he proudly reported to the Syracuse *Post-Standard* (June 1, 1900). "Seven-tenths of the good books of today are written in the West and are published and read in the East." Hamlin Garland in "Literary Emancipation of the West" (*The Forum*, October 1893, reprinted as "Literary Centres" in Garland's collection of essays *Crumbling Idols,* 1894) called for the rejection of European and New England traditions. "Centres of art production are moving westward," he said; "the literary supremacy of the East is passing away" (p. 114 in the latter). Chicago was destined to be the new capital of American literature. He insisted that "literary traditions are weakening all along the line. The old is passing away, the new is coming on. As the old fades away, the strongholds of tradition and classic interest are forgotten and left behind" (p 115). While others in the West were exploring new forms in poetry and novels, Baum gave America's children its first "modernized" fairy tale drawing on the spirit of the West. *The Wizard of Oz* joined Garland's "revolt against the domination of the East over the whole nation" (p. 119). In *The Wonderful Wizard of Oz in American Popular Culture* (Lewiston, N. Y.: Edwin Mellen Press, 1993), Neil Earle called Baum's introduction "almost the self-proclaimed 1776 of children's literature" (p. 66). Baum announces in this declaration of independence of juvenile literature at the turn of the twentieth century that American boys and girls have the unalienable right to the pursuit of happiness in their books.

2. *fairy tales.* The term "fairy tale" entered the English language with the first translations of the *contes de fées* by Comtesse Marie-Chathérine d'Aulnoy (c. 1650–1705) and other members of the court of Louis XIV. The most influential of these French writers was Charles Perrault (1628–1703), a minor bureaucrat who introduced "Little Red Riding Hood," "Cinderella," "Sleeping Beauty," "Puss in Boots," and "Bluebeard" in *Histoires ou contes du temps passé* (1697), known in English as *Tales of Mother Goose.*

Almost from the time they were first available in translation, these stories were viciously attacked as being immoral and thus inappropriate for young readers. The English critic Sarah Trimmer (1741–1810) condemned Perrault's fairy tales in her children's book review, *The Guardian of Education*, warning parents that "the terrific images, which tales of this nature present to the imagination, usually make deep impressions, and injure the tender minds of children, by exciting unreasonable and groundless fears." "Cinderella," for example, instilled in young readers "some of the worst passions that can enter unto the human breast . . . such as envy, jealousy, a dislike to mothers-in-law and half-sisters, vanity, a love of dress etc., etc." America's most popular children's book writer of the time, "Peter Parley" (Samuel Griswold Goodrich, 1793–1860), was also its most vocal critic of fairy stories. He said in *Recollections of a Lifetime* (vol. 1, 1856) that "Puss in Boots" taught that one "may cheat, lie and steal . . . that in order to show gratitude to a friend, we may resort to every kind of meanness and fraud" (p. 167). Jack the Giant Killer was no more than a congenital liar; Goodrich opposed any "sympathy with such a gallant little fellow, especially in combatting giants like Blunderbore, whose floor was covered with human skulls, and whose daintiest food consisted of 'men's hearts, seasoned with pepper and vinegar!' Surely—such is the moral of the tale—we must learn to forgive, nay, to love and approve, wickedness—lying, deception, and murder—when they are employed for good and beneficent purposes! . . . I am convinced that much of the vice and crime in the world are to be imputed in these atrocious books put into the hands of children, and bringing them down, with more or less efficiency, to their own debased moral standard" (pp. 168–69). Arguing that "the elements of nursery books should consist of beauty instead of deformity, goodness instead of wickedness, decency instead of vulgarity," Goodrich produced a long line of dull little children's books containing useful knowledge. Baum wrote *The Wizard of Oz* in part to combat this puritanical strain in nineteenth-century juvenile literature. His modernized fairy tale has had to withstand the assaults of twentieth-century Sarah Trimmers and "Peter Parleys" in their vain attempts to ban it from America's public libraries.

3. *every healthy youngster.* Like L. Frank Baum when he was a child. "I demanded fairy stories when I was a youngster," he told the Philadelphia *North American* (October 3, 1904), "and I was a critical reader, too. One thing I never liked then, and that was the introduction of witches and goblins into the story. I didn't like the little dwarfs in the woods bobbing up with their horrors. That's why you'll never find anything in my fairy tales which frighten a child. I remembered my own feelings well enough to determine that I would never be responsible for a child's nightmare." Baum expresses much the same sentiment in his introduction to *A New Wonderland* (1900; reissued as *The Magical Monarch of Mo*, 1903). "It is the nature of children to scorn realities, which crowd into their lives all too quickly with advancing years," he explains. "Childhood is the time for fables, for dreams, for joy." His stories have no greater purpose than "to excite laughter and to gladden the heart."

4. *The winged fairies of Grimm and Andersen*. Baum, of course, is referring to the fairy tales of brothers Jacob (1785–1863) and Wilhelm (1786–1859) Grimm and Hans Christian Andersen (1805–1875). The Grimm Brothers were German philologists who insisted that they were accurately preserving traditional lore directly from the lips of the German people, but Wilhelm actually reworked and expurgated the tales with each new edition. Andersen was a Danish Romantic poet who invented the majority of his stories. The Brothers Grimm published several editions of their *Kinder- und Hausmärchen* ("Children's and Household Tales") between 1812 and 1856; Andersen issued his *Eventyr* ("Tales") from 1835 right up to the year before he died. "The Grimm brothers were simply collectors and compilers of tales and old folklore," Baum reminded the Milwaukee *Sentinel* (June 16, 1905). "Hans Christian Andersen was the first author to be recognized as a producer of fairy tales, and he became famous in consequence, as there was considerable satisfaction in being able to trace a fairy tale to its legitimate source." The stories of Grimm and Andersen remain the world's most popular fairy tales.

Few "winged fairies" appear in the tales of Grimm and Andersen, for they were largely the invention of French writers. "Stories that are actually concerned primarily with 'fairies,' " admitted J. R. R. Tolkien in "On Fairy Stories" in *Tree and Leaf* (Boston: Houghton Mifflin, 1965), "are relatively rare, and as a rule not very interesting" (p. 6). He, like Baum, avoided "that long line of flower-fairies and fluttering sprites with antennae that I so disliked as a child, and which my children in their turn detested." Their work drew on Faërie, which embraces "many things besides elves and fays, and besides dwarfs, witches, trolls, giants, or dragons; it holds the seas, the sun, and the earth, and all things that are in it: tree and bird, water and stone, wine and bread, and ourselves, mortal men, when we are enchanted."

5. *library*. It is ironic that many librarians and critics of juvenile literature once classified Baum's stories as of only "historical" interest in the field of juvenile books. Martin Gardner did much to undermine this prejudice through "The Librarians of Oz" (*Saturday Review*, April 11, 1959) and "Why Librarians Dislike Oz" (*The American Book Collector*, December 1962). Today the national ban on the Oz books has been lifted, and most libraries have more than just *The Wizard of Oz* on their shelves.

6. *"wonder tales."* Baum may be referring to the common nineteenth-century English translation of the German word *Märchen* and the Danish *eventyr*.

7. *genie*. Like many nineteenth-century critics, Baum lumps the Near Eastern tales of the *Arabian Nights* with European fairy tales. They profoundly influenced the development of the *conte de fées* in France and have been greatly expurgated of their erotic content when published for children. Baum plays with the genie tradition in the Winged Monkeys, the Slaves of the Golden Cap. See Chapter 12, Note 7.

8. *eliminated*. Fortunately, Baum did not eliminate *all* traditional fairy-tale elements from his stories. "The Oz books conform to the accepted pattern far more often than they deviate," observed Russel B. Nye in *The Wizard of Oz and Who He Was*. Baum's "strength as a storyteller for children lay in his unique ability to implement and adapt the familiar apparatus of the older tale by reworking old materials into new forms" (p. 2). An obvious example of his skill at adaptation is the Nome King of *Ozma of Oz* (1907), a traditional character refitted to Baum's needs. (His son Frank Joslyn Baum suggested that his father dropped the "g" from "gnome" because he did not think a child would know how to pronounce it.) As he stretched his storytelling powers, Baum became as adept at writing "old-fashioned" fairy tales like *Queen Zixi of Ix* (1905) as "modernized" ones like the Oz books. "Nobody can write a *new* fairy tale," insisted Andrew Lang in his preface to *The Lilac Fairy Book* (1910); "you can only mix up and dress up the old, old stories, and put the characters into new dresses."

9. *fearsome moral to each tale*. A moral at the end is characteristic of Perrault's fairy tales and Aesop's fables rather than of the stories by Grimm and Andersen. Denslow adopted the high principles of Baum's *Wizard of Oz* in the children's books he produced after their breakup. He modernized classic nursery rhymes in *Denslow's Mother Goose* (1901) by eliminating any disagreeable details. "I believe in pure fun for the children," he explained, "and I believe it can be given them without any incidental gruesomeness." Therefore the Old Woman Who Lived in a Shoe in his edition no longer beats her children but sends them off to bed with kisses. He did not write new material but bowdlerized the old in the ambitious series of "Denslow's Picture Books" he prepared for G. W. Dillingham in 1903 and 1904. "To make children laugh," he said, "you must tell them stories of action. They aren't really fascinated by cruelty—it's action they want." Sounding a bit like "Peter Parley" (see Note 1 above), Denslow described one of these old "horrible and blood-curdling" tales in *Brush and Pencil* (September 1903):

> See what a perfectly outrageous thing is "Jack and the Bean-Stalk." A lad gains admittance to a man's house under false pretense, through lying and deceit, imposing on the sympathy of the man's wife, then he commits theft upon theft. He is a confidence man, a sneak-thief, and a burglar. After which, when the man attempts to defend his property, he is slain by the hero (?), who not only commits murder, but mutilates the corpse, much to the delight of his mother. All childhood classics are not such glaring instances of rapine and murder, but they nearly all have a tendency in that direction, and I am trying to give the kids books that are more healthy in tone.

For Arthur Hosking's *The Artist's Year Book* (Chicago: Fine Arts Building, 1905), Denslow declared that his "aim is to make books for children that are replete with good, clean, wholesome fun and from which all coarseness and vulgarity are excluded." (The letter is now in the Alexander McCook Craighead Collection, United States Military Academy Library, West Point., N.Y.) The Three Bears do not frighten the little girl away, Red Riding Hood's Wolf becomes a watchdog, neither Tom Thumb nor Old Mother Hubbard's Dog die in his retellings. "I don't think I make anything namby-pamby," he said in defense of his methods, "nor do I eliminate the funny element in this work." Baum acknowledges in "What Children Want" (Chicago *Evening Post*, November 29, 1902) that "children are quick to discover and absorb [a moral], provided it is not tacked up like a warning on a signpost."

10. *Modern education.* Although he considered himself "a rather stubborn illiterate," Baum was aware of changes in contemporary education through his four boys. His own upbringing had been relatively conservative. Like many sons of wealthy parents, he was taught at home by English tutors. He also attended Peekskill Military School and Syracuse Classical School, but did not go to college. Princess Ozma wryly explains in *Ozma of Oz* (1907) that "in this country are a number of youths who do not like to work, and the college is

an excellent place for them" (p. 158). Instead Baum entered the family business. "Experience is the only thing that brings knowledge," the Wizard informs the Scarecrow in chapter 15 of *The Wonderful Wizard of Oz*. Maud Gage too went to Syracuse Classical School and studied literature for two years at Cornell before marrying Baum. As for educating their children, the Baums generally agreed with Matilda Joslyn Gage's progressive pedagogical principles. The two older boys attended Mrs. Granger's Kindergarten in Aberdeen, South Dakota, when the kindergarten movement was still in its infancy. In Chicago they studied at the progressive Lewis Institute, a technological school patterned on the Massachusetts Institute of Technology in Cambridge. Frank Joslyn, Robert, and Harry all went to Michigan Military School at Orchard Lake, but Kenneth attended the experimental Interlaken School in La Porte, Indiana, which put into practice the radical ideas of Leo Tolstoy and other modern reformers. All of the Baum boys except Ken went to college. Gage was adamant that none of her grandchildren be baptized or join any church until the individual was old enough to understand what he or she was doing. "I hope Leslie has not been confirmed in regard to something of which she knows nothing," Gage wrote her daughter Helen Leslie Gage about her granddaughter on April 9, 1897. "I most earnestly hope you will use your influence to keep her clear of church entanglements until she *knows* something of the various beliefs of the day, is older, wiser, and can judge from or between conflicting teachings." The Baums did send their four boys to the West Side Ethical Culture Sunday school, which taught morality rather than religion. Fairy tales were part of this instruction, and the school's theories on the subject may have affected Baum's modernized fairy tale.

11. *pleasure.* When Bobbs-Merrill reset the type and replaced Denslow's pictures with new ones by Evelyn Copelman in 1944, "pleasure" became "please." This corruption of Baum's text remains in many subsequent editions of the book.

12. *heart-aches and nightmares are left out.* "I am glad that in spite of his high determination, Mr. Baum failed to keep them out," wrote James Thurber in "The Wizard of Chit[t]enango" (*The New Republic*, December 12, 1934). "Children love a lot of nightmare and at least a little heartache in their books. And they get them in the Oz books. I know that I went through excruciatingly lovely nightmares and heartaches when the Scarecrow lost his straw, when the Tin Woodman was taken apart, when the Saw-Horse broke his wooden leg (it hurt for me, even if it didn't for Mr. Baum)."

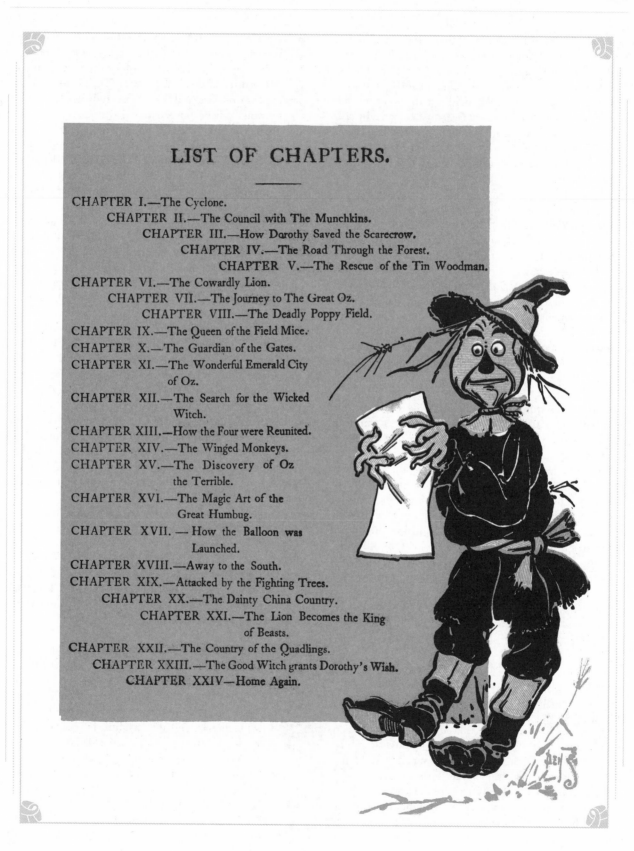

LIST OF CHAPTERS.

Chapter I.
The Cyclone.

Dorothy LIVED IN
the midst of the
great Kansas
prairies, with Uncle Henry,
who was a farmer, and Aunt Em, who was
the farmer's wife. Their house was small,
for the lumber to build it had to be carried by wagon
many miles. There were four walls, a floor
and a roof, which made one room; and this
room contained a rusty looking cooking
stove, a cupboard for the dishes, a table,
three or four chairs, and the beds. Uncle

1.

2.

3.

4.

5.

1. *Dorothy*. The Kansas girl was not the first Dorothy to appear in Baum's work. The little heroine in the very last story ("Little Bun Rabbit") in Baum's very first children's book (*Mother Goose in Prose*, 1897) is another, a "farm girl with all of the qualities of simplicity, common sense, and gentleness that later became identified with the Dorothy of the Oz books" (Roland Baughman, "L. Frank Baum and the 'Oz Books,' " *Columbia Library Columns*, May 1955). When the story was reprinted in *L. Frank Baum's Juvenile Speaker* (1910), her name became Doris. The little heroine of *Dot and Tot of Merryland* (1901) has a common nickname for Dorothy—Dot. And the Queen of Merryland has another—Dolly. Baum may have named Dot's little companion in Merryland Tot from Toto, Dorothy's little companion in Oz.

Dorothy was a popular name at the time, and so many heroines in American fiction were being given it, such as that of Charles E. Carryl's fairy tale *The Admiral's Caravan* (1891). Baum's family always insisted that he did not model his little girl on anyone in particular. Frank Joslyn Baum, the author's oldest son, explained in a letter to *The Baum Bugle* (June 1957):

> Many times during the fifty-seven years since *The Wonderful Wizard of Oz* was first published, many rumors have circulated and some have been printed too, to the effect that my father, L. Frank Baum, had named "Dorothy" of the book after some particular child he knew. One such claim, made by a certain woman [Dorothy Hall Martindale of Michigan] in the Midwest, recently came to my attention. There is no truth in any of the stories. At the time he wrote *The Wizard of Oz* he did not know any girl or woman by the name of Dorothy. It was a name he selected because he liked the sound of it. You see he loves little babies, especially little girl babies. And he wanted very much to have a daughter of his own. But Fate decided otherwise—he had only four boys. But several times, just before the arrival of a child, he had selected a possible name, trusting it would be a girl. The name of "Dorothy" was one such name he hoped to give to a daughter. This he was never able to do. So he used the name for the little Kansas girl who was carried away to the Land of Oz by a cyclone.

Of course, that was not entirely true. Baum did know Dorothy Rountree, the daughter of his friend Harrison H. Rountree, brother-in-law of his publisher Chauncey Williams and the backer of *The Show Window*, Baum's magazine for window trimmers. Perhaps to honor this girl he named the heroine of "Little Bun Rabbit" Dorothy.

Dr. Sally Roesch Wagner offered another theory in "Dorothy Gage and Dorothy Gale" (*The Baum Bugle*, Autumn 1984, pp. 4–6). She said that Baum's niece Matilda Jewell Gage told her that she believed Baum named the character after a sister of hers who died while he was writing the story. Dorothy Louise Gage was born in Bloomington, Illinois, on July 11, 1898, the last child of that generation in the family; she was five months old when she died suddenly on November 11. Her parents, Thomas Clarkson and Sophie Gage, had lost one other child on December 15, 1891; her name was Alice. Baum's wife, Maud, so loved little Dorothy that she was heartbroken when the girl died and she came down from Chicago to attend the funeral. "Dorothy was a perfectly beautiful baby," she wrote her sister Helen Leslie Gage on November 27, 1898. "I could have taken her for my very own and loved her devotedly." That was understandable, since she had no daughters of her own. Wagner implied that in Dorothy of *The Wizard of Oz*, the book he dedicated to his wife, Baum in effect gave Maud a little girl to replace the niece she had just lost. Dorothy Gage in essence became Dorothy Gale.

The reason Baum chose a girl rather than a boy for the story may be found in the following passage from his article "Modern Fairy Tales" (*The Advance*, August 19, 1909):

> Singularly enough, we have no recognized author of fairy literature between Andersen and that of Lewis Carroll, the quaint and clever clergyman who recorded *Alice's Adventures in Wonderland*. Carroll's method of handling fairies was as whimsical as Andersen's was reverential, yet it is but fair to state that the children loved Alice better than any prince or princess that Andersen ever created. The secret of Alice's success lay in the fact that she was a real child, and any normal child could sympathize with her all through her adventures. The story may often bewilder the little one—for it is bound to bewilder us, having neither plot nor motive in its relation—but Alice is doing something every moment, and doing something strange and marvelous, too; so the child follows her with rapturous delight. It is said that Dr. [Charles Lutwidge] Dodgson, the author, was so ashamed of having written a child's book that he would only allow it to be published under the pen name of Lewis Carroll; but it made him famous, even then, and *Alice in Wonderland*, rambling and incoherent as it is, is one of the best and perhaps the most famous of modern fairy tales.

But Dorothy is not an English child. "Both are independent, brave, and practical little girls," noted novelist Alison Lurie in "The Fate of the Munchkins" (*The New York Review of Books*, April 18, 1974), "but Alice, as an upper-middle-class Victorian child, is far more concerned with manners and social status. She worries about the proper way to address a mouse, and is glad she doesn't have to live in a pokey little house like Mabel. Dorothy already lives in a pokey little house. Demographers would class her among the rural poor, but she takes for granted her equality with everyone she meets."

Dorothy is American through and through. And she embodies not only America but the West as well. Baum firmly believed in "the superiority of western women in usefulness over their eastern sisters." Too many ladies of the Atlantic states "sit with idly folded arms or listlessly dallying with fancy work, whose sire is at his wits end to supply the necessities for his family," because "it is still considered a disgrace for young ladies to engage in any kind of regular occupation, and even a married woman loses her social status by engaging in business or following any pursuit which brings her monetary returns." "What a vast difference between these undesirable damsels [of the East] and our brave, helpful western girls!" wrote Baum in the Aberdeen *Saturday Pioneer* (March 15, 1890). "Here a woman delights in being useful; a young lady's highest ambition is to become a bread-winner. And they do." They "have more energy and vitality than those of the east, and . . . there is no nonsense or self pride in their constitutions and they cannot brook idleness when they see before them work to be done which is eminently fitted to their hands." Dorothy embodies this same Western determination and independence in her quest to get back to Kansas. Brian Attebery said in *The Fantasy Tradition in American Literature* (Bloomington: Indiana University Press, 1980, p. 98) that Baum offered the two popular conceptions of the pioneer woman: Aunt Em ("faded and bleak and particularly appealing to local color writers with a naturalistic vision"); and Dorothy ("lively and attractive, drawing her strength from the earth she lives so close to"). There is no nonsense about Dorothy. "The heroine spends little time in pondering who she is, where she is going, or why the world has suddenly turned upside down," noted Justin G. Schiller in his afterword to the 1985 Pennyroyal edition of *The Wonderful Wizard of Oz*; "like the real children of her day, Dorothy accepts the empirical reality of what she experiences, knows what she wants, and sets about doing what needs to be done to achieve it" (p. 262). Nothing will stop this little Kansas girl from getting back home.

She has the indomitable spirit of the early suffragists. When Susan B. Anthony was out in South Dakota in 1890, campaigning for women's rights, she refused to seek shelter in a storm cellar from an approaching twister like the others did. "A little thing like a cyclone doesn't frighten me," she said. See Frances Cranmer Greenman's *Higher than the Sky* (N.Y.: Harper & Bros., 1954, p. 14). Feminists have naturally claimed Dorothy as one of their own. *The Wizard of Oz* is now almost universally acknowledged to be the earliest truly feminist American children's book, because of spunky and tenacious Dorothy. (Even tomboy Jo March marries at the end of *Little Women*!) Homely little Dorothy refreshingly goes out and solves her problem herself rather than waiting patiently like a beautiful heroine in a European fairy tale for someone else, whether prince or commoner, to put things right. Katharine Rogers praised Dorothy in "Liberation for Little Girls" (*Saturday Review*, June 17, 1972, p. 72) for being "a brave, resourceful girl who rescues three male characters and destroys two evil witches." Baum's books are full of "little girls who are enterprising, ingenious, adventurous, or imposingly self-reliant." Some people have criticized Baum as being anti-woman for his gentle satire on militant feminism in General Jinjur and her female Army of Revolt in *The Marvelous Land of Oz* (1904). But they have forgotten that in the end a woman, Glinda the Good, restores a little girl, Princess Ozma, as the rightful ruler of Oz. Baum therefore establishes a matriarchate that would have made his suffragist mother-in-law, Matilda Joslyn Gage, proud. True magic lies with the women in Oz. "The power of men, it is suggested, is illusory," explained Salman Rushdie in his monograph on the MGM movie; "the power of women is real" (p. 42). "In the work I have done with women, in the process of working through their own personal myth structure," explained the clinical psychologist Madonna Kolbenschlag in *Lost in the Land of Oz* (New York: Crossroad, 1994), "I have been amazed at the number of times the Dorothy-script surfaces in the consciousness—sometimes in the dreams—of women in transition or undergoing a major transformation in self-image." Dorothy symbolizes "the spiritual orphan, the one who 'learns by leaving and going where she has to go,' for whom there are no role models and few mentors, who feels alienated from most of the systems created by the dominant male culture" (pp. 18–19). She differs from the conventional heroines of European fairy tales, because she "rescues herself and her companions. She does not depend on 'snaring' a prince or reconciliation with a father-figure in order to improve her situation. . . . there is always a sense in the narrative that Dorothy will be resourceful enough to triumph over adversity" (p. 20). Here was an American girl who "was curious, imaginative, longing for adventure, and bored with routine family life in Kansas. Her sudden translocation to Oz is one of the most wonderful wish fulfillments in all of literature" (p. 127).

But boys like her, too. Baum thought that modern authors of fairy tales had to write primarily for little girls. No doubt he was thinking of his own sons when he told the Chicago *Evening American* (July 22, 1912) that the modern boy "is surrounded by wonders from the very day of his birth. He is probably rocked to sleep by an electric cradle rocker, and when he gets a little older, he is taken out for a spin in his father's automobile. And then later there are the telephone, the wireless and the aeroplane for him to get acquainted with. Girls, it is true, do not take so great an interest in these things, and they are about the only readers that these authors have left." Russel B. Nye argued in *The Wizard of Oz and Who He Was*, "Oz is beyond all doubt a little girl's dream-home. Its atmosphere is feminine, not masculine, with very little of the rowdy, frenetic energy of boys." Those who do appear there are "girls' boys, drawn as little girls assume boys should be. Baum could not make Oz fit boys, nor was he capable of making boys who could fit easily and naturally into Oz society" (pp. 12–13). That is not entirely true if one considers Tip in *The Marvelous Land of Oz* (1904), Ojo in *The Patchwork Girl of Oz* (1913), or Prince Inga in *Rinkitink in Oz* (1916). Many of the most ardent admirers of the Oz books are men. "Because the central human figures in Baum's stories are girls, it is sometimes carelessly assumed that he appeals more to girls than he does to boys," noted Edward Wagenknecht in "Utopia Americana: A Generation Afterwards" (*American Book Collector*, December 1962). "When I was first introduced to *The Wizard of Oz*, I was at that stage in my development (it did not last long) where I imagined I did not like girls, but I cannot recall that this ever affected my devotion to Baum or to Dorothy for a moment. And most of the great Baum dévotées of mature years that I happen to know are not women but men." Gore Vidal agreed. "Dorothy is a perfectly acceptable central character for a boy to read about," he admitted in "On Rereading the Oz Books" (*The New York Review of Books*, October 13, 1977). "She asks the right questions. She is not sappy. . . . She is straight to the point and a bit aggressive." He argued that "surely, for a pre-pube there is not much difference between a boy and a girl protagonist. After all, the central fact of the pre-pube's existence is not being male or female but being a child, much the hardest of all roles to play. During and after puberty, there is a tendency to want a character like oneself."

Since Baum did not model her on any particular child he knew, Dorothy is an Everyman—or Everychild. He offers no detailed description of his

heroine in the Oz books. He likely borrowed some of her characteristics from his Dakota nieces, Leslie Gage, Matilda Jewell Gage, and Magdalena Carpenter. Raylyn Moore, David L. Greene and Dick Martin, Gore Vidal, David McCord, and others have complained about the decline of Dorothy's vocabulary in the later Oz stories, but Baum does not employ "baby talk" as they have insisted but rather a Dakota dialect (" 'spose" for "suppose," " 'splain" for "explain," " 'zactly" for "exactly") that he probably picked up from his nieces when they visited him and Maud at their summer cottage in Macatawa Park, Michigan. Vidal argued in "On Rereading the Oz Books" that by *Ozma of Oz* (1907), "her conversation is full of cute contractions that must have doubled up audiences in Sioux City but were pretty hard going for at least one child forty years ago." Did Vidal have the same problem with *Adventures of Huckleberry Finn* (1884)? Baum left Dorothy's appearance up to the imagination of the illustrator or the reader, but he gives the best description of her personality in *The Emerald City of Oz* (1910):

> This little girl, Dorothy, was like dozens of little girls you know. She was loving and usually sweet-tempered, and had a round rosy face and earnest eyes. Life was a serious thing to Dorothy, and a wonderful thing, too, for she had encountered more strange adventures in her short life than many other girls her age. (p. 22)

She is loved and admired, Baum explains also in *The Emerald City of Oz*, "because she was a simple, sweet and true little girl who was honest to herself and to all whom she met. In this world in which we live simplicity and kindness are the only magic wands that work wonders" (pp. 49–50). The most famous portrayal of Dorothy, of course, is Judy Garland in the 1939 MGM musical, but Anna Laughlin created the role onstage in the 1902 musical extravaganza. Romola Remus was the first screen Dorothy in Baum's *Fairylogue and Radio-Plays* (1908), and Bebe Daniels has been credited with portraying her in two silent Selig one-reelers, *The Wonderful Wizard of Oz* and *Dorothy and the Scarecrow in Oz*, both in 1910. Stephanie Mills was a rousing Dorothy in *The Wiz* in 1975, but Diana Ross played her as a sensitive young woman in the 1978 movie of the Broadway musical. One of the finest Dorothys, however, was little Fairuza Balk in the otherwise disappointing Disney movie *Return to Oz* (1986), based largely on *The Marvelous Land of Oz* (1904) and *Ozma of Oz* (1907).

2. *the great Kansas prairies.* According to the 1902 musical extravaganza of *The Wizard of Oz*, Dorothy lives near Topeka. A letter from her that appears in *The Ozmapolitan* (a flyer advertising *The Marvelous Land of Oz*, 1904) is addressed "Uncle Henry's Farm near Topeka, Kansas." And Aunt Em observes when she and Uncle Henry move to Ozma's palace in *The Emerald City of Oz* (1910), "It beats the Topeka Hotel!" (p. 66).

"Baum locates [Dorothy] swiftly and efficiently in the first sentence of the series," wrote Gore Vidal in "On Rereading the Oz Books" (*The New York Review of Books*, October 13, 1977). He argued, "The style of the first book is straightforward, even formal. There are almost no contractions. . . . There are occasional Germanisms . . . 'What is that little dog you are so tender of?' " Baum's prose strives toward Hamlin Garland's standard as expressed in *Crumbling Idols* (1894): "The West should work in accordance with the fundamental principles of good writing; that is, it should seek to attain the most perfect lucidity, expressiveness, flexibility, and grace. Its technique should be comprehensible, clear in outline, and infinitely suggestive, ready to be submitted to the world, but free to use new forms" (p. 122). In "Why the Wizard of Oz Keeps On Selling" (*Writer's Digest*, December 1952), Frank Joslyn Baum reported that when his father was writing, he always kept in mind the framed motto from the Bible over his writing desk: WHEN I WAS A CHILD I SPAKE AS A CHILD, I UNDERSTOOD AS A CHILD, I THOUGHT AS A CHILD (I Corinthians 13:11). And he followed that advice in writing the first Oz book. Baum had little patience for verbosity and created a special place for wordy people in Rigmarole Town in *The Emerald City of Oz* (1910): " 'If those people wrote books,' Omby Amby remarked with a smile, 'it would take a whole book to say the cow jumped over the moon.' 'Perhaps some of 'em do write books,' asserted the little Wizard. 'I've read a few rigmaroles that might have come from this very town' " (p. 235). Vidal added that Baum's description of the Kansas landscape "would have confirmed John Ruskin's dark view of American scenery." The great English art critic observed, on viewing some paintings by a prominent American painter, that "the ugliness of them is wonderful. I see that they are true studies and that the ugliness of the country must be unfathomable."

Seeking local color for his American fairy tale, Baum did not really write about Kansas but about Dakota Territory, where he lived from 1888 to 1891. He captures much of the same bleakness of the area that Hamlin Garland, from Ordway, Brown County, describes in his 1922 foreword to *Main-Travelled Roads*: "The houses, bare as boxes, dropped on the treeless plains, the barbed-wire fences running at right angles, and the towns mere assemblages of flimsy wooden sheds with painted-pine battlement, produced on me the effect of an almost helpless and sterile poverty." He

added that even at that late date, "there are still wide stretches of territory in Kansas and Nebraska where the farmhouse is a lonely shelter." Baum did not know Kansas well. The only recorded instance of his traveling through the Sunflower State was on tour with the *Maid of Arran* company. He and his wife were not impressed. "I don't see how you can like the West," Maud complained to her brother Thomas Clarkson Gage in South Dakota on November 26, 1882. "I wouldn't be hired to live here. Perhaps I will like Chicago better, but the far west excuse me from it. . . . I don't think much of Kansas as a state, it's N[o] G[ood]. . . . Some of the hotels are dreadful, but I have seen no bugs or grey backs as yet." Baum may have got his picture of Kansas from reading William Allen White's *The Real Issue and Other Stories*, published by his publisher Way & Williams in 1896. "The Story of Aqua Pura" and "A Story of the Highland" in particular share much in common with the opening pages of *The Wizard of Oz*. Former Oz Club secretary Fred M. Meyer noted another indication that Baum was writing about the Dakotas, not Kansas. In *The Road to Oz* (1909), when the Shaggy Man says that he hopes it will snow, Dorothy protests, "If it snowed in August it would spoil the corn and the oats and the wheat; and then Uncle Henry wouldn't have any crops" (pp. 15–16). But Kansans plant winter wheat in the fall and harvest it in June or July; South Dakotans are known for their spring wheat, which they gather in August. At least one writer must have recognized the real locale: Eva Katharine Gibson set her poor imitation of *The Wonderful Wizard of Oz*, *Zauberlinda the Wise Witch* (1901), in the Black Hills of South Dakota.

Of course, many Kansans have objected to Baum's description. When the state adopted the slogan "Land of Ahs," some people protested by calling it the "Land of Blahs." "I'm sure [Baum] didn't mean anything personal," Mark Hunt, director of the Kansas Museum of History, told the New York *Times* (October 9, 1989), "but there are times that we think he did." Dick Buzbee, publisher of the Hutchinson (Kansas) *News*, crusaded against *The Wizard of Oz*, because "all the nasty things that happen to [Dorothy] are in Kansas." (Perhaps he never read the book or saw the movie?) Former senator and Republican presidential candidate Robert Dole was quoted in the *Congressional Record* (October 23, 1991) as telling his colleagues, "What awaits visitors to Kansas is the real thing . . . certainly not the Hollywood Kansas of *The Wizard of Oz*." Yet the Seward County Historical Society in Liberal restored a turn-of-the-century farmhouse to serve as Dorothy's House, and there have been plans for years to erect a Wizard of Oz Theme Park in Wyandotte County. "Kansans might not always appreciate Baum for choosing Kansas as the setting of *The*

Wizard of Oz," concluded Thomas Fox Averill in "Oz and Kansas Culture" (*Kansas History,* Spring 1989). "But they should at least appreciate that Baum also gave them Dorothy, a person strong enough, with enough brains, heart, and courage to endure the bleak and forbidding Kansas he created. He also gave us a big portion of Kansas folklore, and a genuine part of the Kansas and American mind."

3. *Uncle Henry . . . and Aunt Em.* When Baum wrote *The Wizard of Oz,* American writers were just recognizing that the West was not always as romantic as the dime novels said. The historian Frederick Jackson Turner declared the official end of the American frontier at the 1893 World's Columbia Exposition, and much of the romance and glamour of the Old West died with it. Hamlin Garland was a leader in the new realistic school that depicted life as it was, not as it should have been. William Dean Howells found Garland's influential *Main-Travelled Roads* (1891) to be "full of those gaunt, grim, sordid, pathetic, ferocious figures, whom our satirists find so easy to caricature as Hayseeds, and whose blind groping for fairer conditions is so grotesque to the newspapers and so menacing to the politicians." Aunt Em and Uncle Henry belong to that pitiful race of Americans. They exemplify the naturalist writers' belief that environment profoundly alters character. It is not a pretty picture, but a sympathetic one. Baum knew about many Aunt Ems and Uncle Henrys during his years in Aberdeen, South Dakota. He saw firsthand how drought ruined lives, how the land showed no mercy to its inhabitants. "The lonesomest sound, for me, is the whine of the prairie wind through a window-screen in a farmhouse kitchen," Aberdeen artist Frances Cranmer Greenman recalled these years in her memoir *Higher than the Sky* (N.Y.: Harper & Bros., 1954). "The loneliest sight I ever saw was, as our grumbling freight train stopped on the prairie to catch its breath, a weather-beaten woman, her gray gingham dress whipped in the wind, standing by the door of her weather-beaten house and gazing with hopeless eyes at the nothingness around her" (p. 20). Another forlorn farmwife told Susan B. Anthony that the hardest thing about life on the prairie was "to sit in our little sod houses at night and listen to the wolves howl over the graves of our babies. The howl of a wolf is the cry of a child from the grave" (pp. 20–21). The hard life of Dorothy's foster parents paralleled that of Baum's in-laws, Julia Gage and James Duguid "Frank" Carpenter of Edgeley, North Dakota. Like Aunt Em, Julia Carpenter had been a pretty, lively bride when she left Fayetteville, New York, to start a new life far away from family and friends. Julia Carpenter kept a diary of her life on the prairie, which Elizabeth Hampsten edited and published in *To All Enquiring*

Friends: Letters, Diaries and Essays in North Dakota 1880–1910 (Grand Forks, N.D.: University of North Dakota, 1979, pp. 199–252). And it was far different from that described by Laura Ingalls Wilder of De Smet, South Dakota, in her famous Little House books. A woman cook told Julia, as they were passing through Jamestown on June 16, 1882, "what a dreadful country it was, not fit for a woman, how lonely she was." She soon found out for herself how horrible it could be. "This is *awful country,*" she wrote on January 1, 1884, "and I want to live East." Frank Carpenter often left his wife alone for days on end as he sought work, and their nearest neighbors were fifteen to twenty miles away. "Alone all day and night again," Julia noted in her diary on April 14, 1884. "*Dreadfully, dreadfully* forlorn. Can't stand being alone so much." Her husband sought comfort in drink and gambling, was abusive, and eventually committed suicide. Julia's mind had been going and finally snapped. She died in a sanatorium. Late in life when an occultist asked her how her eyes got so bad, she said, "Looking so hard across the prairie for another human being." The Carpenters were much on Baum's mind when he was writing *The Wizard of Oz.* Homesteading proved to be too hard for them, and in 1899 they had to leave the farm and move into town.

"Some commentators have made, I think, too much of Baum's parentless children," Gore Vidal argued in "On Rereading the Oz Books" (*The New York Review of Books,* October 13, 1977). "The author's motive seems to me to be not only obvious but sensible. A child separated from loving parents for any length of time is going to be distressed, even in a magic story. But aunts and uncles need not be taken too seriously." But Dorothy *does* take her aunt and uncle seriously. John Algeo suggested in "The Names of Oz" (in Edward Callary's *From Oz to the Onion Patch,* DeKalb, Ill.: North Central Name Society, 1986) that "Em" comes from "M," "the initial of Baum's wife, Maud, and of his mother-in-law Matilda [Joslyn Gage], and is also the first letter of the word 'mother.' Aunt Em is the archetypal feminine, the eternal female parent, the long-suffering Mother" (p. 133). Matilda Joslyn Gage's husband's name was Henry. Also, "M" could stand for Magdalena, Julia Carpenter's daughter, and "Henry" for Harry, her son. Of course, suggesting these correspondences is no more than an amusing parlor game, for Baum likely chose these names as representative of a certain type of Midwesterner with whom he was familiar. Uncle Henry and Aunt Em have come to symbolize the stern American farmer and his wife as much as the couple in Grant Wood's famous painting *American Gothic* have.

4. *Their house.* Baum describes a typical claim shanty of the period. Compare Dorothy's farmhouse with the Carpenter home near Edgeley, North Dakota, as described in Julia's diary:

> Our house consists of two rooms, the main part 12' x 16' with a closet taken out. Outside door and window facing the south, window facing the west, door in the north leading into the kitchen. The outside of the windows covered with green mosquito netting, door has a green wire screen, the windows have blue cambric curtains and newspaper lambrequins fringed. The floor is covered with an old velvet carpet formerly used at home. The bedstead is a light yellow wood, made up with the white spread, pillow shams, etc., covered with mosquito netting. The bedstead stands on an alcove formed by the closet. Over the head of the bed are several pictures of Frank Baum and others, plaques, clock etc. Over the mantel are pictures of Mother, T. C., and Maud. At one end of the bed stands a bureau, in front of the south window is a table, behind the door a stand. In one corner stands two large dry goods boxes. In other parts of the room are my blue rocker, Frank's rocker given by Helen. . . . A small looking-glass and one or two pictures finish the furniture of the room. . . . The kitchen is a "lean-to" reached by two steps. Its furniture is a large cupboard, a table covered with oilcloth, four chairs, three shelves, etc. This room has two windows, one facing east, the road, the other facing north. The outer door is at the west end. A little distance back of the house is a sod barn, for our four mules. . . . Northwest of the house is a shallow well. (Hampsten, *To All Enquiring Friends*, p. 212)

5. *the lumber to build it had to be carried by wagon many miles.* The Carpenters too had to carry the lumber by wagon from Ellendale, North Dakota, to their homestead, a day's journey, to build their little house on the prairie in 1882.

Henry and Aunt Em had a big bed in one corner, and Dorothy a little bed in another corner. There was no gar-ret at all, and no cellar—except a small hole, dug in the ground, called a cyclone cellar, where the family could go in case one of those great whirlwinds arose, mighty enough to crush any building in its path. It was reached by a trap-door in the middle of the floor, from which a ladder led down into the small, dark hole.

When Dorothy stood in the doorway and looked around, she could see nothing but the great gray prairie on every side. Not a tree nor a house broke the broad sweep of flat country that reached the edge of the sky in all directions. The sun had baked the plowed land into a gray mass, with little cracks running through it. Even the grass was not green, for the sun had burned the tops of the long blades until they were the same gray color to be seen everywhere. Once the house had been painted, but the sun blistered the paint and the rains washed it away, and now the house was as dull and gray as every-thing else.

When Aunt Em came there to live she was a young, pretty wife. The sun and wind had changed her, too. They had taken the sparkle from her eyes and left them a sober gray; they had taken the red from her cheeks and lips, and they were gray also. She was thin and gaunt, and never smiled, now. When Dorothy, who was an orphan, first came to her, Aunt Em had been so startled

6. *gray*. Garland argued in *Crumbling Idols* (1894) that the new writer of the West "spontaneously reflects the life which goes on around him." This was achieved through local color with "such quality of texture and background that it could not have been written in any other place or by any one else but a native." It required "a statement of life as indigenous as the plant-growth . . . that every tree and bird and mountain shall be dear and companionable and necessary, not picturesque; the tourist cannot write the local novel" (pp. 52–55). For Baum the local color of Kansas was gray. "The word 'gray' appears nine times in the space of four paragraphs," Martin Gardner observed in Note 1 of *The Wizard of Oz and Who He Was*. "Baum is clearly contrasting the grayness of life on the Kansas farm, and the solemnity of Uncle Henry and Aunt Em, with the color and gaiety of Oz." While capturing some of the solemnity of prairie life of Garland's *Main-Travelled Roads* (1891), Baum uses color sparingly and symbolically here in much the way that Stephen Crane does in his work. "And yet, what color does convey/So passionless a sense as gray?" asked Baum in his poem "A Sonnet to My Lady's Eye" (Chicago *Sunday Times-Herald*, October 25, 1896; reprinted in *By the Candelabra's Glare*, 1898, p. 20). "It is out of this greyness—the gathering, cumulative greyness of that bleak world—that calamity comes," argued Salman Rushdie in his 1992 monograph on the 1939 movie. "The tornado is the greyness gathered together and whirled about and unleashed, so to speak, against itself" (p. 16).

7. *in all directions*. "This is the plain American style at its best," Gore Vidal wrote in praise of this description in "On Rereading the Oz Books." The novelist Cathleen Schine in "America as Fairyland" (*The New York Times Book Review*, June 7, 1985) called it "a bleak, flat slap across the flushed face of children's literature." In "Gopher Prairie and Emerald City" (*The Baum Bugle*, Winter 1982, p. 14), Dr. Eugene J. Fisher of New York University noted the similarity between the bleakness of Baum's Kansas farm and that in Sinclair Lewis's Gopher Prairie in *Main Street* (1920): "She saw the prairie, flat in giant patches or rolling in long hummocks. The width and bigness of it began to frighten her. It spread out so; it went on so uncontrollable; she could never know it." The people are also "as drab as their houses, as flat as their fields." Julia Carpenter likewise recorded in her diary on June 15, 1882, that "as far as the eye could reach, not a tree or shrub could be seen."

by the child's laughter that she would scream and press her hand upon her heart whenever Dorothy's merry voice reached her ears; and she still looked at the little girl with wonder that she could find anything to laugh at.

Uncle Henry never laughed. He worked hard from morning till night and did not know what joy was. He was gray also, from his long beard to his rough boots, and he looked stern and solemn, and rarely spoke.

8.   It was Toto that made Dorothy laugh, and saved her from growing as gray as her other surroundings. Toto was not gray; he was a little black dog, with long, silky hair and small black eyes that twinkled merrily on either side of his funny, wee nose. Toto played all day long, and Dorothy played with him, and loved him dearly.

To-day, however, they were not playing. Uncle Henry sat upon the

9.   door-step and looked anxiously at the sky, which was even grayer than usual. Dorothy stood in the door with Toto in her arms, and looked at the sky too. Aunt Em was washing the dishes.

From the far north they heard a

8. *Toto*. Early settlers on the vast lonely prairie often relied on pets to keep them company, since neighbors were few and far between. Julia Gage Carpenter bought a kitten who became her greatest comfort with her husband away so much of the time. Toto was a popular name for dogs in the nineteenth century; in France it is a common nickname, often for little boys. Remarkably Baum (likely at the director Julian Mitchell's suggestion) replaced Dorothy's dog with a spotted calf named Imogene in the 1902 musical extravaganza. "I regret that one favorite character of the children—the dog Toto—will be missing," he told the Chicago *Record-Herald* (June 10, 1902). "We found Toto an impossibility from the dramatic viewpoint, and reluctantly abandoned him. But we put the cow in his place. It may seem a long jump from a dog to a cow, but in the latter animal we have a character that really ought to amuse the youngsters exceedingly, and the eccentric creature accompanies Dorothy on her journey from Kansas just as Toto did in the book." The reason was purely practical: It was far easier for an actor to impersonate a cow than a dog (although Nana was a popular character in James M. Barrie's *Peter Pan* of 1904). Fred Stone's brother Edwin played Imogene until his sudden death in 1903; Joseph Schrode took the part afterward. "*I couldn't stand Toto* [in the 1939 movie]," insisted Rushdie in his monograph on the picture. "I still can't." He considered the dog "that little yapping hairpiece of a creature, that meddlesome rug! . . . That Toto should be the film's one true object of love has always rankled. Useless (though satisfying) to protest: nobody, now, can rid me of that turbulent toupée" (pp. 17–18). But Rushdie admired how "L. Frank Baum, excellent fellow, gave the dog a distinctly minor role: it [*sic*] kept Dorothy happy, and when she was not, it had a tendency to 'whine dismally': not an endearing trait. Its only real important contribution to the narrative of Baum's story came when it accidentally knocked over the screen behind which the Wizard stood concealed [in Chapter 15]." But Rushdie forgot that Toto makes at least two other important contributions to the narrative: He is responsible for Dorothy's trip to Oz in the cyclone (Chapter 1) and her failure to return to Kansas in the Wizard's balloon (Chapter 17).

Although Baum probably intended Toto to be a mongrel, illustrators have depicted him as various breeds. Writer Daniel P. Mannix identified Denslow's dog as a Cairn terrier. John R. Neill, who succeeded Denslow as the Imperial Illustrator of Oz, portrayed Toto as the then fashionable Boston bulldog in *The Road to Oz* (1909) and *The Emerald City of Oz* (1910). Neill played with his predecessor's conceptions of the little Kansas girl and her dog in *The Road to Oz*. When they discover in the Tin Woodman's garden statues of themselves just as they "had first appeared in the Land of Oz" (p. 162), Neill's slim, elegant Dorothy and Toto laugh at Denslow's comparatively dumpy portrayals complete with the date "1900" and a sea horse on each pedestal. (See illustration, p. lxiv.) But Neill drew him as a shaggy black breed in the later Oz books. Dogs are now often called Toto after Dorothy's little companion, just like the cocker spaniel Maud Baum had at Ozcot years after her husband's death. While serving in France during World War I, Captain Frank Joslyn Baum noted in his diary with amusement how a fellow officer referred to fleas as "totos"!

9. *looked anxiously at the sky*. "Out on this wide prairie, where not a tree or a building obscures the horizon in any direction, we are ever watching its clouds," wrote Helen Leslie Gage in "The Dakota Cyclone" (Syracuse *Weekly Express*, June 29, 1887). Baum may well have consulted this article when he wrote *The Wizard of Oz*, for he shares some details of the Kansas cyclone with his sister-in-law's description of one she observed out in Edgeley, North Dakota, where the Carpenters lived.

low wail of the wind, and Uncle Henry and Dorothy could see where the long grass bowed in waves before the coming storm. There now came a sharp whistling in the air from the south, and as they turned their eyes that way they saw ripples in the grass coming from that direction also.

Suddenly Uncle Henry stood up.

10. "There's a cyclone coming, Em," he called to his wife; "I'll go look after the stock." Then he ran toward the sheds where the cows and horses were kept.

Aunt Em dropped her work and came to the door. One glance told her of the danger close at hand.

"Quick, Dorothy!" she screamed; "run for the cellar!"

Toto jumped out of Dorothy's arms and hid under the bed, and the girl started to get him. Aunt Em, badly frightened, threw open the trap-door in the floor and climbed down the ladder into the small, dark hole. Dorothy caught Toto at last, and started to follow her aunt. When she was half way across the room there came a great shriek from the wind, and the house shook so hard that she lost her footing and sat down suddenly upon the floor.

11. A strange thing then happened.

The house whirled around two or three times and rose slowly through the air. Dorothy felt as if she were going up in a balloon.

The north and south winds met where the house stood, and made it the exact center of the cyclone. In the

10. *cyclone*. Baum may have set his story during the summer, for that is when cyclones are most prevalent. Gore Vidal suggested in "The Wizard of the 'Wizard' " (*The New York Review of Books*, September 29, 1977) that Baum may have had in mind one especially destructive cyclone that destroyed two Kansas towns in 1893, killing thirty-one people. When *The Wizard of Oz* first came out, Professor Willis L. Moore, chief of the United States Weather Bureau, wrote an anxious letter to the publishers:

> When I consider the circulation it must have, I regret that the term "cyclone" was used when the term "tornado" was meant. I have been laboring earnestly to correct the improper use of these words. A tornado is nearly always an incident to a cyclone and usually occurs in the southeast quadrant of a cyclonic storm. Cyclones are not necessarily dangerous, while tornadoes are always destructive. A cyclone always covers a wide extent of country, sometimes as much as 1,000 miles, while the path of a tornado is very narrow, seldom more than one mile and frequently not more than 100 yards. The author is not to blame for this mistake, for the public has usually insisted upon an improper use of these terms to such an extent that I fear scientists will be compelled to change their nomenclature. If your little book had used the correct word it would have been of considerable assistance to science, instead of perpetuating an unfortunate error. ("The Scientist and the Fairy Book," Chicago *Journal,* September 20, 1900)

Speaking on behalf of the George M. Hill Company, Frank K. Reilly promised Professor Willis that the mistake would be changed in the next edition, but it never was. The word "cyclone" still is commonly used to mean a tornado, a hurricane, or any other destructive windstorm. Aware of this meteorological discrepancy, Aleksandr Volkov changed Baum's cyclone to a hurricane in his 1939 Russian "translation" of *The Wizard of Oz*. Baum's niece Matilda Jewell Gage once protested that her uncle could not have been describing Dakota in *The Wizard of Oz*. She insisted that when *she* was a little girl "there never *were* any tornadoes or cyclones any where but in Kansas! That was the place—that was what Kansas was famous for." The papers were full of reports about Kansas cyclones, but the Dakotas too were famous for their cyclones in the late nineteenth century. Cyclone cellars were common out there, and Julia Carpenter wrote in her diary instructions of what to do in case a cyclone or tornado hit. Baum did witness at least one semi-cyclone in Aberdeen, South Dakota, on May 23, 1890. "Taken altogether," he reported the next day in the *Saturday Pioneer*, "it was quite a sensational episode for Aberdeen, and demonstrates the fact that even in our glo-rious climate, removed as we are for the most part from violent elemental disturbances, we are not wholly exempt from the milder sort of cyclones." Another one just missed hitting Chicago on May 30, 1896, when Baum lived there. Most children today know cyclones (or tornadoes) through *The Wizard of Oz*.

Baum's fairy tale was not the very first children's book to use a cyclone as means of passage to wonderland. The actor Richard Mansfield (with whom Maud Baum's cousin Blanche Weaver toured in the first American production of *Cyrano de Bergerac*) had one carry two little girls, Beatrice and Jessie, to a whimsical place in *Blown Away* (1897). His "nonsense narrative without rhyme and reason" was a poor imitation of *Alice in Wonderland* and is now forgotten. Some American readers have found a cyclone too prosaic a means to travel to fairyland, too commonplace for a wonder tale. This criticism of the book may be due to nothing more than local prejudice. "Here in America," admitted Carol Ryrie Brink, the Newbery Medal–winning author of *Caddie Woodlawn* (1935), in "Some Forgotten Children's Books" (*South Dakota Library Bulletin*, April–June 1948), "we show the liveliest interest in the strange adventures of a little girl in a rabbit hole or a marionette in the stomach of a whale, yet we are likely to disapprove of a Kansas girl being carried off in a cyclone to a fictitious land. This is probably because we are not acquainted with interiors of English rabbit holes nor Italian whales, but we know for certain that no Kansas cyclone ever took a child further than Topeka or Emporia." Oz is only for dreamers and not for the literal-minded.

11. *A strange thing then happened*. It was not so strange as it may seem. Helen Leslie Gage in her article "The Dakota Cyclone" (Syracuse *Weekly Express*, June 29, 1887) described what happened when a funnel-shaped cloud struck a house in North Dakota:

> Boards began to fly against the sides, the house creaked and groaned and the old gentleman also started for the cellar. When on the second step the house went off its foundation, knocking him along with it. The house stood facing due west; it was carried a little above the ground to the southeast, where it struck the earth and then was lifted over two or three feet north and set down at an angle of forty-five degrees, piling up the earth in a bank to the windows. . . . Everything in the pantry lay on the floor with the marble-top table lying in the midst, and the dog cowering in the corner.

She also mentioned how the wind seized another house and caught up a claim shanty and 'shook its occupants about.

middle of a cyclone the air is generally still, but the great pressure of the wind on every side of the house raised it up higher and higher, until it was at the very top of the cyclone; and there it remained and was carried miles and miles away as easily as you could carry a feather.

It was very dark, and the wind howled horribly around her, but Dorothy found she was riding quite easily. After the first few whirls around, and one other time when the house tipped badly, she felt as if she were being rocked gently, like a baby in a cradle.

Toto did not like it. He ran about the room, now here, now there, barking loudly; but Dorothy sat quite still on the floor and waited to see what would happen.

Once Toto got too near the open trap-door, and fell in; and at first the little girl thought she had lost him. But soon she saw one of his ears sticking up through the hole, for the strong pressure of the air was keeping him up so that he could not fall. She crept to the hole, caught Toto by the ear, and dragged him into the room again; afterward closing the trap-door so that no more accidents could happen.

Hour after hour passed away, and slowly Dorothy got over her fright; but she felt quite lonely, and the wind shrieked so loudly all about her that she nearly became deaf. At first she had wondered if she would be dashed to pieces when the house fell again; but as the hours passed and nothing terrible happened, she stopped worrying and

12. *he could not fall.* "The author of the chronicle of Dorothy's adventures explains that the same force which held up the house held up Toto," wrote Norman E. Gilbert in J. Malcolm Bird's *Einstein's Theories of Relativity and Gravitation* (New York: Scientific American Publishing, 1922, pp. 338–39), "but this explanation is not necessary. Dorothy was now floating through space, and house and dog were subject to the same forces of gravitation which gave them identical motions. Dorothy must have pushed the dog onto the floor and in doing so must herself have floated to the ceiling whence she might have pushed herself to the floor. In fact gravitation was apparently suspended and Dorothy was in a position to have tried certain experiments which Einstein has never tried because he was never in Dorothy's unique positions." Although Baum does not actually say whether or not this actually happened to Dorothy, it may well occur when the cyclone transports her to Oz. Cosmonauts and astronauts have experienced this same "weightlessness" in outer space.

resolved to wait calmly and see what the future would bring. At last she crawled over the swaying floor to her bed, and lay down upon it; and Toto followed and lay down, beside her.

In spite of the swaying of the house and the wailing of the wind, Dorothy soon closed her eyes and fell fast asleep.

13. *asleep.* One of the unforgivable changes made in the 1939 MGM film was the revelation at the end that Dorothy's adventure in Oz was merely a dream. That was already a literary cliché by 1900, cribbed from Lewis Carroll's *Alice* books. A reviewer in *The Bookman* that December classified current fairy stories into two categories—those concerned with winged fairies, such as folk tales, and those that occur in dreamland, such as *Alice in Wonderland*. The Christmas books for 1900 reflected these traditions: fairy tale collections from Andrew Lang and others, and new stories such as *The Dream Fox Story Book*, *The Road to Nowhere*, and *The Little Dreamer's Adventures*, all forgotten now. (Lang said in the 1910 preface to *The Lilac Fairy Book* that he thought "very tiresome" the writer of a new fairy tale in which "the little boy or girl wakes up and finds he has been dreaming.") The only new American fantasy not dependent on these two conventions that was published that season and is still read today is *The Wonderful Wizard of Oz*. One reason for the success of Baum's story with young readers is that Oz is "a real truly live place," even if it was not for MGM Studios.

While Oz is unquestionably a real place, Baum did recognize the ambiguity of fairyland when he, as "Laura Bancroft," wrote in the preface to *Policeman Bluejay* (1908)

that "in a fairy story it does not matter whether one is awake or not. You must accept it as you would a fragrant breeze that cools your brow, a draught of sweet water, or the delicious flavor of a strawberry; and be grateful for the pleasure it brings you, without stopping to question its source."

Located on the map of the Land of Oz and its surrounding countries, designed by Baum and printed as the back endpaper of *Tik-Tok of Oz* (1914), is a curious little place labeled "The Kingdom of Dreams." It is the only one that does not appear in any of Baum's writings. However, a possible reference to it is in *Ozma of Oz* (1907), where Dorothy falls asleep in the Caverns of the Nome King and enters "the land of dreams" (p. 190).

"The immediately important thing about the Land of Oz," argued Robert A. Heinlein in his introduction to Samuel Mines's *Startling Stories* (London: Cassell, 1954), "is not the question of whether or not it exists in solid reality in some fold of the continua but the fact that Oz is a vastly entertaining place. Like youth itself, the Land of Oz is too much fun to be limited to the kids. If there is still a trace of 'Just imagine' left in your heart, then let us turn here and travel down the Yellow Brick Road toward the Emerald City, where all things are possible and no speculations are barred."

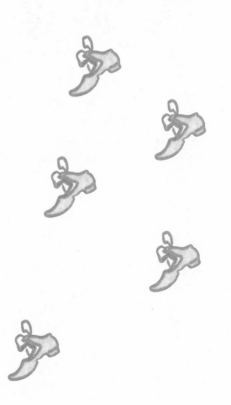

This picture of Dorothy and Toto is a detail of Denslow's
drawing for the title pages of the four
Songs of Father Goose folios that the
George M. Hill Company issued in 1900.
Private collection.

1. *a shock.* Science fiction enthusiasts have argued that the Land of Oz lies in a parallel universe in another dimension, another world that may be the same size and occupy the same space as Earth. Entry is often accompanied by a violent upheaval or a sudden feeling of uneasiness at the momentary meeting between the two worlds. A note to Barbara Hughes's "The Deadly Desert" (*The Baum Bugle*, Autumn 1968, p. 15) suggests that Dorothy's awakening by a shock may be evidence of just such a connection. All recorded journeys from Earth to Oz by other than magical means are associated with violent physical upheavals. Dorothy herself travels by air, water, and earth: the cyclone in *The Wizard of Oz*, the storm at sea in *Ozma of Oz* (1907), and the earthquake in *Dorothy and the Wizard in Oz* (1908). That Oz is on another planet was indicated in the early publicity for *The Marvelous Land of Oz* (1904); the Philadelphia *North America* published "exclusives" from Mars and elsewhere about the approach of the Scarecrow and his friends to America for days before Baum's "Queer Visitors from the Marvelous Land Oz" comic page commenced on November 28, 1904. Baum may or may not have actually written these. When the National Radio Astronomy Observatory at Green Bank, West Virginia, began searching for signs of life in distant solar systems through intergalactic radio waves in 1960, the program was named "Project Ozma" after the princess in *The Marvelous Land of Oz* (1904), because the land of Oz is far, far away, hard to get to, and inhabited by strange creatures.

But Oz may not be on some other planet or in the realm of Faërie, that shadowy realm of Celtic mythology. *The Wizard of Oz* is technically a *voyage imaginaire* or a traveler's tale like *The Travels of Sir John Mandeville* (1375), Daniel Defoe's *Robinson Crusoe* (1719), and Jonathan Swift's *Gulliver's Travels* (1726). J. R. R. Tolkien in *Tree and Leaf* (Boston: Houghton Mifflin, 1965) explained that these imaginary lands contain "marvels to be seen in this world in some other region in our own time and space: distance only conceals them" (p. 12). Oz is somewhere out there. One just has to seek it like the Isles of the Blest, St. Brendan's Island, Prospero's domain, or James Hilton's Shangri-La. Mary Devlin in "The Great Cosmic Fairy Tale" (*Gnosis Magazine,* Fall 1996) noted the similarity between the Land of Oz and the Land of Og, one of the kingdoms of the lost continent of Lemuria which famous psychic Edgar Cayce said he discovered in a trance. The Ork declares in *The Scarecrow of Oz* (1915) that "it is astonishing how many little countries there are, hidden away in the cracks and corners of this big globe of Earth. If one travels, he may find some new country at every turn, and a good many of them have never yet been put upon the maps" (p. 91). The possibilities are endless!

A likely inspiration for Oz was the legendary lost continent of Atlantis. Plato spoke of this mythical island at the mouth of the Mediterranean from which all Western philosophy, religion, and culture are said to originate, but which eventually was consumed by the sea. Ignatius Donnelly's *Atlantis* (1882) did much to revive interest in the myth in Baum's time; and the Ramayana Brotherhood, the branch of the Theosophical Society in Chicago to which the Baums belonged, followed what it called the old Altlantean Brotherhood of Hermes. Its leader Dr. William P. Phelan claimed that he could contact Atlantis in a trance. Matilda Joslyn Gage, Baum's mother-in-law, believed she was a reincarnated Atlantean priest! Oz, like Atlantis, is a land that Time has forgot, where witches and wizards still dwell and "civilization" has yet to invade. Under the name "Floyd Akers" in *The Boy Fortune Hunters in Yucatan* (1910), Baum played with the belief that survivors from Atlantis settled in Central America.

The most popular theory of the actual location of Oz is that it must be somewhere in the South Pacific. In Baum's unproduced and unpublished play *The Girl from Oz* (1909), a character says that Oz is "some island far away in the Pacific." In the short story "Nelebel's Fairyland" (*The Russ*, June 1905), the heroine travels east from the Forest of Burzee, which is on the same continent as Oz, to Coronado Bay, California. While on an ocean voyage to Australia in *Ozma of Oz* (1907), Dorothy gets marooned on the shores of the continent where Oz is located. Some people, like Oz Club member Sonia B. Brown in "Have We Discovered Oz?" (*The Baum Bugle*, Spring 1980), have argued unconvincingly that Oz *is* Australia. See also John Algeo's "Australia as the Land of Oz" (*American Speech*, Spring 1990) for other parallels between the two places.

Wherever it may lie, the Land of Oz, because it is fairyland, is known to mortals only through the travels of a fortunate few. Baum says that the fairies blessed Dorothy at her birth (*The Emerald City of Oz*, 1910, p. 22); this in part explains why she happens to visit Oz while it remains hidden to most mortals. "If there were no such place as Oz, how could I write stories about it?" Baum replied to one inquisitive little reader on December 4, 1916. "But I can't get there myself, never having been invited, and Dorothy says that you and I must both wait for an invitation and she's not sure Ozma will ever give us one. But, my dear friend, if you keep longing for something better and brighter you are sure to attain it in time. Be brave and courageous and you may discover something better than the Fairyland of Oz."

People were always asking Baum where Oz was. The cartoonist Walt McDougall wrote with tongue in cheek in "L. Frank Baum Studied by McDougall" (St. Louis *Post Dispatch*, July 30, 1904) that Baum "spent hours revealing to me the beauties of *The Wizard of Oz* and explaining how he

1.

She WAS AWAKENED by a shock, so sudden and severe that if Dorothy had not been lying on the soft bed she might have been hurt. As it was, the jar made her catch her breath and wonder what had happened; and Toto put his cold little nose into her face and whined dismally. Dorothy sat up and noticed that the house was not moving; nor was it dark, for the bright sunshine came in at the window, flooding the little room. She sprang from her bed and

2.

with Toto at her heels ran and opened the door.

The little girl gave a cry of amazement and looked

came to think of the book. I tried to discourage him by introducing him to people who would ask him whether the accent was on the 'o' or the 'z,' and where Oz is situated; but upon obtaining a grave answer that 'Oz was the domain of children, young and old, wherever they may be found,' they would regard him with suspicion and flee from him, avoiding Baum and myself thereafter." Shel Silverstein had another answer. "Do you want to visit the wonderful far-off Land of Oz," he asked in *Uncle Shelby's ABZ Book* (New York: Simon & Schuster, 1961), "where the Wizard lives and scarecrows can dance and the road is made of yellow bricks and everything is emerald green? Well, you *can't* because there is no Land of Oz and there is no Tin Woodsman [*sic*] and there is no Santa Claus! Maybe someday you can go to Detroit."

Many science fiction writers have expressed their appreciation of Baum's work. "It occurs to me," admits the young Martian heroine of Robert A. Heinlein's *Podkayne of Mars* (1963), "that my most vivid conceptions of Earth come from the Oz stories—and when you come down to it, I suppose that isn't too reliable a source. I mean, Dorothy's conversations with the Wizard are instructive—but about *what*? When I was a child I believed every word of my Oz tapes; but now I am no longer a child and I do not truly suppose that a whirlwind is a reliable means of transportation, nor that one is likely to encounter a Tin Woodman on a road of yellow brick" (p. 107). Heinlein makes other references to Oz in *Glory Road* (1964) and *The Number of the Beast* (1980). According to Keith Laumer's *The Otherside of Time* (1965), Earth separated from another world in the year 1814. When his hero Brion Bayard enters this parallel universe, he discovers a red leather-bound book entitled *The Sorceress of Oz* by one "Lyman F. Baum" (p. 77). It has the date 1896 and the printer's imprint Wiley & Cotton of New York, New Orleans, and Paris (Reilly & Britton of Chicago in another universe?). The frontispiece is in the manner of W. W. Denslow and depicts "Sorana the Sorceress" surrounded by a band of Nomes; the capital of the story's fairyland is the Sapphire City. Most curious of all, in this other universe, "Lyman F. Baum" died in 1897! Philip José Farmer took enormous liberties with Baum's Land of Oz in his adult "sequel" to *The Wizard of Oz, A Barnstormer in Oz* (1982). So too did film director John Boorman in his science fiction movie *Zardoz* (1974), starring Sean Connery. Inspired by *The Wizard of Oz*, a trickster creates a god called Zardoz, an enormous stone head. He is exposed like Oz himself when the hero finds a copy of *The Wonderful Wizard of Oz* in an abandoned library.

Perhaps the most ardent Oz fan among important science fiction writers is Ray Bradbury. He has expressed his affection for Baum and Oz in prefaces to Raylyn Moore's *Wonderful Wizard, Marvelous Land* (Bowling Green, Ohio: Bowling Green University Popular Press, 1974) and the 1999 "Kansas Centennial Edition" of *The Wonderful Wizard of Oz*, published by the University Press of Kansas and illustrated with wood engravings by Michael McCurdy. In "The Exiles" (in *The Illustrated Man*, 1951), Bradbury's impassioned protest against book banning, L. Frank Baum is one of the "forbidden authors," like Washington Irving, Edgar Allan Poe, Charles Dickens, Nathaniel Hawthorne, Lewis Carroll, and Henry James, who "find themselves shunted off to Mars as the non-dreamers, the super-psychological technicians, the book burners of the future, advance through towns and libraries, tossing the last of the great dreams into the fire." The story concludes with the fall of the Emerald City as the last Oz book goes up in flames:

> "I remember. Yes, now I do. A long time back. When I was a child. A book I read. A story. Oz, I think it was. Yes. Oz. *The Emerald City of Oz*. . . ."
>
> "Oz?"
>
> "Yes, Oz, that's what it was. I saw it just now, like in the story. I saw it fall."
>
> "Smith!"
>
> "Yes, sir?"
>
> "Report to the ship's doctor."

Bradbury predicted in his preface to *Wonderful Wizard, Marvelous Land* that "when the cities die, in their present form at least, and we head out into Eden again, which we must and we will, Baum will be waiting for us" (p. xviii).

Some readers have suspected that Dorothy has actually died and her trip to Oz is an out-of-body experience, not too far-fetched an idea when one considers Baum's interest in the occult and reincarnation. "What is called 'death' by people is not death," Matilda Joslyn Gage wrote her grandson Harry Carpenter on January 21, 1897. "You are more alive than ever you were after what is called death. Death is only a journey, like going to another country. You are alive when you travel to Aberdeen [South Dakota] just as much as when you stay in Edgeley [North Dakota, where he lived], and it is the same with what is called death. After people have been gone for awhile, they come back and live in another body, in another family and have another name. Sometimes they live in another country and nation." Dorothy has surely gone on to another plane of existence when the cyclone takes her to Oz.

2. *opened the door*. One of the imaginative touches of the 1939

MGM movie occurred when the cyclone dropped Dorothy's house in Oz. The Kansas sequences were filmed in sepia, but when Judy Garland opened the door, the screen suddenly changed to brilliant Technicolor in Munchkinland. This burst of color, which continued until the last section of the film when it suddenly converted back to sepia on Dorothy's awakening in Kansas, was one of the most dramatic uses of Technicolor in its early years. The effect was just as startling when the picture was first shown on NBC in the early years of color television in the 1950s. But the MGM movie was not the very first film to make this transition from monochrome to color in the same picture. The Kansas sequence of Ted Eshbaugh's early 1933 Technicolor cartoon of *The Wizard of Oz* was shot in black and white only, but the screen turned to color when Dorothy literally landed in Oz. Unfortunately a dispute with Technicolor prevented the short from being distributed, so it was all but forgotten when the MGM picture came out in 1939.

about her, her eyes growing bigger and bigger at the wonderful sights she saw.

3. The cyclone had set the house down, very gently—for a cyclone—in the midst of a country of marvelous beauty. There were lovely patches of green sward all about, with stately trees bearing rich and luscious fruits. Banks of gorgeous flowers were on every hand, and birds with rare and brilliant plumage sang and fluttered in the trees and bushes. A little way off was a small brook, rushing and sparkling along between green banks, and murmuring in a voice very grateful to a little girl who had lived so long on the dry, gray prairies.

While she stood looking eagerly at the strange and beautiful sights, she noticed coming toward her a group of the queerest people she had ever seen. They were not as big as the grown folk she had always been used to; but neither were they very small. In fact, they seemed about as tall

4. as Dorothy, who was a well-grown child for her age, although they were, so far as looks go, many years older.

5. Three were men and one a woman, and all were oddly dressed. They wore round hats that rose to a small point a foot above their heads, with little bells around the brims that tinkled sweetly as they moved. The hats of the men were blue; the little woman's hat was white, and she wore a white gown that hung in plaits from her shoulders; over it were sprinkled little stars that glistened in the sun like diamonds. The men were dressed in blue, of the same

3. *a country of marvelous beauty.* This fairyland is like the country of Beulah in John Bunyan's *Pilgrim's Progress* (1678), "whose air was very sweet and pleasant. . . . Yea, here they heard continually the singing of birds, and saw every day the flowers appear in the earth." Clinical psychologist Madonna Kohlbenschlag in *Lost in the Land of Oz* (New York: Crossroad, 1994) called *The Wizard of Oz* "a modern *Pilgrim's Progress*, a book of disillusionment and spiritual restoration" (p. 103). Baum knew well this famous Calvinist tract. (He even makes a bad pun about John Bunyan and bunions in *The Scarecrow of Oz*, 1914, p. 50.) This Puritan classic profoundly affected nineteenth-century American children's literature, from Louisa May Alcott's *Little Women* (1868) to Frances Hodgson Burnett's *Two Little Pilgrims' Progress* (1897). Bunyan's Protestant allegory was recommended reading to children who attended Centenary Methodist Episcopal Church, the Baum family's place of worship in Syracuse, New York. But little Frank Baum likely agreed with Huckleberry Finn that the book's "statements was interesting but tough."

4. *a well-grown child for her age.* Baum puts the child at ease by making the people of this strange land the same size as herself. She is immediately on an equal footing with them. Since Baum had no particular child in mind as Lewis Carroll did when he wrote *Alice in Wonderland*, Dorothy's exact age is difficult to determine. "Dorothy speaks not at all the way a grownup might think a child should speak," noted Gore Vidal in "On Rereading the Oz Books" (*The New York Review of Books*, October 13, 1977), "but like a sensible somewhat literal person." According to *The Tin Woodman of Oz* (1918), Princess Ozma appears to be fourteen or fifteen years old, Dorothy much younger. "She had been a little girl when she first came to the Land of Oz," Baum continues, "and she was a little girl still, and would never seem to be a day older while she lived in this wonderful fairyland" (p. 156). This suggests that she could not have been much older than ten years when she came to live in Oz in *The Emerald City of Oz* (1910). If each succeeding story (with the exception of *The Marvelous Land of Oz,* in which she does not appear) is a year in her short young life, she may have been no more than five or six years old when took her first trip to Oz. Denslow pictures a child no older than that and dresses her in frocks suited to this age at the turn of the century. Frank Joslyn Baum said in "Why the Wizard of Oz Keeps On Selling" (*Writer's Digest*, December 1952) that his father wrote the book for children two to six years old.

5. *Three were men.* These gentlemen stand in for the three Shining Ones, who befriend and advise Christian early on his journey in *Pilgrim's Progress*. These Munchkins afforded Denslow his first opportunity in the book "to parade rows of figures across the pages like comic friezes, but with each tiny figure amusingly individualized by some feature or item of clothing" (Baum and MacFall, *To Please a Child*, p. 150). Other examples of Denslow's comic chorus lines are the Winkies, Hammer-Heads, and Glinda's Guards.

6. shade as their hats, and wore well polished boots with a deep roll of blue at the tops. The men, Dorothy thought, were about as old as Uncle Henry, for two of them had beards. But the little woman was doubtless much older: her face was covered with wrinkles, her hair was nearly white, and she walked rather stiffly.

When these people drew near the house where Dorothy was standing in the doorway, they paused and whispered among themselves, as if afraid to come farther. But the little old woman walked up to Dorothy, made a low bow and said, in a sweet voice,

7. "You are welcome, most noble Sorceress, to the land of the Munchkins. We are so grateful to you for having
8. killed the wicked Witch of the East, and for setting our people free from bondage."

Dorothy listened to this speech with wonder. What could the little woman possibly mean by calling her a sorceress, and saying she had killed the wicked Witch of the East? Dorothy was an innocent, harmless little girl, who had been carried by a cyclone many miles from home; and she had never killed anything in all her life.

But the little woman

6. *blue at the tops.* A more detailed description of the native costume of the Munchkins is offered in *The Patchwork Girl of Oz* (1913):

> [The boy] wore blue silk stockings, blue knee-pants with gold buckles, a blue ruffled waist and a jacket of bright blue braided with gold. His shoes were of blue leather and turned up at the toes, which were pointed. His hat had a peaked crown and a flat brim, and around the brim was a row of tiny golden bells that tinkled when he moved. . . . Instead of shoes, the old man wore boots with turnover tops and his blue coat had wide cuffs of gold braid. (pp. 23–24)

Baum defines his secondary world by giving each locality of Oz not only its unique name but also its favorite color and descriptions of its native costume and customs. "I began with enthusiasm," Austrian artist Lisbeth Zwerger said of her illustrating the 1996 North-South edition, "but the project proved to be a real challenge. Baum's precise details—his vivid description of the Munchkins, for example—make an illustrator superfluous."

7. *most noble Sorceress.* Their initial mistake is not as far-fetched as it may seem, for at one time a person of any age could be suspected of practicing witchcraft. "During the height of witchcraft persecution," noted Matilda Joslyn Gage in *Woman, Church, and State*, "hundreds of little ones were condemned as witches. Little girls of ten, eight, and seven years are mentioned; blind girls, infants and even young boys were among the numbers who thus perished" (p. 232).

8. *setting our people free from bondage.* Salman Rushdie asked in his monograph on the MGM movie, "Is [the Munchkin Country] not a mite too pretty, too kempt, too sweetly sweet for a place that was, until moments before Dorothy's arrival, under the absolute power of the evil and dictatorial Witch of the East? How is it that this squashed Witch had no castle? How could her despotism have left so little mark upon the land? Why are the Munchkins so relatively unafraid, hiding only briefly before they emerge, and giggling while they hide? The heretical thought occurs: maybe the Witch of the East *wasn't as bad as all that*" (p. 42). Rushdie considered her no worse than the Italian Fascist dictator Benito Mussolini, for "she certainly kept the streets clean, the houses painted and in good repair, and no doubt such trains as there might be, running on time. Moreover, and again unlike her sister, she seems to have ruled without the aid of soldiers, policemen or any other regiments of repression. Why, then, was she so hated? I only ask." Of course, Baum does not fill in all the details of her oppressive rule. A common flawed defense of the American slave system was the argument that some slaves were actually *happy* under their masters. The main houses on Southern plantations were usually painted and in good repair and the streets often clean, and the trains tended to operate on schedule in Dixie. Perhaps so, but slavery is still slavery however deceptively pleasant outward appearances might be.

evidently expected her to answer; so Dorothy said, with hesitation,

"You are very kind; but there must be some mistake. I have not killed anything."

"Your house did, anyway," replied the little old woman, with a laugh; "and that is the same thing. See!" she continued, pointing to the corner of the house; "there are her two toes, still sticking out from under a block of wood."

Dorothy looked, and gave a little cry of fright. There, indeed, just under the corner of the great beam the house rested on, two feet were sticking out, shod in silver shoes with pointed toes.

"Oh, dear! oh, dear!" cried Dorothy, clasping her hands together in dismay; "the house must have fallen on her. What ever shall we do?"

"There is nothing to be done," said the little woman, calmly.

"But who was she?" asked Dorothy.

"She was the wicked Witch of the East, as I said," answered the little woman. "She has held all the Munchkins in bondage for

9. *silver shoes.* Baum may have been inspired by Christian's admonition to By-Ends in *Pilgrim's Progress* that one "must also own religion in his rags, as well as when in his silver slippers." (By-ends later refers to "golden slippers in the sunshine.") Baum's Silver Shoes became the Ruby Slippers in the 1939 MGM movie, the invention of the Australian-born screenwriter Noel Langley. Aljean Harmetz in *The Making of the Wizard of Oz* (1977, pp. 40–41) dated their introduction specifically to Langley's fourth script of May 14, 1938. They were decorated with nothing more than red sequins glued to conventional pumps, yet the surviving pairs have had a bizarre history beyond the movie as recorded in Rhys Thomas's *The Ruby Slippers of Oz* (Los Angeles: Table Weaver Publishing, 1989). The last pair to come up for auction sold for $666,000 at Christie's East in 2000, and another are currently on permanent exhibition at the Smithsonian Institution in Washington, D.C. To commemorate the fiftieth anniversary of the movie in 1989, the jeweler Harry Winston made a pair of ruby slippers of real gems said to be worth $3 million, the entire cost of the 1939 musical. In "*The Wizard of Oz*: Therapeutic Rhetoric in a Contemporary Media Ritual" (*Quarterly Journal of Speech*, February 1989), David Payne pointed out that according to Freudian analysis, "slippers" symbolize the vagina and "red" menstrual blood. But Margaret Hamilton, who played both Wicked Witches of the East and West, had grown up on the Oz books, so she asked the producer Mervyn LeRoy during the shooting of the 1939 movie why MGM did not stick to Baum's story in this instance. He told her simply that in Technicolor red stood out better against the Yellow Brick Road than silver would have.

10. *the Munchkins.* Since no notes survive for the composition of *The Wonderful Wizard of Oz*, any explanation of the names of Oz is mere speculation. There is probably a good dose of Munchausen, the eighteenth-century semi-legendary German baron whose name is now synonymous with the fabulous, in the Munchkins. Like the other names of the four countries of Oz, Munchkin ends in a diminutive, referring to the size of the natives. Brian Attebery in *The Fantasy Tradition in American Literature* (Bloomington: Indiana University Press, 1980, p. 89) wondered if Baum might have been thinking of *Münch Kind*, the statue known as the *Munich Child* that looks down from the town hall in the capital of Bavaria. Also, blue is the "official" color of Bavaria. Aleksandr Volkov in his 1939 Russian "translation" of *The Wizard of Oz* called the Munchkins *Zhevuny*, the Munchers. The word "Munchkin" has entered the language. The tenth edition of *Merriam-Webster's Collegiate Dictionary* (Springfield, Mass.: Merriam-Webster, 1998) defines one as "a person who is notably small and often endearing." The second edition of the *Random House Webster's Collegiate Dictionary* (New York: Random House, 1999) agrees that a Munchkin is "a small person, esp. one who is dwarfish or elfin in appearance." But the fourth edition of *Webster's New World Dictionary* (New York: Macmillan, 1999) adds some odd details not suggested by Baum's text: "an imaginary being having a small human form and a dutiful, amiable, innocuous nature"; and one "who keeps busy doing things that are often unimportant, unnecessary, or annoying"! Munchkins are now the name of the popular Dunkin' Donuts doughnut holes.

many years, making them slave for her night and day. Now they are all set free, and are grateful to you for the favour."

"Who are the Munchkins?" enquired Dorothy.

11. "They are the people who live in this land of the East, where the wicked Witch ruled."

"Are you a Munchkin?" asked Dorothy.

12. "No; but I am their friend, although I live in the land of the North.   When they saw the Witch of the East was
13. dead the Munchkins sent a swift messenger to me, and I
14. came at once.   I am the Witch of the North."

"Oh, gracious!" cried Dorothy; "are you a real witch?"

"Yes, indeed;" answered the little woman.   "But I
15. am a good witch, and the people love me.   I am not as powerful as the wicked Witch was who ruled here, or I should have set the people free myself."

"But I thought all witches were wicked," said the girl, who was half frightened at facing a real witch.

16. "Oh, no; that is a great mistake.   There were only
17. four witches in all the Land of Oz, and two of them, those who live in the North and the South, are good witches.   I know this is true, for I am one of them myself, and cannot be mistaken.   Those who dwelt in the East and the West were, indeed, wicked witches; but now that you have killed one of them, there is but one wicked Witch in all the Land
18. of Oz—the one who lives in the West."

"But," said Dorothy, after a moment's thought, "Aunt

11. *this land of the East.* A common error in the later Oz books and elsewhere is the reversal of the Munchkin Country to the West and the Winkie Country to the East. The source for this confusion is the Map of the Marvelous Land of Oz that served as the front endpaper of *Tik-Tok of Oz* (1914) and in which the two countries switch places. Baum was to blame, for he designed it himself. The earliest Oz map was a hand-colored slide used in the 1908 *Fairylogue and Radio-Plays.* Is it possible that when Baum was preparing the new one, he consulted this slide and hastily looked at it backward, which of course reversed the two countries? James E. Haff and Dick Martin diligently studied all the vagaries of Oz geography to produce for the International Wizard of Oz Club updated and accurate Maps of the Marvelous Land of Oz and the Surrounding Countries which located every place mentioned in the long Oz series, and in its correct spot. They placed the Munchkins in the East and the Winkies in the West as stated in the first Oz book.

Baum wrote quickly and not always carefully. It seems unlikely he reread a story once it was published or even when it was still in manuscript. Writers are notorious for their careless errors. Probably the most famous instance is Daniel Defoe's reporting that Robinson Crusoe strips to swim back to the shipwreck, and then he fills up his pockets with biscuits. Mark Twain could not remember what he called Becky Thatcher in *The Adventures of Tom Sawyer* (1876) when he began *Adventures of Huckleberry Finn* (1884). "Baum was simply not a minutely consistent writer," explained Edward Wagenknecht in *The Baum Bugle* (Spring 1974), "and anybody who could 'harmonize' the Oz books might be safely trusted to perform the same service for the Four Gospels." Gore Vidal admitted in "On Rereading the Oz Books" (*The New York Review of Books,* October 13, 1977), "I used to spend a good deal of time worrying about the numerous inconsistencies in the sacred text. From time to time, Baum himself would try to rationalize errors but he was far too quick and careless a writer ever to create the absolutely logical mad worlds that Lewis Carroll or E. Nesbitt did." Cathleen Schine reported in "America as Fairyland" (*The New York Times Book Review,* June 6, 1985) that, oddly, several people who had read the series when children told her that they considered all the discrepancies "as one of the most compelling aspects of the Oz books—Baum's illogic made them think."

12. *the land of the North.* Not until the second Oz book, *The Marvelous Land of Oz* (1904), does Baum disclose the favorite color and name of the land of the North—the purple Country of the Gillikins, employing another diminutive. It is similar to "Gilligren," the hero of "Sing a Song o' Sixpence" in Baum's *Mother Goose in Prose* (1897). Martin Gardner suggested that the purple country of the North may have derived its name from the purple gillyflower of New England.

13. *a swift messenger.* Fred M. Meyer, a former Oz Club secretary, noted that this messenger must have been swift indeed if he was able to summon the Good Witch of the North just minutes after Dorothy's house landed on the Wicked Witch of the East. Perhaps it was a bird who carried the news north.

14. *the Witch of the North.* Her name in the 1902 musical extravaganza was Locasta, likely director Julian Mitchell's invention rather than Baum's. Ruth Plumly Thompson called the Good Witch of the North Tattypoo in *The Giant Horse of Oz* (1928) and provided her with a remarkable history of her own not indicated by Baum in his stories. Aleksandr Volkov named her Villina in his Russian "translation" of *The Wizard of Oz.* The 1939 MGM movie combined the Good Witch of the North and Glinda the Good Witch of the South into Glinda the Witch of the North, played by Billie Burke, who at fifty-three embodied both age and beauty.

15. *a good witch.* Baum plays with conventional wisdom throughout *The Wizard of Oz.* Most people of his time thought all witches were wicked, knowledge probably gleaned from Grimm and Andersen fairy tales. "The word 'witch,' " Gage argued in *Woman, Church, and State,* "formerly signified a woman of superior knowledge" (p. 236). It meant no more than "wise woman." Gage was well aware of the standard Christian conception: "A witch was held to be a woman who had deliberately sold herself to the evil one, who delighted in injuring others, and who, for the purpose of enhancing the enormity of her evil acts, chose the Sabbath day for the performance of her most impious rites" (p. 217). But, Gage insisted, "Under catholicism, those condemned as sorcerers and witches, as 'heretics,' were in reality the most advanced thinkers of the christian ages" (p. 247). Baum acknowledges this belief in "The Witchcraft of Mary-Marie" in *Baum's American Fairy Tales* (1908) that witches "sell their souls to Satan, in return for a knowledge of witchcraft" (p. 45). But he did not believe in Satan. He commented in an editorial in the Aberdeen *Saturday Pioneer* (October 18, 1890) that "the absurd and legendary devil is the enigma of the Church." The closest equivalent of Baum's Good Witch in European tradition is the pagan sorceress. A witch serves Satan, a sorceress serves herself. Baum must have known this distinction: in the later Oz books, Glinda the Good Witch becomes Glinda the Sorceress.

Recent fundamentalists have not agreed. On October 24,

1986, a federal judge in Greeneville, ruled that Tennessee, schools violated the Constitution by requiring fundamentalist Christians to use textbooks containing literature that offended their religious beliefs. Among this "anti-Christian" literature was *The Wizard of Oz,* which dared to portray Good Witches and taught that intelligence, love, and courage are individually developed rather than God-given. Other Christians have not been so sanctimonious, and some preachers have actually based sermons on teachings in *The Wizard of Oz.* The Presbyterian minister Frederick Buechner said in *The Magnificent Defeat* (New York: Seabury Press, 1966) that *The Wizard of Oz* "seems to me not only the greatest fairy tale that this nation has produced but one of its great myths" (pp. 51–56). See also Buechner's "The Gospel as Fairy Tale" in *Telling the Truth* (New York: Harper & Row, 1977). "[Dorothy's] passage along the Yellow Brick Road has a narrative function not unlike that of the Jewish and Christian passage either through the life cycle as individuals or through history as communities," said Dr. Paul Nathanson as quoted by the New York *Times* (November 28, 1991) during the annual convention of the American Academy of Religion in Kansas City. He considered her situation to be like the expulsion from the Garden of Eden and the exile of the Jews from the Promised Land. In July 1995, Judy Atwell, an associate in the vocation unit of the Presbyterian Church USA, used *The Wizard of Oz* in an educational workshop for high school students and adult advisers from around the world at Purdue University, Lafayette, Indiana, because the story crosses national, ethnic, gender, and generational lines. And in February 1996, the Pontifical Council on Social Communications of the Catholic Church at the Vatican chose the 1939 MGM movie of *The Wizard of Oz* as one of forty-five movies that best represent the church's perspective. Even Ray Bolger, who played the Scarecrow in the 1939 MGM musical, interpreted the story in traditional Christian terms in "A Lesson from Oz" (*Guideposts,* March 1982).

Baum thought clergymen tended to be verbose and ramble on, and he had as little respect for them as he did for college professors. (He would have been amused by Dr. Nathanson's declaration that *The Wizard of Oz* is "a cosmogonic myth that is also eschatological"!) When the Shaggy Man visits Rigmarole Town in *The Emerald City of Oz* (1910), where the people cannot say even a simple "yes" or "no" to a question, he observes, "Some of the college lecturers and ministers are certainly related to these people. . . . [I]f one can't talk clearly and straight to the point, they send him to Rigmarole Town; while Uncle Sam lets him roam around wild and free, to torture innocent people" (pp. 235–36). In "Modern Fairy Tales" (*The Advance,* August 19, 1909), Baum criticized a popular divine in New York City who "made a ponderous attempt to do his duty by the lambs of his flock by preaching a special sermon to children every month. 'My children,' he said, on one of those painful occasions, 'I propose to give you this morning an epitome of the life of St. Paul. Perhaps some of you, my children, do not know what the word 'epitome' means. Now 'epitome,' my children, is in its signification synonymous with 'synopsis.' " The appeal of Oz has not been limited merely to the members of the various branches of the Christian faith. Vernon Crawford argued in *From Confucius to Oz* (New York: Donald I. Fine, 1988) that "the virtues taught by Confucius were in actuality the characteristics that were sought by the Scarecrow, the Tin Woodman, and the Lion, in *The Wizard of Oz.*" There is even *The Zen of Oz* by Joey Green (Los Angeles: Renaissance Books, 1998). Baum's great-granddaughter Dr. Gita Dorothy Morena used the story as a metaphor for her personal spiritual growth in *The Wisdom of Oz* (San Diego: Inner Connections Press, 1998).

16. *that is a great mistake.* Because the devil plays no part in Baum's stories, his witches and wizards must be judged by their individual natures rather than by the source of their occult powers. They can be "good" or "bad," depending upon how they use their knowledge. The same is true for immortals, according to the Theosophical theory of Elementals. Mme. Blavatsky argued in *Isis Unveiled* (Vol. 1, 1878, p. xxviii) that "dæmons" means "all kinds of spirits, whether good or bad, human or otherwise." When Rob accidentally summons up the Demon of Electricity in *The Master Key* (1901), the boy exclaims that he had "always understood that demons were bad things." "Not necessarily," his visitor replies. "If you will take the trouble to consult your dictionary, you will find that demons can be either good or bad, like any other class of beings. Originally all demons were good, yet of later years people have come to consider all demons evil. I do not know why. Should you read Hesiod, you will find he says:

> Soon was a world of holy demons made,
> Aerial sprites, by great Juno, designed,
> To be on earth the guardians of mankind." (pp. 16–17)

Only in the Christian era were these spirits classified as evil. When a traveler suggests to the little girl in "The Witchcraft of Mary-Marie" in *Baum's American Fairy Tales* (1908) that she learn witchcraft, the child cries in astonishment, "I'm not old enough. Witches, you know, are withered dried-up old hags. . . . And they sell their souls to Satan." But she is quickly corrected:

> One might think that you knew all about witches, to hear you chatter. But your words prove you to be very ignorant of the subject. You may find good people and bad people in

the world; and so, I suppose, you may find good witches and bad witches. But I must confess most of the witches I have known were very respectable, and famous for their kind actions. (pp. 45–46)

The speaker turns out to be a good witch herself.

17. *Oz.* A number of theories as to the origin of the word "Oz" have been suggested since the initial publication of *The Wonderful Wizard of Oz.* "The word Oz came out of Mr. Baum's mind, just as did his queer characters," Maud Baum insisted in a letter to Jack Snow, on June 21, 1943. "No one or anything suggested the word—or any person. *This is a fact."* The generally accepted story as described in Baum and MacFall's *To Please a Child* (pp. 106–10) concerns a small filing cabinet in the Baum home. One evening while Baum was telling his boys and their friends a story about a little girl named Dorothy who was carried off by a Kansas cyclone to a fairyland, one of the children asked him what was the name of the strange country. Looking about the room, his eye fell upon the drawers of the filing cabinet, which were labeled "A-N" and O-Z." He told the children it was the Land of Oz. This account may well have been the fabrication of his son Frank Joslyn Baum, for it varies in significant details from the earliest-known published version of the filing cabinet story. That was a Bobbs-Merrill press release announcing its reissue of *The Wonderful Wizard of Oz* as *The New Wizard of Oz* (1903) that appeared in *Publishers Weekly* (April 18, 1903) and many newspapers:

> I have a little cabinet letter file on my desk that is just in front of me. I was thinking and wondering about a title for the story, and had settled on "Wizard" as part of it. My gaze was caught by the gilt letters on the three drawers of the cabinet. The first was A-G; the next drawer was labeled H-N; and on the last were the letters O-Z. And "Oz" it at once became.

But even this account is not entirely trustworthy. Baum must have come up with the word sometime before considering the final name for the book, for "Oz" was part of several titles for the story even before "Wizard" was ever considered (see Introduction, pages xxxviii–xxxix). "Father tried and discarded many names for his land, writing at his rolltop desk," Harry Neal Baum told Joseph Haas in "The Wonderful Writer of Oz" (Chicago *Daily News*, April 17, 1965), "and one day he glanced at its three file drawers and was inspired." Curiously, on the bookshelf behind the Wond'rous Wise Man in Maxfield Parrish's picture in *Mother Goose in Prose* (1897) sits a volume of *Household Book of Repartee*, marked on the spine "A to N." But where is O to Z? (See illustration on page xxvii.)

Several less prosaic theories have been proposed. In *The Wizard of Oz and Who He Was* (p. 37), Gardner noted the similarity between the Land of Oz and the Land of Uz, where Job lived. Because he was an admirer of the works of Charles Dickens, whose pseudonym was Boz, Baum may have merely dropped the B for Baum and been left with "Oz." Or does it come from Shelley's "Ozymandias" (Greek for Egyptian pharoah Ramses II)? Celia Catlett Anderson suggested another in "The Comedians of Oz" (*Studies in American Humor*, Winter 1986–1987): "The Old Testament Deity's self-description, 'I am the alpha and the omega'—alpha-omega equals A-Z, equals Oz." Jack Snow, in his introduction to *Who's Who in Oz* (1954), preferred to think that Baum liked stories that caused the reader to exclaim with "Ohs" and "Ahs" of wonder. The word "Oz" can be pronounced either way. Baum's personal pronunciation is indicated in the following verse sung by Oz in the unpublished first dramatization of *The Wizard of Oz,* written in 1901:

> Hear me, fear me! Never dare to cheer me!
> I'm the greatest necromancer ever was!
> All my deeds with magic reek,
> I'm the whole thing, so to speak!
> I'm the Wonderful Wizard of Oz!

Fred Stone, who originated the role of the Scarecrow in the 1902 musical extravaganza of *The Wizard of Oz*, told the Los Angeles *Sunday Times* (June 13, 1943) about the time a second-rate road company of the show passed through San Francisco and a local bartender was asked if Oz was pronounced "Ohs" or "Ahs." "I pronounce it rotten," was the reply.

Gardner disclosed in his "Mathematical Games" column (*Scientific American*, February 1972) a likely unintended correlation between Baum's home state and the name of the fairyland, noting that Oz Club member Mary Scott discovered that a one-step word shift from the abbreviation of New York produces Oz:

$$N \rightarrow Y$$
$$O \rightarrow Z$$

After that column appeared, Gardner learned that another one-step word shift discloses the abbreviation of the home state of Ruth Plumly Thompson, the second Royal Historian of Oz:

$$O \rightarrow P$$
$$Z \rightarrow A$$

In the same article, Gardner diagrammed the possible alphabetical symmetry of the word "WIZARD." Baum reveals in *Dorothy and the Wizard in Oz* (1908) that the word "Oz" means "Great and Good" (p. 196).

18. *the one who lives in the West.* A quick survey of the other books in the series shows that there have been far more than four witches in the saga of Oz. There are various types with different specialties. Mombi the Witch in *The Marvelous Land of Oz* (1904) is said to be no more than a sorceress or a wizardess, because the Good Witch of the North forbids any other witch, good or bad, in her country. Mrs. Yoop of *The Tin Woodman of Oz* (1918) and Red Reera of *Glinda of Oz* (1920) are Yookoohoos who are experts in transformations, and Coo-ee-oh, also of *Glinda of Oz,* is the only Krumbic Witch in the world. *Dorothy and the Wizard in Oz* (1908, p.196) discloses that there were once four Wicked Witches who each ruled one of the four countries of Oz. The Good Witch of the North conquered the Wicked Witch of the North, Mombi; Glinda conquered the Wicked Witch of the South. But who is she? Perhaps Blinkie of *The Scarecrow of Oz* (1914), who lives in Jinxland with a band of witches who may have fled with her when Glinda came to power.

19. *years and years ago.* This statement repeats the sentiment expressed in the poem "Who's Afraid" in *By the Candelabra's Glare* (1898, p. 74):

> Who's afraid?
> Ev'ry Giant now is dead—
> Jack has cut off ev'ry head.
> Ev'ry Goblin, known of old,
> Perished years ago I'm told.
> Ev'ry Witch, on broomstick riding,
> Has been burned or is in hiding.
> Ev'ry dragon, seeking gore.
> Died an age ago—or more.
> Ev'ry horrid Bogie Man
> Lives in far-off·Yucatan.
> Burglars dare not venture near
> When they know that papa's here.
> Lions now you only see
> Caged in the menagerie.
> And the Grizzly Bear can't hug
> When he's made into a rug—
> Who's afraid?

Baum abridged this verse when he reprinted it in *Father Goose, His Book* (1899).

20. *civilized.* Baum presents a curious paradox: Although Kansas is civilized, it is a wasteland; Oz is untamed and a paradise. Western technology has not made the desert bloom. Like many of his contemporaries, Baum was skeptical of what modern civilization had wrought. Progress has a bad tendency of encroaching on one's freedoms. One

need only recall Huckleberry Finn's lighting out for the territory to avoid being "sivilized." Baum may speak of "modernized fairy tales" and "progressive fairies," but he did not entirely embrace modern progress. He did not feel that change for its own sake was necessarily good. His mother-in-law, Matilda Joslyn Gage, refused to believe that history always moved forward, as the social Darwinians said; she thought that certain ancient periods were far superior to anything in the modern era. The so-called savage people so often proved more civilized than the so-called civilized nations. "One of your writers has said, with truth, that among civilized people things are seldom what they seem," observes the Demon of Electricity in Baum's *The Master Key* (1901, p. 93). Baum considered the cultured classes to be snobby, deceitful, superficial. One of the prairie dogs in *Prairie-Dog Town* (one of the "Twinkle Tales" by "Laura Bancroft," 1906) defines civilization as "a very big word which means some folks have found a better way to live than other folks" (p. 5). And what sort of life was that? "To become civilized," explains the King of Foxville in *The Road to Oz* (1909), "means to dress as elaborately and prettily as possible, and to make a show of your clothes so your neighbors will envy you, and for that reason both civilized foxes and civilized humans spend most of their time dressing themselves" (p. 56).

Baum explores the nature of civilization in the introduction to *The Enchanted Island of Yew* (1903), one of his old-fashioned once-upon-a-time fairy tales. When Man was young, he lived in the Golden Age. "In the old days, when the world was young," Baum explains, "there were no automobiles nor flying-machines to make one wonder; nor were there railway trains, nor telephones, nor mechanical inventions of any sort to keep people keyed up to a high pitch of excitement. Men and women lived simply and quietly. They were Nature's children, and breathed fresh air into their lungs instead of smoke and coal gas; and tramped through green meadows and deep forests instead of riding in street cars; and went to bed when it was dark and rose with the sun—which is vastly different from the present custom" (pp. 1–2). Man was helpless then, but he had the fairies to protect him; now they are shy and seldom seen by modern mortals. "Great cities had been built and great Kingdoms established. Civilization had won the people, and they no longer robbed or fought or indulged in magic arts, but were busily employed and leading respectable lives" (p. 242). But at what cost? Is life any better, are people any happier than when Man was young? Fortunately, the Land of Oz was never civilized, so its people are not all busily employed and leading respectful lives. Oz belongs to another era, that of the ancient matriarchate (Mother-rule) as described by Matilda Joslyn Gage in *Woman, Church, and State* (1893), where women held the real power. All the

Em has told me that the witches were all dead—years and   19.
years ago."

"Who is Aunt Em?" inquired the little old woman.

"She is my aunt who lives in Kansas, where I came
from."

The Witch of the North seemed to think for a time,
with her head bowed and her eyes upon the ground. Then
she looked up and said,

"I do not know where Kansas is, for I have never heard
that country mentioned before. But tell me, is it a civilized   20.
country?"

"Oh, yes;" replied Dorothy.

"Then that accounts for it. In the civilized countries
I believe there are no witches left; nor wizards, nor sorceresses, nor magicians. But, you see, the Land of Oz has
never been civilized, for we are cut off from all the rest of
the world. Therefore we still have witches and wizards
amongst us."

"Who are the Wizards?" asked Dorothy.

"Oz himself is the Great Wizard," answered the   21., 22.
Witch, sinking her voice to a whisper. "He is more powerful than all the rest of us together. He lives in the City   23.
of Emeralds."

Dorothy was going to ask another question, but just
then the Munchkins, who had been standing silently by,
gave a loud shout and pointed to the corner of the house
where the Wicked Witch had been lying.

men in the story seem flawed. Even the Wizard is not so Great as first assumed.

Marius Bewley in "Oz Country" (*The New York Review of Books*, December 3, 1964) suspected that Baum was sympathetic to Jeffersonian agrarianism, a system in which each citizen tends to his own garden and shuns national and foreign affairs. Oz is largely an agrarian kingdom, a pastoral paradise with just one city, the Emerald City, in the center. Much of it is untilled and still wilderness, like much of Central New York where Baum was born. Baum did believe in the American dream of rugged individualism, each man his own maker. "I am convinced," observes the Scarecrow in *The Marvelous Land of Oz* (1904), "that the only people worthy of consideration in this world are the unusual ones. For the common folks are like the leaves of a tree, and live and die unnoticed." Then adds the pretentious Woggle-Bug, "Spoken like a philosopher!" (p. 188). But Baum is not necessarily in favor of elitism. He says the exact opposite elsewhere, in *Rinkitink in Oz* (1916): "The poor and humble man who lives unnoticed and unknown . . . is the only one who can appreciate the joy of living" (p. 220). It is all just a matter of opinion. As the Cowardly Lion puts it in *The Lost Princess of Oz* (1917), "To be individual, my friends, to be different from others, is the only way to become distinguished from the common herd. Let us be glad, therefore, that we differ from one another in form and in disposition. Variety is the spice of life and we are various enough to enjoy one another's company; so let us be content" (p. 148). To be an individual, to be different, does not make one better than anyone else. Dorothy's three companions—the Scarecrow, the Tin Woodman, and the Cowardly Lion—exemplify the Horatio Alger myth of "getting on." Each one is in effect a self-made man: Despite their faults and the tremendous odds they encounter, they go out to seek their fortunes and get what they want. Such a personal philosophy enabled Baum to keep going through all the trials and tribulations of his own age.

The Good Witch of the North has good reason to suspect "civilization." It was in the most "advanced" nations that the all-out slaughter of suspected witches and wizards was accomplished. Matilda Joslyn Gage reported in *Woman, Church, and State* (1893) that thousands of women died "the horrid death of fire for a crime which never existed save in the imagination of those persecutors, and which grew in their imagination from a false belief in woman's extraordinary wickedness, based upon the false theory as to original sin" (p. 228). She said that their accusers and persecutors were motivated by every kind of self-interest including "greed, malice, envy, hatred, fear, the desire of clearing one's self from suspicion" (p. 243). The most brutal tortures were employed for "the repression of woman's intellect, knowledge being held as evil and dangerous in

her hands" (p. 243). One hundred thousand women were said to be executed under Francis I, the patron of Leonardo da Vinci; there were nine million persons after 1484. The Salem witch trials took place in Puritan New England in the late seventeenth century; the last execution in Scotland was in 1722; and it was not until the reign of George II, in 1736, that the English Parliament repealed the statute against anyone accused of conjuration, witchcraft, sorcery, or enchantment. And this was not before, Gage insisted, "a holocaust of women were sacrificed, victims of the ignorance and barbarity of the church, which thus retarded civilization and delayed spiritual progress for many hundred years" (p. 237). As history has demonstrated into the twenty-first century, barbarism is not practiced solely by the barbarians.

21. *Oz himself.* According to *Dorothy and the Wizard in Oz* (1908, p. 196), Oz was always the name of the ruler of the Land of Oz when it was under one head. If the monarch happened to be a woman, her name was Ozma. Prior to the Wizard's arrival in Oz, it was ruled by a grandfather of Princess Ozma, the present ruler. Mombi the Witch enchanted him and his son when she and the other Wicked Witches took over the four countries of Oz. But then the Royal History gets hazy. According to *The Marvelous Land of Oz* (1904, pp. 240–41), Pastoria, Ozma's father, was ruler of the Emerald City long before the Wizard came to Oz, but this may have been just a way of making the book consistent with the 1902 musical extravaganza, in which Pastoria was introduced to battle the Wizard for control of the Emerald City. Everywhere else the Wizard is credited with having built the capital of Oz. Mombi also serves as Ozma's guardian before her enchantment is broken by Glinda the Good, who proclaims the girl the rightful ruler of Oz. Robert R. Pattrick explored the sometimes thorny pre-Dorothean history of Oz in his collection of essays *Unexplored Territory in Oz* (Kinderhook, Ill.: International Wizard of Oz Club, 1963).

22. *the Great Wizard.* The ratio of one wizard to four witches in Oz is lower than it was in Europe during the Inquisition. "A wizard was rare," reported Matilda Joslyn Gage in *Woman, Church, and State*; "one writer declaring that to every hundred witches but one wizard was found" (p. 224). Another source said, "To one wizard 10,000 witches." According to the Venetian folklore, there were fewer wizards in part due to the devil's decision "to always tempt women instead of men, because through ambition or a desire for revenge, they yield more easily." Consequently, far more women were suspected of witchcraft and put to death.

"What is it?" asked the little old woman; and looked, and began to laugh. The feet of the dead Witch had disappeared entirely and nothing was left but the silver shoes.

"She was so old," explained the Witch of the North, "that she dried up quickly in the sun. That is the end of her. But the silver shoes are yours, and you shall have them to wear." She reached down and picked up the shoes, and after shaking the dust out of them handed them to Dorothy.

24.

"The Witch of the East was proud of those silver shoes," said one of the Munchkins; "and there is some charm connected with them; but what it is we never knew."

Dorothy carried the shoes into the house and placed them on the table. Then she came out again to the Munchkins and said,

"I am anxious to get back to my Aunt and Uncle, for I am sure they will worry about me. Can you help me find my way?"

The Munchkins and the Witch first looked at one

23. *City of Emeralds*. Baum may have chosen the emerald as the predominant jewel of the enchanted capital of Oz to honor his mother's ancestral homeland, Ireland, "the Emerald Isle." It is also Baum's own birthstone, the traditional one for the month of May.

24. *dust*. As Oz Club member David L. Greene suggested in a letter, Baum may well have been thinking of the Biblical phrase "For dust thou art and unto dust shalt thou return" (Genesis 3:19), often repeated at traditional Christian burials. Baum may be emphasizing the fact the Witch was so old and evil that a good thump on the head sent her remains scattering in the wind.

25. *desert*. It took Baum several Oz books to determine the exact nature of this great sandy waste. It still is traversable in *The Marvelous Land of Oz* (1904), as when Mombi the Witch in the guise of a Griffin tries to escape Glinda the Good by fleeing across it. But by *The Road to Oz* (1909, p. 126), a sign warns travelers of its dangers:

> ALL PERSONS ARE WARNED
> NOT TO VENTURE UPON THIS DESERT
> For the Deadly Sands Will Turn Any
> Living Flesh to Dust in an Instant. Beyond
> This Barrier is the
> LAND OF OZ
> But no one can Reach that Beautiful Country because of
> these Destroying Sands.

On the map of the Land of Oz that appears on the endpapers of *Tik-Tok of Oz* (1914), Baum divides the surrounding desert like the countries of Oz into four geographical areas, each with its own name. Although the entire wasteland is generally known as the "Deadly Desert," that technically refers only to that portion that touches the Winkie Country on the West. In the North is the "Impassable Desert," in the South the "Great Sandy Waste." The desert bordering the Munchkin Country to the East is the "Shifting Sands." "These ingredients of the topography of Oz—the impassable barrier, the four-sidedness, the symbolic colors, the circle, and the center—are also ingredients of a mandala," argued John Algeo in "Oz and Kansas: A Theosophical Quest" (in Susan R. Gannon and Ruth Anne Thompson's *Proceedings of the Thirteenth Annual Conference of the Children's Literature Association*, Kansas City: University of Missouri, 1988). "Mandalas are eastern diagrams representing the human psyche and the world of illusion—the manifold, beautiful, enticing, but also frightening world in which we live. And that is what Oz is."

26. *Quadlings*. Like the other names of the peoples of Oz, "Quadling" ends in a diminutive. If "quad" means "four,"

then a free translation of this word might be "a small inhabitant of the fourth country." Or was it the name of a friend or acquaintance of Baum's? When *The Annotated Wizard of Oz* first came out, a woman from Canada wrote that her maiden name was Quadling.

27. *Winkies*. Although "wink" usually means to blink (the Winkies "wink" in Volkov's Russian books), the name of the yellow land of Oz may instead refer to the colloquial expression meaning a little bit of light. After all, as revealed in Chapter 12, the Country of the West is "where the sun sets." In parts of Great Britain and the United States, "winkie" is a children's pet name for the index finger, and Baum affectionately called his own boys his "kiddiwinkles." The name of the land of the West also suggests William Miller's famous nursery rhyme "Wee Willie Winkie," said to be the nickname of William of Orange.

28. *one, two, three*. Three is traditionally a mystic number and an important element in much of the magic performed throughout this story.

29. *a slate, on which was written in big, white chalk marks*. Slates and white chalk were the basic writing tools of schoolchildren at the turn of the century. But most modern readers probably will not recognize "slate-writing" as a form of automatic or spirit writing, the only specific occult practice Baum mentions in the story. A medium puts a piece of chalk or a pencil between two slates in hope that some unseen power will write a message from the Great Beyond. Charles Webster Leadbetter explained in his Theosophical manual *The Astral Plane* (1898) that "the fragment of pencil enclosed between two slates is guided by the spirit hand, of which only just the tiny points sufficient to grasp it are materialized" (p. 96).

30. *Is your name Dorothy*. Dorothy *Gale* to be exact. Her last name first appeared in the script for the 1902 musical extravaganza. It may have been the invention of the director, Julian Mitchell, or the script doctor, Glen Macdonough, to set up the following weak joke:

> DOROTHY: My name is Dorothy, and I am one of the Kansas Gales.
> SCARECROW: That accounts for your breezy manner.

The girl signs "Dorothy Gale" to a letter printed in *The Ozmapolitan* (see Chapter 1, Note 2). Actually Denslow used the full name before Baum did, in the comic page "Dorothy's Christmas Tree" in the Minneapolis *Journal* and other papers, December 10, 1904. (See the Denslow

another, and then at Dorothy, and then shook their heads.

"At the East, not far from here," said one, "there is a great desert, and none could live to cross it."

25.

"It is the same at the South," said another, "for I have been there and seen it. The South is the country of the Quadlings."

26.

"I am told," said the third man, "that it is the same at the West. And that country, where the Winkies live, is ruled by the wicked Witch of the West, who would make you her slave if you passed her way."

27.

"The North is my home," said the old lady, "and at its edge is the same great desert that surrounds this land of Oz. I'm afraid, my dear, you will have to live with us."

Dorothy began to sob, at this, for she felt lonely among all these strange people. Her tears seemed to grieve the kind-hearted Munchkins, for they immediately took out their handkerchiefs and began to weep also. As for the little old woman, she took off her cap and balanced the point on the end of her nose, while she counted "one, two, three" in a solemn voice. At once the cap changed to a slate, on which was written in big, white chalk marks:

28.

29.

"LET DOROTHY GO TO THE CITY OF EMERALDS."

The little old woman took the slate from her nose, and, having read the words on it, asked,

"Is your name Dorothy, my dear?"

30.

"Yes," answered the child, looking up and drying her tears.

"Then you must go to the City of Emeralds. Perhaps Oz will help you."

"Where is this City?" asked Dorothy.

"It is exactly in the center of the country, and is ruled by Oz, the Great Wizard I told you of."

"Is he a good man?" enquired the girl, anxiously.

"He is a good Wizard. Whether he is a man or not I cannot tell, for I have never seen him."

"How can I get there?" asked Dorothy.

"You must walk. It is a long journey, through a country that is sometimes pleasant and sometimes dark and terrible. However, I will use all the magic arts I know of to keep you from harm."

"Won't you go with me?" pleaded the girl, who had begun to look upon the little old woman as her only friend.

"No, I cannot do that," she replied; "but I will give you my kiss, and no one will dare injure a person who has been kissed by the Witch of the North."

She came close to Dorothy and kissed her gently on the forehead Where her lips touched the girl they left a round, shining mark, as Dorothy found out soon after.

31.

32.

"The road to the City of Emeralds is paved with yellow brick," said the Witch; "so you cannot miss it. When you get to Oz do not be afraid of him, but tell your story and ask him to help you. Good-bye, my dear."

Appendix, color section, No. 20.) Baum did not add Gale to her name until the third title *Ozma of Oz* (1907, p. 15).

31. *a round, shining mark*. Baum may have recalled that the second of the Shining Ones whom Christian meets in *Pilgrim's Progress* "set a mark on his forehead." Earle J. Coleman suggested in "Oz as Heaven and Other Philosophical Questions" (*The Baum Bugle,* Autumn 1980) that Baum and Bunyan may be recalling Ezekiel 9, in which the Lord commanded that those who are marked on the forehead will be protected by Him. Although the Good Witch of the North is not powerful enough to defeat the Wicked Witch of the West, her kiss symbolizes abstract Good, which is stronger than Evil. This very kiss is an important part of Ruth Plumly Thompson's *The Wishing Horse of Oz* (1935).

32. *yellow brick*. What would be more logical than a yellow brick road to travel on through the blue countryside to a green city? Yet many commentators have tried to associate this highway literally with the phrase "streets paved with gold," such as American cities were often metaphorically said to have. Yellow brick was a common building materi-al in the late-nineteenth-century United States: The famous Dakota Hotel at Seventy-second Street in New York City was made of yellow brick in 1882; when the old Metropolitan Opera House at Thirty-ninth Street was rebuilt in 1892, it became known as the Yellow Brick Brewery. Aberdeen, South Dakota, had a yel-low brick "castle" which was finished soon after the Baums left in 1891. Although this is the most famous road in Oz, it is not the only one made of yellow bricks. Tip and Jack Pumpkinhead follow one through the purple Gillikin Country to the Emerald City in *The Marvelous Land of Oz* (1904). The Munchkin Country has another one traveled by Scraps and Ojo in *The Patchwork Girl of Oz* (1913). No one has yet determined how many yellow brick roads there must be in the yellow Winkie Country.

The three Munchkins bowed low to her and wished her a pleasant journey, after which they walked away through the trees. The Witch gave Dorothy a friendly little nod, whirled around on her left heel three times, and straightway disappeared, much to the surprise of little Toto, who barked after her loudly enough when she had gone, because he had been afraid even to growl while she stood by.

33. But Dorothy, knowing her to be a witch, had expected her to disappear in just that way, and was not surprised in the least.

33. *not surprised in the least.* A similar reaction to a magical disappearance occurs in "The Queen of Quok" in *American Fairy Tales* (1901). When the Slave of the Royal Bedstead (a genie who presents the boy king with a magic purse that never empties) vanishes, the young King of Quok admits, "I expected that, yet I am sorry he did not wait to say good-by." What the critic Roger Sale in "L. Frank Baum, and Oz" (*Hudson Review*, Winter 1972–1973) said of the opening of *Ozma of Oz* (1907) is equally true of these early chapters of *The Wizard of Oz*:

What is so enthralling about all this is the instinctive rightness of Baum's talent; he moves, totally without self-consciousness, from a real world to an improbable world to a magic world. The sentences come easily, and imply they were no harder to write than it would be to take the journey they describe. Dorothy herself has no tricks or mechanical skills, but she commands a large presence just by responding [to] and accepting each new detail with the same unshakable curiosity with which she faced the last. We do not classify each situation according to how realistic or magical it is because Dorothy and Baum do not; instead, they take each one as it comes since, as we have always known and are being shown afresh, that is the way to get out of pretty fixes.

Chapter III
How Dorothy saved
the Scarecrow.

WHEN DOROTHY WAS left alone she began to feel hungry. So she went to the cupboard and cut herself some bread, which she spread with butter. She gave some to Toto, and taking a pail from the shelf she carried it down to the little brook and filled it with clear, sparkling water. Toto ran over to the trees and began to bark at the birds sitting there. Dorothy went to get him, and saw such delicious fruit hanging from the branches that she gathered some of it, finding it just what she wanted to help out her breakfast.

Then she went back to the house, and having helped

herself and Toto to a good drink of the cool, clear water, she set about making ready for the journey to the City of Emeralds.

1.   Dorothy had only one other dress, but that happened to be clean and was hanging on a peg beside her bed. It
2. was gingham, with checks of white and blue; and although the blue was somewhat faded with many washings, it was still a pretty frock. The girl washed herself carefully, dressed herself in the clean gingham, and tied her pink sunbonnet on her head. She took a little basket and filled it with bread from the cupboard, laying a white cloth over the top. Then she looked down at her feet and noticed how old and worn her shoes were.

"They surely will never do for a long journey, Toto," she said. And Toto looked up into her face with his little black eyes and wagged his tail to show he knew what she meant.

At that moment Dorothy saw lying on the table the silver shoes that had belonged to the Witch of the East.

"I wonder if they will fit me," she said to Toto. "They
3. would be just the thing to take a long walk in, for they could not wear out."

She took off her old leather shoes and tried on the
4. silver ones, which fitted her as well as if they had been made for her.

Finally she picked up her basket.

1. *only one other dress*. But Denslow draws three—the one she is wearing, the blue-and-white checked one, and the dotted one shown in the opening pages of the book. (See also Chapter 23, Note 1.)

2. *gingham*. A cheap, light printed cotton cloth often worn in summer by American women and girls of the period, usually in the country. Baum is emphasizing the very ordinariness of his young heroine, though she is slayer of the Wicked Witch and liberator of the Munchkins.

3. *they could not wear out*. Baum may be recalling that the Three Shining Ones show Christian in the armory at House Beautiful of Bunyan's *Pilgrim's Progress* "shoes that would not wear out." See Note 4 below.

4. *fitted her as well as if they had been made for her*. Surely the Wicked Witch of the West wore a bigger shoe than Dorothy does! Baum may have recalled the famous seven-league boots worn by le petit Poucet, or Hop o' My Thumb, in Charles Perrault's *Histories ou contes du temps passé* (1697). These, like the Silver Shoes, are enchanted, so when the tiny boy puts on the ogre's big boots, "they fitted his feet and legs as well as if they had been made on purpose for him." All the other clothes of Oz fit Dorothy just as well. Baum may be reemphasizing the fact that Dorothy is the same size as the natives of this strange country.

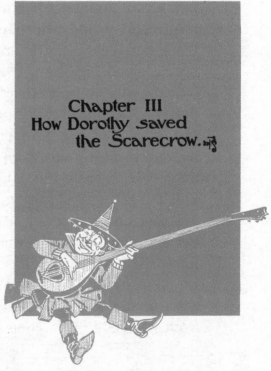

This chapter title page was originally drawn for Chapter 2. Denslow pasted a paper label with the new title over the old on the pen-and-ink drawing (now in the Henry Goldsmith collection, the Prints and Drawings Department, the New York Public Library).

"Come along, Toto," she said, "we will go to the Emerald City and ask the great Oz how to get back to Kansas again."

5.   She closed the door, locked it, and put the key carefully in the pocket of her dress. And so, with Toto trotting along soberly behind her, she started on her journey.

There were several roads near by, but it did not take her long to find the one paved with yellow brick. Within a short time she was walking briskly toward the Emerald City, her silver shoes tinkling merrily on the hard, yellow roadbed. The sun shone bright and the birds sang sweet and Dorothy did not feel nearly as bad as you might think a little girl would who had been suddenly whisked away from her own country and set down in the midst of a strange land.

She was surprised, as she walked along, to see how pretty the country was about her. There were neat fences at the sides of the road, painted a dainty blue color, and beyond them were fields of grain and vegetables in abundance. Evidently the Munchkins were good farmers and able to raise large crops. Once in a while she would pass a house, and the people came out to look at her and bow low as she went by; for everyone knew she had been the means of destroying the wicked witch and setting them free from bondage. The houses

5. *key.* No matter how strange her situation, Dorothy always acts like a tidy, meticulous, well-behaved little girl. Although she may never see her house again, she probably does exactly what Aunt Em and Uncle Henry have always taught her to do when she leaves the house. "Dorothy may still have this key," speculated Gardner in Note 5 of *The Wizard of Oz and Who He Was*. "It would be interesting to know if the old farm house is still standing at the spot where the cyclone left it."

Having locked the door behind her, Dorothy is now ready to set off on her quest to get back home to Kansas. Many readers have noted how the story follows the simple threefold mythic path of the classical hero as defined by Joseph Campbell in his highly influential *The Hero with a Thousand Faces* (Cleveland: World, 1956)—Separation, Descent, and Return. Oddly, Campbell never considered *The Wizard of Oz* in any of his writings, and yet it beautifully reflects his theories. Dorothy follows much the same pattern described in Campbell's book: She is carried away to the threshold of adventure (the cyclone); meets a protective figure, usually an old woman (the Good Witch of the North); is provided with talismans (the Silver Shoes, the Good Witch's kiss, the Golden Cap); meets helpers (the Scarecrow, the Tin Woodman, the Cowardly Lion); goes through a series of tests (Kalidahs, Deadly Poppy Field, Fighting Trees, Hammer-Heads); goes through a supreme ordeal (killing the Wicked Witch of the West); gains her reward (the trip back to Kansas); and makes her final return. Because of her age, however, Dorothy does not undergo a sacred marriage, father atonement, or apotheosis. And she does not "bestow boons." Those belong to other heroes and other times.

6. of the Munchkins were odd looking dwellings, for each was round, with a big dome for a roof. All were painted
7. blue, for in this country of the East blue was the favorite color.

Towards evening, when Dorothy was tired with her long walk and began to wonder where she should pass the night, she came to a house rather larger than the rest. On the green lawn before it many men and women were dancing. Five little fiddlers played as loudly as possible and the people were laughing and singing, while a big table near by was loaded with delicious fruits and nuts, pies and cakes, and many other good things to eat.

The people greeted Dorothy kindly, and invited her to supper and to pass the night with them; for this was the home of one of the richest Munchkins in the land, and his friends were gathered with him to celebrate their freedom from the bondage of the wicked witch.

Dorothy ate a hearty supper and was waited upon by the rich Munchkin himself, whose name was Boq. Then she sat down upon a settee and watched the people dance.

When Boq saw her silver shoes he said,

"You must be a great sorceress."

"Why?" asked the girl.

"Because you wear silver shoes and have killed the wicked witch. Besides, you have white in your frock, and
8. only witches and sorceresses wear white."

6. *odd looking dwellings.* Denslow, rather than Baum, defines the fanciful architecture of Oz by introducing human characteristics to the houses and other buildings of the fairyland. This personification is in perfect harmony with Baum's story, and John R. Neill eagerly retains it in his pictures for the subsequent Oz books. It has all the bizarre whimsy and wild extravagance of the Italian Mannerist style (particularly the Orsini Gardens at Bomarzo and the Palazzo Zuccari in Rome). The personification of buildings was also evident contemporaneously in Art Nouveau. This style carried to comic excess is evident in Neill's "Battle of the Houses," Chapter 20 of Neill's *The Wonder City of Oz* (1940).

7. *blue was the favorite color.* Each country of Oz has its own distinct color, possibly because that is how maps distinguish one area from another. Baum advises in the opening of *A New Wonderland* (1900; reissued as *The Magical Monarch of Mo*, 1903) that if cartographers would put the Beautiful Valley "on the maps of our geographies and paint it pink or light green, and print a big round dot where the King's castle stands, it would be easy enough to point out to you its exact location" (p. 5). Martin Gardner recalled a passage in the third chapter of Mark Twain's *Tom Sawyer Abroad* (1894) which discusses these colors of geography books. Noticing that the ground below is green as they float over in a balloon, Huck Finn says to Tom:

> "I know by the color [where we are]. We're right over Illinois. And you can see for yourself that Indiana ain't right."
> "I wonder what's the matter with you, Huck. You know by the color?"
> "Yes, of course I do."
> "What's the color got to do with it?"
> "It's got everything to do with it. Illinois is green. Indiana is pink. . . . I've seen it on the map and it's pink. You show me any pink down there, if you can. No, sir, it's green. . . . there ain't no two states the same color."

Gore Vidal observed in "The Wizard of the 'Wizard'" (*The New York Review of Books*, September 29, 1977) that this partition of the Land of Oz into geometric shapes, each with its own particular color, has "the effect, exactly, of a certain kind of old-fashioned garden where flower beds are laid out symmetrically and separated from one another by 'winding paths covered with white gravel.'" Baum tended just such a flower garden at Ozcot, his home in Hollywood.

There is no great symbolic meaning to the color scheme of Oz, and Baum seems not to have consulted his mother-in-law Matilda Joslyn Gage's "Colors and Their Meaning" (*Continental Monthly*, August 1864). But it is not arbitrary

either. The change from one region to another follows the principles of color theory. Each of the three major countries visited in *The Wizard of Oz* has a primary color, one of the three from which all others derive. Dorothy and her companions do not journey directly from one primary color to another. Instead their path passes through a secondary one. To get to the West, they must go through the green countryside around the Emerald City, merely a link between the blue land of the Munchkins and the yellow Winkie Country. They also traverse from the Winkie Country to Glinda's Castle in the red South by way of the Emerald City; the wild countryside they visit before arriving in the Quadling Country is brown. It is made from all three primary colors or mixing green with red. The standard color wheel puts blue to the right (East), yellow to the left (West), and red at the bottom (South), like the Munchkins, Winkies, and Quadlings. Here is a diagram of the geography of Oz based upon this theory:

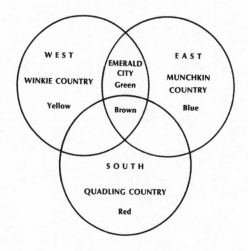

Baum published William M. Couran's "The Scientific Arrangement of Color," in the September and October 1898 issues of his trade magazine *The Show Window*. Baum wrote his own summary of its principles in Chapter 5 of *The Art of Decorating Dry Goods Stores and Windows* (1900) at the time he was working on *The Wizard of Oz*.

The color scheme also follows the passing seasons: The grays of winter yield to the blues, reds, and greens of spring, followed by the yellows and greens of summer, then the browns and reds of autumn, and finally the return to gray on Dorothy's homecoming.

8. *only witches and sorceresses wear white.* Although some European covens wore white in the Middle Ages, Baum is again playing with conventions. Black then was generally

considered evil and white was good. "Black was hated as the color of the devil," Gage explained in *Woman, Church, and State* (p. 217), so it was known as the witch color. But she also made a distinction between "black" and "white" magic: " 'Magic' whether brought about by the aid of spirits or simply through an understanding of secret natural laws, is of two kinds, 'white' and 'black,' according as its intent and consequences are evil or good, and in this respect does not differ from the use made of the well-known laws of nature, which are ever of good or evil character, in the hands of good and evil persons" (p. 236). Maetta the Sorceress of *A New Wonderland* (1900; later *The Magical Monarch of Mo*, 1903) and the good witch of "The Witchcraft of Mary-Marie" in *Baum's American Fairy Tales* (1908) wear white, like the Good Witches of the North and South. Another witch, the dangerous Mrs. Yoop in *The Tin Woodman of Oz* (1918), wears "silver robes embroidered with gay floral designs" (p. 70). But MGM made Glinda the Good Witch wear pink, like a good fairy. Evidently Wicked Witches do *not* wear white in Oz: Denslow depicts the one in the West in black and yellow, but Baum makes no such distinction in his text.

9. *never seen a dog before.* A similar reaction occurs when a dog named Prince visits the lovely Valley of Mo in *The Magical Monarch of Mo* (1903). There are no dogs in Oz either, but there must have been in Oz at one time. According to the Map of the Land of Oz and its surrounding countries (prepared by James E. Haff and Dick Martin for the International Wizard of Oz Club), the only place beyond the mountains of Mo and the great desert is the Land of Oz. (To cross the desert at the point dividing Oz and Mo must have at one time been easier than at other spots. The Foolish Donkey of *The Magical Monarch of Mo* visits Oz before Glinda sets up her Barrier of Invisibility that cuts it off from the rest of the world in 1910 in *The Emerald City of Oz*, as revealed in 1913 in *The Patchwork Girl of Oz*, p. 93.) Prince must have come from the Land of Oz. Also, the Saw-Horse kicks a green dog who dares to bark at it when the queer creature arrives in the Emerald City in *The Marvelous Land of Oz* (1904, p. 69).

"My dress is blue and white checked," said Dorothy, smoothing out the wrinkles in it.

"It is kind of you to wear that," said Boq. "Blue is the color of the Munchkins, and white is the witch color; so we know you are a friendly witch."

Dorothy did not know what to say to this, for all the people seemed to think her a witch, and she knew very well she was only an ordinary little girl who had come by the chance of a cyclone into a strange land.

When she had tired watching the dancing, Boq led her into the house, where he gave her a room with a pretty bed in it. The sheets were made of blue cloth, and Dorothy slept soundly in them till morning, with Toto curled up on the blue rug beside her.

She ate a hearty breakfast, and watched a wee Munchkin baby, who played with Toto and pulled his tail and crowed and laughed in a way that greatly amused Dorothy. Toto was a fine curiosity to all the people, for they had never seen a dog before.

9.

"How far is it to the Emerald City?" the girl asked.

"I do not know," answered Boq, gravely, "for I have never been there. It is better for people to keep away from Oz, unless they

This picture of the Scarecrow first appeared in *Denslow's A B C Book* (New York: G. W. Dillingham, 1903), illustrating the following doggerel by Denslow:

S is for Scarecrow
who lives in the corn,
That the crows think so foolish
they laugh him to scorn.

He is obviously the same one Dorothy found in the Munchkin's cornfield.
Private collection.

10. *a Scarecrow*. This Munchkin Scarecrow could have come right out of any American cornfield. Like Hans Christian Andersen, Baum had that uncanny ability to relate his fairyland to the immediacy of a child's world through the little details of his story. (Andersen describes the soldier's new wealth in "The Tinder Box" in terms of all the rocking horses, tin soldiers, and sugar pigs one could buy.) Other examples of "homely, American things that you'd hardly expect in Fairyland" (as Clifton Fadiman called them in his afterword to the 1962 Macmillan edition) are a funnel for a hat, an oilcan, and the big clothes basket used for the Wizard's balloon. "The American scarecrow had its heyday in the latter part of the nineteenth century,"

reported Neal Avon in *Ephemeral Folk Figures* (New York: Clarkson N. Potter, 1969). "There was a time in America when no rustic scene would have seemed complete without some representation of this spectral image standing guard among the farmer's crops, but they are rare today. Science now has more effective ways of discouraging marauding crows." Baum's first glimpse of a scarecrow may well have been while growing up at Rose Lawn, the family farm outside Syracuse, New York. "When I was a boy," Baum told the Philadelphia *North American* (October 3, 1904), "I was tremendously interested in scarecrows. They always seemed to my childish imagination as just about to wave their arms, straighten up and stalk across the field on their long legs. I lived on a farm, you know. It was natural then, that my first character in this animated life series was the Scarecrow, on whom I have taken revenge for all the mystic feeling he once inspired." Also out in the country, Baum and his younger brother Harry Clay set up a printing press in the barn and issued a few numbers of an amateur newspaper, *The Rose Lawn Home Journal*. Baum wrote much of the material himself, including the following charade that appeared in the September 1, 1871, issue:

My FIRST expresses much alarm
Or sense of some approaching harm.
My SECOND's heard at early morn;
Or seen amid the new sown corn
Unless my WHOLE in strange array
Frightens th' intruding thief away.

The answer is "Scare-Crow," apparently Baum's earliest writing on the subject. Fred A. Stone created the role of the Scarecrow in the 1902 musical extravaganza of *The Wizard of Oz*. It made him a musical comedy star, and he devoted a chapter to the show in his autobiography, *Rolling Stone* (1943). "I used to be so happy when little folks shook my limp fingers and patted the straw filling in my chest," Stone wrote in a letter in the 1920 Bobbs-Merrill edition of *The New Wizard of Oz*. "Dorothy Gale was my good friend too and when a baby girl came to my house one day I named her 'Dorothy' after my little playmate in Oz." Dorothy Stone grew up to be a musical comedy performer like her father and appeared in several shows with him. The silent comedian Larry Semon portrayed the Scarecrow in the poor 1925 Chadwick picture; Semon had been a cartoonist who worked with John R. Neill on the Philadelphia *North American*. Ray Bolger, whose favorite book growing up in Boston was *The Wizard of Oz*, proved to be as nimble a dancer as Stone in the 1939 MGM musical. Hinton Battle had the part in the 1975 Broadway musical *The Wiz*; Michael Jackson was the Scarecrow in the 1978 film, his only major movie role to date.

have business with him. But it is a long way to the
Emerald City, and it will take you many days. The
country here is rich and pleasant, but you must pass
through rough and dangerous places before you reach the
end of your journey."

This worried Dorothy a little, but she knew that only
the great Oz could help her get to Kansas again, so she
bravely resolved not to turn back.

She bade her friends good-bye, and again started
along the road of yellow brick. When she had gone several miles she thought she would stop to rest, and so
climbed to the top of the fence beside the road and sat
down. There was a great cornfield beyond the fence, and
and not far away she saw a Scarecrow, placed high on a   10.
pole to keep the birds from the ripe corn.

Dorothy leaned her chin upon her hand and gazed
thoughtfully at the Scarecrow. Its head was a small sack
stuffed with straw, with eyes, nose and mouth painted on
it to represent a face. An old, pointed blue hat, that had
belonged to some Munchkin, was perched on this head,
and the rest of the figure was a blue suit of clothes, worn
and faded, which had also been stuffed with straw. On
the feet were some old boots with blue tops, such as every
man wore in this country, and the figure was raised above
the stalks of corn by means of the pole stuck up its back.

While Dorothy was looking earnestly into the queer,
painted face of the Scarecrow, she was surprised to see

Carroll, a master of nonsense, loved puns while recognizing that others did not share his taste. When the King of Hearts makes a pun in *Alice in Wonderland* (1865), there is dead silence in the courtroom; likewise, the Snark "looks gravely at a pun." Current critics tend to share Johnson's view in spite of the frequency of verbal jokes in the writings of James Joyce, Vladimir Nabokov, and other modernists. Baum admits in *The Marvelous Land of Oz* (1904) that so many people turn in disgust at the hearing of a pun, but (with tongue in cheek) he offers his best defense through the Woggle-Bug:

> A joke derived from a play upon words is considered among educated people to be eminently proper . . . our language contains many words having a double meaning; and . . . to pronounce a joke that allows both meanings of a certain word, proves the joker a person of culture and refinement, who has, moreover, a thorough command of the language." (p. 160)

But then this is the Woggle-Bug speaking, one of the most pompous characters in all the Oz books.

Sketch of Fred A Stone as the Scarecrow drawn by Denslow and signed by the actor, 1902.
Courtesy W. W. Denslow Papers, Special Collections, Syracuse University Library.

11. *a rather husky voice.* The first of many puns throughout the story. Ever since boyhood, Baum had a terrible weakness for them. He used to torment his family and friends with his jokes, and his four sons inherited his sense of humor. Although children enjoy them, most modern critics of juvenile literature generally agree that these plays on words lower the literary value of a work. They fail to recognize that puns test the mental agility of young readers just learning new vocabulary. The common complaint is that puns contain only facile verbal relations, while true wit depends on shrewdly drawn intellectual connections. Yet Elizabethans highly prized puns; Shakespeare is full of them. But the pun had lost most of its favor by the eighteenth century, when Joseph Addison called it false wit and Samuel Johnson ranked it the lowest form of humor. Lewis

This picture of the Scarecrow first appeared on the front cover of *The New Wizard of Oz* (Indianapolis: Bobbs-Merrill, 1903). *Courtesy Willard Carroll Collection.*

one of the eyes slowly wink at her.   She thought she must have been mistaken, at first, for none of the scarecrows in Kansas ever wink; but presently the figure nodded its head to her in a friendly way.   Then she climbed down from the fence and walked up to it, while Toto ran around the pole and barked.

"Good day," said the Scarecrow, in a rather husky voice.   11.

"Did you speak?" asked the girl, in wonder.

"Certainly," answered the Scarecrow; "how do you do?"

"I'm pretty well, thank you," replied Dorothy, politely; "how do you do?"

"I'm not feeling well," said the Scarecrow, with a smile, "for it is very tedious being perched up here night and day to scare away crows."

"Can't you get down?" asked Dorothy.

"No, for this pole is stuck up my back. If you will please take away the pole I shall be greatly obliged to you."

Dorothy reached up both arms and lifted the figure off the pole; for, being stuffed with straw, it was quite light.

"Thank you very much," said the Scarecrow, when he had been set down on the ground. "I feel like a new man."

Dorothy was puzzled at this, for it sounded queer to

hear a stuffed man speak, and to see him bow and walk along beside her.

"Who are you?" asked the Scarecrow, when he had stretched himself and yawned, "and where are you going?"

"My name is Dorothy," said the girl, "and I am going to the Emerald City, to ask the great Oz to send me back to Kansas."

"Where is the Emerald City?" he enquired; "and who is Oz?"

"Why, don't you know?" she returned, in surprise.

"No, indeed; I don't know anything. You see, I am stuffed, so I have no brains at all," he answered, sadly.

"Oh," said Dorothy; "I'm awfully sorry for you."

"Do you think," he asked, "If I go to the Emerald City with you, that the great Oz would give me some

12.   brains?"

"I cannot tell," she returned; "but

13.   you may come with me, if you like. If Oz will not give you

12. *brains.* Baum is playing with the absurdity of a soft-headed, straw-stuffed man longing for a brain like other people. Much of the charm and wit of *The Wizard of Oz* relies on Baum's irony and amusing incongruity. Gareth B. Matthews in *Philosophy and the Young Child* (Cambridge, mass.: Harvard University Press, 1980) called Baum "a master of philosophical whimsy" (p. 59). The Scarecrow is the Divine Fool, a simpleton who makes good by his natural wits. He is the one who solves most of the problems encountered along the Yellow Brick Road, but he relies on common sense rather than dubious theory. Baum also plays with sages who, like the Wise Men of Gotham, are rarely as bright as everyone else assumes them to be; he introduces the Wise Donkey and the Foolish Owl in *The Patchwork Girl of Oz* (1913) as well as the pitiful Frogman in *The Lost Princes of Oz* (1917). The best example of empty pomposity in the Oz stories is the thoroughly educated but highly magnified Woggle-Bug of *The Marvelous Land of Oz* (1904).

Folk tales often describe the quest for the one thing that will make a person whole. It is usually some unattainable object like the Holy Grail or an improbable one like a brain for a scarecrow. In her chapter on psychic growth in Carl G. Jung's *Man and His Symbols* (New York: Doubleday, 1964), M.-L. Franz defines this search as the process of individuation. Matilda Joslyn Gage argued in *Woman, Church, and State* (1893) that "the growth of a personal will" was "the most important end to be attained in the history of man's evolution. . . . Under Will, man decides for himself, escaping from all control that hinders his personal development" (p. 234). One's imperfection can only be solved within oneself. That is the metaphysical conclusion of "The Fishman and His Soul" in Oscar Wilde's *The House of Pomegranates* (1891). On being separated from the fisherman, the soul goes in search of God and is led to a room in the temple of an enchanted country where it finds only a mirror. The astronaut encounters much the same experience in Stanley Kubrick's film of Arthur C. Clarke's *2001: A Space Odyssey* (1968). The Scarecrow likewise learns on the discovery of Oz the Terrible that what he seeks has really always been within him.

Another underlying theme begins here. In one sense, Dorothy's three companions embody the three basic qualities—brain, heart, and courage—that Baum desires she should carry with her not only on her journey to the Great Oz but throughout her life. These are three virtues that she must cultivate within herself just as the Scarecrow, the Tin Woodman, and the Cowardly Lion must do so individually.

13. *you may come with me, if you like.* The structure of the tale at this point becomes reminiscent of many folk tales, from the Grimms' "How Six Made Their Way Through the World" to "The Five Chinese Brothers," in which the poor hero gathers together a band of odd characters on his travels. It is not evident at first exactly to what good use they may be put, but in the end they come through to help the hero overcome all obstacles just as Dorothy's companions do. The Chicago *Evening Post* (September 20, 1900) noted that Dorothy "keeps adding to her train" like Henny-Penny in the English nursery tale. Jonathan Cott in his introduction to the 1994 Barefoot Books edition of *The Wizard of Oz* saw similarities between Dorothy and her friends and a monk and his animal companions in the Chinese novel *The Journey to the West* (known as *Monkey*) and the winged pilgrims of a twelfth-century Persian fable, *The Conference of the Birds*. The last seems particularly pertinent: When the birds find God, they learn that He is themselves, for "He who knows his self knows his Lord." Diana Ross, who played Dorothy in the 1978 movie of *The Wiz*, argued in her memoir, *Secrets of a Sparrow* (New York: Villard Books, 1993), that each of her three companions signifies "a different aspect of Dorothy's essence." "The Scarecrow was a representation of Dorothy's hunger for knowledge, the part of her that longed to know more about life and living," the singer explained. "The Tinman personified Dorothy's craving for love, the search for her heart, the deep need in her (in all of us, for that matter) to increase her capacity to give and to receive love. And the Lion, the supposedly mean old lion, was yet another part of Dorothy's psyche. His loud and aggressive roars, designed to distance people by projecting fear and rage into their hearts, was merely a cover-up of his own fears and rage, an armoring to protect the sweetness and vulnerability of his, and of course Dorothy's, gentle heart" (p. 187).

any brains you will be no worse off than you are now."

"That is true," said the Scarecrow. "You see," he continued, confidentially, "I don't mind my legs and arms and body being stuffed, because I cannot get hurt. If anyone treads on my toes or sticks a pin into me, it doesn't matter, for I can't feel it. But I do not want people to call me a fool, and if my head stays stuffed with straw instead of with brains, as yours is, how am I ever to know anything?"

"I understand how you feel," said the little girl, who was truly sorry for him. "If you will come with me I'll ask Oz to do all he can for you."

"Thank you," he answered, gratefully.

They walked back to the road, Dorothy helped him over the fence, and they started along the path of yellow brick for the Emerald City.

Toto did not like this addition to the party, at first. He smelled around the stuffed man as if he suspected there might be a nest of rats in the straw, and he often growled in an unfriendly way at the Scarecrow.

"Don't mind Toto," said Dorothy, to her new friend; "he never bites."

"Oh, I'm not afraid," replied the Scarecrow, "he can't hurt the straw. Do let me carry that basket for you. I shall not mind it, for I can't get tired. I'll tell you a secret," he continued, as he walked along; "there is only one thing in the world I am afraid of."

"What is that?" asked Dorothy; "the Munchkin farmer who made you?"

"No," answered the Scarecrow; "it's a lighted match."   14.

14. *a lighted match*. It is surprising that Baum did nothing with this observation later in the story. But the 1939 MGM movie has the Wicked Witch of the West set the Scarecrow on fire, an action which provokes Dorothy to douse her thoroughly with water. This accident exonerates the girl for the "murder" of the Wicked Witch.

This picture of the Scarecrow appeared
on a trade card, c. 1910.
Private collection.

Chapter IV.
~The Road through
the Forest.~

After A FEW HOURS the road began to be rough, and the walking grew so difficult that the Scarecrow often stumbled over the yellow brick, which were here very uneven. Sometimes, indeed, they were broken or missing altogether, leaving holes that Toto jumped across and Dorothy walked around. As for the Scarecrow, having no brains he walked straight ahead, and so stepped into the holes and fell at full length on the hard bricks. It never hurt him, however, and Dorothy would pick him up and set him upon his feet again, while he joined her in laughing merrily at his own mishap.

The farms were not nearly so well cared for here as they were farther back. There were fewer houses and fewer fruit trees, and the farther they went the more dismal and lonesome the country became.

At noon they sat down by the roadside, near a little brook, and Dorothy opened her basket and got out some bread. She offered a piece to the Scarecrow, but he refused.

"I am never hungry," he said; "and it is a lucky thing I am not. For my mouth is only painted, and if I should cut a hole in it so I could eat, the straw I am stuffed with would come out, and that would spoil the shape of my head."

Dorothy saw at once that this was true, so she only nodded and went on eating her bread.

"Tell me something about yourself, and the country you came from," said the Scarecrow, when she had finished her dinner. So she told him all about Kansas, and how gray everything was there, and how the cyclone had carried her to this queer land of Oz. The Scarecrow listened carefully, and said,

"I cannot understand why you should wish to leave this beautiful country and go back to the dry, gray place you call Kansas."

"That is because you have no brains," answered the girl. "No matter how dreary and gray our homes are, we people of flesh and blood would rather live there than in

1. any other country, be it ever so beautiful.   There is no place like home."

The Scarecrow sighed.

"Of course I cannot understand it," he said.   "If your heads were stuffed with straw, like mine, you would probably all live in the beautiful places, and then Kansas would have no people at all.   It is fortunate for Kansas that you have brains."

"Won't you tell me a story, while we are resting?" asked the child.

The Scarecrow looked at her reproachfully, and answered,

"My life has been so short that I really know nothing whatever.   I was only made day before yesterday.   What happened in the world before that time is all unknown to me.   Luckily, when the farmer made my head, one of the first things he did was to paint my ears, so that I heard what was going on.   There was another Munchkin with him, and the first thing I heard was the farmer saying,

"'How do you like those ears?'

"'They aren't straight,' answered the other.

"'Never mind,' said the farmer; 'they are ears just the same,' which was true enough.

"'Now I'll make the eyes,' said the farmer.   So he painted my right eye, and as soon as it was finished I found myself looking at him and at everything around me with a

2. great deal of curiosity, for this was my first glimpse of the world.

1. *be it ever so beautiful. There is no place like home.* Baum appears to be playing with the famous sentiment of John Howard Payne's 1823 song "Home, Sweet Home": "Be it ever so humble, there's no place like home." Baum made a bad pun of this song in *The Emerald City of Oz* (1910) by calling a march played in the Tin Woodman's honor "There's No Plate like Tin" (p. 250). Baum's irony was apparently lost on the makers of the famous movie. Arthur Freed, assistant to the producer Mervyn LeRoy, was responsible for making "There's No Place Like Home" the theme of the 1939 MGM picture. He argued that "Dorothy is only motivated by one object in Oz; that is, to get back home to her Aunt Em, and every situation should be related to this main drive." He was adamant that Dorothy repeat "There's No Place Like Home" when she clicks her heels together three times. "The major fault we found [in the picture]," complained Howard Rushmore in *The Daily Worker* (August 18, 1939), "was the weak climax with the too obvious moral that little boys and girls should never leave their backyards; a moral that falls a trifle flat for no tot (or adult) doesn't wish for at least a roundtrip ticket to the land of Oz after seeing how attractive Mervyn LeRoy has made it." Salman Rushdie agreed. In his monograph on the picture, he argued that this "cutesy slogan" "is the least convincing idea in the film (it's one thing for Dorothy to want to get home, quite another that she can only do so by eulogizing the ideal state which Kansas so obviously is not)" (p. 14). But home is not the landscape but a condition. Margaret Hamilton, who played the Wicked Witch of the West, defined it in "There's No Place Like Oz" (*Children's Literature*, vol. 10, 1982) as "the place where we belong, where we are welcome, where there is love and understanding and acceptance waiting for us when we come. Home, where we can shed our cares and share our troubles and feel safe and protected."

2. *my first glimpse of the world.* "The problem of language aside," S. J. Sackett observed in "The Utopia of Oz," "it would be difficult to imagine a better description of the awakening of a new mind, the first initial marks upon the *tabula rasa*, than the following account told by the Scarecrow to Dorothy, of his early moments." Sackett interpreted this as Baum's answer to "the unchangeability of human nature."

> The key to the problem is epistemology. You must assume with [John] Locke that the mind at birth is a *tabula rasa*, an empty page; that there are no innate ideas, no Jungian archetypes, or other inherited memories. According to this theory the individual's environment will completely mold his personality, for he has no inherited psychological characteristics. Each experience he has will form his personality, little by little.

It has already been shown how the environment battered Aunt Em and Uncle Henry. Sackett likewise considered the process by which the Sawhorse comes to life in *The Marvelous Land of Oz* (1904, pp. 47–51) as "well worth reading as an account of the way one sensation after another marks the empty page of the mind at birth."

3. *the other a little bigger*. "Both Denslow and Neill," observed Gardner in Note 6 of *The Wizard of Oz and Who He Was*, "drew the Scarecrow with a larger left eye, showing a respect for the text of the Royal History that has not been shared by other Oz illustrators." When the Oz artist Dick Martin read this, he vowed to take better care in the future to adhere to Baum's text whenever he drew the Scarecrow. This emphasis on the left eye is one of several examples in Baum's writing of sinistrality, the preference of the left over the right parts of the body. There is no mystical or deep psychological reason for this: Baum himself was left-handed. When Ojo in *The Patchwork Girl of Oz* (1914) declares that he is unlucky because he is left-handed, the Tin Woodman slyly speaks for the author when he replies, "Many of our greatest men are that way" (p. 329).

"'That's a rather pretty eye,' remarked the Munchkin who was watching the farmer; 'blue paint is just the color for eyes.'

"'I think I'll make the other a little bigger,' said the farmer; and when the second eye was done I could see much better than before. Then he made my nose and my mouth; but I did not speak, because at that time I didn't know what a mouth was for. I had the fun of watching them make my body and my arms and legs; and when they fastened on my head, at last, I felt very proud, for I thought I was just as good a man as anyone.

"'This fellow will scare the crows fast enough,' said the farmer; 'he looks just like a man.'

"'Why, he is a man,' said the other, and I quite agreed with him. The farmer carried me under his arm to the cornfield, and set me up on a tall stick, where you found me. He and his friend soon after walked away and left me alone.

"I did not like to be deserted this way; so I tried to walk after them, but my feet would not touch the ground, and I was forced to stay on that pole. It was a lonely life to lead, for I had nothing to think of, having been made such a little while before. Many crows and other birds flew into the cornfield, but as soon as they saw me they flew away again, thinking I was a Munchkin; and this pleased me and made me feel that I was quite an important person. By and by an old crow flew near me, and after looking at me carefully he perched upon my shoulder and said,

"'I wonder if that farmer thought to fool me in this clumsy manner.   Any crow of sense could see that you are only stuffed with straw.' Then he hopped down at my feet and ate all the corn he wanted.   The other birds, seeing he was not harmed by me, came to eat the corn too, so in a short time there was a great flock of them about me.

"I felt sad at this, for it showed I was not such a good Scarecrow after all; but the old crow comforted me, saying: 'If you only had brains in your head you would be as good a man as any of them, and a better man than some of them.   Brains are the only things worth having in this world, no matter whether one is a crow or a man.'

"After the crows had gone I thought this over, and decided I would try hard to get some brains. By good luck, you came along and pulled me off the stake, and from what you say I am sure the great Oz will give me brains as soon as we get to the Emerald City."

"I hope so," said Dorothy, earnestly, "since you seem anxious to have them."

"Oh yes; I am anxious," returned the Scarecrow.   "It is such an uncomfortable feeling to know one is a fool."

4. *Brains are the only thing worth having in this world, whether one is a crow or a man.* Spoken like a true philosopher! Jack Zipes accurately observed in his notes to the 1998 Penguin Twentieth-Century Classics edition that "the Scarecrow will utter truisms, platitudes, and proverbs, indicating that he is more insightful than he thinks he is and much brighter than the others around him" (p. 368). He is also capable of a few Sam Goldwynisms ("Count me out!") or Yogi Berraisms ("It's *déjà vu* all over again!"), as below when he states the obvious: "If this road goes in, it must come out."

5. *as soon as we get to the Emerald City.* Baum relates a somewhat different version of this history in "The Scarecrow Tells a Fairy Tale to Children and Hears an Equally Marvelous True Story," one of the "Queer Visitors from the Marvelous Land of Oz" comic pages, which appeared in Sunday newspapers on November 27, 1904:

> You must know, my dears, that in the Land of Oz everything has life that can become of use by living. Now, I do not know of what use a live Scarecrow can be unless he serves to amuse children; but it is a fact that, as soon as the farmer had stuffed me into the shape of a man, and made me a head by using this excellent cotton sack, I began to realize that I was a part of the big world and had come to life.
>
> Of course, I could not see, nor hear, nor talk at first, but the farmer brought a paint pot and a brush, and upon the front surface of my head, where a face properly belongs, he began to paint. First he made this left eye, which you observe is a beautiful circle, with a dot in the center of it. The first object I saw with this eye was the farmer himself, and, you may be sure, I watched him carefully as he painted my other eye. I have always considered that man an artist; otherwise he could not have made me so handsome. My right eye is even finer than the left; and, after making it, the farmer gave me this exquisite nose, with which I gathered the scent of the wild flowers and the new-mown hay and the furrows of sweet and fertile earth. Next my mouth was manufactured, so excellently shaped that I have never ceased to be proud of it; but I could not then speak, for I knew no words by which to express my feelings. Then followed these lovely ears, which completed my features. And now I heard the loud breathing of the farmer, who was fat and inclined to asthma, and the twittering songs of the birds and the whisper of the winds as they glided across the meadows, and the chatter of the field mice—and many other pleasant and delightful sounds.
>
> Indeed, I now believed myself fully the equal of the man who had made me; but the idea was soon dispelled when the farmer sat me upon the stout pole in the cornfield. And then walked away with his paint pot and left me. I tried at once to follow, but my feet would not touch the earth, and so I could not escape from the pole.
>
> Near me was a stile, and people crossing the fields would stop at the stile and converse; so that by listening to them I soon learned how to speak properly. I had a fine view of the country from my elevation, and plenty of time to examine it curiously. Moreover, the crows often came and perched upon my head and shoulders and talked of the big world they had seen; so my education was unusually broad and diverse. I longed to see the big world of Oz for myself, and my real mission in life—to scare the crows—seemed to be a failure. The crows even grew fond of me and spoke to me pleasantly while they dug up the grains of the corn the farmer had planted.

His whole life changed when a little girl from Kansas took pity on him and lifted him off his pole.

6. *to know one is a fool.* Socrates argued that if he seemed to be wiser than the average man, it was because he knew his own ignorance. In a revision of this chapter, titled "The Scarecrow's Story," that appears in *The Juvenile Speaker* (1910), Baum added the following:

> I realize at present that I'm only an imitation of a man, and I assure you it's a very uncomfortable feeling to know one is a fool. It seems to me that a body is only a machine for brains to direct, and those who have no brains themselves are liable to be directed by the brains of others.
>
> But I may be wrong. I'm only a Scarecrow, you know. (p. 76)

"Well," said the girl, "let us go." And she handed the basket to the Scarecrow.

There were no fences at all by the road side now, and the land was rough and untilled. Towards evening they came to a great forest, where the trees grew so big and close together that their branches met over the road of yellow brick. It was almost dark under the trees, for the branches shut out the daylight; but the travellers did not stop, and went on into the forest.

"If this road goes in, it must come out," said the Scarecrow, "and as the Emerald City is at the other end of the road, we must go wherever it leads us."

"Anyone would know that," said Dorothy.

"Certainly; that is why I know it," returned the Scarecrow. "If it required brains to figure it out, I never should have said it."

After an hour or so the light faded away, and they found themselves stumbling along in the darkness. Dorothy could not see at all, but Toto could, for some dogs see very well in the dark; and the Scarecrow declared he could see as well as by day. So she took hold of his arm, and managed to get along fairly well.

"If you see any house, or any place where we can pass the night," she said, "you must tell me; for it is very uncomfortable walking in the dark."

Soon after the Scarecrow stopped.

"I see a little cottage at the right of us," he said, "built of logs and branches. Shall we go there?"

"Yes, indeed;" answered the child. "I am all tired out."

So the Scarecrow led her through the trees until they reached the cottage, and Dorothy entered and found a bed of dried leaves in one corner. She lay down at once, and with Toto beside her soon fell into a sound sleep. The Scarecrow, who was never tired, stood up in another corner and waited patiently until morning came.

7.

7. *the cottage*. Dorothy and the Scarecrow meet the apparent owner of this vacant house in the next chapter. It lacks a conventional bed, for he, like the Scarecrow, never sleeps.

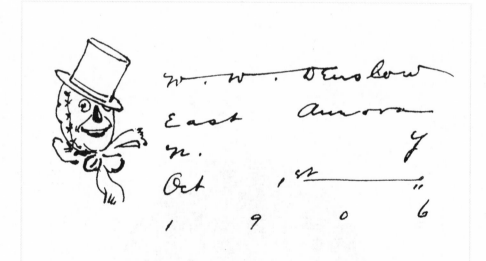

Denslow drew this sketch of the Scarecrow while visiting the Roycroft Shops, East Aurora, New York, 1906.
Courtesy Justin G. Schiller.

Chapter V.
The Rescue of
the Tin Woodman

1. *to be made of flesh.* This philosophical discussion beautifully sets up the discovery of a man of tin in the forest.
Baum combined portions of the previous and present chapters to form "An Adventure in Oz," published in *L. Frank
Baum's Juvenile Speaker* (1910) revised as follows:

> Presently she brought a cup of water from the brook and
> drank it.
>
> "You people of flesh and blood," remarked the
> Scarecrow, who had been watching her, "take a good deal
> of trouble to keep alive. You must eat and drink and sleep,
> and those are three things that a straw man need not worry
> about. However, you have brains, and it is worth a lot of
> bother to be able to think properly."
>
> "Yes," said Dorothy; "take it altogether, I'm glad I'm not
> straw." (pp. 25–26)

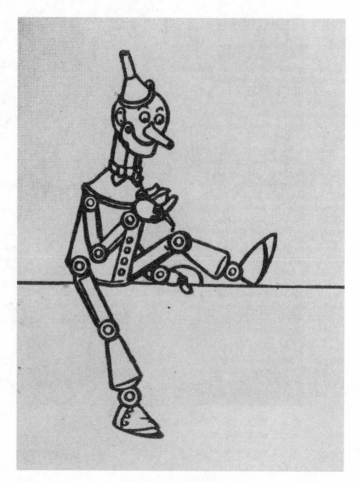

This picture of the Tin Woodman first appeared on the back
cover of *The New Wizard of Oz*
(Indianapolis: Bobbs-Merrill, 1903).
Courtesy Willard Carroll Collection.

When

DOROTHY awoke the sun was shining through the trees and Toto had long been out chasing birds and squirrels. She sat up and looked around her. There was the Scarecrow, still standing patiently in his corner, waiting for her.

"We must go and search for water," she said to him.

"Why do you want water?" he asked.

"To wash my face clean after the dust of the road, and to drink, so the dry bread will not stick in my throat."

"It must be inconvenient to be made of flesh," said the Scarecrow, thoughtfully; "for you must sleep, and eat and

1.

2. *a man made entirely of tin*. Another example of whimsical incongruity. Baum told the Philadelphia *North American* (October 3, 1904) that he named the second of Dorothy's companions the Tin Woodman "because of the oddity of a woodman made of tin." Harry Neal Baum had another story of how his father came to think of the Tin Woodman. Sometime before he began writing children's stories, Baum was asked to set up of a hardware-store window. "He wanted to create something eye-catching," his son told Joseph Haas for the article "A Little Bit of 'Oz' in Northern Indiana" (Indianapolis *Times*, May 3, 1965), "so he made a torso out of a washboiler, bolted stovepipe arms and legs to it and used the underside of a saucepan for a face. He topped it with a funnel hat and what would become the inspiration for Tin Woodman was born." Tin men also served as signs for nineteenth-century American tinsmith shops.

The Tin Woodman is only one of many mechanical men who clank through Baum's books. "One of Baum's major contributions to the tradition of the fantasy tale," explained Nye in *The Wizard of Oz and Who He Was*, "is his recognition of the inherent wonder of the machine, his perception of the magic of *things* in themselves. . . . By transforming the talking beasts of ancient folk tales into talking machines, Baum grafted twentieth century technology to the fairy tale tradition. The useful, friendly, companionable creatures of Oz became part of the child's family life, much as the automobile was becoming integrated into contemporary American society" (pp. 7–8). He had faith in this new technology, for, as Nye pointed out, "At no time did Baum allow the machines of Oz to get out of control" (p. 8). Other notable examples of these mechanical men are the Cast-Iron Man in *A New Wonderland* (1900), Mr. Split in *Dot and Tot of Merryland* (1901), and his not-too-distant relatives Tik-Tok (whose prototype is the clockwork man of *Father Goose, His Book*, 1899) and the Giant-with-the-Hammer, both built by Smith & Tinker in *Ozma of Oz* (1907).

drink.   However, you have brains, and it is worth a lot of bother to be able to think properly."

They left the cottage and walked through the trees until they found a little spring of clear water, where Dorothy drank and bathed and ate her breakfast.   She saw there was not much bread left in the basket, and the girl was thankful the Scarecrow did not have to eat anything, for there was scarcely enough for herself and Toto for the day.

When she had finished her meal, and was about to go back to the road of yellow brick, she was startled to hear a deep groan near by.

"What was that?" she asked, timidly.

"I cannot imagine," replied the Scarecrow; "but we can go and see."

Just then another groan reached their ears, and the sound seemed to come from behind them.   They turned and walked through the forest a few steps, when Dorothy discovered something shining in a ray of sunshine that fell between the trees.   She ran to the place, and then stopped short, with a cry of surprise.

One of the big trees had been partly chopped through, and standing beside it, with an uplifted axe in his hands, was a man made entirely of tin.   His head and arms and legs were jointed upon his body, but he stood perfectly motionless, as if he could not stir at all.

Dorothy looked at him in amazement, and so did the

3. *rusted*. Technically, only iron rusts, but other metals during corrosion are commonly said to "rust." Aleksandr Volkov, associate professor at the Moscow Institute of Nonferrous Metals and Gold, who did the first Russian "translation" of *The Wizard of Oz* in 1939, naturally recognized this error and renamed Baum's character Zheleznyi Drovosek, the Iron Woodcutter.

A Metropolitan Life Insurance advertisement in *National Geographic* (November 1954) likened the rusting of the Tin Woodman's joints to arthritis, the stiffening of the human body joints. The ad stressed proper medical care to keep them "flexible and workable." Sometimes the pain is so great that they have to be replaced with metal ones by surgery much in the same way parts of the Tin Woodman's body became tin.

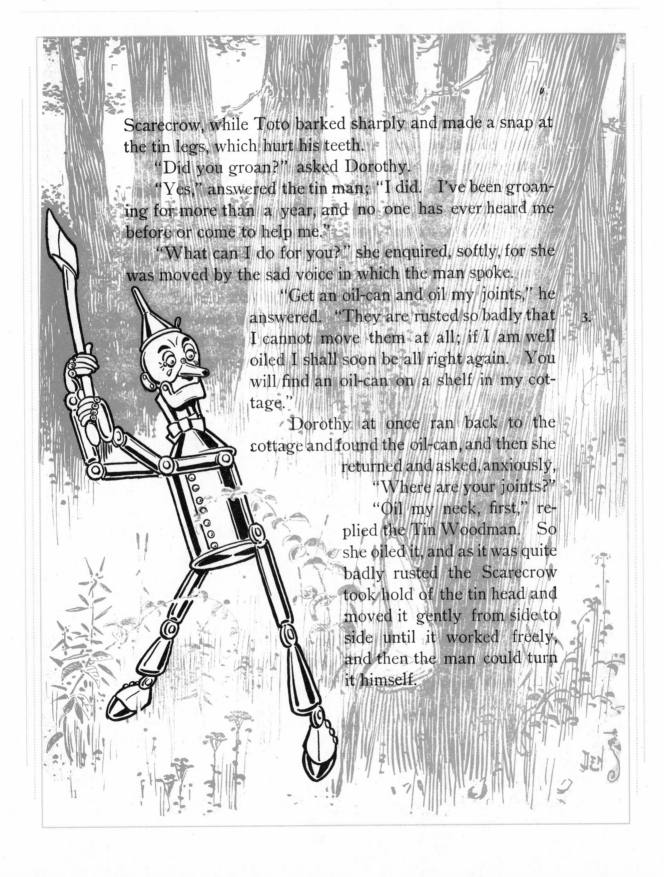

Scarecrow, while Toto barked sharply and made a snap at the tin legs, which hurt his teeth.

"Did you groan?" asked Dorothy.

"Yes," answered the tin man; "I did. I've been groaning for more than a year, and no one has ever heard me before or come to help me."

"What can I do for you?" she enquired, softly, for she was moved by the sad voice in which the man spoke.

"Get an oil-can and oil my joints," he answered. "They are rusted so badly that I cannot move them at all; if I am well oiled I shall soon be all right again. You will find an oil-can on a shelf in my cottage."

Dorothy at once ran back to the cottage and found the oil-can, and then she returned and asked, anxiously,

"Where are your joints?"

"Oil my neck, first," replied the Tin Woodman. So she oiled it, and as it was quite badly rusted the Scarecrow took hold of the tin head and moved it gently from side to side until it worked freely, and then the man could turn it himself.

"Now oil the joints in my arms," he said. And Dorothy oiled them and the Scarecrow bent them carefully until they were quite free from rust and as good as new.

The Tin Woodman gave a sigh of satisfaction and lowered his axe, which he leaned against the tree.

"This is a great comfort," he said. "I have been holding that axe in the air ever since I rusted, and I'm glad to be able to put it down at last. Now, if you will oil the joints of my legs, I shall be all right once more."

So they oiled his legs until he could move them freely; and he thanked them again and again for his release, for he seemed a very polite creature, and very grateful.

"I might have stood there always if you had not come along," he said; "so you have certainly saved my life. How did you happen to be here?"

"We are on our way to the Emerald City, to see the great Oz," she answered, "and we stopped at your cottage to pass the night."

"Why do you wish to see Oz?" he asked.

"I want him to send me back to Kansas; and the Scarecrow wants him to put a few brains into his head," she replied.

The Tin Woodman appeared to think deeply for a moment. Then he said:

"Do you suppose Oz could give me a heart?"

"Why, I guess so," Dorothy answered; "it would be as easy as to give the Scarecrow brains."

"True," the Tin Woodman returned. "So, if you will allow me to join your party, I will also go to the Emerald City and ask Oz to help me."

"Come along," said the Scarecrow, heartily; and Dorothy added that she would be pleased to have his company. So the Tin Woodman shouldered his axe and they all passed through the forest until they came to the road that was paved with yellow brick.

The Tin Woodman had asked Dorothy to put the oil-can in her basket. "For," he said, "if I should get caught in the rain, and rust again, I would need the oil-can badly."

It was a bit of good luck to have their new comrade join the party, for soon after they had begun their journey again they came to a place where the trees and branches grew so thick over the road that the travellers could not pass. But the Tin Woodman set to work with his axe and chopped so well that soon he cleared a passage for the entire party.

Dorothy was thinking so earnestly as they walked along that she did not notice when the Scarecrow stumbled into a hole and rolled over to the side of the road. Indeed, he was obliged to call to her to help him up again.

"Why didn't you walk around the hole?" asked the Tin Woodman.

"I don't know enough," replied the Scarecrow, cheerfully. "My head is stuffed with straw, you know, and that is why I am going to Oz to ask him for some brains."

4.

4. *I don't know enough.* Here is the first opportunity the Scarecrow has to use his intelligence; he fails dismally. But he learns by doing. Previously he has had no experiences on which to base his judgment. He has had no memory, no mark on his *tabula rasa*, to remind him of how to act. A child must fall down once in a while and get up and go on. This mistake will act as a lesson to the Scarecrow, for from now on he will recall this experience to avoid a recurrence. It will encourage him to use his newfound judgment in other situations.

5. *the son of a woodman.* Denslow draws the Tin Woodman with his tin bow tie, tall tin collar, tin spats, and jauntily placed funnel hat as more urbane and dapper than the usual lumberjack. The Boston *Beacon* (September 29, 1900) said in its review of *The Wonderful Wizard of Oz* that the Tin Woodman looked like Kaiser Wilhelm of Germany. His cosmopolitan appearance makes a fine contrast with the country-bumpkinish Scarecrow. "I made twenty-five sketches of those two monkeys before I was satisfied with them," Denslow recalled. "You may well believe that there was a great deal of evolution before I got that golf ball in the Scarecrow's ear or the funnel on the Tin Man's head. I experimented and tried out all sorts of straw waistcoats and sheet-iron cravats before I was satisfied" ("Denslow: Denver Artist, Originator of Scarecrow and Tin Man," Denver *Republican*, September 4, 1904). The funnel hat was probably Denslow's invention, for Baum never mentions it in this story. But he does in the later Oz books. Denslow may have picked it up from medieval and Renaissance painting, where simpletons wear funnels on their heads to indicate their stupidity.

6. *When I grew up.* This does not agree with subsequent knowledge of aging and death in Oz. The following account appears in *The Tin Woodman of Oz* (1918):

> Oz was not always a fairyland, I am told. Once it was much like other lands, except it was shut in by a dreadful desert of sandy wastes that lay all around it, thus preventing its people from all contact with the rest of the world. Seeing this isolation, the fairy band of Queen Lurline, passing over Oz while on a journey, enchanted the country and so made it a Fairyland. And Queen Lurline left one of her fairies to rule this enchanted Land of Oz, and then passed on and forgot all about it.
>
> From that moment on no one in Oz ever died. Those who were old remained old; those who were young and strong did not change as years passed them by; the children remained children always, and played and romped to their hearts' content, while all the babies lived in their cradles and were tenderly cared for and never grew up. So people

in Oz stopped counting how old they were in years, for years made no difference in their appearance and could not alter their station. They did not get sick, so there were no doctors among them. Accidents might happen to some, on rare occasions, it is true, and while no one could die naturally, as other people do, it was possible that one might be totally destroyed. Such incidents, however, were very unusual, and so seldom was there anything to worry over that the Oz people were as happy and contented as can be. (pp. 156–57)

This enchantment affected those from the outside world in the same way, "so Dorothy . . . seemed just the same sweet little girl she had been when first she came to this delightful fairyland." And since Dorothy never aged, Baum could extend the series indefinitely. This new concept of Oz may have been merely wish fulfillment on Baum's part, for when he wrote it he was getting older and not in the best of health. The kingdom was quite different under the Wizard's reign. Perhaps when the rightful ruler of Oz, like the Fisher King, was away, the country regressed to its preenchanted state. See Note 8 below.

7. *a wood-chopper.* His name is Nick Chopper, before and after he became a man of tin, as disclosed in *The Marvelous Land of Oz* (1904, p. 117). The name came from the 1902 musical extravaganza, in which Nick (from "Niccolo") Chopper sang an interpolated song, "Niccolo's Piccolo." David C. Montgomery portrayed him in that production, and Oliver Hardy in the same role was a highlight of the 1925 Chadwick silent picture of *The Wizard of Oz*. Of course, the best-known Tin Woodman is Jack Haley in the 1939 MGM musical. The tap dancer Tiger Haynes played him on Broadway in *The Wiz* in 1975, and a nimble Nipsey Russell took the part in the 1978 movie version.

8. *father died.* "The many references in this book to the deaths of men and beasts are hard to reconcile with our later knowledge concerning the extreme difficulty of 'destroying' any living beings in Oz," commented Gardner in Note 7 of *The Wizard of Oz and Who He Was.* Of course, all that changes when Ozma is restored to the throne of Oz. "The image of Death occurs again and again," observed Justin G. Schiller in his afterword to the 1985 Pennyroyal edition of *The Wizard of Oz*, "usually in relation to protecting innocent creatures from savage or malevolent forces: Kalidahs fall upon jagged rocks, the wildcat who chased the queen of the field mice is decapitated" (pp. 263–64). See also Chapter 9, Note 1. Even Baum is not sure how far the power of protection extends in the land of Oz after Ozma takes the throne. He admits in *The Magic of Oz* (1919) that "it is doubtful whether those who come to Oz from the out-

"Oh, I see;" said the Tin Woodman. "But, after all, brains are not the best things in the world."

"Have you any?" enquired the Scarecrow.

"No, my head is quite empty," answered the Woodman; "but once I had brains, and a heart also; so, having tried them both, I should much rather have a heart."

"And why is that?" asked the Scarecrow.

"I will tell you my story, and then you will know."

So, while they were walking through the forest, the Tin Woodman told the following story:

"I was born the son of a woodman who chopped down trees in the forest and sold the wood for a living. When I grew up I too became a wood-chopper, and after my father died I took care of my old mother as long as she lived. Then I made up my mind that instead of living alone I would marry, so that I might not become lonely.

"There was one of the Munchkin girls who was so beautiful that I soon grew to love her with all my heart. She, on her part, promised to marry me as soon as I could earn enough money to build a better house for her; so I set to work harder than ever. But the girl lived with an old woman who did not want her to marry anyone, for she

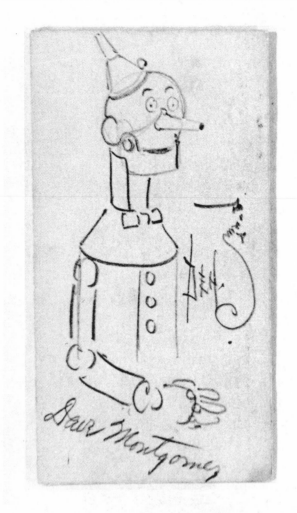

Sketch of Dave Montgomery as the Tin Woodman
drawn by Denslow and signed by the actor, 1902.
*Courtesy the W. W. Denslow Papers, Special Collections, Syracuse
University Library.*

side world . . . will live forever or cannot be injured. Even Ozma is not sure about this, and so the guests of Ozma from other lands are always carefully protected from any danger, so as to be on the safe side" (p. 83). Jack Snow wrote a clever story around this dilemma, "Murder in Oz," which describes the "death" of Ozma and its aftermath. Originally written for *Ellery Queen's Mystery Magazine*, it was first serialized in *The Baum Bugle* (October–Christmas 1959).

9. *one of the Munchkin girls.* Baum called her Beatrice Fairfax in the first draft of the *Wizard of Oz* play he submitted to Fred Hamlin. (See also Chapter 22, Note 6.) But

when the show was finally produced in Chicago in 1902, she became Cynthia Cynch, the Lady Lunatic, a burlesque of Shakespeare's Ophelia, gone mad over the loss of her lover Niccolo Chopper the Tin Woodman. (One of the women who played her during the play's long run, Allene Crater, captured the heart of the Scarecrow, Fred Stone, and married him.) When the Tin Woodman finally resolves to seek and marry his long-lost love in *The Tin Woodman of Oz* (1918), her name is given as Nimmee Aimee.

10. *to love her.* Another theme Baum came to believe should be kept out of his "modernized" fairy tales was romance. "Love, as depicted in literature," he said in the St. Louis *Republic* (May 30, 1903), "is a threadbare and unsatisfactory topic which children can comprehend neither in its esoteric nor exoteric meaning. Therefore it has no place in their storybooks." (John Ruskin had much the same opinion, writing in his introduction to an 1868 edition of *German Popular Tales* that the word "love," "in the modern child-story, is too often restrained and darkened into the hieroglyph of an evil mystery, troubling the sweet peace of youth with premature gleams of uncomprehended passion, and flitting shadows of unrecognized sin.") But when Baum wrote *The Wizard of Oz*, he had not yet eliminated all romance from his children's books. Besides the love of the Tin Woodman and the girl, there is the marriage of Gayelette and Quelala in Chapter 14. There are other love stories in *Tik-Tok of Oz* (1914) and *The Scarecrow of Oz* (1915), because these stories were based respectively on a musical extravaganza and a motion picture that were aimed at adults as well as at children. Baum knew he had to be cautious in his treatment of them. "In *The Scarecrow* I introduced a slightly novel theme, for me, in the love and tribulations of Pon the gardener's son and the Princess Gloria," he admitted to his publishers on January 17, 1916. "It smacked a bit of the Andersen fairy tales [although it came from the Grimms' "Iron John"] and I watched its effect upon my readers. They accepted it gleefully, with all the rest, it being well within their comprehension." Baum treats the Tin Woodman's quest for his lost love in *The Tin Woodman of Oz* (1918) in a more unconventional and whimsical way than he does the romances in those other books.

11. *an old woman.* Baum does not mention this old woman in his second script for the *Wizard of Oz* extravaganza, but suggests that the Tin Woodman's beloved is the servant of the Wicked Witch of the East. Having declared, "No Love-making allowed in these Dominions," the evil hag discovers the lovers in each other's arms and turns him into a tin man to prevent him from marrying the girl. "An old woman" is never mentioned in *The Tin Woodman of Oz* either, in which the Tin Woodman recalls a slightly different history from that in *The Wizard of Oz*. The girl actually worked for the Wicked Witch of the East, who, not wishing to lose her servant to the young woodman, enchanted his axe, which cut off his limbs. Each part was then replaced by the tinsmith. Furious that he survived each of these mishaps, the witch finally made the axe chop his body in half. And not content even with that, she "rushed up and seized the axe and chopped my body into several small pieces" (p. 26). But the faithful girl dutifully gathered them up for the tinsmith, who now made him a new body out of metal. Finally the Witch had his head chopped off and ran off with it. This head reappears with startling results in Chapter 18 of *The Tin Woodman of Oz*.

This picture of the Wicked Witch of the East comes from one
of the six panels of a lithographed wallpaper frieze of
characters from the musical extravaganza *The Wizard
of Oz*, drawn by W. W. Denslow, c. 1910.
Courtesy Willard Carroll Collection.

was so lazy she wished the girl to remain with her and do the cooking and the housework. So the old woman went to the wicked Witch of the East, and promised her two sheep and a cow if she would prevent the marriage. Thereupon the wicked Witch enchanted my axe, and when I was chopping away at my best one day, for I was anxious to get the new house and my wife as soon as possible, the axe slipped all at once and cut off my left leg.

"This at first seemed a great misfortune, for I knew a one-legged man could not do very well as a wood-chopper.

12., 13. So I went to a tin-smith and had him make me a new leg out of tin. The leg worked very well, once I was used to it; but my action angered the wicked Witch of the East, for she had promised the old woman I should not marry the pretty Munchkin girl. When I began chopping again my axe slipped and cut off my right leg. Again I went to the tinner, and again he made me a leg out of tin. After this the enchanted axe cut off my arms, one after the other; but, nothing daunted, I had them replaced with tin ones. The wicked Witch then made the axe slip and cut

14. off my head, and at first I thought that was the end of me. But the tinner happened to come along, and he made me a new head out of tin.

"I thought I had beaten the wicked Witch then, and I worked harder than ever; but I little knew how cruel my enemy could be. She thought of a new way to kill my love for the beautiful Munchkin maiden, and made my axe

12. *tin-smith*. He is called Ku-Klip in *The Tin Woodman of Oz* (p. 22). The Tin Woodman's fate reminded Mary Devlin in "The Great Cosmic Fairy Tale" (*Gnosis Magazine,* Fall 1996) of the story of the Celtic hero Nuada, who loses a hand in combat, which the Divine Smith replaces with a silver one. One of the most unusual and yet fascinating episodes in all the Oz stories is the Tin Woodman's return to the tin-smith's shop, where he encounters his former head. (It may have been suggested by one of Baum's favorite stories, the more whimsical "The King's Head and the Purple Dragon" in *A New Wonderland*, 1900.) In addition to building the Tin Woodman, Ku-Klip constructs Captain Fyter, the Tin Soldier, who also falls in love with the Munchkin maiden and suffers the same fate as Nick Chopper. Gardner saw in this Ozian *Doppelgänger* "profound metaphysical questions concerning personal identity." These are increased when one considers that Baum originally wanted to call the book "The Twin Tin Woodman of Oz." Ku-Klip, like Dr. Frankenstein, tries to patch together a flesh-and-blood human being, but with disastrous results. The unsociable Chopfyte, made of the spare parts of both Nick Chopper and Captain Fyter, is a man who is literally "always someone else." Nye in *The Wizard of Oz and Who He Was* (1957) interpreted the creation of this unpleasant individual as Baum's commentary "on techno-logical overdevelopment, which may undo the unwary in America as it does in Oz" (p. 8).

13. *a new leg out of tin.* Several readers have com-pared the reconstruction of the Tin Woodman's body with Plutarch's parable of the Ship of Theseus.

Martin Gardner recounted it in "*The Tin Woodman of Oz,* An Appreciation" (*The Baum Bugle*, Fall 1996, p. 15): "Over decades, parts of a ship are gradually replaced by new parts. This occurs in such small increments that sailors never doubt they are living on he same ship. Imagine that the old parts are preserved and later reassembled. Which is now the 'real' ship?" Gardner wondered if Baum's interest in Theosophy and reincarnation might have affected what Gardner calls the "Tin Woodman problem": "If in our next incarnation we have a completely different body and brain, in what sense are we the same person who lived earlier?" Gareth B. Matthews pointed out in *Philosophy and the Young Child* (Cambridge, Mass.: Harvard University Press, 1980, p. 60) that Baum adds two important elements not linked to the Ship of Theseus: the replacement of tin for flesh, rather than like for like; and his memory of what he had once been. Technically, the Tin Woodman is not a robot: He is a *living* being, though not of flesh and blood. Paul M. Abrahm and Stuart Kenter said in "Tik-Tok and the Three Laws of Robotics" (*Science Fiction Studies*, March 1978) that after the tinsmith, "a combined internist and prosthetic engineer," got through with him, the woodman "was, inside and out . . . a veritable showcase of successful spare-part surgery—the ultimate in cyborgs." The Tin Woodman of Oz is the first bionic man. In preparing a wood engraving for this chapter in the 1985 Pennyroyal Press edition of *The Wizard of Oz*, Barry Moser cleverly followed the very same process in his manufacture of the Tin Woodman: "I began with a human figure and then 'tinned' it and made it mechanical" (May 16, *Forty-seven Days to Oz*).

14. *the end of me.* The Tin Woodman explains in *The Tin Woodman of Oz* (1918) why it was *not* the end of him: "In the Land of Oz . . . no one can ever be killed. A man with a wooden leg or a tin leg is still the same man; and, as I lost parts of my meat body by degrees, I always remained the same person as in the beginning, even though in the end I was all tin and no meat" (pp. 29–30).

slip again, so that it cut right through my body, splitting me into two halves. Once more the tinner came to my help and made me a body of tin, fastening my tin arms

15.
16. and legs and head to it, by means of joints, so that I could move around as well as ever. But, alas! I had now no heart, so that I lost all my love for the Munchkin girl, and did

17. not care whether I married her or not. I suppose she is still living with the old woman, waiting for me to come after her.

"My body shone so brightly in the sun that I felt very proud of it and it did not matter now if my axe slipped, for it could not cut me. There was only one danger—that my joints would rust; but I kept an oil-can in my cottage and took care to oil myself whenever I needed it. However, there came a day when I forgot to do this, and, being

18.

caught in a rainstorm, before I thought of the danger my joints had rusted, and I was left to stand in the woods until you came to help me. It was a terrible thing to undergo, but during the year I stood there I had time to think that the greatest loss I had known was the loss of my heart. While I was in love I was the happiest man on earth; but no one can love who has not a

15. *I could move around as well as ever.* Being entirely made of tin has its advantages. "I was a much better man than ever," he recalls in *The Tin Woodman of Oz*, "for my body could not ache or pain me, and I was so beautiful and bright that I had no need of clothing. Clothing is always a nuisance, because it soils and tears and has to be replaced; but my tin body only needs to be oiled and polished" (p. 26).

16. *I had now no heart.* Baum may well be speaking for himself when he has the Tin Woodman say, "While I was in love I was the happiest man on earth." Maud Gage Baum was his first and only love, and he dedicated his most important book to her, *The Wonderful Wizard of Oz*. Henry M. Littlefield offered in "The Wizard of Oz: Parable on Populism" (*American Quarterly*, Spring 1964) a prosaic interpretation of the Tin Woodman's story. It is no more than "a Populist view of evil eastern influences on honest labor." By replacing his flesh with tin, "eastern witchcraft dehumanized a simple laborer so that the faster and better he worked the more quickly he became a kind of machine." But the Wicked Witch does not want him to work at all! She does not turn him into a machine to make him labor better and harder. She wants to destroy him and his love for the girl. Littlefield's attempt to explain *The Wizard of Oz* in terms of the times in which it was written often strains for dubious historical allusions. "A fairy tale is not an allegory," insisted Scottish author George MacDonald in "The Fantastic Imagination" in *A Dish of Orts* (1893). "He must be an artist indeed who can, in any mode, produce a strict allegory that is not a weariness to the spirit." It is pointless to try to restrict Baum's broad use of metaphor to a Populist manifesto. All the pieces do not fit neatly into a coherent political allegory. Baum was too wise for that.

17. *did not care whether I married her or not.* Ironically, she now loved him even more than ever. According to *The Tin Woodman of Oz*, she informed him that "you will make the best husband any girl could have. I shall not be obliged to cook for you, for now you do not eat; I shall not have to make your bed, for tin does not tire or require sleep; when we go to a dance, you will not get weary before the music stops and say you want to go home. All day long, while you are chopping wood in the forest, I shall be able to amuse myself in my own way—a privilege few wives enjoy. There is no temper in your new head, so you will not get angry with me. Finally, I shall take pride in being the wife of the only live Tin Woodman in all the world!" He proudly concludes that this speech proves that the girl "was as wise as she was brave and beautiful" (p. 29).

18. *a rainstorm.* Was the Wicked Witch of the West responsible for this shower? Witches have traditionally been blamed for severe changes in the weather. In the 1959 revision of his Russian "translation" of *The Wizard of Oz*, Aleksandr Volkov has the Wicked Witch of the East conjure up the storm which brings Elli (Dorothy) to the Magic Land (Oz).

19.

20.

heart, and so I am resolved to ask Oz to give me one. If he does, I will go back to the Munchkin maiden and marry her."

Both Dorothy and the Scarecrow had been greatly interested in the story of the Tin Woodman, and now they knew why he was so anxious to get a new heart.

"All the same," said the Scarecrow, "I shall ask for brains instead of a heart; for a fool would not know what to do with a heart if he had one."

21.

"I shall take the heart," returned the Tin Woodman; "for brains do not make one happy, and happiness is the best thing in the world."

22.

Dorothy did not say anything, for she was puzzled to know which of her two friends was right, and she decided if she could only get back to Kansas and Aunt Em it did not matter so much whether the Woodman had no brains and the Scarecrow no heart, or each got what he wanted.

What worried her most was that the bread was nearly gone, and another meal for herself and Toto would empty the basket. To be sure neither the Woodman nor the Scarecrow ever ate anything, but she was not made of tin nor straw, and could not live unless

23.

she was fed.

19. *to ask Oz to give me one*. That a man of cold, hollow metal should desire a soft and tender heart is another case of whimsical irony in the story. The Tin Woodman embodies the Romantic rebellion against the Industrial Age. He cannot love because he has been turned into a machine himself; only by getting back in touch with that human part of him he has lost, his heart, can he be whole again. Marc Barasch in "The Healing Road to Oz" (*Yoga Journal,* November/December 1991) viewed the Tin Woodman's history, more than that of any of the others in the story, as a metaphor for that of many of his patients: "a deep split between a tinny outer persona and an unheard inner self; an investment of all emotional energy in outer objects—relationships, careers—leaving a hollowness within; and a physical catastrophe that paradoxically awakens them to the healing power of their own authentic being."

20. *marry her*. Baum added some puns to this conversation when he revised the chapter as "The Heart of a Man of Tin" in *L. Frank Baum's Juvenile Speaker* (1910):

> "Perhaps," said Dorothy, "she won't care very much for a tin husband."
>
> "Perhaps not," sighed the tin man; "yet I am brighter than most husbands, and am considered a polished gentleman." (p. 38)

Not until the twelfth Oz book, *The Tin Woodman of Oz* (1918), does he attempt to fulfill his promise to marry the girl.

21. *best thing in the world*. This dispute between the Scarecrow and the Tin Woodman brings to mind a similar discussion in Plato's dialogue "Charmides": Socrates speaks of a dream he has had of universal knowledge, but he then reverts to the opinion that knowledge does not bring happiness.

22. *which of her two friends was right*. Dorothy is perplexed because she is confronted with the ancient philosophical question of having to choose between the dictates of the rational mind and those of the emotional heart. Her two companions present the opposing views of the Age of Reason and the Romantic Movement. "Together they symbolize inner unity of body and soul, the complete man in Aristotelian terms," noted Justin G. Schiller in his afterword to the 1985 Pennyroyal edition of *The Wonderful Wizard of Oz*, "perhaps also the passing from adolescence into adulthood" (p. 265). This debate reminded John Algeo in "*The Wizard of Oz*: The Perilous Journey" (*The American Theosophist*, October 1986) of H. P. Blavatsky's "The Two Paths" in *The Voice of the Silence* (1889), in which she compares the intellectual Doctrine of the Eye to the compassionate Doctrine of the Heart. Baum offers a wise compromise: At the end of *The Marvelous Land of Oz* (1904), the Scarecrow and the Tin Woodman vow never to part. They still bicker about which is better, brain or heart. But Princess Ozma wisely concludes, "You are both rich, my friends, and your riches are the only riches worth having—the riches of content!"

23. *she was fed*. Dorothy's response is just like a child's. Her solution is purely practical: So long as she has something to eat, she will let others argue over the finer points of philosophy. Metaphysics does not feed bellies. Baum implies that Dorothy need not worry, for she already has a brain and a heart—in the persons of the Scarecrow and the Tin Woodman—to guide her. In regard to this discussion, Martin Gardner wondered in his introduction to the 1960 Dover edition of *The Wonderful Wizard of Oz* if T. S. Eliot had partly in mind the Tin Woodman and the Scarecrow of Oz when he wrote in "The Hollow Men," "We are the stuffed men/We are the hollow men."

Chapter VI.
The Cowardly
Lion.

ALL THIS TIME DOROTHY and her companions had been walking through the thick woods. The road was still paved with yellow brick, but these were much covered by dried branches and dead leaves from the trees, and the walking was not at all good.

There were few birds in this part of the forest, for birds love the open country where there is plenty of sunshine; but now and then there came a deep growl from some wild animal hidden among the trees. These sounds made the little girl's heart beat fast, for she did not know what made them; but Toto knew, and he walked close to Dorothy's side, and did not even bark in return.

"How long will it be," the child asked of the Tin Woodman, "before we are out of the forest?"

"I cannot tell," was the answer, "for I have never been to the Emerald City.   But my father went there once, when I was a boy, and he said it was a long journey through a dangerous country, although nearer to the city where Oz dwells the country is beautiful.   But I am not afraid so long as I have my oil-can, and nothing can hurt the Scarecrow, while you bear upon your forehead the mark of the good Witch's kiss, and that will protect you from harm."

"But Toto!" said the girl, anxiously; "what will protect him?"

"We must protect him ourselves, if he is in danger," replied the Tin Woodman.

Just as he spoke there came from the forest a terrible roar, and the next moment a great Lion bounded into the road.   With one blow of his paw he sent the Scarecrow spining over and over to the edge of the road, and then he struck at the Tin Woodman with his sharp claws. But, to the Lion's surprise, he could make no impression on the tin, although the Woodman fell over in the road and lay still.

Little Toto, now that he had an enemy to face, ran barking toward the Lion, and the great beast had opened his mouth to bite the dog, when Dorothy, fearing Toto would be killed, and heedless of danger, rushed forward and slapped the Lion upon his nose as hard as she could, while she cried out:

1.

"Don't you dare to bite Toto! You ought to be ashamed of yourself, a big beast like you, to bite a poor little dog!"

"I didn't bite him," said the Lion, as he rubbed his nose with his paw where Dorothy had hit it.

"No, but you tried to," she retorted. "You are nothing but a big coward."

2.

"I know it," said the Lion, hanging his head in shame; "I've always known it. But how can I help it?"

"I don't know, I'm sure. To think of your striking a stuffed man, like the poor Scarecrow!"

"Is he stuffed?" asked the Lion, in surprise, as he watched her pick up the Scarecrow and set him upon his feet, while she patted him into shape again.

"Of course he's stuffed," replied Dorothy, who was still angry.

"That's why he went over so easily," remarked the Lion. "It astonished me to see him whirl around so. Is the other one stuffed, also?"

"No," said Dorothy, "he's made of tin." And she helped the Woodman up again.

"That's why he nearly blunted my claws," said the Lion. "When they scratched against the tin it made a

1. *slapped the Lion upon his nose*. Dorothy treats him just as she would a naughty kitten or a bad puppy. She probably has disciplined Toto in that very same manner. The Cowardly Lion often acts like an enormous house pet. Of course, Baum was not the first person to describe the animal in this manner. According to Edward Topsell in *The History of Four-Footed Beasts* (1607), the lion whom Androcles befriended smelled the man as a dog would and wagged his tail; Topsell also reported that in Libya lions were brought up in houses like dogs.

2. *a big coward*. The Lion, like Dorothy's other companions, embodies a whimsical paradox. The author is again playing with the reader's preconceptions, but Denslow once implied that he rather than Baum came up with the character. "In order to get another element of fun, we introduced the Cowardly Lion," he said. "Lions are usually conceived to be pretty ferocious. The fun of the thing, as I saw it, was to make him a coward" ("Denslow: Denver Artist, Originator of Scarecrow and Tin Man," Denver *Republican*, September 4, 1904). There are other gentle lions in legend and literature. In heraldry, a lion with his tail hanging between his legs indicates a coward. The legends of Androcles and Saint Jerome concern lions tamed when thorns are removed from their paws. The Cowardly Lion is also reminiscent of Una's lion in Edmund Spenser's *Faerie Queene* (Book I, Canto iii). The gentle lion has a place in American art as well, in Edward Hicks's paintings such as *The Peaceable Kingdom,* in which the lion literally lies down with the lamb.

One of the highlights of the MGM film was Bert Lahr's hilarious performance as the Cowardly Lion. "Not all characters from children's literature, of course, are ruined by conversion to stage or screen," observed William K. Zinsser in "John Dolittle, M. D., Puddleby-on-the-Marsh" (*The New York Times Children's Book Review*, November 6, 1966). "On the contrary, the Cowardly Lion of Oz, thanks to one of those genetical surprises that occasionally tweak the nose of science, looked more authentic when the part was played by Bert Lahr than if it had been taken by a lion." Despite his fine reviews, Lahr immediately deserted Hollywood for Broadway. "How many lion parts are there?" he asked. John Lahr's fine biography of his father, *Notes on a Cowardly Lion* (1969), devotes considerable space to a discussion of the MGM film and its effect on his life and career. Ted Ross deservedly won a Tony Award for his portrayal of the Cowardly Lion in the 1975 Broadway production of *The Wiz*, and he reprised the role in the 1978 movie.

TIN WOODMAN

This picture of the Tin Woodman appeared
on a trade card, c. 1910.
Private collection.

cold shiver run down my back.   What is that little animal you are so tender of?"

"He is my dog, Toto," answered Dorothy.

"Is he made of tin, or stuffed?" asked the Lion.

"Neither.   He's a—a—a meat dog," said the girl.

3.

"Oh.   He's a curious animal, and seems remarkably small, now that I look at him.   No one would think of biting such a little thing except a coward like me," continued the Lion, sadly.

"What makes you a coward?" asked Dorothy, looking at the great beast in wonder, for he was as big as a small horse.

"It's a mystery," replied the Lion.   "I suppose I was born that way.   All the other animals in the forest naturally expect me to be brave, for the Lion is everywhere thought to be the King of Beasts.   I learned that if I roared very loudly every living thing was frightened and got out of my way. Whenever I've met a man I've been awfully scared; but I just roared at him, and he has always run away as fast as he could go.   If the elephants and the tigers and the bears had ever tried to fight me, I should have run myself—I'm such a

4.

3. *a meat dog.* This discussion reveals that Dorothy's three companions, besides personifying the qualities of courage, intelligence, and kindness, also represent the three states of nature—animal, vegetable, and mineral. Baum used the word "meat" to distinguish his flesh-and-blood characters from the purely fanciful ones like the Scarecrow and the Tin Woodman. "Each new character furthers the plot," explained Gore Vidal in "On Rereading the Oz Books" (*The New York Review of Books*, October 13, 1977). "Each is essentially a humor. Each, when he speaks, strikes the same simple, satisfying note." John Algeo suggested in "*The Wizard of Oz*: The Perilous Journey" (*The American Theosophist*, October 1986) that the three companions represent manas (thinking), kama (feeling), and sthula sharira (doing), quoting a statement by the Theosophist leader Annie Besant: "There is no danger that dauntless courage cannot conquer; there is no trial that spotless purity cannot pass through; there is no difficulty that strong intellect cannot surmount." Algeo argued that the highly polished Tin Woodman represents "spotless purity," but the virtue reflects more on his sensibility within than on his outward appearance.

4. *King of Beasts.* Although this belief goes back to ancient times and was prevalent in the Middle Ages, it was not until the Renaissance that it become part of a highly sophisticated system. In such works as Raymond de Symonde's *Natural Theology* (1550) and William Peacham's *The Compleat Gentleman* (1622) the lion as King of Beasts fitted neatly into their system of primates. In every class of every level of existence, there is a superior creature. The eagle is chief of the birds, the dolphin or whale (although mammals) head of the fish, the lion the king of the beasts. Gelli in his *Circe* (1548) and some other authorities of the period considered the elephant the king of beasts,

but most people think of the lion as the animal primate. See also Chapter 11, Note 26.

The Lion's dilemma is reminiscent of that of Wellington De Boots, a character in Joseph Stirling Coyne's once popular comedy *Everybody's Friend* (1859), in which Baum appeared when a young man. De Boots confesses in the end that he is "an impostor—a humbug—a swindle." Because he was named after the Duke of Wellington, who defeated Napoleon at Waterloo, "I have been obliged to support the courageous character attached to the name, with the smallest amount of pluck that ever fell to the lot of mortal man." He possesses, in reality, "not the heart of a lion, but a mouse—the meekest of mice." But, he adds, "the fault's not mine—nature and my grandfathers and grandmothers are alone to blame." Like the Cowardly Lion (and Oz the Terrible himself), Wellington De Boots is not what others think he must be, so he has been forced to perpetuate a fraud to live up to their expectations.

5. *heart disease.* This is one of several jokes about heart ailments throughout the story. But did Baum suffer from a defective heart, as his son Frank Joslyn insisted in *To Please a Child*? Other members of the family denied it, and no known contemporary records confirm it.

6. *the Lion.* A revision of this chapter that appeared in *L. Frank Baum's Juvenile Speaker* (1910) adds the following:

> "No," declared Dorothy, "that doesn't 'splain it. I guess it's lion nature, because it's human nature. Out West in Kansas, where I live, they always say that the cowboy that roars the loudest and claims he's the baddest man, is sure to be the biggest coward of all." (p. 61)

Baum is playin with the moral from Aesop's fable: "Barking dogs seldom bite."

coward; but just as soon as they hear me roar they all try to get away from me, and of course I let them go."

"But that isn't right. The King of Beasts shouldn't be a coward," said the Scarecrow.

"I know it," returned the Lion, wiping a tear from his eye with the tip of his tail; "it is my great sorrow, and makes my life very unhappy. But whenever there is danger my heart begins to beat fast."

5.

"Perhaps you have heart disease," said the Tin Woodman.

"It may be," said the Lion.

"If you have," continued the Tin Woodman, "you ought to be glad, for it proves you have a heart. For my part, I have no heart; so I cannot have heart disease."

6.

"Perhaps," said the Lion, thoughtfully, "if I had no heart I should not be a coward."

"Have you brains?" asked the Scarecrow.

"I suppose so. I've never looked to see," replied the Lion.

"I am going to the great Oz to ask him to give me some," remarked the Scarecrow, "for my head is stuffed with straw."

"And I am going to ask him to give me a heart," said the Woodman.

"And I am going to ask him to send Toto and me back to Kansas," added Dorothy.

"Do you think Oz could give me courage?" asked the cowardly Lion.

"Just as easily as he could give me brains," said the Scarecrow.

"Or give me a heart," said the Tin Woodman.

"Or send me back to Kansas," said Dorothy.

"Then, if you don't mind, I'll go with you," said the Lion, "for my life is simply unbearable without a bit of courage."

"You will be very welcome," answered Dorothy, "for you will help to keep away the other wild beasts. It seems to me they must be more cowardly than you are if they allow you to scare them so easily."

"They really are," said the Lion; "but that doesn't make me any braver, and as long as I know myself to be a coward I shall be unhappy."

So once more the little company set off upon the journey, the Lion walking with stately strides at Dorothy's side. Toto did not approve this new comrade at first, for he could not forget how nearly he had been crushed between the Lion's great jaws; but after a time he became more at ease, and presently Toto and the Cowardly Lion had grown to be good friends.

During the rest of that day there was no other adventure to mar the peace of their journey. Once, indeed, the Tin Woodman stepped upon a beetle that was crawling along the road, and killed the poor little thing. This made the Tin Woodman very unhappy, for he was always careful not to hurt any living creature; and as he walked along he wept several tears of sorrow and regret. These tears ran slowly down his face and over the hinges of his jaw, and there they rusted. When Dorothy presently asked him a question the Tin Woodman could not open his mouth, for his jaws were tightly rusted together. He became greatly frightened at this and made many motions to Dorothy to relieve him, but she could not understand. The Lion was also puzzled to know what was wrong. But the Scarecrow seized the oil-can from Dorothy's basket and oiled the Woodman's jaws, so that after a few moments he could talk as well as before.

"This will serve me a lesson," said he, "to look where I step. For if I should kill another bug or beetle I should surely cry again, and crying rusts my jaw so that I cannot speak."

Thereafter he walked

7.

7. *lesson*. This is the first instance in which the Tin Woodman realizes the consequences of a heartless act. From this moment on he will be as kind and loving as if he did in fact have a heart.

8. *unkind to anything*. The Tin Woodman sounds like a disciple of the eighteenth-century cult of sensitivity. He would agree with the sentiments of the sentimental English poet William Cowper (1731–1800):

> I would not enter on my list of friends,
> Though graced with polished manners and fine sense,
> Yet wanting sensibility, the man
> Who needlessly sets foot upon a worm.

His concerns recall those of the German Romantic hero of Goethe's *The Sorrows of Young Werther* (1774), who obsesses that "the most harmless walk costs the lives of thousands of the poor, minute worms; *one* step of your foot annihilates the painstaking construction of ants, and stamps a small world into an ignominious grave." Baum provides a home for such anxious individuals, suffering from "foolish fears, and worries over nothing, with a mixture of nerves and ifs," in Flutterbudget Center of the Gillikin County in *The Emerald City of Oz* (1910, p. 242). "I—I pricked my finger with a needle while I was sewing, and—and the blood came!" declares one of these flighty people. "And now I'll have blood-poisoning, and the doctors will cut off my finger, and that will give me a fever and I shall die!" (p. 239). Baum is clearly expressing his own belief that even the lowliest creature has its place in the universe. But he does not insist that a beetle is of equal value or on the same level as a man. The minister in "The Wonderful Pump" in *American Fairy Tales* (1901) explains to a farmer and his wife who have received a great deal of money from the ruler of the insects: "Even bugs which can speak have no consciences and can't tell the difference between right and wrong." But Baum does not believe this, for he has the beetle befriended by the farmer's wife admit, "Bugs value their lives as much as human beings." Therefore they too should be treated with kindness. In "The Mandarin and the Butterfly," also in *American Fairy Tales*, the villain informs his captive, "Butterflies do not have souls and, therefore, cannot live again." Death is the end of everything for them. Yet a butterfly deserves kindness just as does any other of God's creatures. The Tin Woodman is so kind-hearted, explains the Wizard in *The Emerald City of Oz* (1910), that when "a fly happens to light upon his tin body he doesn't rudely brush it off, as some people might do; he asks it politely to find some other resting place" (p. 250). And in *The Patchwork Girl of Oz* (1913), the Tin Woodman, as Emperor of the Winkies, refuses to allow a boy to take the wing from a yellow butterfly for a potion to restore his uncle back to life. He cannot bear for even a butterfly to suffer. Another fine example of this cultivation of "sensibility" is the Tin Woodman's crying at the loss of the Wizard in his balloon in Chapter 16.

9. *I must be very careful*. Baum is being ironic in suggesting that those with hearts are not as kind as this hollow man of tin. Martin Gardner noted in *The Wizard of Oz and Who He Was* that "the Tin Woodman is so concerned over his lack of heart that his 'Reverence for Life' exceeds that of a Schweitzer" (p. 25).

Denslow drew this illustration of the Scarecrow and the Tin Woodman for the new title page of *The New Wizard of Oz*, issued by Bobbs-Merrill in 1903.

Private collection.

very carefully, with his eyes on the road, and when he saw a tiny ant toiling by he would step over it, so as not to harm it. The Tin Woodman knew very well he had no heart, and therefore he took great care never to be cruel or unkind to anything.

8.

"You people with hearts," he said, "have something to guide you, and need never do wrong; but I have no heart, and so I must be very careful, When Oz gives me a heart of course I needn't mind so much."

9.

This sketch of the Scarecrow appears in the copy of *The Wonderful Wizard of Oz* that
W. W. Denslow and L. Frank Baum signed for Charles Warren Stoddard, 1900.
Courtesy the Houghton Library, Harvard University.

1. *They were obliged to camp out that night under a large tree in the forest.* In his 1939 Russian "translation" of *The Wizard of Oz*, Aleksandr Volkov inserted an entirely new chapter between those about the Tin Woodman and the Cowardly Lion. A sign in the forest (traveler, hurry! round this bend in the road will be fulfilled all you desire!) fools Elli (Dorothy) into being captured by an ogre, who ties her up, lays her out on the kitchen table, and sharpens a big knife with which he intends to butcher her. Of course, her companions rescue the girl, but this unpleasant adventure is inconsistent with Baum's conviction that modernized fairy tales should be free of all stereotyped characters and any horrible and bloodcurdling incidents. This apocryphal episode resembles the more amusing imprisonment of Dorothy by the giant Crinklink in *Little Dorothy and Toto* (1913), but it is unlikely Volkov knew this relatively obscure "Little Wizard Story."

2. *I should certainly weep.* Despite his lack of a heart, the Tin Woodman is still able to express concern for all living creatures; evidently he has learned from the experience that closed the last chapter. But his moral position remains ambiguous. Is it kinder to have Dorothy starve rather than let his jaws rust from crying? He suffers from an excess of sensitivity, because he has no heart to guide him. One suspects that the Tin Woodman is expressing the sentiments of the author, who cared nothing for hunting or fishing. Baum's love of wildlife is reflected in many passages in his stories. He indicated in the introduction to *Policeman Bluejay* (1908) that "if a little tenderness for the helpless animals and birds is acquired with the amusement, the value of the tales will be doubled."

3. *nuts.* "Oz was free from many of the fads which have attracted much attention in the outside world," S. J. Sackett wrote in "The Utopia of Oz." "At one time, however, Dorothy was taken by an idea which was rather close to vegetarianism." He cited a passage in Chapter 2 of *Ozma of Oz* (1907), but a close look at Dorothy's diet in *The Wizard of Oz* reveals no meat of any kind. The Tin Woodman's views expressed above may reflect Baum's reservations about eating animals. His mother-in-law, shortly before she died in 1898, embraced vegetarianism and on April 14, 1897, gave a lecture titled "The Influence of Food upon Character" at the West Side Branch of the Chicago Vege-

tarian Society. "There are a great many millions of people who never eat meat at all," Matilda Joslyn Gage informed her grandson Harry Carpenter on January 21, 1897. "They think all life—even of animals, birds, and insects—is sacred. They think it is very wrong to kill anything that lives. They also think it is bad for anyone to eat flesh food." And she felt it was as good for one's health as for one's soul. Baum himself, however, was not a vegetarian.

4. *His padded hands were so clumsy.* Notice how skillfully Baum fills his tale with little easily missed but defining items which vividly bring his characters to life and give a heightened sense of reality to the story. Martin Gardner in "*The Tin Woodman of Oz*: An Appreciation" (*The Baum Bugle*, Fall 1996) likewise noted "Baum's constant attention to small details that gives verisimilitude to what otherwise would be preposterous fantasy." These reflect the child reader's immediate world. "The Road of Yellow Bricks has missing holes over which the Scarecrow stumbles," observed writer Daniel P. Mannix in a letter of August 25, 1982, "he has trouble picking up nuts with his padded fingers, Dorothy has to be fed during the journey (ever hear of the people *having* to eat in fairyland journeys?), it gets cold at night and they need a fire, and so on. The point is not that in America children have to eat, get cold, and there are potholes in the roads; the point is that all these details make Oz a real place." The fears and foibles of Dorothy's friends that the author so carefully describes help to mold their peculiar and distinctive personalities on the journey to the Great Oz.

5. *burn him up.* In contrast to this danger, the scarecrow in Nathaniel Hawthorne's short story "Feathertop: A Moralized Legend" remains living only so long as a spark remains burning in the pipe given him by an old witch who made him. There are similarities between the manufacture of Feathertop and that of Baum's Scarecrow. Marius Bewley noted in "Oz Country" (*The New York Review of Books*, December 3, 1964) that on reading the Oz books "one becomes aware of allegorical themes and attitudes that put one in mind of Hawthorne's short stories." Jack Pumpkinhead of *The Marvelous Land of Oz* (1904) too has much in common with Hawthorne's Feathertop. Cynthia Hearn Dorfman suggested that "Mombi," the name of the witch who brought Jack Pumpkinhead, may be derived from "Mother Rigby," that of the witch who invented Feathertop.

They WERE obliged to camp out that night under a large tree in the forest, for there were no houses near. The tree made a good, thick covering to protect them from the dew, and the Tin Woodman chopped a great pile of wood with his axe and Dorothy built a splendid fire that warmed her and made her feel less lonely. She and Toto ate the last of their bread, and now she did not know what they would do for breakfast.

"If you wish," said the Lion, "I will go into the forest

and kill a deer for you. You can roast it by the fire, since your tastes are so peculiar that you prefer cooked food, and then you will have a very good breakfast."

"Don't! please don't," begged the Tin Woodman. "I should certainly weep if you killed a poor deer, and then my jaws would rust again."

But the Lion went away into the forest and found his own supper, and no one ever knew what it was, for he didn't mention it. And the Scarecrow found a tree full of nuts and filled Dorothy's basket with them, so that she would not be hungry for a long time. She thought this was very kind and thoughtful of the Scarecrow, but she laughed heartily at the awkward way in which the poor creature picked up the nuts. His padded hands were so clumsy and the nuts were so small that he dropped almost as many as he put in the basket. But the Scarecrow did not mind how long it took him to fill the basket, for it enabled him to keep away from the fire, as he feared a spark might get into his straw and burn him up. So he kept a good distance away from the flames, and only came near to cover Dorothy with dry leaves when she lay down to sleep. These kept her very snug and warm and she slept soundly until morning.

When it was daylight the girl bathed her face in a little rippling brook and soon after they all started toward the Emerald City.

This was to be an eventful day for the travellers. They had hardly been walking an hour when they saw before them a great ditch that crossed the road and divided the forest as far as they could see on either side. It was a very wide ditch, and when they crept up to the edge and looked into it they could see it was also very deep, and there were many big, jagged rocks at the bottom. The sides were so steep that none of them could climb down, and for a moment it seemed that their journey must end.

"What shall we do?" asked Dorothy, despairingly.

"I haven't the faintest idea," said the Tin Woodman; and the Lion shook his shaggy mane and looked thoughtful. But the Scarecrow said:

"We cannot fly, that is certain; neither can we climb down into this great ditch. Therefore, if we cannot jump over it, we must stop where we are."

"I think I could jump over it," said the Cowardly Lion, after measuring the distance carefully in his mind.

"Then we are all right," answered the Scarecrow, "for you can carry us all over on your back, one at a time."

"Well, I'll try it," said the Lion. "Who will go first?"

"I will," declared the Scarecrow; "for, if you found that you could not jump over the gulf, Dorothy would be

6.

killed, or the Tin Woodman badly dented on the rocks below. But if I am on your back it will not matter so much, for the fall would not hurt me at all."

"I am terribly afraid of falling, myself," said the Cowardly Lion, "but I suppose there is nothing to do but try it. So get on my back and we will make the attempt."

The Scarecrow sat upon the Lion's back, and the big beast walked to the edge of the gulf and crouched down.

"Why don't you run and jump?" asked the Scarecrow.

"Because that isn't the way we Lions do these things," he replied. Then giving a great spring, he shot through the air and landed safely on the other side. They were all greatly pleased to see how easily he did it, and after the Scarecrow had got down from his back the Lion sprang across the ditch again.

7.

Dorothy thought she would go next; so she took Toto in her arms and climbed on the Lion's back, holding tightly to his mane with one hand. The next moment it seemed as if she was flying through the air; and then, before she had time to think about it, she was safe on the other side. The Lion went back a third time and got the Tin Woodman, and then they all sat down for a few moments to give the beast a chance to rest, for his great leaps had made his breath short, and he panted like a big dog that has been running too long.

8.

They found the forest very thick on this side, and it looked dark and gloomy. After the Lion had rested they started along the road of yellow brick, silently wondering, each in his own mind, if ever they would come to the end of the woods and reach the bright sunshine again. To add to their discomfort, they soon heard strange noises in the depths of the forest, and the Lion whispered to them that it was in this part of the country that the Kalidahs lived.

"What are the Kalidahs?" asked the girl.

"They are monstrous beasts with bodies like bears and heads like tigers," replied the Lion; "and with claws so long and sharp that they could tear me in two as easily as I could kill Toto. I'm terribly afraid of the Kalidahs."

6. *we must stop where we are.* Note that this is the first instance in which the Scarecrow uses his head; his fall into the hole in the road taught him to think before acting.

7. *across the ditch again.* This is the first opportunity the Lion has to prove his bravery, and he succeeds beautifully. Surely he always had the ability to be courageous. He proves Ernest Hemingway's dictum that courage is grace under pressure.

8. *like a big dog that has been running too long.* Baum also compares the Lion to cats elsewhere in the story. He reassures the young child reader that there is nothing to fear from this beast who is as harmless as a house pet.

9. *bodies like bears and heads like tigers*. The Kalidahs may have inspired the famous chant "Lions and tigers and bears! Oh my!" in the 1939 MGM musical. Jack Snow speculated in *Who's Who in Oz* (1954) that the name Kalidah came from "kaleidoscope," the popular children's toy that creates ever-changing patterns from transparent shapes and mirrors. Or perhaps it is an ironic use of the Greek *kalos eidos* (from which "kaleidoscope" comes), which means "beautiful form." These monsters could have come from the pages of a children's "turn up" or transformation book in which various animals and people exchange heads and other parts of the body at the flip of a flap. The strangest of all these creatures in the Oz series are the Li-Mon-Eags of *The Magic of Oz* (1919), part lion, monkey, eagle, and wild ass, who are really the Nome King and Munchkin lad Kiki Aru in disguise. Jorge Luis Borges noted in *The Book of Imaginary Beasts* (New York: E. P. Dutton, 1969) how mythical creatures are created from "a combination of parts of real beasts, and the possibilities of permutation are infinite." Baum reports in *The Emerald City of Oz* (1910), "The Kalidahs . . . had once been fierce and bloodthirsty, but even they were now nearly all tamed, although at times one or another of them would get cross and disagreeable" (p. 32). One of the wild Kalidahs does show up in Chapter 9 of *The Magic of Oz* (1919), where they are described as "the most powerful and ferocious beasts in all Oz" (p. 104). Reilly & Britton was concerned that the creatures might have appeared elsewhere in the series, so Baum assured the publishers on November 2, 1918, "The Kalidahs do not appear in any of my books except *The Wizard*—and not much about them there."

"I'm not surprised that you are," returned Dorothy "They must be dreadful beasts."

The Lion was about to reply when suddenly they came to another gulf across the road; but this one was so broad and deep that the Lion knew at once he could not leap across it.

So they sat down to consider what they should do, and after serious thought the Scarecrow said,

"Here is a great tree, standing close to the ditch. If the Tin Woodman can chop it down, so that it will fall to the other side, we can walk across it easily."

"That is a first rate idea," said the Lion. "One would almost suspect you had brains in your head, instead of straw."

The Woodman set to work at once, and so sharp was his axe that the tree was soon chopped nearly through. Then the Lion put his strong front legs against the tree and pushed with all his might, and slowly the big tree tipped and fell with a crash across the ditch, with its top branches on the other side.

They had just started to cross this queer bridge when a sharp growl made them all look up, and to their horror they saw running toward them two great beasts with bodies like bears and heads like tigers.

"They are the Kalidahs!" said the Cowardly Lion, beginning to tremble.

"Quick!" cried the Scarecrow, "let us cross over."

So Dorothy went first, holding Toto in her arms; the Tin Woodman followed, and the Scarecrow came next. The Lion, although he was certainly afraid, turned to face the Kalidahs, and then he gave so loud and terrible a roar that Dorothy screamed and the Scarecrow fell over backwards, while even the fierce beasts stopped short and looked at him in surprise.

But, seeing they were bigger than the Lion, and remembering that there were two of them and only one of him, the Kalidahs again rushed forward, and the Lion crossed over the tree and turned to see what they would do next. Without stopping an instant the fierce beasts also began to cross the tree, and the Lion said to Dorothy,

"We are lost, for they will surely tear us to pieces with their sharp claws. But stand close behind me, and I will fight them as long as I am alive."

"Wait a minute!" called the Scarecrow. He had been thinking what was best to be done, and now he asked the Woodman to chop away the end of the tree that rested on their side of the ditch. The Tin Woodman began to use his axe at once, and, just as the two Kalidahs were nearly across, the tree fell with a crash into the gulf, carrying the ugly, snarling brutes with it, and both were dashed to pieces on the sharp rocks at the bottom.

"Well," said the Cowardly Lion, drawing a long breath of relief, "I see we are going to live a little while longer, and I am glad of it, for it must be a very uncomfortable

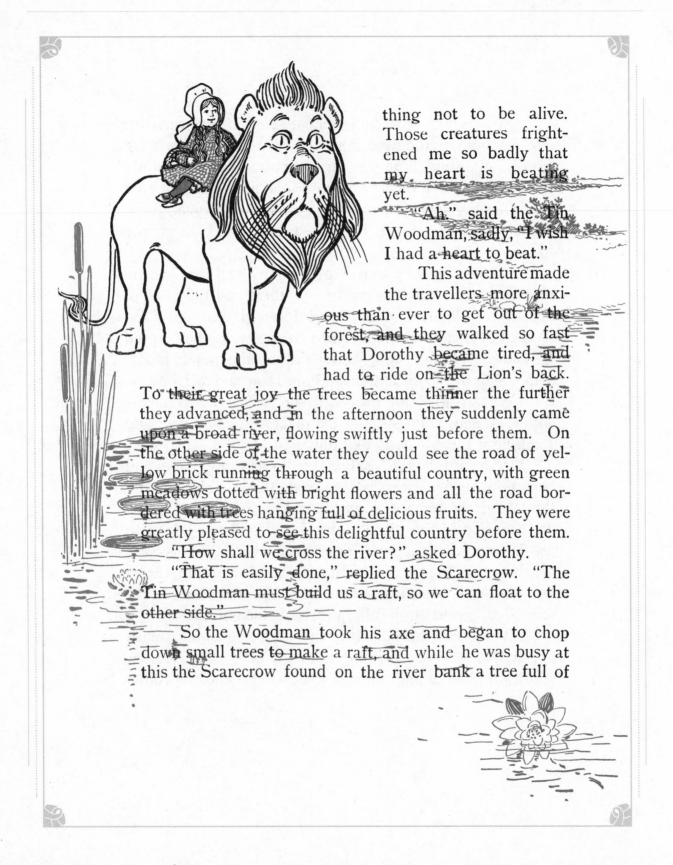

thing not to be alive. Those creatures frightened me so badly that my heart is beating yet."

"Ah," said the Tin Woodman, sadly, "I wish I had a heart to beat."

This adventure made the travellers more anxious than ever to get out of the forest, and they walked so fast that Dorothy became tired, and had to ride on the Lion's back.

To their great joy the trees became thinner the further they advanced, and in the afternoon they suddenly came upon a broad river, flowing swiftly just before them. On the other side of the water they could see the road of yellow brick running through a beautiful country, with green meadows dotted with bright flowers and all the road bordered with trees hanging full of delicious fruits. They were greatly pleased to see this delightful country before them.

"How shall we cross the river?" asked Dorothy.

"That is easily done," replied the Scarecrow. "The Tin Woodman must build us a raft, so we can float to the other side."

So the Woodman took his axe and began to chop down small trees to make a raft, and while he was busy at this the Scarecrow found on the river bank a tree full of fine fruit. This pleased Dorothy, who had eaten nothing but nuts all day, and she made a hearty meal of the ripe fruit.

But it takes time to make a raft, even when one is as industrious and untiring as the Tin Woodman, and when night came the work was not done. So they found a cozy place under the trees where they slept well until the morning; and Dorothy dreamed of the Emerald City, and of the good Wizard Oz, who would soon send her back to her own home again.

Chapter VIII.
The Deadly Poppy Field.

Our LITTLE PARTY of travellers awakened next morning refreshed and full of hope, and Dorothy breakfasted like a princess off peaches and plums from the trees beside the river. Behind them was the dark forest they had passed safely through, although they had suffered many discouragements; but before them was a lovely, sunny country that seemed to beckon them on to the Emerald City.

To be sure, the broad river now

cut them off from this beautiful land; but the raft was nearly done, and after the Tin Woodman had cut a few more logs and fastened them together with wooden pins, they were ready to start. Dorothy sat down in the middle of the raft and held Toto in her arms. When the Cowardly Lion stepped upon the raft it tipped badly, for he was big and heavy; but the Scarecrow and the Tin Woodman stood upon the other end to steady it, and they had long poles in their hands to push the raft through the water.

They got along quite well at first, but when they reached the middle of the river the swift current swept the raft down stream, farther and farther away from the road of yellow brick; and the water grew so deep that the long poles would not touch the bottom.

"This is bad," said the Tin Woodman, "for if we cannot get to the land we shall be carried into the country of the wicked Witch of the West, and she will enchant us and make us her slaves."

"And then I should get no brains," said the Scarecrow.

"And I should get no courage," said the Cowardly Lion.

"And I should get no heart," said the Tin Woodman.

"And I should never get back to Kansas," said Dorothy.

"We must certainly get to the Emerald City if we can," the Scarecrow continued, and he pushed so hard on his long pole that it stuck fast in the mud at the bottom of the river, and before he could pull it out again, or let go, the raft was swept away and the poor Scarecrow left clinging to the pole in the middle of the river.

"Good bye!" he called after them, and they were very sorry to leave him; indeed, the Tin Woodman began to cry, but fortunately remembered that he might rust, and so dried his tears on Dorothy's apron.

Of course this was a bad thing for the Scarecrow.

"I am now worse off than when I first met Dorothy," he thought. "Then, I was stuck on a pole in a cornfield, where I could make believe scare the crows, at any rate; but surely there is no use for a Scarecrow stuck on a pole in the middle of a river. I am afraid I shall never have any brains, after all!"

Down the stream the raft floated, and the poor Scarecrow was left far behind. Then the Lion said:

"Something must be done to save us. I think I can swim to the shore and pull the raft after me, if you will only hold fast to the tip of my tail."

So he sprang into the water and the Tin Woodman caught fast hold of his tail, when the Lion began to swim with all his might toward the shore. It was hard work, although he was so big; but by and by they were drawn out of the current, and then Dorothy took the Tin Woodman's long pole and helped push the raft to the land.

They were all tired out when they reached the shore at last and stepped off upon the pretty green grass, and they also knew that the stream had carried them a long way past the road of yellow brick that led to the Emerald City.

"What shall we do now?" asked the Tin Woodman, as the Lion lay down on the grass to let the sun dry him.

"We must get back to the road, in some way," said Dorothy.

"The best plan will be to walk along the river bank until we come to the road again," remarked the Lion.

So, when they were rested, Dorothy picked up her basket and they started along the grassy bank, back to the road from which the river had carried them. It was a lovely country, with plenty

1. *They were all tired out.* All except the Tin Woodman, who, not being made of flesh and blood, never tires.

This picture of a toy Tin Woodman first appeared in *Denslow's A B C Book* (New York: G. W. Dillingham, 1903), illustrating the following doggerel by Denslow:

> T is the Tin
> that they make into toys,
> That walk by themselves
> and puzzle small boys.

Another one of these toys peers out of Santa's bag in *Denslow's Night Before Christmas* (New York: G. W. Dillingham, 1902). (See color plate 1 in the Denslow Appendix.)
Private collection.

of flowers and fruit trees and sunshine to cheer them, and had they not felt so sorry for the poor Scarecrow they could have been very happy.

They walked along as fast as they could, Dorothy only stopping once to pick a beautiful flower; and after a time the Tin Woodman cried out,

"Look!"

Then they all looked at the river and saw the Scarecrow perched upon his pole in the middle of the water, looking very lonely and sad.

"What can we do to save him?" asked Dorothy.

The Lion and the Woodman both shook their heads, for they did not know. So they sat down upon the bank and gazed wistfully at the Scarecrow until a Stork flew by, which, seeing them, stopped to rest at the water's edge.

"Who are you, and where are you going?" asked the Stork.

"I am Dorothy," answered the girl; "and these are my friends, the Tin Woodman and the Cowardly Lion; and we are going to the Emerald City."

"This is n't the road," said the Stork, as she twisted her long neck and looked sharply at the queer party.

"I know it," returned Dorothy, "but we have lost the Scarecrow, and are wondering how we shall get him again."

"Where is he?" asked the Stork.

"Over there in the river," answered the girl.

"If he wasn't so big and heavy I would get him for you," remarked the Stork.

2. *Stork.* Some of Baum's most tender and most personal writing concerns the stork legend. One of the seven valleys of Merryland in *Dot and Tot of Merryland* (1901) is the Valley of Babies, where blossoms fall from the sky and unfold their petals to disclose a sleeping child within each flower; then the storks care for these infants until they are ready to be winged into the world. In the dedication copy of *The Road to Oz* (1909) that the writer gave his first grandson, Joslyn Stanton ("Tik-Tok") Baum, he wrote the following brief sweet fantasy to honor the boy's birth:

> Once on a time the Storks brought a baby to Frank Joslyn and Helen Snow Baum, and the baby was so smiling and sweet and merry that he won his way to all hearts—those of strangers as well as of his doting relatives. For, as the Stork was flying Earthward, it met the Love Fairy, who stopped to kiss the babe; and next the Laughing Fay tossed it in his arms; and then Glinda the Good blessed it and decreed it happiness. So on the Stork flew with its burden until it passed the Emerald City, where the Shaggy Man took the Love Magnet from the Great Gates and pressed it against the infant's brow.
>
> And so, what do you think will be the fate of this youngster—so favored by the fairies? I know. He will find in life joy and gladness and prosperity, and since he has touched the Love Magnet he will win all hearts. It is so decreed.

"He isn't heavy a bit," said Dorothy, eagerly, "for he is stuffed with straw; and if you will bring him back to us we shall thank you ever and ever so much."

"Well, I'll try," said the Stork; "but if I find he is too heavy to carry I shall have to drop him in the river again."

So the big bird flew into the air and over the water till she came to where the Scarecrow was perched upon his pole.   Then the Stork with her great claws grabbed the Scarecrow by the arm and carried him up into the air and back to the bank, where Dorothy and the Lion and the Tin Woodman and Toto were sitting.

When the Scarecrow found himself among his friends again he was so happy that he hugged them all, even the Lion and Toto; and as they walked along he sang "Tol-de-ri-de-oh!" at every step, he felt so gay.

"I was afraid I should have to stay in the river for-ever," he said, "but the kind Stork saved me, and if I ever get any brains I shall find the Stork again and do it some kindness in return."

"That's all right," said the Stork, who was flying along beside them.   "I always like to help anyone in trouble. But I must go now, for my babies are waiting in the nest for me.   I hope you will find the Emerald City and that Oz will help you."

"Thank you," replied Dorothy, and then the kind Stork flew into the air and was soon out of sight.

They walked along listening to the singing of the

3. *"Tol-de-ri-de-oh."* Judith Brownlow, a college classmate, noted the similarity between the Scarecrow's phrase and the last line in the refrain to a seventeenth-century ballad, "A carrion crow sat on an oak" (first published as early as 1796 and frequently included in collections of Mother Goose rhymes):

> With a heigh ho! the carrion crow!
> Sing tol de rol, de riddle row!

It seems appropriate that the Scarecrow would know this song. N. N. Razgovorova's commentary to *The Wonderful Wizard of Oz* in Tatyana Dmitrievna Venediktova's English-language compilation *The Marvelous Land of Oz* (Moscow: Raduga, 1986, p. 371) mentioned another possible source, the refrain of a version of "The Ox-Driving Song," known in different parts of America:

> To my roll, to my roll, to my ride-e-o
> To my rid-e-u, to my reed-e-o,
> To my roll, to my roll, to my ri-de-e-o.

bright-colored birds and looking at the lovely flowers which now became so thick that the ground was carpeted

4.   with them. There were big yellow and white and blue and purple blossoms, besides great clusters of scarlet poppies, which were so brilliant in color they almost dazzled Dorothy's eyes.

"Aren't they beautiful?" the girl asked, as she breathed in the spicy scent of the flowers.

"I suppose so," answered the Scarecrow. "When I

5.   have brains I shall probably like them better."

"If I only had a heart I should love them," added the Tin Woodman.

"I always did like flowers," said the Lion; "they seem so helpless and frail. But there are none in the forest so bright as these."

They now came upon more and more of the big scarlet poppies, and fewer and fewer of the other flowers; and soon they found themselves in the midst of a great meadow of poppies. Now it is well known that when there are many of these flowers together their odor is so

6.   powerful that anyone who breathes it falls asleep, and if the sleeper is not carried away from the scent of the flowers he sleeps on and on forever. But Dorothy did not know this, nor could she get away from the bright red flowers that were everywhere about; so presently her eyes grew heavy and she felt she must sit down to rest and to sleep.

4. *big yellow and white and blue and purple blossoms.* Although one may at first suspect that this is another indication that Baum has not yet decided that the flora and fauna take on the favorite color of a region of Oz, Susan Wolstenholme in her notes to the 1997 Oxford edition of *The Wonderful Wizard of Oz* offered a curious explanation for this seeming inconsistency: "The friends are lost here, and have been brought off-course by the river. The flowers' different colors here indicate that they are meandering around the geographical center of Oz—possibly just around the Emerald City—and that the borders are close together at this point" (p. 270).

5. *I shall probably like them better.* Earle J. Coleman argued in "Oz as Heaven and Other Philosophical Questions (*The Baum Bugle,* Autumn 1980) that this discussion "generates the question of whether aesthetic judgments are fundamentally cognitive rather than grounded upon sense or feelings. Immanuel Kant, for example, inclines toward the latter; contemporary conceptional artists defend the former." It furthers the debate between the head and the heart that the Scarecrow and the Tin Woodman introduced in Chapter 5. See Chapter 5, Note 22.

6. *their odor is so powerful that anyone who breathes it falls asleep.* Baum likely had in mind the Enchanted Ground that Christian must pass through to get to the Land of Beulah and the Celestial City in *Pilgrim's Progress*, "a certain country, whose air naturally tended to make one drowsy." He warns his companion Hopeful not to nap, "lest sleeping, we never awake more." The scarlet poppy has traditionally been associated with sleep and death since ancient times. Because of their color, scarlet poppies were said to grow from the blood of the slain, for they were often seen on battlefields. When Demeter (Ceres) sought her daughter Proserpine (Persephone) in the underworld, the gods gave her a poppy to smell to let her sleep, and these flowers sprang from her footsteps. Scarlet poppies also suggest the blood of Christ. Of course, opium and its derivatives come from poppy seeds. It produces the most extraordinary dreams, but can cause addiction. Opium was once a common ingredient in laudanum and other painkillers just as cocaine was an ingredient of Coca-Cola. It was also widely smoked for pleasure in bohemian circles. Not until the early twentieth century were opium-containing patent medicines taken off the open market in America, and strict laws were introduced against the international traffic in opium. The poppy was also a common device of Art Nouveau, for it was considered one of the most beautiful of all flowers. John R. Neill often portrayed Princess Ozma with scarlet poppies in her hair, but this was a bow to the current fashion rather than any reference to the Deadly Poppy Field. The Wicked Witch of the West enchants the poppies in the 1939 MGM musical. It is ironic that once Dorothy and her friends have finally emerged from the dark and dangerous forest to the fresh air and bright sunshine, they encounter the most dangerous obstacle on their journey to the emerald city, these seemingly helpless and frail flowers.

Legends and literature are full of references to malevolent vegetation. The upas tree of Java supposedly drips and breathes poison, its seductive fragrance killing creatures for miles around. The kerzra flower of Persia likewise poisons anyone who dares to smell its intoxicating perfume. Captain Arkwright supposedly discovered a death flower on the island of El Banoor on a voyage to the South Pacific in 1581. Nathaniel Hawthorne's short story "Rappaccini's Daughter" tells of a garden whose odor kills everyone but the immune Beatrice. It is surprising that someone as fond of flowers as Baum was should introduce so many hostile plants into the Oz books. There are the dangerous vegetable people who dwell in great greenhouses underground, the evil Mangaboos of *Dorothy and the Wizard in Oz* (1908). The natives of the Rose Kingdom, as introduced in *Tik-Tok of Oz* (1914), are of the same terrible family as the Mangaboos; they are beautiful but heartless. Not even the Shaggy Man's Love Magnet can convince them to treat their visitors better. *The Patchwork Girl of Oz* (1913) seems to be especially overgrown with deadly vegetation. Around the bend on the Yellow Brick Road in Chapter 10 lies a patch of man-eating plants, like enormous Venus flytraps that attack unsuspecting travelers in the Munchkin Country. But perhaps the worst of all were to appear in a suppressed chapter from the same book. "The Garden of Meats" was so disturbing that the publishers asked Baum to delete it, and he readily agreed. The text does not survive, but the illustrations that do suggest that here was a place where vegetables grew people for *their* food. See Dick Martin's "The Garden of Meats: A Lost Episode of Ozian History" (*The Baum Bugle,* Christmas 1966).

But the Tin Woodman would not let her do this.

"We must hurry and get back to the road of yellow brick before dark," he said; and the Scarecrow agreed with him. So they kept walking until Dorothy could stand no longer. Her eyes closed in spite of herself and she forgot where she was and fell among the poppies, fast asleep.

"What shall we do?" asked the Tin Woodman.

"If we leave her here she will die," said the Lion. "The smell of the flowers is killing us all. I myself can scarcely keep my eyes open and the dog is asleep already."

It was true; Toto had fallen down beside his little mistress. But the Scarecrow and the Tin Woodman, not being made of flesh, were not troubled by the scent of the flowers.

"Run fast," said the Scarecrow to the Lion, "and get out of this deadly flower-bed as soon as you can. We will bring the little girl with us, but if you should fall asleep you are too big to be carried."

So the Lion aroused himself and bounded forward as fast as he could go. In a moment he was out of sight.

"Let us make a chair with our hands, and carry her," said the Scarecrow. So they picked up Toto and put the dog in Dorothy's lap, and then they made a chair with their hands for the seat and their arms for the arms and carried the sleeping girl between them through the flowers.

On and on they walked, and it seemed that the great carpet of deadly flowers that surrounded them would never end. They followed the bend of the river, and at last came upon their friend the Lion, lying fast asleep among the poppies. The flowers had been too strong for the huge beast and he had given up, at last, and fallen only a short distance from the end of the poppy-bed, where the sweet grass spread in beautiful green fields before them.

"We can do nothing for him," said the Tin Woodman, sadly; "for he is much too heavy to lift. We must leave him here to sleep on forever, and perhaps he will dream that he has found courage at last."

"I'm sorry," said the Scarecrow; "the Lion was a very good comrade for one so cowardly. But let us go on."

They carried the sleeping girl to a pretty spot beside the river, far enough from the poppy field to prevent her breathing any more of the poison of the flowers, and here they laid her gently on the soft grass and waited for the fresh breeze to waken her.

Denslow drew this illustration specially for the endpapers of *The New Wizard of Oz*
(Indianapolis: Bobbs-Merrill, 1903).
Private collection.

"W^e CANNOT BE FAR from the road of yellow brick, now," remarked the Scarecrow, as he stood beside the girl, "for we have come nearly as far as the river carried us away."

The Tin Woodman was about to reply when he heard a low growl, and turning his head (which worked beautifully on hinges) he saw a strange beast come bounding over the grass towards them. It was, indeed, a great, yellow wildcat, and the Woodman thought it must be chasing something, for its ears were lying close to its head and its mouth was wide open, showing two rows of ugly teeth, while its red eyes glowed like balls of fire. As it came nearer the Tin

Woodman saw that running before the beast was a little gray field-mouse, and although he had no heart he knew it was wrong for the wildcat to try to kill such a pretty, harmless creature.

So the Woodman raised his axe, and as the wildcat 1. ran by he gave it a quick blow that cut the beast's head clean off from its body, and it rolled over at his feet in two pieces.

The field-mouse, now that it was freed from its enemy, stopped short; and coming slowly up to the Woodman it said, in a squeaky little voice,

"Oh, thank you! Thank you ever so much for saving my life."

"Don't speak of it, I beg of you," replied the Woodman. "I have no heart, you know, so I am careful to help all those who may need a friend, even if it happens to be only a mouse."

"Only a mouse!" cried the little animal, indignantly; 2. "why, I am a Queen—the Queen of all the field-mice!"

"Oh, indeed," said the Woodman, making a bow.

"Therefore you have done a great deed, as well as a brave one, in saving my life," added the Queen.

At that moment several mice were seen running up as fast as their little legs could carry them, and when they saw their Queen they exclaimed,

"Oh, your Majesty, we thought you would be killed! How did you manage to escape the great Wildcat?" and

1. *cut the beast's head clean off from its body.* Although the Oz books generally avoid the many horrors found in the tales of Grimm and Andersen, the occasional decapitations in this story have horrified modern critics of juvenile literature who feel that children's books should be free of all violence. Yet children still enjoy stories like Charles Perrault's "Little Red Riding Hood" and "Bluebeard" with all their Freudian undertones and suffer no deeply disturbing psychological consequence from reading them. Dr. Bruno Bettelheim challenged his fellow child therapists by arguing in *The Uses of Enchantment* (New York: Alfred A. Knopf, 1976) that fairy tales are necessary for the healthy development of the young mind. He believed that "more can be learned from them about the inner problems of human beings, and of the right solutions to their predicaments in any society, than from any other type of story within a child's comprehension" (p. 5). "Gruesome as the story is," he insisted, " 'Bluebeard,' like all fairy stories . . . teaches deep down a higher morality or humanity" (p. 302). But even he preferred the Grimms' "Little Red Cap," in which the girl is saved, to the darker, more tragic "Little Red Riding Hood," "with its anxiety-producing ending." Perrault's version, in which the child dies, "is devoid of escape, recovery, and consolation" (p. 167). In this seeming contradiction between theory and practice, Baum shares Andrew Lang's attitude toward violence in his preface to *The Violet Fairy Book* (1910): "I hate cruelty: I never put a wicked stepmother in a barrel and send her tobogganing down a hill. It is true that Prince Ricardo *did* kill the Yellow Dwarf; but that was in fair fight, sword in hand, and the dwarf, peace to his ashes! *died in harness.*" Baum commented elsewhere on the Tin Woodman's self-contradictory nature of being able to weep profusely over the killing of a beetle one minute and then swiftly decapitate a wildcat the next. "The Tin Woodman was usually a peaceful man," Baum explained in *The Marvelous Land of Oz* (1904), "but when occasion required he could fight as fiercely as a Roman gladiator" (p. 219). Children demand justice, and no one is unduly punished or torment-

ed in *The Wizard of Oz.* There is no gratuitous violence or cruelty in the story, and much of it that remains is quite mild when compared to that in other fairy tales. The violences in Oz did not trouble poet David McCord. "If the Tin Woodman has to destroy a pack of wolves [in Chapter 12], he does it with his axe," he explained in *Twentieth Century Children's Writers* (Detroit: St. James Press, 1978). "But there is no picture of the heap; no gory mess; nothing but these simple words." He noted that "in the present era of ever-increasing global violence, [Oz] is possibly all the more surprising and welcome (compared with TV and the comics, for example) as a place devoid of bloodshed" (p. 91).

Baum was more cautious in the subsequent Oz books than he had been in *The Wizard of Oz.* The mayhem in these stories, if not entirely eliminated, is minimized. In his essay "Modern Fairy Tales" (*The Advance*, August 19, 1909), Baum further refined his definition of suitable reading for children as any not "marred by murders or cruelties, by terrifying characters, or by mawkish sentimentality, love or marriage." His publishers proudly stated that the policy of the Oz series was "No Baum story ever sent a child to bed to troubled dreams." In his preface to Raylyn Moore's *Wonderful Wizard Marvelous Land* (Bowling Green, Ohio: Bowling Green University Popular Press, 1974), Ray Bradbury accused Baum of being "a spirited man with a nice old grandma's soul" (p. xvi).

2. *Queen of all the field-mice.* Baum explored the same theme in "The Wonderful Pump" of *American Fairy Tales* (1901): A poor farm woman saves a beetle who turns out to be the king of all the insects, and he uses his special powers to reward her for her kindness. Oz Club member David L. Greene compared this incident about the Tin Woodman and the Queen of the Field Mice to Roman writer Aulus Gellius's fable about Androcles and the Lion, in which one kindness is repaid by another. The *Pañcatantra,* the Indian fable collection, includes a variant of Aesop's "The Lion and the Mouse" in which a large number of mice come to the lion's aid and gnaw the ropes that bind him.

they all bowed so low to the little Queen that they almost stood upon their heads.

"This funny tin man," she answered, "killed the Wildcat and saved my life. So hereafter you must all serve him, and obey his slightest wish."

"We will!" cried all the mice, in a shrill chorus. And then they scampered in all directions, for Toto had awakened from his sleep, and seeing all these mice around him he gave one bark of delight and jumped right into the middle of the group. Toto had always loved to chase mice when he lived in Kansas, and he saw no harm in it.

But the Tin Woodman caught the dog in his arms and held him tight, while he called to the mice: "Come back! come back! Toto shall not hurt you."

At this the Queen of the Mice stuck her head out from a clump of grass and asked, in a timid voice,

"Are you sure he will not bite us?"

"I will not let him," said the Woodman; "so do not be afraid."

One by one the mice came creeping back, and Toto did not bark again, although he tried to get out of the Woodman's arms, and would have bitten him had he not known very well he was made of tin. Finally one of the biggest mice spoke.

"Is there anything we can do," it asked, "to repay you for saving the life of our Queen?"

"Nothing that I know of," answered the Woodman; but the Scarecrow, who had been trying to think, but could not because his head was stuffed with straw, said, quickly,

"Oh, yes; you can save our friend, the Cowardly Lion, who is asleep in the poppy bed."

"A Lion!" cried the little Queen; "why, he would eat us all up."

"Oh, no;" declared the Scarecrow; "this Lion is a coward."

"Really?" asked the Mouse.

"He says so himself," answered the Scarecrow, "and he would never hurt anyone who is our friend. If you will help us to save him I promise that he shall treat you all with kindness."

"Very well," said the Queen, "we will trust you. But what shall we do?"

"Are there many of these mice which call you Queen and are willing to obey you?"

"Oh, yes; there are thousands," she replied.

"Then send for them all to come here as soon as possible, and let each one bring a long piece of string."

The Queen turned to the mice that attended her and told them to go at once and get all her people. As soon as they heard her orders they ran away in every direction as fast as possible.

"Now," said the Scarecrow to the Tin Woodman, "you must go to those trees by the river-side and make a truck that will carry the Lion."

So the Woodman went at once to the trees and began to work; and he soon made a truck out of the limbs of trees, from which he chopped away all the leaves and branches. He fastened it together with wooden pegs and made the four wheels out of short pieces of a big tree-trunk. So fast and so well did he work that by the time the mice began to arrive the truck was all ready for them.

They came from all directions, and there were thousands of them: big mice and little mice and middle-sized mice; and each one brought a piece of string in his mouth. It was about this time that Dorothy woke from her long sleep and opened her eyes. She was greatly astonished to find herself lying upon the grass, with thousands of mice standing around and looking at her timidly. But the Scarecrow told her about everything, and turning to the dignified little Mouse, he said,

"Permit me to introduce to you her Majesty, the Queen."

Dorothy nodded gravely and the Queen made a courtesy, after which she became quite friendly with the little girl.

The Scarecrow and the Woodman now began to fasten the mice to the truck, using the strings they had brought. One end of a string was tied around the neck

3. *"Permit me to introduce you to her Majesty, the Queen."*
But Denslow draws the Tin Woodman, rather than the
Scarecrow, introducing Dorothy to the Queen of the Field
Mice in the color plate of this scene.

of each mouse and the other end to the truck. Of course the truck was a thousand times bigger than any of the mice who were to draw it; but when all the mice had been harnessed they were able to pull it quite easily. Even the Scarecrow and the Tin Woodman could sit on it, and were drawn swiftly by their queer little horses to the place where the Lion lay asleep.

After a great deal of hard work, for the Lion was heavy, they managed to get him up on the truck. Then

the Queen hurriedly gave her people the order to start, for she feared if the mice stayed among the poppies too long they also would fall asleep.

At first the little creatures, many though they were, could hardly stir the heavily loaded truck; but the Woodman and the Scarecrow both pushed from behind, and they got along better. Soon they rolled the Lion out of the poppy bed to the green fields, where he could breathe the sweet, fresh air again, instead of the poisonous scent of the flowers.

4., 5.

4. *poppy bed*. Another pun: The Lion went to sleep in, appropriately, a flower bed.

5. *to the green fields*. The only original stage business of the 1902 musical extravaganza incorporated into the 1939 MGM film is the snowstorm, created by the Good Witch, to break the spell of the Deadly Poppy Field. This transformation scene was one of the highlights of the show and closed the first act. See illustration on page lxii.

6. *homes*. The queen has strayed far from her home. She and her subjects return in *The Marvelous Land of Oz* (1904), where they live in a village in the Winkie Country in the West rather than in the Munchkin Country in the East.

Dorothy came to meet them and thanked the little mice warmly for saving her companion from death. She had grown so fond of the big Lion she was glad he had been rescued.

Then the mice were unharnessed from the truck and scampered away through the grass to their homes. The Queen of the Mice was the last to leave.

"If ever you need us again," she said, "come out into the field and call, and we shall hear you and come to your assistance. Good bye!"

"Good bye!" they all answered, and away the Queen ran, while Dorothy held Toto tightly lest he should run after her and frighten her.

After this they sat down beside the Lion until he should awaken; and the Scarecrow brought Dorothy some fruit from a tree near by, which she ate for her dinner.

6.

This illustration was the front endpaper design of the Hill edition.

Chapter X.
The Guardian
of the Gate.

It WAS SOME TIME BEFORE THE Cowardly Lion awakened, for he had lain among the poppies a long while, breathing in their deadly fragrance; but when he did open his eyes and roll off the truck he was very glad to find himself still alive.

"I ran as fast as I could," he said, sitting down and yawning; "but the flowers were too strong for me. How did you get me out?"

Then they told him of the field-mice, and how they had generously saved him from death; and the Cowardly Lion laughed, and said,

"I have always thought myself very big and terrible; yet such small things as flowers came near to killing me,

1. *such small animals as mice have saved my life.*
This sentiment reflects the moral of Aesop's
fable "The Lion and the Mouse": "The least
may help the greatest." Baum has added a
corollary through the Deadly Poppy
Field: "The weak may destroy the
strong." The unproduced first draft
of his *Wizard of Oz* play proved that
Baum must have been thinking of
Aesop's fable in the rescue of
the Cowardly Lion. "Once
this lion saved my life," confesses the Queen of the Field
Mice, "and now I can return the
favor."

2. *Land of Oz.* Dorothy is referring to the green countryside surrounding the Emerald City, the land overseen by
Oz the Wizard; she has been in the country known as Oz
ever since her house landed on the Wicked Witch of the
East. But in exploring Baum's ambiguous use of the word
in "The Meaning of Oz" (*The Baum Bugle*, Autumn 1871),
Oz Club member Jay Delkin charged that the author had
decided on using "Oz" only as the Wizard's proper name
long before he decided on a name for the book; he never
once called the country Oz nor referred to Oz as "the Wizard of Oz" except in the title. But that is not consistent with
the entire text. Baum appears to have used "Oz" inter-
changeably for the Wizard *and* the entire country.

1. and such small animals as mice have saved my life. How strange it all is! But, comrades, what shall we do now?"

"We must journey on until we find the road of yellow brick again," said Dorothy; "and then we can keep on to the Emerald City."

So, the Lion being fully refreshed, and feeling quite himself again, they all started upon the journey, greatly enjoying the walk through the soft, fresh grass; and it was not long before they reached the road of yellow brick and turned again toward the Emerald City where the great Oz dwelt.

The road was smooth and well paved, now, and the country about was beautiful; so that the travelers rejoiced in leaving the forest far behind, and with it the many dangers they had met in its gloomy shades.

PLATE 1
Title Page

PLATE 2

"She caught Toto by the ear."

PLATE 3

"I am the Witch of the North."

PLATE 4

"You must be a great sorceress."

PLATE 5

"Dorothy gazed thoughtfully at the Scarecrow."

PLATE 6

" 'I was only made yesterday,' said the Scarecrow."

PLATE 7

" 'This is a great comfort,' said the Tin Woodman."

PLATE 8
"You ought to be ashamed of yourself!"

PLATE 9

"The tree fell with a crash into the gulf."

PLATE 10

"The Stork carried him up into the air."

PLATE 11

"Permit me to introduce to you her Majesty, the Queen."

PLATE 12

"The Lion ate some of the porridge."

PLATE 13

"The Eyes looked at her thoughtfully."

PLATE 14

"The Soldier with the green whiskers led them through the streets."

PLATE 15

"The Monkeys wound many coils about his body."

PLATE 16

"The Tinsmiths worked for three days and four nights."

PLATE 17

"The Monkeys caught Dorothy in their arms and flew away with her."

PLATE 18

"Exactly so! I am a humbug."

PLATE 19

" 'I feel wise, indeed,' said the Scarecrow."

PLATE 20

"The Scarecrow sat on the big throne."

PLATE 21

"The branches bent down and twined around him."

PLATE 22
"These people were all made of china."

PLATE 23

"The Head shot forward and struck the Scarecrow."

PLATE 24

"You must give me the Golden Cap."

Once more they could see fences built beside the road; but these were painted green, and when they came to a small house, in which a farmer evidently lived, that also was painted green. They passed by several of these houses during the afternoon, and sometimes people came to the doors and looked at them as if they would like to ask questions; but no one came near them nor spoke to them because of the great Lion, of which they were much afraid. The people were all dressed in clothing of a lovely emerald green color and wore peaked hats like those of the Munchkins.

2. "This must be the Land of Oz," said Dorothy, "and we are surely getting near the Emerald City."

"Yes," answered the Scarecrow; "everything is green here, while in the country of the Munchkins blue was the favorite color. But the people do not seem to be as friendly as the Munchkins and I'm afraid we shall be unable to find a place to pass the night."

"I should like something to eat besides fruit," said the girl, "and I'm sure Toto is nearly starved. Let us stop at the next house and talk to the people."

So, when they came to a good sized farm house, Dorothy walked boldly up to the door and knocked. A woman opened it just far enough to look out, and said,

"What do you want, child, and why is that great Lion with you?"

"We wish to pass the night with you, if you will allow us," answered Dorothy; "and the Lion is my friend and comrade, and would not hurt you for the world."

"Is he tame?" asked the woman, opening the door a little wider.

"Oh, yes;" said the girl, "and he is a great coward, too; so that he will be more afraid of you than you are of him."

"Well," said the woman, after thinking it over and taking another peep at the Lion, "if that is the case you may come in, and I will give you some supper and a place to sleep."

So they all entered the house, where there were, besides the woman, two children and a man. The man had hurt his leg, and was lying on the couch in a corner. They seemed greatly surprised to see so strange a company, and while the woman was busy laying the table the man asked,

"Where are you all going?"

"To the Emerald City," said Dorothy, "to see the Great Oz."

"Oh, indeed!" exclaimed the man. "Are you sure that Oz will see you?"

"Why not?" she replied.

"Why, it is said that he never lets any one come into his presence. I have been to the Emerald City many times, and it is a beautiful and wonderful place; but I have never been permitted to see the Great Oz, nor do I know of any living person who has seen him."

"Does he never go out?" asked the Scarecrow.

"Never. He sits day after day in the great throne room of his palace, and even those who wait upon him do not see him face to face."

"What is he like?" asked the girl.

"That is hard to tell," said the man, thoughtfully. "You see, Oz is a great Wizard, and can take on any form he wishes. So that some say he looks like a bird; and some say he looks like an elephant; and some say he looks like a cat. To others he appears as a beautiful fairy, or a brownie, or in any other form that pleases him. But who the real Oz is, when he is in his own form, no living person can tell."

"That is very strange," said Dorothy; "but we must try, in some way, to see him, or we shall have made our journey for nothing."

"Why do you wish to see the terrible Oz?" asked the man.

3. *a beautiful fairy, or a brownie*. This passage and the "winged" lady in the next chapter suggest that Baum as yet had not yet entirely eliminated the "stereotyped" fairy from his fairy tales. Baum admits in "The Ryl" in *Baum's American Fairy Tales* (1908) that both the winged fairy and the brownie do have a place in children's books, though not necessarily in his. The Ryl is one of the "servants of nature," but when mistaken for a fairy, he snaps, "Do you see any wings growing out of my body? Do you see any golden hair flowing over my shoulders, or any gauzy cobweb skirts floating about my form in graceful folds?" That was the cliché for a fairy. "Really now," he says on being called a "brownie," "do I look like one of those impossible, crawly, mischievous elves? Is my body ten times bigger than it should be? Do my legs look like toothpicks and my eyes like saucers?" Baum, of course, is describing the brownie as created by the Canadian artist Palmer Cox (1840–1924). His "Brownie" books were best-sellers in their day, and the format of Baum's *Father Goose, His Book* (1899) was in part based on them. (So popular were Cox's drawings that Denslow imitated them with his "Inland Gnomes" in 1894 for *The Inland Printer* as calling cards and other decorations. See illustration on page lvii.) That Baum had Cox in mind is apparent from the Ryl's explanation: "Old nurses prefer to talk about those stupid fairies and hobgoblins, and never mention ryls to the children. And the people who write fairy tales and goose books and brownie books and such rubbish sit down at writing-tables and invent all sorts of impossible and unbelievable things" (pp. 176–77). Cox is the author of the "brownie books," and Baum (of course) is the author of "fairy tales and goose books."

Baum had broadened his view of the traditional fairy by the time he wrote "Modern Fairy Tales" (*The Advance*, August 19, 1909):

> I once asked a little fellow, a friend of mine, to tell me what a "fairy" is. He replied, quite promptly, "A fairy has wings, and is much like an angel, only smaller." Now that, I believe is the general conception of fairies; and it is a pretty conception, is it not? Yet we know the family of immortals generally termed "fairies" has many branches and includes fays, sprites, elves, nymphs, ryls, knooks, gnomes, brownies and many more subdivisions. There is no blue book or history of the imaginative little creatures to guide us in classifying them, but they all have their uses and peculiar characteristics; as, for example, the little ryls, who carry around paint-pots, with which they color, most brilliantly and artistically, the blossoms of the flowers.

4. *no living person can tell*. This is how unsophisticated people try to comprehend the unknowable. Gods are famous for being shape-shifters like the Wizard. God has appeared in different ways to different people throughout history, including bird, elephant, and cat. The word "Oz" could be replaced by "God" without falsifying the statements expressed here. "Fairy" and "brownie" too arose as terms to explain the unexplainable. "Every normal human being," argued W. H. Auden in the "Afterword" to George MacDonald's *The Light Princess* (New York: Farrar, Straus & Giroux, 1967), "is interested in two kinds of worlds: the Primary, everyday world which he knows through his senses and a Secondary world or worlds, which he not only can create in his imagination, but also cannot stop himself creating. A person incapable of imagining another than that given him by his senses is subhuman, and a person who identified his imaginary world with the world of sensory fact has become insane." The fairy tale evolved to fulfill the basic human need to express this secondary world, whether spiritual or purely imaginative. Dorothy has the remarkable ability to pass effortlessly from one to the other.

Baum evidently considered shape-shifting one of the blacker arts of sorcery, since such transformations are based on illusions and deceptions. Shape-shifters are the werewolves and vampires of the horror stories. "I never deal in transformations," declares Glinda the Good in *The Marvelous Land of Oz* (1904), "for they are not honest, and no respectable sorceress likes to make things appear to be what they are not. Only unscrupulous witches use the art" (p. 273). Baum invented a specific kind of witch who specializes in transformations, the Yookoohoo. One of these, Mrs. Yoop, the terrible Giantess of *The Tin Woodman of Oz* (1918), describes herself as "an Artist in Transformations" (p. 73). Red Reera of *Glinda of Oz*, "who assumes all sorts of forms sometimes changing her for several times in a day, according to her fancy" (p. 206), is less malevolent than Mrs. Yoop, for "all her wonderful powers are used for her own selfish amusement." But, adds another character, "What her real form may be we do not know." These women practice the same branch of witchcraft as Circe, the sorceress in the *Odyssey* who transforms unsuspecting travelers into pigs. Not only women indulge in this sort of sorcery: the Munchkin lad Kiki Aru, assisted by the Nome King, gets into all kinds of mischief with a magic word in *The Magic of Oz* (1919). Perhaps the most terrifying creatures in the entire Oz canon are the Phanfasms of *The Emerald City of Oz* (1910). They belong to the race of Erbs, "the most powerful and merciless of all the evil spirits" (p. 126), who constantly change their forms at will from the horrible to the beautiful and back again.

Meyer Levin noticed in "Oz" (*Hollywood Tribune*, August 21, 1939) odd similarities between Baum's story and "one of the most abstract philosophic novels of modern times," Franz Kafka's *The Castle* (1926). "For *The Castle* is the tale of a man who comes to a certain mountain, in the hope of obtaining an interview with the lord of the castle,"

"I want him to give me some brains," said the Scarecrow, eagerly.

"Oh, Oz could do that easily enough," declared the man. "He has more brains than he needs."

"And I want him to give me a heart," said the Tin Woodman.

"That will not trouble him," continued the man, "for Oz has a large collection of hearts, of all sizes and shapes."

"And I want him to give me courage," said the Cowardly Lion.

"Oz keeps a great pot of courage in his throne room," said the man, "which he has covered with a golden plate, to keep it from running over. He will be glad to give you some."

5.

"And I want him to send me back to Kansas," said Dorothy.

"Where is Kansas?" asked the man, in surprise.

"I don't know," replied Dorothy, sorrowfully; "but it is my home, and I'm sure it's somewhere."

"Very likely. Well, Oz can do anything; so I suppose he will find Kansas for you. But first you must get to see him, and that will be a hard task; for the great Wizard does not like to see anyone, and he usually has his own way. But what do you want?" he continued, speaking to Toto. Toto only wagged his tail; for, strange to say, he could not speak.

6.

The woman now called to them that supper was ready,

Levin explained, "but as he penetrates further toward his object, it becomes mysteriously apparent that no one has actually seen the head of the Castle, and there is a suspcion that he does not exist. Yet in his search and progress toward the Castle, the man acquires most of the things for which he yearned: a wife, a home, a place in the community."

5. *a great pot of courage*. In Chapter 16, however, the Wizard stores his "courage" in green bottles.

6. *he could not speak*. Gardner explained in Note 11 of *The Wizard of Oz and Who He Was*, "In *Tik-Tok of Oz* (p. 268) we discover that Toto was capable of speaking the moment he entered Oz. He just didn't feel like it." Aleksandr Volkov differed with the author on this point in his 1939 "translation" of *The Wizard of Oz*. "Baum leaves Toto dumb," he explained, "but in that world where all creatures can talk, not only birds and beasts, but people made of tin and straw, I thought that the clever and loyal Toto ought also to speak, and so in my writing he does."

7. *food for horses*. The Lion seems to be recalling Dr. Samuel Johnson's wry entry under "Oats" in his *Dictionary of the English Language* (1755): "A grain, which in England is generally given to horses, but in Scotland supports the people."

8. *dazzled by their brilliancy*. With an economy of language, Baum describes the mystery and majesty of a fairy city. It must be a remarkable sight indeed to dazzle the painted eyes of a scarecrow! This glimpse of the Emerald City suggests another bejeweled metropolis, the Celestial City of *Pilgrim's Progress*, which is "builded of pearls and precious stones, also the street thereof was paved with gold." Baum's description evokes another capital, Camelot, as described by Alfred Lord Tennyson in *Gareth and Lynette* (1872):

> The damp hill-sides were quicken'd into green,
> And the live green had kindl'd into flowers,
> For it was the time of Easterday.
> So, when their feet were planted on the plain,
> That broaden'd toward the base of Camelot,
> Far off they saw the silvery-misty morn
> Rolling her smoke about the Royal mount,
> That rose between the forest and the field.
> At times the spires and turrets half-way down
> Prick'd thro the mist; at times the great gate shone
> Only, that open'd on the field below. . . .

so they gathered around the table and Dorothy ate some delicious porridge and a dish of scrambled eggs and a plate of nice white bread, and enjoyed her meal. The Lion ate some of the porridge, but did not care for it, saying it was made from oats and oats were food for horses, not for lions. The Scarecrow and the Tin Woodman ate nothing at all. Toto ate a little of everything, and was glad to get a good supper again.

7.

The woman now gave Dorothy a bed to sleep in, and Toto lay down beside her, while the Lion guarded the door of her room so she might not be disturbed. The Scarecrow and the Tin Woodman stood up in a corner and kept quiet all night, although of course they could not sleep.

The next morning, as soon as the sun was up, they started on their way, and soon saw a beautiful green glow in the sky just before them.

"That must be the Emerald City," said Dorothy.

As they walked on, the green glow became brighter and brighter, and it seemed that at last they were nearing the end of their travels. Yet it was afternoon before they came to the great wall that surrounded the City. It was high, and thick, and of a bright green color.

In front of them, and at the end of the road of yellow brick, was a big gate, all studded with emeralds that glittered so in the sun that even the painted eyes of the Scarecrow were dazzled by their brilliancy.

8.

There was a bell beside the gate, and Dorothy pushed

the button and heard a silvery tinkle sound within. Then the big gate swung slowly open, and they all passed through and found themselves in a high arched room, the walls of which glistened with countless emeralds.

Before them stood a little man about the same size as the Munchkins. He was clothed all in green, from his head to his feet, and even his skin was of a greenish tint. At his side was a large green box.

When he saw Dorothy and her companions the man asked,

"What do you wish in the Emerald City?"

"We came here to see the Great Oz," said Dorothy.

The man was so surprised at this answer that he sat down to think it over.

"It has been many years since anyone asked me to see Oz," he said, shaking his head in perplexity. "He is powerful and terrible, and if you come on an idle or foolish errand to bother the wise reflections of the Great Wizard, he might be angry and destroy you all in an instant."

"But it is not a foolish errand, nor an idle one," replied the Scarecrow; "it is important. And we have been told that Oz is a good Wizard."

"So he is," said the green man; "and he rules the Emerald City wisely and well. But to those who are not honest, or who approach him from curiosity, he is most terrible, and few have ever dared ask to see his face. I am the Guardian of the Gates, and since you demand to see the Great Oz I must take you to his palace. But first you must put on the spectacles."

"Why?" asked Dorothy.

"Because if you did not wear spectacles the brightness and glory of the Emerald City would blind you. Even those who live in the City must wear spectacles night and day. They are all locked on, for Oz so ordered it when the City was first built, and I have the only key that will unlock them."

He opened the big box, and Dorothy saw that it was filled with spectacles of every size and shape. All of them had green glasses in them. The Guardian of the gates found a pair that would just fit Dorothy and put them over her eyes. There were

9.

10.

9. *the Guardian of the Gates.* Florence Ryerson and Edgar Allan Woolf suggested in their revision of Noel Langley's screenplay for the 1939 MGM picture that the role of the Wizard be expanded to let the same actor play the Guardian of the Gates, the cabbie with the Horse of a Different Color, and the Soldier with the Green Whiskers in various disguises. They believed that Frank Morgan needed more screen time, so that the audience would not "feel cheated because they didn't see enough of him." This solution was a clever way of reinforcing Baum's point that Oz is a master of deception. A later Royal Historian of Oz, Jack Snow, actually combined the Guardian of the Gates and the Soldier with the Green Whiskers into one character in *The Magical Mimics in Oz* (1946).

10. *All of them had green glasses in them.* Sunglasses were not so common then as today, because people usually used visors to shade their eyes from bright light. The blind and other people with serious vision problems were the ones who generally wore tinted spectacles in the street. Austrian artist Lisbeth Zwerger, who illustrated the 1996 North-South edition of *The Wizard of Oz*, admitted that "even though green is my favorite color, I was so intimidated by the need to paint all the scenes in the Emerald City in shades of green that it seemed as though the book would never be completed. The idea of including a pair of green-tinted glasses saved the project. It allowed me much greater freedom. I have tried to meet the challenge of bringing something new to Baum's marvelous story, and in the end I greatly enjoyed my stay in the land of Oz." Each copy of the book contained a little pair of green paper spectacles inserted in the back endpaper.

two golden bands fastened to them that passed around the back of her head, where they were locked together by a little key that was at the end of a chain the Guardian of the Gates wore around his neck. When they were on, Dorothy could not take them off had she wished, but of course she did not want to be blinded by the glare of the Emerald City, so she said nothing.

Then the green man fitted spectacles for the Scarecrow and the Tin Woodman and the Lion, and even on little Toto; and all were locked fast with the key.

Then the Guardian of the Gates put on his own glasses and told them he was ready to show them to the palace. Taking a big golden key from a peg on the wall he opened another gate, and they all followed him through the portal into the streets of the Emerald City.

Chapter XI.
The Wonderful Emerald City of OZ.

Even WITH EYES protected by the green spectacles Dorothy and her friends were at first dazzled by the brilliancy of the wonderful City. The streets were lined with beautiful houses all built of green marble and studded everywhere with sparkling emeralds. They walked over a pavement of the same green marble, and where the blocks were joined together were rows of emeralds, set closely, and glittering in the brightness of the sun. The window panes were of green glass; even the sky above the City had a green tint, and the rays of the sun were green.

There were many people, men, women and children,

1.

2.

1. *the wonderful City.* The Emerald City of Oz (1910, p. 29) gives some indication of the size of the capital of the country: 9,654 buildings and 57,318 citizens. The Emerald City may have in part been inspired by the White City, the ideally designed metropolis of the 1893 World's Columbian Exposition in Chicago. It had special significance for both Baum and Denslow: The fair brought Baum to Chicago in 1891 and Denslow in 1893. "It is literally stunning, the immensity of the thing," Denslow noted in his diary of May 3. "Miles of ground covered with tremendous and artistic buildings. My first thoughts were, knowing that they are only intended for short use of six months, was what a magnificent ruin they must make when all is finished." Denslow spent nearly every day of the exposition at the White City, sketching the sights and characters for the Chicago *Herald.* Baum went often with Maud and the boys and sometimes on his own, so he knew well all the marvels it held. There were all sorts of eccentric entertainments and amusements, such as Buffalo Bill's Wild West Show and the belly dancer Little Egypt, and performers varied from the pianist Ignace Paderewski to the pugilist James J. Corbett. This world's fair introduced cotton candy, Cracker Jack, and the Ferris wheel. Like the Emerald City, the White City seemed to spring up suddenly out of nowhere in the center of the country from the swamps along the lake. The shops and vendors along the Midway Pleasance were as lively as those in the capital of Oz. The glittering emeralds may have been suggested by the little lights all over the White City that were lit up at night. In *Two Little Pilgrims' Progress* (1897), Frances Hodgson Burnett compared the White City to the City Beautiful in Bunyan's *Pilgrim's Progress,* and the effect of the electric lights at night was quite extraordinary. Burnett said that after dark the White City seemed to be set "with myriads of diamonds, all alight. Endless chains of jewels seemed strung and wound about it. The Palace of Flowers held up a great crystal of light glowing against the dark blue of the sky, towers and domes were crowned and diademed, thousands of jewels hung among the masses of leaves, or reflected themselves, sparkling in the darkness of the lagoons, fountains of molten jewels sprung up, and flamed and changed" (p. 171). Denslow even borrowed the general architecture of the White City, an eclectic blending of European and Near Eastern elements with towers and minarets and banners flying everywhere, for the Emerald City.

2. *many people.* According to *The Magic of Oz* (1919, p. 54), an inhabitant of the Emerald City is an "Ozmie," perhaps a misprint for "Ozmite," the now generally accepted name. A native of the Land of Oz is an "Ozite" (*Dorothy and the Wizard in Oz,* 1908, p. 224; and *The Emerald City of Oz,* 1910, p. 30).

3. *lemonade.* Though hardly a teetotaler, Baum was so fond of this drink that the Los Angeles *Evening Herald* (April 17, 1913) called him "the champion long-distance lemonade consumer of the local rialto." When a child came over to Ozcot, his home in Hollywood, California, Maud Baum often made up a pitcher, and the Royal Historian and his little visitor sat in the garden, talking and drinking their lemonade.

4. *green pennies.* Probably copper coins, which often turn green. The wonderful things that Baum describes in the shops of the wonderful Emerald City of Oz are exactly what a child might notice and buy with her pennies. Currency, as a part of the economy of Oz, exists only in the earliest of Baum's Oz stories. While in the Jackdaws' Nest in Chapter 19 of *The Marvelous Land of Oz* (1904), the Scarecrow gets stuffed with dollar bills of various denominations, and the Tin Woodman appoints him his Royal Treasurer at story's end. But Baum finally acknowledged in a letter to a young reader on February 8, 1919, that "the Scarecrow stuffed with money . . . was a bad mistake." As the series progresses, Princess Ozma abolishes currency by royal decree. The Tin Woodman explains why in *The Road to Oz* (1909):

> Money in Oz! Money in Oz! . . . What a queer idea! Did you suppose we are so vulgar as to use money here? . . . If we used money to buy things with, instead of love and kindness and the desire to please one another, then we should be no better than the rest of the world. . . . Fortunately money is not known in the Land of Oz at all. We have no rich, and no poor; for what one wishes the others all try to give him, in order to make him happy, and no one in all Oz cares to have more than he can use. (pp. 164–65)

Baum may have done away with money in Oz because of his own increasing financial troubles, which finally resulted in his having to file for bankruptcy two years after he wrote the above passage.

Prior to the success of *The Wizard of Oz,* the Baums went through some lean years. In his autobiography (*The Baum Bugle,* Christmas 1970), Baum's son Robert recalled conditions in Chicago just before his father turned to writing children's books:

> Money was not very plentiful and a penny went a long way. When I would ask Father or Mother for money, which was not very often, I would get a penny and go over to the candy store or grocery store to see what I could buy. Standing in front of the case I would ask "How many of these for a penny?" And it was surprising what a penny would buy.

walking about, and these were all dressed in green clothes and had greenish skins. They looked at Dorothy and her strangely assorted company with wondering eyes, and the children all ran away and hid behind their mothers when they saw the Lion; but no one spoke to them. Many shops stood in the street, and Dorothy saw that everything in them was green. Green candy and green pop-corn were offered for sale, as well as green shoes, green hats and green clothes of all sorts. At one place a man was selling green lemonade, and when the children bought it Dorothy could see that they paid for it with green pennies.

There seemed to be no horses nor animals of any kind; the men carried things around in little green carts, which they pushed before them. Everyone seemed happy and contented and prosperous.

The Guardian of the Gates led them through the streets until they came to a big building, exactly in the middle of the City, which was the Palace of Oz, the Great Wizard. There was a soldier before the door, dressed in a green uniform and wearing a long green beard.

"Here are strangers," said the Guardian of the Gates to him, "and they demand to see the Great Oz."

"Step inside," answered the soldier, "and I will carry your message to him."

So they passed through the Palace gates and were led into a big room with a green carpet and lovely green furniture set with emeralds. The soldier made them all

Not very good candy, probably, but sweet and satisfying to the taste. . . . Red letter days were when Father would come home from a sales trip and we would ask for a penny and he would magnanimously hand out a nickel. And all the things a nickel would buy, quite enough to upset our digestions for the next few days. (pp. 19–20)

5. *no horses.* Suzanne Rahn reported in her monograph on *The Wizard of Oz* (p. 49) that for cleanliness' sake, horses were barred from the fairgrounds of the World's Columbian Exposition in Chicago in 1893. Baum may simply be recalling that the only means of transport through the White City was by foot or in boats through the canals.

6. *animals of any kind.* But, as revealed in the very last line of this chapter, the Emerald City is not entirely devoid of livestock. The hen who lays a green egg contradicts the later Oz books in which Billina the Yellow Hen of *Ozma of Oz* (1907) is said to be the only chicken in Oz.

7. *wearing a long green beard.* The official title of the Soldier with the Green Whiskers in *The Marvelous Land of Oz* (1904, p. 94) is "the Royal Army of Oz," but not until the third Oz book, *Ozma of Oz* (1907, p. 261), is his name given—Omby Amby. He had been called Timothy Alfalfa in the 1902 *Wizard of Oz* musical extravaganza, but the character was cut from the show. Ruth Plumly Thompson renamed him Wantowin Battles in *Ozoplaning with the Wizard of Oz* (1939). Having gone to the Peekskill Military School for two years, Baum understandably had a low opinion of the military—the officers, not the soldiers. Oddly, he sent his three older boys to the Michigan Military School, Orchard Lake, Michigan. The Soldier with the Green Whiskers is Baum's gentle jab at the army. This soldier is

more for show than for battle, and Denslow adds a nice touch with the bouquet of flowers in his musket. In his fancy uniform and long green whiskers, he is more like a member of a military band than a warrior. He turns out to be woefully inadequate as a fighter when General Jinjur and her Army of Revolt invade the Emerald City in *The Marvelous Land of Oz.* He confesses to the female rebels that "my gun isn't loaded . . . for fear of accidents. And I've forgotten where I hid the powder and shot to load it with. But if you'll wait a short time I'll try to hunt them up" (p. 86). The illustrator John R. Neill draws a plug in his musket like a pop gun. Princess Ozma's Army of Oz is not much better in *Ozma of Oz* (1907): twenty-six officers and just one private, Omby Amby. He has cut off his whiskers when Ozma promotes him to Captain General, but grown them back by *The Patchwork Girl of Oz* (1913).

8. *his screen.* Remember this screen, for it plays an important part in the events of Chapter 15. It is one of several small but pertinent details in this and the following chapter that foreshadow the discovery of Oz, the Terrible.

9. *The soldier now blew upon a green whistle.* This seems to be the most common way of summoning someone in Oz. The Wicked Witch of the West has a silver whistle, as does Dorothy to call the Queen of the Field Mice in Chapter 14.

10. *a young girl.* Her name is Jellia Jamb ("Jelly or jam?") in *The Marvelous Land of Oz* (p. 77). When Ruth Plumly Thompson gathers together the characters from *The Wizard of Oz* for a reunion in *Ozoplaning with the Wizard of Oz* (1939), Jellia Jamb becomes the heroine of the story, the only time in all the long Oz series.

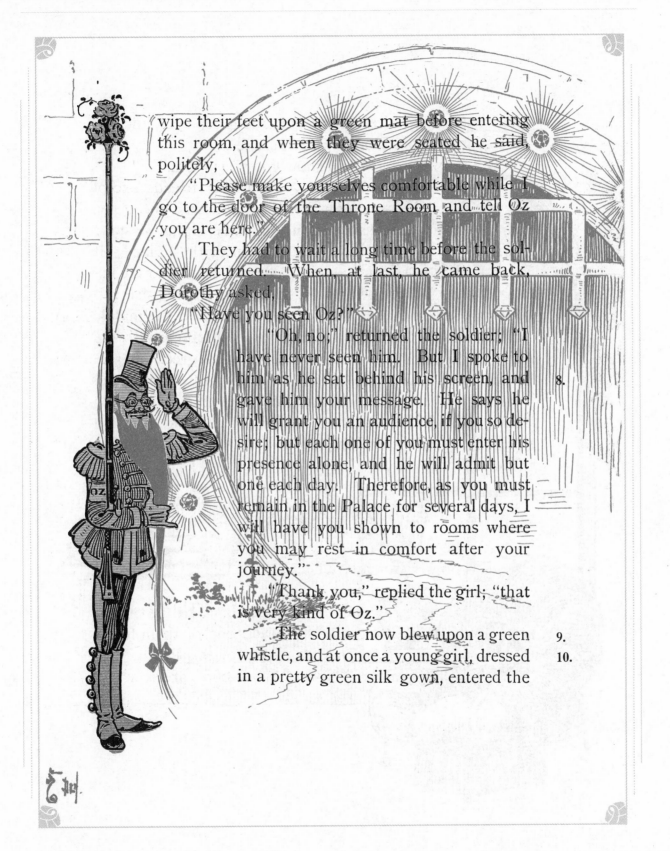

wipe their feet upon a green mat before entering this room, and when they were seated he said, politely,

"Please make yourselves comfortable while I go to the door of the Throne Room and tell Oz you are here."

They had to wait a long time before the soldier returned. When, at last, he came back, Dorothy asked,

"Have you seen Oz?"

"Oh, no;" returned the soldier; "I have never seen him. But I spoke to him as he sat behind his screen, and gave him your message. He says he will grant you an audience, if you so desire; but each one of you must enter his presence alone, and he will admit but one each day. Therefore, as you must remain in the Palace for several days, I will have you shown to rooms where you may rest in comfort after your journey."

"Thank you," replied the girl; "that is very kind of Oz."

The soldier now blew upon a green whistle, and at once a young girl, dressed in a pretty green silk gown, entered the

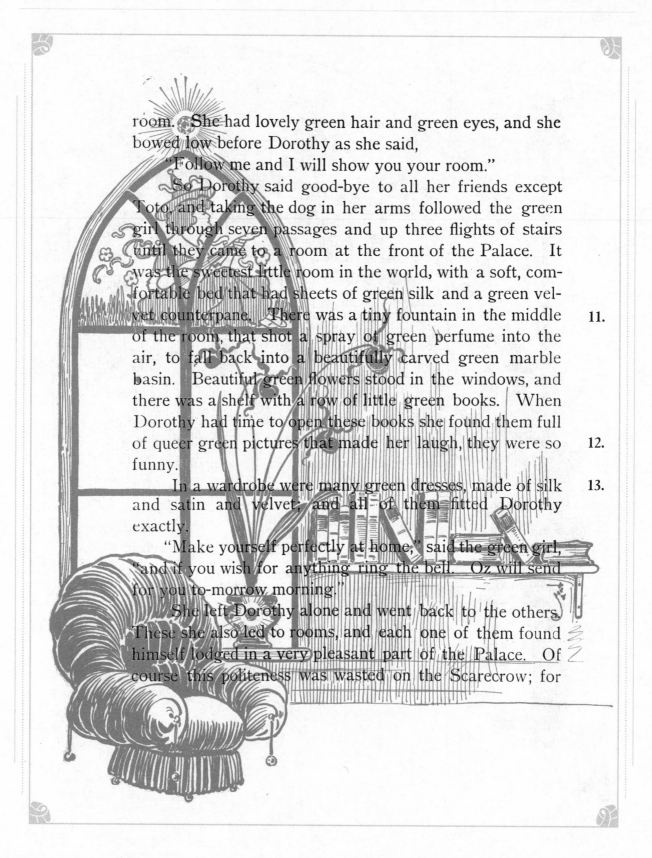

room. She had lovely green hair and green eyes, and she bowed low before Dorothy as she said,

"Follow me and I will show you your room."

So Dorothy said good-bye to all her friends except Toto, and taking the dog in her arms followed the green girl through seven passages and up three flights of stairs until they came to a room at the front of the Palace. It was the sweetest little room in the world, with a soft, comfortable bed that had sheets of green silk and a green velvet counterpane. There was a tiny fountain in the middle of the room, that shot a spray of green perfume into the air, to fall back into a beautifully carved green marble basin. Beautiful green flowers stood in the windows, and there was a shelf with a row of little green books. When Dorothy had time to open these books she found them full of queer green pictures that made her laugh, they were so funny.

In a wardrobe were many green dresses, made of silk and satin and velvet, and all of them fitted Dorothy exactly.

"Make yourself perfectly at home," said the green girl, "and if you wish for anything ring the bell. Oz will send for you to-morrow morning."

She left Dorothy alone and went back to the others. These she also led to rooms, and each one of them found himself lodged in a very pleasant part of the Palace. Of course this politeness was wasted on the Scarecrow; for

11.

12.

13.

when he found himself alone in his room he stood stupidly in one spot, just within the doorway, to wait till morning. It would not rest him to lie down, and he could not close his eyes; so he remained all night staring at a little spider

14.   which was weaving its web in a corner of the room, just as if it were not one of the most wonderful rooms in the world. The Tin Woodman lay down on his bed from force of habit, for he remembered when he was made of flesh; but not being able to sleep he passed the night moving his joints up and down to make sure they kept in good working order. The Lion would have preferred a bed of dried leaves in the forest, and did not like being shut up in a room; but he had too much sense to let this worry him, so he sprang upon the bed and rolled himself

15.   up like a cat and purred himself asleep in a minute.

The next morning, after breakfast, the green maiden came to fetch Dorothy, and she dressed her in one of the prettiest gowns—made of green brocaded satin. Dorothy put on a green silk apron and tied a green ribbon around Toto's neck, and they started for the Throne Room of the Great Oz.

First they came to a great hall in which were many ladies and gentlemen of the court, all dressed in rich costumes.

16.   These people had nothing to do but talk to each other, but they always came to

11. *counterpane*. Bedspread today.

12. *queer green pictures*. Could these little green books with queer green pictures be copies of *The Wonderful Wizard of Oz*? The first edition was bound in apple green cloth and full of queer green pictures too, particularly in the Emerald City chapters. It would have made Dorothy laugh to see herself portrayed in Denslow's funny pictures. This supposition is reminiscent of a device in the *nouveau roman* and other modern literature. Michel Butor's *La Modification* (1957), like Marcel Proust's *À la recherche du temps perdu* (1913–1927), ends with the narrator deciding to write the same story the reader has just finished; the scattered pages left on the hero's table at the close of Alain Robbe-Grillet's *Dans le labyrinthe* (1959) may just be *Dans le labyrinthe* in manuscript.

13. *silk and satin and velvet*. Quite a contrast to Dorothy's usual gingham. Like all the clothes in Oz, they are just her size. They must be the native costume of the inhabitants of the Emerald City. "There were many people on these walks—men, women, and children—all dressed in handsome garments of silk or satin or velvet, with beautiful jewels," Baum reports in *The Road to Oz* (1909). "Better even than this: all seemed happy and contented, for their faces were smiling and free from care, and music and laughter might be heard on every side" (pp. 190–91).

14. *a little spider which was weaving its web*. Notice how beautifully Baum constructs a sense of reality by bringing the fantasy back to earth through precise, commonplace detail. This is a skill he demonstrates throughout the writing of *The Wizard of Oz*. "Reality and unreality are so entwined that it is often difficult to know where one leaves off and the other begins," wrote Frank J. Baum in "Why the Wizard of Oz Keeps On Selling" (*Writer's Digest*, December 1952).

15. *purred himself asleep*. Of course, lions do not purr. Baum is merely reinforcing the image of the Cowardly Lion as a big gentle house cat.

16. *These people had nothing to do but talk to each other*. Like most nobility, the author implies. Baum may have been aware that in ancient Egyptian temples nobles were kept outside the sacred chamber in a separate room. "Baum's deep affection for the monarchy and the trappings of royalty that runs through all the books reflects a facet of sensibility shared by many nineteenth century Americans," wrote Bewley in his revision of "Oz Country" in *Masks and Mirrors* (New York: Atheneum, 1970, p. 261). Perhaps, but it is only a superficial respect here. Baum has his doubts as to their worth as well.

17. *ask to see him.* Many readers have noticed the Biblical overtones to this chapter. Oz Club member David L. Greene noted that when Jehovah appeared in a burning bush in Exodus, Moses was too afraid to gaze upon the face of God and covered his eyes. Obviously, the Wizard wishes his people to think of him as a god. They believe he changes his form at will, and he is in general a mystery to them. One must be worthy to have an audience with him, but few are chosen. Had Dorothy not had the Silver Shoes and the Good Witch's kiss, she might never have been admitted. If he were indeed a god, then the discovery of Oz, the Terrible, in Chapter 15 would be bitter indeed.

Baum plays with "seeing" with Carrollian logic in this passage. While the courtiers wonder if she will actually be permitted an audience with the Great Oz, Dorothy naively concludes that he will let her look upon him. The soldier, however, takes her literally and infers that Oz will be able to look at her even if she cannot look upon him. It becomes quite clear in Chapter 15 why the Wizard refuses to meet with his people.

18. *a great light.* Baum may well have intended this to be an electric light. The wizard in *A New Wonderland* (1900, p. 134) has one in his dwelling. The 1893 World's Columbian Exposition was famous for being illuminated by electricity and did much to popularize Thomas A. Edison's marvelous invention. In 1900, electricity was still one of the world's great untapped wonders. Electric lights are found everywhere in Baum's fairy tales. Mermaid palaces are lit by electrical jellyfish in *The Sea Fairies* (1910). "We use electric lights in our palaces," reports one of the sea maidens, "and have done so for thousands of years—long before the earth people knew of electric lights" (p. 92). Of all the lovely ladies in the palace of the Queen of Light in *Tik-Tok of Oz* (1914), Electra is "the most beautiful," so that "both Sunlight and Daylight regarded Electra with envy and were a little jealous of her" (p. 130).

Baum followed *The Wonderful Wizard of Oz* with his one experiment in science fiction, *The Master Key* (1901), his "electrical fairy tale" in which a boy accidentally summons the Demon of Electricity to do his bidding. The young hero was inspired by Baum's son Robert, who recalled his fascination with electricity in his autobiography:

> I was interested in anything of a mechanical nature and up in the large attic . . . I had a workshop in which I made many things . . . but my special pet projects I worked out in my own room, which was in the back of the house on the second floor. My parents really must have been quite lenient with me, because I bored holes all through the house and installed wires to operate my various gadgets. For instance, when I wanted privacy in my room, I got it by the very simple expedient of installing a wire from a spark coil and battery to the inside handle of my door. When anyone from the outside took hold of the handle and turned it, contact was made and caused him to change his mind about entering.
>
> I also rigged up an apparatus which I attached to our gas lights so that by pushing a button the gas was turned on, and an electric spark ignited it. As I was still going to the Lewis [Institute], and we now lived much further away, I had to leave home early in the morning, so I rigged up an annunciator drop in the kitchen to simplify matters to me. As soon as I got out of bed, I pushed a button in my room and the annunciator came down with a sign saying, "START BREAKFAST." This was the signal to our cook and, by the time I got down, my breakfast was ready.

Lenient indeed! "Rob fills the house with electrical batteries and such truck," Baum reported to his brother Harry on April 8, 1900, "and we are prepared to hear a bell ring whenever we open a door or step on a stair." Much of this chaos was captured in the opening chapters of *The Master Key.*

Baum's interest in mechanical inventions nearly matched his son's, and he had faith in the potentials of electricity, just then coming of age. "Electricity is destined to become the motive power of the world," Mr. Joslin speaks for Baum in *The Master Key.* "The future advance of civilization will be along electrical lines" (pp. 2–3).

wait outside the Throne Room every morning, although they were never permitted to see Oz. As Dorothy entered they looked at her curiously, and one of them whispered,

"Are you really going to look upon the face of Oz the Terrible?"

"Of course," answered the girl, "if he will see me."

"Oh, he will see you," said the soldier who had taken her message to the Wizard, "although he does not like to have people ask to see him. Indeed, at first he was angry, and said I should send you back where you came from. Then he asked me what you looked like, and when I mentioned your silver shoes he was very much interested. At last I told him about the mark upon your forehead, and he decided he would admit you to his presence." 17.

Just then a bell rang, and the green girl said to Dorothy,

"That is the signal. You must go into the Throne Room alone."

She opened a little door and Dorothy walked boldly through and found herself in a wonderful place. It was a big, round room with a high arched roof, and the walls and ceiling and floor were covered with large emeralds set closely together. In the center of the roof was a great 18. light, as bright as the sun, which made the emeralds sparkle in a wonderful manner.

But what interested Dorothy most was the big throne of green marble that stood in the middle of the room. It

19. *I am Oz, the Great and Terrible.* Baum's Oz is as bombastic as Shelley's Ozymandias:

> My name is Ozymandias, king of kings:
> Look on my works, ye Mighty, and despair!

Compare this meaning of "Oz" to that mentioned in Chapter 2, Note 17: "Great and Good." The Wizard's title is reminiscent of "the most evil character in all the Oz books" (as both Nye and Bewley noted), the First and Foremost, ruler of the dreaded Phanfasms in *The Emerald City of Oz* (1910). "That beautifully sinister title," observed Bewley in "Oz Country," "sums up the ultimate meaning of Oz history. The aggrandizement of the individual and private self at the expense of others is the root of all evil." That is also true of Oz, the Great and Terrible, now addressing Dorothy, the Small and Meek.

20. *Dorothy, the Small and Meek.* No better reply could have been chosen. Poor mortals seeking aid from gods or mighty rulers often feign humility to curry favor.

was shaped like a chair and sparkled with gems, as did everything else. In the center of the chair was an enormous Head, without body to support it or any arms or legs whatever. There was no hair upon this head, but it had eyes and nose and mouth, and was bigger than the head of the biggest giant.

As Dorothy gazed upon this in wonder and fear the eyes turned slowly and looked at her sharply and steadily. Then the mouth moved, and Dorothy heard a voice say:

"I am Oz, the Great and Terrible. Who are you, and why do you seek me?"   19.

It was not such an awful voice as she had expected to come from the big Head; so she took courage and answered,

"I am Dorothy, the Small and Meek. I have come to you for help."   20.

The eyes looked at her thoughtfully for a full minute. Then said the voice:

"Where did you get the silver shoes?"

"I got them from the wicked Witch of the East, when my house fell on her and killed her," she replied.

"Where did you get the mark upon your forehead?" continued the voice.

"That is where the good Witch of the North kissed me when she bade me good-bye and sent me to you," said the girl.

Again the eyes looked at her sharply, and they saw she was telling the truth. Then Oz asked,

"What do you wish me to do?"

"Send me back to Kansas, where my Aunt Em and Uncle Henry are," she answered, earnestly. "I don't like your country, although it is so beautiful. And I am sure Aunt Em will be dreadfully worried over my being away so long."

The eyes winked three times, and then they turned up to the ceiling and down to the floor and rolled around so queerly that they seemed to see every part of the room. And at last they looked at Dorothy again.

"Why should I do this for you?" asked Oz.

"Because you are strong and I am weak; because you are a Great Wizard and I am only a helpless little girl," she answered.

"But you were strong enough to kill the wicked Witch of the East," said Oz.

"That just happened," returned Dorothy, simply; "I could not help it."

"Well," said the Head, "I will give you my answer. You have no right to expect me to send you back to Kansas unless you do something for me in return. In this country everyone must pay for everything he gets. If you wish me to use my magic power to send you home again you must do something for me first. Help me and I will help you."

"What must I do?" asked the girl.

"Kill the wicked Witch of the West," answered Oz.

"But I cannot!" exclaimed Dorothy, greatly surprised.

"You killed the Witch of the East and you wear the silver shoes, which bear a powerful charm. There is now but one Wicked Witch left in all this land, and when you can tell me she is dead I will send you back to Kansas—but not before."

The little girl began to weep, she was so much disappointed; and the eyes winked again and looked upon her anxiously, as if the Great Oz felt that she could help him if she would.

"I never killed anything, willingly," she sobbed; "and even if I wanted to, how could I kill the Wicked Witch? If you, who are Great and Terrible, cannot kill her yourself, how do you expect me to do it?"

"I do not know," said the Head; "but that is my answer, and until the Wicked Witch dies you will not see your Uncle and Aunt again. Remember that the Witch is Wicked—tremendously Wicked —and ought to be killed. Now go, and do not ask to see me again until you have done your task."

Sorrowfully Dorothy left the Throne Room and went back

21.

21. *looked upon her anxiously*. This suggests that the Head is not so terrible as it appears. It is almost human! The eyes nearly implore Dorothy to kill the Wicked Witch of the West for the Wizard's sake.

22. *wings*. This is the only appearance of a traditional fairy in any of Baum's Royal History of Oz. Note that Denslow's lovely lady does *not* wear wings. She bears a striking resemblance to John R. Neill's depiction of Princess Ozma in *Ozma of Oz* (1907) and subsequent Oz books. Aleksandr Volkov made her a mermaid in his 1939 Russian "translation."

where the Lion and the Scarecrow and the Tin Woodman were waiting to hear what Oz had said to her.

"There is no hope for me," she said, sadly, "for Oz will not send me home until I have killed the Wicked Witch of the West; and that I can never do."

Her friends were sorry, but could do nothing to help her; so she went to her own room and lay down on the bed and cried herself to sleep.

The next morning the soldier with the green whiskers came to the Scarecrow and said,

"Come with me, for Oz has sent for you."

So the Scarecrow followed him and was admitted into the great Throne Room, where he saw, sitting in the emerald throne, a most lovely lady. She was dressed in green silk gauze and wore upon her flowing green locks a crown of jewels. Growing from her shoulders were wings, gorgeous in color and so light that they fluttered if the slightest breath of air reached them.

22.

When the Scarecrow had bowed, as prettily as his straw stuffing would let him, before this beautiful creature, she looked upon him sweetly, and said,

"I am Oz, the Great and Terrible. Who are you, and why do you seek me?"

Now the Scarecrow, who had expected to see the great Head Dorothy had told him of, was much astonished; but he answered her bravely.

"I am only a Scarecrow, stuffed with straw. Therefore I have no brains, and I come to you praying that you will put brains in my head instead of straw, so that I may become as much a man as any other in your dominions."

"Why should I do this for you?" asked the lady.

"Because you are wise and powerful, and no one else can help me," answered the Scarecrow.

"I never grant favors without some return," said Oz; "but this much I will promise. If you will kill for me the Wicked Witch of the West I will bestow upon you a great many brains, and such good brains that you will be the wisest man in all the Land of Oz."

"I thought you asked Dorothy to kill the Witch," said the Scarecrow, in surprise.

"So I did. I don't care who kills her. But until she is dead I will not grant your wish. Now go, and do not seek me again until you have earned the brains you so greatly desire."

The Scarecrow went sorrowfully back to his friends and told them what Oz had said; and Dorothy was surprised to find that the great Wizard was not a Head, as she had seen him, but a lovely lady.

"All the same," said the Scarecrow, "she needs a heart as much as the Tin Woodman."

On the next morning the soldier with the green whiskers came to the Tin Woodman and said,

"Oz has sent for you.   Follow me,"

So the Tin Woodman followed him and came to the great Throne Room.   He did not know whether he would find Oz a lovely lady or a Head, but he hoped it would be the lovely lady.   "For," he said to himself, "if it is the Head, I am sure I shall not be given a heart, since a head has no heart of its own and therefore cannot feel for me.   But if it is the lovely lady I shall beg hard for a heart, for all ladies are themselves said to be kindly hearted."

But when the Woodman entered the great Throne Room he saw neither the Head nor the Lady, for Oz had taken the shape of a most terrible Beast.   It was nearly as big as an elephant, and the green throne seemed hardly strong enough to hold its weight.   The Beast had a head like that of a rhinoceros, only there were five eyes in its face.   There were five long arms growing out of its body and it also had five long, slim legs.   Thick, woolly hair covered every part of it, and a more dreadful looking monster could not be imagined.   It was fortunate the Tin Woodman had no heart at that moment, for it would have beat loud and fast from terror.   But being only tin, the Woodman was not at all afraid, although he was much disappointed.

"I am Oz, the Great and Terrible," spake the Beast, in a voice that was one great roar.   "Who are you, and why do you seek me?"

23.

23. *a most terrible Beast*. Literature and legend are full of such creatures, made up of parts of various animals. There is the Great Beast (Satan) of the Book of Revelation, with seven heads and ten horns. Baum's Beast is as horrible as Apollyon, the monster in *Pilgrim's Progress*, "with scales like a fish . . . wings like a dragon, feet like a bear, and out of his belly came fire and smoke, and his mouth was as the mouth of a lion." Baum created all sorts of conglomerate beasts in his stories. They may be the transformations of magicians, like the Li-Mon-Eags in *The Magic of Oz* (1919), or natural creatures in the wild, like the Hip-po-Gy-Raf in *The Tin Woodman of Oz* (1918). In the unproduced first draft for the musical extravaganza of *The Wizard of Oz*, Baum replaced this most terrible Beast with "a huge crab-like beast," perhaps because it would have been easier to reproduce onstage than the bizarre monster in the story. Neither of these creatures nor any of the Wizard's disguises appeared in the final production.

Denslow began drawing the most terrible Beast, but Baum apparently thought it too terrible for the children's books and had him abandon it. Denslow drew over it in ink the color plate of the Soldier with the Green Whiskers leading the four travelers through the streets of the Emerald City. The original pencil sketch of the monster can just barely be seen on the original drawing in the Henry Goldsmith Collection, Prints and Drawings Division, the New York Public Library. Few subsequent illustrators have ever depicted this third transformation of the Wizard.

24. *loving heart*. "The Wizard failed to keep his promise," explained Gardner in Note 14 of *The Wizard of Oz and Who He Was*. "We learn in *The Tin Woodman of Oz* (p. 31) that it was a 'kind' but not a 'loving' heart." This is indicated in Chapter 16 when the Tin Woodman receives his heart and asks, "But is it a kind heart?" and the Wizard replies, "Oh, very!" The Tin Woodman confesses in *The Tin Woodman of Oz* that the reason he failed to return immediately to the girl after he received his heart was that he could not love her "any more than I did when I was heartless" (p. 31).

25. *to give us what we desire*. The Lion comments on the irony of their situation. Had each only gone before the other in sequence, all of their problems might have been solved. The Scarecrow could have appealed to the great Head's intellect for a brain, the Tin Woodman might have wooed the lovely lady for a heart, and the Lion could have challenged the Beast to a battle of strength for some courage. Each could have shown a different form of Oz that he already knew how to use the gift he so desired. As it happens, he is confronted with one he can neither comprehend nor overcome.

"I am a Woodman, and made of tin. Therefore I have no heart, and cannot love. I pray you to give me a heart that I may be as other men are."

"Why should I do this?" demanded the Beast.

"Because I ask it, and you alone can grant my request," answered the Woodman.

Oz gave a low growl at this, but said, gruffly,

"If you indeed desire a heart, you must earn it."

"How?" asked the Woodman.

"Help Dorothy to kill the Wicked Witch of the West," replied the Beast. "When the Witch is dead, come to me, and I will then give you the biggest and kindest and most loving heart in all the Land of Oz."

24.

So the Tin Woodman was forced to return sorrowfully to his friends and tell them of the terrible Beast he had seen. They all wondered greatly at the many forms the great Wizard could take upon himself, and the Lion said,

"If he is a beast when I go to see him, I shall roar my loudest, and so frighten him that he will grant all I ask. And if he is the lovely lady, I shall pretend to spring upon her, and so compel her to do my bidding. And if he is the great Head, he will be at my mercy; for I will roll this head all about 25. the room until he promises to give us what we desire. So be of good cheer my friends, for all will yet be well."

The next morning the soldier with the green whiskers led the Lion to the great Throne Room and bade him enter the presence of Oz.

The Lion at once passed through the door, and glancing around saw, to his surprise, that before the throne was a Ball of Fire, so fierce and glowing he could scarcely bear to gaze upon it. His first thought was that Oz had by accident caught on fire and was burning up; but, when he tried to go nearer, the heat was so intense that it singed his whiskers, and he crept back tremblingly to a spot nearer the door.

Then a low, quiet voice came from the Ball of Fire, and these were the words it spoke:

"I am Oz, the Great and Terrible. Who are you, and why do you seek me?" And the Lion answered,

"I am a Cowardly Lion, afraid of everything. I come to you to beg that you give me courage, so that in reality I may become the King of Beasts, as men call me."

"Why should I give you courage?" demanded Oz.

"Because of all Wizards you are the greatest, and alone have power to grant my request," answered the Lion.

26. *a Ball of Fire*. The Wizard may be aware of the popular belief, as expressed by Edward Topsell in *The History of Four-Footed Beasts* (1607), that lions are afraid of fire and cannot bear to look at it. Baum's choice of these four particular transformations of Oz, the Great and Terrible, may not have been arbitrary. They follow the Great Chain of Being of the Middle Ages and Renaissance. Baum may have been acquainted with this system through his occult studies. The theory was that all things of this world, from God to the least of inanimate objects, were linked in a descending order. This chain was then divided into classes, and each of these had its individual primate. The Wizard himself, as ruler of the Emerald City, is at the apex of Ozian society and therefore can transform into the primates of other classes. Fire holds the highest place among elements, the head among the members of the body. Robert Kirk argued in his *Secret Commonwealth* (1691) that the fairy belongs to "a Middle Nature betwixt Man and Angel." It is the most perfect of humanlike beings of the visible world. It is the Elemental of the Air, the highest form of all earthly spirits, and thus the primate of Elementals. The Beast may be the Great Beast of the Book of Revelation (as mentioned in Note 23), the primate of monsters. The residue of this system survives in poetic metaphor. (See E. M. W. Tillyard's *The Elizabethan World Picture*, London: Chatto & Windus, 1956; and Arthur O. Lovejoy's *The Great Chain of Being*, Cambridge, Mass.: Harvard University Press, 1936.)

27. *a low, quiet voice*. This description already betrays the true nature of Oz the Wizard when unmasked in Chapter 15.

28. *Dorothy dried her eyes.* Notice how cleverly Baum undercuts the little girl's tears. A similar incident occurs in Chapter 18 when the Tin Woodman must have his tears wiped away lest he rust, for he feels it his solemn duty to weep at the passing of the Wizard of Oz from the Emerald City.

The Ball of Fire burned fiercely for a time, and the voice said,

"Bring me proof that the Wicked Witch is dead, and that moment I will give you courage. But so long as the Witch lives you must remain a coward."

The Lion was angry at this speech, but could say nothing in reply, and while he stood silently gazing at the Ball of Fire it became so furiously hot that he turned tail and rushed from the room. He was glad to find his friends waiting for him, and told them of his terrible interview with the Wizard.

"What shall we do now?" asked Dorothy, sadly.

"There is only one thing we can do," returned the Lion, "and that is to go to the land of the Winkies, seek out the Wicked Witch, and destroy her."

"But suppose we cannot?" said the girl.

"Then I shall never have courage," declared the Lion.

"And I shall never have brains," added the Scarecrow.

"And I shall never have a heart," spoke the Tin Woodman.

"And I shall never see Aunt Em and Uncle Henry," said Dorothy, beginning to cry.

"Be careful!" cried the green girl, "the tears will fall on your green silk gown, and spot it."

So Dorothy dried her eyes and said,

28.

"I suppose we must try it; but I am sure I do not want to kill anybody, even to see Aunt Em again."

"I will go with you; but I'm too much of a coward to kill the Witch," said the Lion.

"I will go too," declared the Scarecrow; "but I shall not be of much help to you, I am such a fool."

"I haven't the heart to harm even a Witch," remarked the Tin Woodman; "but if you go I certainly shall go with you."

Therefore it was decided to start upon their journey the next morning, and the Woodman sharpened his axe on a green grindstone and had all his joints properly oiled. The Scarecrow stuffed himself with fresh straw and Dorothy put new paint on his eyes that he might see better. The green girl, who was very kind to them, filled Dorothy's basket with good things to eat, and fastened a little bell around Toto's neck with a green ribbon.

They went to bed quite early and slept soundly until daylight, when they were awakened by the crowing of a green cock that lived in the back yard of the palace, and the cackling of a hen that had laid a green egg.

Chapter XII.
The Search for the
Wicked Witch

1. *no longer green.* This is no surprise when one learns in Chapter 15 the true nature of the magic of the Emerald City. Denslow's pictures strictly adhere to this detail in the text.

2. *Wicked Witch of the West.* Margaret Hamilton, who grew up on the Oz books and immortalized the role in the 1939 MGM musical, will always be regarded as the quintessential Wicked Witch of the West. Of course, her green-skinned witch is more traditional than Baum's, being in part based upon the evil stepmother in Walt Disney's *Snow White and the Seven Dwarfs* (1936). She cackles, dresses all in black, has a tall peaked hat and a large beaked nose, and rides a broom. Appropriately, the pop artist Andy Warhol had Hamilton pose for "The Witch" in *Myths,* his series of silkscreen prints issued in 1981. Barry Moser depicted the evil crone as Hamilton's old Hollywood friend Nancy Reagan in the 1985 Pennyroyal Press edition. "Baum's images are sometimes so corny," he complained on May 3, in *Forty-seven Days to Oz,* "that it seems impossible to develop an image which isn't dumb and transparent." And Moser did just that in his portrait of the Wicked Witch of the West.

The SOLDIER WITH THE green whiskers led them through the streets of the Emerald City until they reached the room where the Guardian of the Gates lived. This officer unlocked their spectacles to put them back in his great box, and then he politely opened the gate for our friends.

"Which road leads to the Wicked Witch of the West?" asked Dorothy.

"There is no road," answered the Guardian of the Gates; "no one ever wishes to go that way."

"How, then, are we to find her?" enquired the girl.

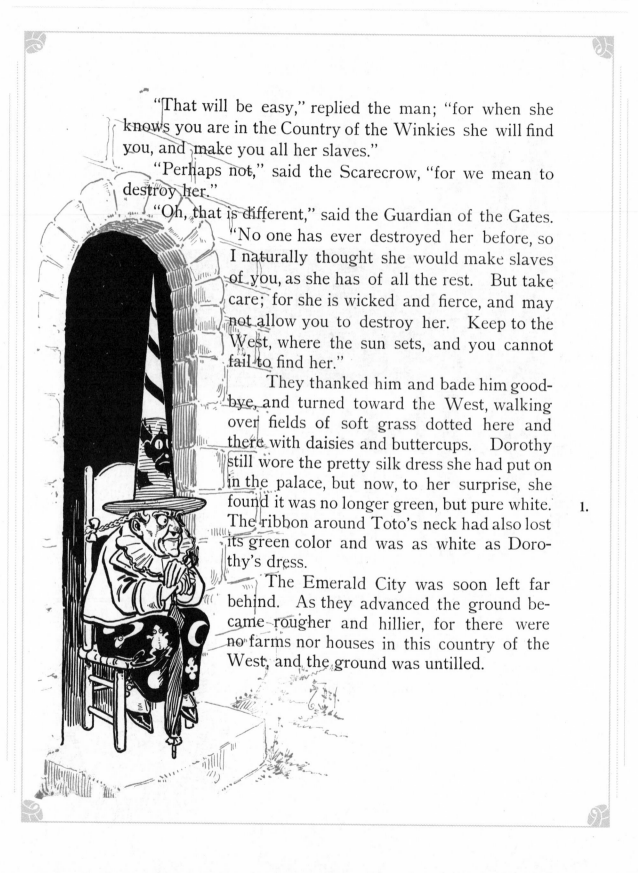

"That will be easy," replied the man; "for when she knows you are in the Country of the Winkies she will find you, and make you all her slaves."

"Perhaps not," said the Scarecrow, "for we mean to destroy her."

"Oh, that is different," said the Guardian of the Gates. "No one has ever destroyed her before, so I naturally thought she would make slaves of you, as she has of all the rest. But take care; for she is wicked and fierce, and may not allow you to destroy her. Keep to the West, where the sun sets, and you cannot fail to find her."

They thanked him and bade him good-bye, and turned toward the West, walking over fields of soft grass dotted here and there with daisies and buttercups. Dorothy still wore the pretty silk dress she had put on in the palace, but now, to her surprise, she found it was no longer green, but pure white. The ribbon around Toto's neck had also lost its green color and was as white as Doro-thy's dress.

The Emerald City was soon left far behind. As they advanced the ground be-came rougher and hillier, for there were no farms nor houses in this country of the West, and the ground was untilled.

In the afternoon the sun shone hot in their faces, for there were no trees to offer them shade; so that before night Dorothy and Toto and the Lion were tired, and lay down upon the grass and fell asleep, with the Woodman and the Scarecrow keeping watch.

Now the Wicked Witch of the West had but one eye, yet that was as powerful as a telescope, and could see everywhere. So, as she sat in the door of her castle, she happened to look around and saw Dorothy lying asleep, with her friends all about her. They were a long distance off, but the Wicked Witch was angry to find them in her country; so she blew upon a silver whistle that hung around her neck.

2.

At once there came running to her from all directions a pack of great wolves. They had long legs and fierce eyes and sharp teeth.

"Go to those people," said the Witch, "and tear them to pieces."

"Are you not going to make them your slaves?" asked the leader of the wolves.

"No," she answered, "one is of tin, and one of straw; one is a girl and another a Lion. None of them is fit to work, so you may tear them into small pieces."

"Very well," said the wolf, and he dashed away at full speed, followed by the others.

It was lucky the Scarecrow and the Woodman were wide awake and heard the wolves coming.

3. *forty wolves, and forty times*. "Forty wolves," "forty crows," and "forty bees" play with the Biblical number for "many." The Great Flood lasted forty days and forty nights; Christ fasted in the wilderness for forty days and forty nights. The centipede—the word means "one-hundred-footed"—is "forty-footed" in the Near East. The Wicked Witch's hordes are like three plagues upon the land, representing three states of animals: beast (wolf), bird (crow), and bug (bee). Oddly, Barry Moser in the 1985 Pennyroyal edition drew a coyote as leader of the wolves and a raven as king of the crows, different creatures from those Baum describes.

"This is my fight," said the Woodman; "so get behind me and I will meet them as they come."

He seized his axe, which he had made very sharp, and as the leader of the wolves came on the Tin Woodman swung his arm and chopped the wolf's head from its body, so that it immediately died. As soon as he could raise his axe another wolf came up, and he also fell under the sharp edge of the Tin Woodman's weapon. There were forty wolves, and forty times a wolf was killed; so that at last they all lay dead in a heap before the Woodman.

3.

Then he put down his axe and sat beside the Scarecrow, who said,

"It was a good fight, friend."

They waited until Dorothy awoke the next morning. The little girl was quite frightened when she saw the great pile of shaggy wolves, but the Tin Woodman told her all.

She thanked him for saving them and sat down to breakfast, after which they started again upon their journey.

Now this same morning the Wicked Witch came to the door of her castle and looked out with her one eye that could see afar off.   She saw all her wolves lying dead, and the strangers still travelling through her country.   This made her angrier than before, and she blew her silver whistle twice.

Straightway a great flock of wild crows came flying toward her, enough to darken the sky.   And the Wicked Witch said to the King Crow,

"Fly at once to the strangers; peck out their eyes and tear them to pieces."

The wild crows flew in one great flock toward Dorothy and her companions.   When the little girl saw them coming she was afraid.   But the Scarecrow said,

"This is my battle; so lie down beside me and you will not be harmed."

So they all lay upon the ground except the Scarecrow, and he stood up and stretched out his arms.   And when the crows saw him they were frightened, as these birds always are by scarecrows, and did not dare to come any nearer.   But the King Crow said,

"It is only a stuffed man.   I will peck his eyes out."

The King Crow flew at the Scarecrow, who caught it by the head and twisted its neck until it died.   And then another crow flew at him, and the Scarecrow twisted its neck also.   There were forty crows, and forty times the Scarecrow twisted a neck, until at last all were lying dead beside him.   Then he called to his companions to rise, and again they went upon their journey.

When the Wicked Witch looked out again and saw all her crows lying in a heap, she got into a terrible rage, and blew three times upon her silver whistle.

Forthwith there was heard a great buzzing in the air, and a swarm of black bees came flying towards her.

"Go to the strangers and sting them to death!" commanded the Witch, and the bees turned and flew rapidly until they came to where Dorothy and her friends were walking. But the Woodman had seen them coming and the Scarecrow had decided what to do.

"Take out my straw and scatter it over the little girl and the dog and the lion," he said to the Woodman, "and the bees cannot sting them." This the Woodman did, and as Dorothy lay close beside the Lion and held Toto in her arms, the straw covered them entirely.

The bees came and found no one but the Woodman to sting, so they flew at him and broke off all their stings against the tin, without hurting the Woodman at all. And as bees cannot live when their stings are broken that was the end of the black bees, and they lay scattered thick about the Woodman, like little heaps of fine coal.

Then Dorothy and the Lion got up, and the girl helped the Tin Woodman put the

4. *a swarm of black bees.* Settlers of the vast American West often battled wolves, crows, and bees just like Dorothy and her companions. The Wicked Witch's bees may have inspired two deleted scenes from the 1939 MGM picture: the Tin Man beehive and the "Jitterbug" number. The Wicked Witch's desire to use the Tin Man as a beehive was not an entirely idle threat in the original cut of the picture. Just as he is about to set off down the Yellow Brick Road with Dorothy and the Scarecrow after the witch disappeared in a puff of red smoke, the Tin Man hears a buzzing in his chest and two bees fly out of his mouth! "The Jitterbug" was a song Harold Arlen and E. Y. "Yip" Harburg wrote for the Haunted Forest sequence. A blue-and-pink mosquito gives Dorothy and her three companions the "jitters" as they break into an exhaustive dance with all the trees shivering to the music before the Winged Monkeys descend upon them. Although this elaborate, complex scene took five weeks to shoot at a cost of $80,000, it was cut after the first preview. All that remains is the Wicked Witch's line "I've sent a little insect on ahead to take the fight out of them. . . ." When Margaret Hamilton asked producer Mervyn LeRoy why the studio excised the number from the final picture, he told her they did not want to date the picture. The recent "jitterbug" dance craze would not last forever. Hamilton then asked LeRoy how long he thought the picture might last, and he said at least ten years. "You're crazy!" she told him. Both scenes are included in *The Wizard of Oz: The Screenplay* (New York: Delta, 1989).

5. *a Golden Cap.* It seems appropriate that since the Wicked Witch of the West possessed a pair of magic shoes made of silver, the Wicked Witch of the East should have an enchanted talisman of her own made of gold. Enchanted caps appear everywhere in folklore, often associated with magic transportation. Perseus had an invisible helmet, Odysseus a cap of darkness, Jack the Giant Killer a cap of knowledge. *The History of Fortunatus*, a popular seventeenth-century chapbook derived from a Dutch legend, describes one that will take the hero anywhere he may wish when he puts it on. Richard Burton describes in *The Anatomy of Melancholy* (1628) another one similar to the Wicked Witch's Golden Cap: "King Erricus, of Sweden, had an enchanted Cap, by virtue of which, and some magical murmur or whispering terms, he could command spirits, trouble the air, and make the wind stand which way he would; insomuch that when there was any great wind or storm, the common people were wont to say, the King now had on his conjuring Cap." Jack Zipes mentioned in his notes to the 1998 Penguin Twentieth-Century Classics edition of *The Wonderful World of Oz* another possibility in "The True History of Little Goldenhood," an obscure variant of "Little Red Riding Hood" that Baum may have been familiar with in Andrew Lang's *The Red Fairy Book* (1890). (Harry Baum recalled copies of Lang's fairy books around the house when he was growing up.) This magic hood, made of a ray of sunshine, protects the child by burning the Wolf's tongue when foolish little Blanchette puts her head into his mouth. The same book includes a retelling of the Volsunga Saga, in which Sigurd dons the Helm of Dread, a golden helmet which renders its wearer invisible. The Golden Cap can be spotted briefly in the 1939 MGM movie: When Glinda's snowstorm destroys the Deadly Poppy Field, the furious Wicked Witch throws the cap across the throne room.

6. *the Winged Monkeys.* Although they do not act as protectors under the power of the Golden Cap, the Winged Monkeys are probably another species of Baum's animal fairies. "Why should not the animals have their Fairies, as well as mortals?" he demanded in his "Prologue" to "Animal Fairy Tales" (*The Delineator*, January 1905), Baum's response to Rudyard Kipling's *Jungle Books* (1894–1895). "Why should their tales not interest us as those concerning the Fairies of our own race?" This series includes several of the best short stories Baum ever wrote. The Fairy Beavers of *John Dough and the Cherub* (1906) also belong to these races of animal immortals.

The Winged Monkeys may serve a similar function as the familiars of European witches. Certain spells and magic words could conjure a band of "divining familiars" to foretell the future. Of course, the Winged Monkeys determine, rather than merely predict, what will happen.

7. *obey any order they were given.* The Winged Monkeys, slaves of the Golden Cap, are the "modernized" equivalent of the "stereotyped" genies of the *Arabian Nights* who obey whoever summons them by a wonderful lamp, whether a poor fisherman or a lad like Aladdin. Genies too are often limited to just three wishes per bearer.

straw back into the Scarecrow again, until he was as good as ever. So they started upon their journey once more.

The Wicked Witch was so angry when she saw her black bees in little heaps like fine coal that she stamped her foot and tore her hair and gnashed her teeth. And then she called a dozen of her slaves, who were the Winkies, and gave them sharp spears, telling them to go to the strangers and destroy them.

The Winkies were not a brave people, but they had to do as they were told; so they marched away until they came near to Dorothy. Then the Lion gave a great roar and sprang toward them, and the poor Winkies were so frightened that they ran back as fast as they could.

When they returned to the castle the Wicked Witch beat them well with a strap, and sent them back to their work, after which she sat down to think what she should do next. She could not understand how all her plans to destroy these strangers had failed; but she was a powerful Witch, as well as a wicked one, and she soon made up her mind how to act.

There was, in her cupboard, a Golden Cap, with a 5. circle of diamonds and rubies running round it. This Golden Cap had a charm. Whoever owned it could call three times upon the Winged Monkeys, who would obey 6., 7. any order they were given. But no person could command these strange creatures more than three times.

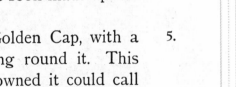

Twice already the Wicked Witch had used the charm of the Cap. Once was when she had made the Winkies her slaves, and set herself to rule over their country. The Winged Monkeys had helped her do this. The second time was when she had fought against the Great Oz himself, and driven him out of the land of the West. The Winged Monkeys had also helped her in doing this. Only once more could she use this Golden Cap, for which reason she did not like to do so until all her other powers were exhausted. But now that her fierce wolves and her wild crows and her stinging bees were gone, and her slaves had been scared away by the Cowardly Lion, she saw there was only one way left to destroy Dorothy and her friends.

So the Wicked Witch took the Golden Cap from her cupboard and placed it upon her head. Then she stood upon her left foot and said, slowly,

"Ep-pe, pep-pe, kak-ke!"

Next she stood upon her right foot and said,

"Hil-lo, hol-lo, hel-lo!"

After this she stood upon both feet and cried in a loud voice,

"Ziz-zy, zuz-zy, zik!"

Now the charm began

to work. The sky was darkened, and a low rumbling sound was heard in the air. There was a rushing of many wings; a great chattering and laughing; and the sun came out of the dark sky to show the Wicked Witch surrounded by a crowd of monkeys, each with a pair of immense and powerful wings on his shoulders.

One, much bigger than the others, seemed to be their leader. He flew close to the Witch and said,

"You have called us for the third and last time. What do you command?"

"Go to the strangers who are within my land and destroy them all except the Lion," said the Wicked Witch. "Bring that beast to me, for I have a mind to harness him like a horse, and make him work."

"Your commands shall be obeyed," said the leader; and then, with a great deal of chattering and noise, the Winged Monkeys flew away to the place where Dorothy and her friends were walking.

8. *Ep-pe, pep-e, kak-ke.* "My wife has called my attention," wrote Gardner in Note 15 of *The Wizard of Oz and Who He Was*, "to the close similarity of this incantation to 'ipecac,' the name of a once popular household emetic still sold in drugstores."

9. *Hil-lo, hol-lo, hel-lo.* Apparently the magic of the charm lies in part in the change in vowels. Another example occurs in *Prince Mud-Turtle* (1906) by "Laura Bancroft": "Uller, aller; oller; oller!" (p. 32). Other incantations have been formed through the alteration of consonants, as in the charm of the Powder of Life in *The Marvelous Land of Oz* (1904): "Weaugh! Teaugh! Peaugh!" (p. 20).

10. *Ziz-zy, zuz-zy, zik.* Compare this line with the incantation of *A New Wonderland* (1900): "Gizzle, guzzle, goo!" (p. 46). The last line of the Golden Cap's charm is related to traditional counting-out rhymes, like "One-ery, two-ery, Ziccary, zan!"; "Eeny, meeny, miney, mo!"; and "Onesy, twosy, three!" Perhaps the witch queen of *Queen Zixi of Ix* (1905) said it best. When asked what a particular charm means, Zixi, disguised as "Miss Trust," replies: "No one knows; and therefore it is a fine incantation" (p. 153). As Richard Cavendish reported in *The Black Arts* (New York: G. P. Putnam's Sons, 1967, p. 130), incantations generally have no meaning (even though they may derive from meaningful rituals, as in "hocus-pocus" from a line in the Latin mass, *Hoc est corpus meum*); their importance lies in the fact that they *sound* impressive.

Some of the Monkeys seized the Tin Woodman and carried him through the air until they were over a country thickly covered with sharp rocks. Here they dropped the poor Woodman, who fell a great distance to the rocks, where he lay so battered and dented that he could neither move nor groan.

Others of the Monkeys caught the Scarecrow, and with their long fingers pulled all of the straw out of his clothes and head. They made his hat and boots and clothes into a small bundle and threw it into the top branches of a tall tree.

The remaining Monkeys threw pieces of stout rope around the Lion and wound many coils about his body and head and legs, until he was unable to bite or scratch or struggle in any way. Then they lifted him up and flew away with him to the Witch's castle, where he was placed in a small yard with a high iron fence around it, so that he could not escape.

But Dorothy they did not harm at all. She stood, with Toto in her arms, watching the sad fate of her comrades and thinking it would soon be her turn. The leader of the Winged Monkeys flew up to her, his long, hairy arms stretched out and his ugly face grinning terribly; but he saw the mark of the Good Witch's kiss upon her forehead and stopped short, motioning the others not to touch her.

"We dare not harm this little girl," he said to them, "for she is protected by the Power of Good, and that is

11.   greater than the Power of Evil.   All we can do is to carry
her to the castle of the Wicked Witch and leave her there."

So, carefully and gently, they lifted Dorothy in their
arms and carried her swiftly through the air until they
came to the castle, where they set her down upon the
front door step.   Then the leader said to the Witch,

"We have obeyed you as far as we were able.   The
Tin Woodman and the Scarecrow are destroyed, and the
Lion is tied up in your yard.   The little girl we dare not
harm, nor the dog she carries in her arms.   Your power
over our band is now ended, and you will never see us
again."

Then all the Winged Monkeys, with much laughing
and chattering and noise, flew into the air and were soon
out of sight.

The Wicked Witch was both surprised and worried
when she saw the mark on Dorothy's forehead, for she

11. *greater than the Power of Evil.* Herein lies the secret of this and every other fairy tale. The triumph of Good over Evil is, as Roger Samber declared in his dedication to his English translation of Charles Perrault's fairy tales as *Histories of Past Time*s (1729), "the true End and Design of Fable." Perrault himself recognized this when he wrote in his introduction to his tales in verse:

> We see them [the children] sad and depressed as long as the hero and heroine are unlucky and shouting with joy when the time for their happiness arrives; in the same way, having endured impatiently the property of the wicked man and woman, they are overjoyed when they see them finally punished as they deserved. (Quoted from Jacques Barchelon and Henry Petit's introduction, *The Authentic Mother Goose Fairy Tales and Nursery Rhymes*, Chicago: Allan Swallow, 1960.)

Andrew Lang agreed. "Courage, beauty, youth, kindness, have many trials, but they always win the battle," he argued in his introduction to *The Pink Fairy Book* (1897); "while witches, giants, unfriendly cruel people, are on the losing end. So it ought to be, and so, on the whole, it is and will be; and that is all the moral of fairy tales." Baum admitted in "Modern Fairy Tales" (*The Advance*, August 19, 1909) that "never has a fairy tale lived, if one has been told or written, wherein the good did not conquer evil and virtue finally reign supreme." Likewise, in *The Life and Adventures of Santa Claus* (1902), he argued that "it is the Law that while Evil, unopposed, may accomplish terrible deeds, the powers of Good can never be overthrown when opposed to Evil" (p. 117).

knew well that neither the Winged Monkeys nor she, her-self, dare hurt the girl in any way. She looked down at Dorothy's feet, and seeing the Silver Shoes, began to tremble with fear, for she knew what a powerful charm belonged to them. At first the Witch was tempted to run away from Dorothy; but she happened to look into the child's eyes and saw how simple the soul behind them was, and that the little girl did not know of the wonderful power the Silver Shoes gave her. So the Wicked Witch laughed to herself, and thought, "I can still make her my slave, for she does not know how to use her power." Then she said to Dorothy, harshly and severely,

"Come with me; and see that you mind everything I tell you, for if you do not I will make an end of you, as I did of the Tin Woodman and the Scarecrow."

Dorothy followed her through many of the beautiful rooms in her castle until they came to the kitchen, where the Witch bade her clean the pots and kettles and sweep the floor and keep the fire fed with wood.

12.

Dorothy went to work meekly, with her mind made up to work as hard as she could; for she was glad the Wicked Witch had decided not to kill her.

13.

With Dorothy hard at work the Witch thought she would go into the court-yard and harness the Cowardly Lion like a horse; it would amuse her, she was sure, to make him draw her chariot whenever she wished to go to drive. But as she opened the gate the Lion gave a loud

12. *keep the fire fed with wood.* Notice how different is Baum's Wicked Witch, a decidedly American variant, from the ones in European folklore. She does not threaten to eat Dorothy as does the one who captures Hansel and Gretel. The worst thing she can think of is to make Dorothy do housework! The Good Witch's kiss conveniently protects Dorothy, so she does not have to suffer any of the tortures that befall others in the old stories. Children may not like to clean the pots and kettles and sweep the floor and keep the fire supplied with wood, but these household chores do not induce nightmares. Dorothy is like Charles Perrault's Cinderella, who must do all the cleaning for her wicked stepmother and cruel stepsisters.

13. *not to kill her.* "Many Western farmers have held these same grim thoughts in less mystical terms," observed Henry M. Littlefield in "The Wizard of Oz: Parable on Populism" (*American Quarterly*, Spring 1964). "The Witch of the West uses natural forces to achieve her ends; she is Baum's version of satient and malign nature." These forces take the forms of her wolves, crows, and bees, all of which have tormented American settlers. "If the Witch of the West is a diabolical force of Darwinian or Spencerian nature, then another contravening force may be counted upon to dispose of her. Dorothy destroys the evil Witch by angrily dousing her with a bucket of water. Water, that precious commodity which the drought-ridden farmers on the great plains needed so badly, and which if correctly used could create an agricultural paradise, or at least dissolve a wicked witch. Plain water brings an end to malign nature in the West." Baum knew well the importance of water on the prairie from the time he lived in Aberdeen, South Dakota.

roar and bounded at her so fiercely that the Witch was afraid, and ran out and shut the gate again.

"If I cannot harness you," said the Witch to the Lion, speaking through the bars of the gate, "I can starve you. You shall have nothing to eat until you do as I wish."

So after that she took no food to the imprisoned Lion; but every day she came to the gate at noon and asked,

"Are you ready to be harnessed like a horse?"

And the Lion would answer,

"No.   If you come in this yard I will bite you."

The reason the Lion did not have to do as the Witch wished was that every night, while the woman was asleep Dorothy carried him food from the cupboard. After he had eaten he would lie down on his bed of straw, and Dorothy would lie beside him and put her head on his soft, shaggy mane, while they talked of their troubles and tried to plan some way to escape.   But they could find no way to get out of the castle, for it was constantly guarded by the yellow Winkies, who were the slaves of the Wicked Witch and too afraid of her not to do as she told them.

14. The girl had to work hard during the day, and often the Witch threatened to beat her with the same old umbrella she always carried in her hand. But, in truth, she did not dare to strike Dorothy, because of the mark upon her forehead. The child did not know this, and was full of fear for herself and Toto. Once the Witch struck Toto a blow with her umbrella and the brave little dog flew at her

14. *umbrella*. Considering her fear of water and the fate of the Wicked Witch of the West, it seems eminently suitable that she should carry an umbrella rather than a broom, the common implement usually associated with witches, as in the 1939 MGM musical.

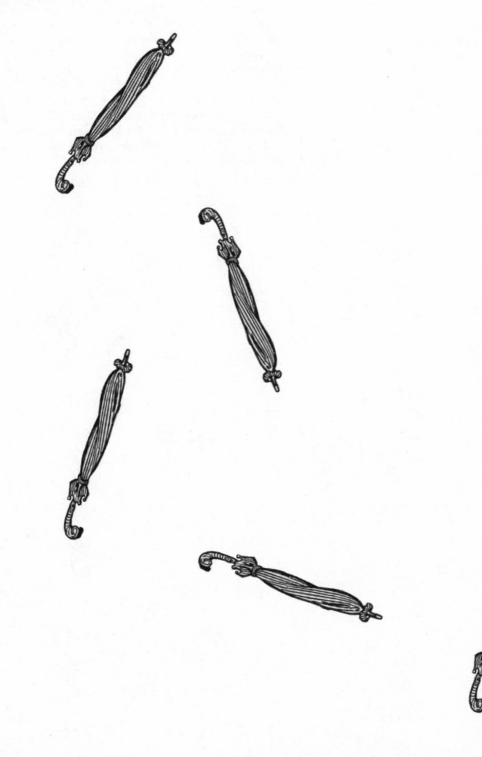

15. *The Witch was too much afraid of the dark.* Baum is, of course, being ironic again. Surely the only thing anyone should be scared of in the castle is the Wicked Witch herself! Baum undercuts the illusion of her being the quintessence of evil by showing how she too suffers some childish fears. There is really nothing there for her to be scared of, but one only fears what one does not know. The Winkies are still in terror of the Wicked Witch, although most of her powers are gone. In Chapter 15, Dorothy and her companions face what they think is the most dreadful form of Oz, the Great and Terrible—the empty Throne Room. The Wicked Witch of the West is clearly not evil incarnate as are the witches of European folklore. They are like forces of nature, while Baum's witch has her little human frailties. She is typical of Baum's villains. She is selfish, petty, and mean, just like a spoiled child.

and bit her leg, in return.   The Witch did not bleed where she was bitten, for she was so wicked that the blood in her had dried up many years before.

Dorothy's life became very sad as she grew to understand that it would be harder than ever to get back to Kansas and Aunt Em again.   Sometimes she would cry bitterly for hours, with Toto sitting at her feet and looking into her face, whining dismally to show how sorry he was for his little mistress.   Toto did not really care whether he was in Kansas or the Land of Oz so long as Dorothy was with him; but he knew the little girl was unhappy, and that made him unhappy too.

Now the Wicked Witch had a great longing to have for her own the Silver Shoes which the girl always wore. Her Bees and her Crows and her Wolves were lying in heaps and drying up, and she had used up all the power of the Golden Cap; but if she could only get hold of the Silver Shoes they would give her more power than all the other things she had lost.   She watched Dorothy carefully, to see if she ever took off her shoes, thinking she might steal them.   But the child was so proud of her pretty shoes that she never took them off except at night and when she took her bath.   The Witch was too much afraid of the dark to dare go in Dorothy's room at night to take the shoes, and her dread of water was greater than her fear of the dark, so she never came near when Dorothy was bathing.   Indeed, the old Witch never touched water, nor ever let water touch her in any way.

15.

But the wicked creature was very cunning, and she finally thought of a trick that would give her what she wanted. She placed a bar of iron in the middle of the kitchen floor, and then by her magic arts made the iron invisible to human eyes. So that when Dorothy walked across the floor she stumbled over the bar, not being able to see it, and fell at full length. She was not much hurt, but in her fall one of the Silver Shoes came off, and before she could reach it the Witch had snatched it away and put it on her own skinny foot.

The wicked woman was greatly pleased with the success of her trick, for as long as she had one of the shoes she owned half the power of their charm, and Dorothy could not use it against her, even had she known how to do so.

The little girl, seeing she had lost one of her pretty shoes, grew angry, and said to the Witch,

"Give me back my shoe!"

"I will not," retorted the Witch, "for it is now my shoe, and not yours."

"You are a wicked creature!" cried Dorothy. "You have no right to take my shoe from me."

"I shall keep it, just the same," said the Witch, laughing at her,

"and some day I shall get the other one from you, too."

This made Dorothy so very angry that she picked up the bucket of water that stood near and dashed it over the Witch, wetting her from head to foot.

Instantly the wicked woman gave a loud cry of fear; and then, as Dorothy looked at her in wonder, the Witch began to shrink and fall away.

"See what you have done!" she screamed. "In a minute I shall melt away."

"I'm very sorry, indeed," said Dorothy, who was truly frightened to see the Witch actually melting away like brown sugar before her very eyes.

"Didn't you know water would be the end of me?" asked the Witch, in a wailing, despairing voice. **16.**

"Of course not," answered Dorothy; "how should I?"

"Well, in a few minutes I shall be all melted, and you will have the castle to yourself. I have been wicked in my day, but I never thought a little girl like you would **17.** ever be able to melt me and end my wicked deeds. Look **18.** out—here I go!"

With these words the Witch fell down in a brown, melted, shapeless mass and began to spread over the clean boards of the kitchen floor. Seeing that she had really melted away to nothing, Dorothy drew another bucket of water and threw it over the mess. She then swept it all **19.** out the door. After picking out the silver shoe, which

16. *"Didn't you know water would be the end of me?"* Dorothy should have known this. "It is a well known fact," Robert Bruns wrote in a note to his poem "Tam O'Shanter, a Tale" of 1790, "that witches, or any evil spirits, have no power to follow a poor wight any farther than the middle of the next running stream." When Tam O'Shanter stumbles upon a witches' Sabbath in the woods, he flees on horseback and escapes their wrath because "a running stream they dare na cross." Accused witches were often tested by ordeal by water. It was considered to be the most decisive proof of witchcraft, because man cannot deceive the element of water. The suspect was bound and flung into a river; if she floated, she was guilty and could be executed by fire. This method of justice appeared as early as 1950 B.C., in the Code of Hammurabi; the French courts carried it out with conclusive results as late as June 1696. Baum refers to "the ducked witches of years ago" in the Aberdeen *Saturday Pioneer* (March 29, 1890).

Many students of Oz believe that the magic in Baum's books may be rationally explained, that it is based on certain scientific principles and is no more than an extension of natural laws. Dr. Douglas A. Rossman argued in "On the Liquidation of Witches" (*The Baum Bugle*, Spring 1969) that the melting of the Wicked Witch of the West was due to hydrolysis. Adhesion, the sticking together of molecules in contact with each other, may be broken down either by water or by some other powerful force, like that of a house falling from the sky. Like the Wicked Witch of the East, the Wicked Witch of the West is so old and dried-up that she cannot even bleed; she has no bodily liquids to combat strong outside influences. Little is keeping the molecules together. Only her black arts have kept her from literally falling apart. Water breaks down the weak adhesion of her body, and she melts into a brown, shapeless mass. The impact of Dorothy's house landing on the Wicked Witch of the East breaks down her molecular structure,

and she crumbles into dust. Celia Catlett Andersen noted in "The Comedians of Oz" (*Studies in American Humor,* Winter 1986–1987) that the Wicked Witch of the West "is justly destroyed by that emblem of household drudgery, a bucketful of water." A slightly revised version of this chapter appeared as "Melting a Wicked Witch" in *L. Frank Baum's Juvenile Speaker* (1911).

17. *a little girl like you.* Apparently she never read "Hansel and Gretel," in which another enterprising child just as neatly disposes of a wicked witch. "As long as children believe in witches," argued Dr. Bruno Bettelheim in *The Uses of Enchantment* (New York: Alfred A. Knopf, 1976), "they need to be told stories in which children, by being ingenious, rid themselves of these persecuting figures of their imagination" (p. 166).

18. *Look out—here I go!* But is Dorothy guilty of murder? Several elementary schools have recently put her on trial for killing the Wicked Witch of the West. According to "Junior Barristers Square Off over Dorothy's Deadly Deed" (*Orange County* [Calif.] *Register*, June 5, 1992), the girl was judged in class by a jury of her peers—fourth-, fifth-, and sixth-graders. It is a clever way of teaching students the fundamentals of the American judicial system. Dorothy usually gets off. But she really should learn how to control her temper!

19. *She then swept it all out the door.* What a swift, clean, efficient way to get rid of Evil! "Even failing all else, there is an object lesson in tidiness here for children," commented Raylyn Moore in *Wonderful Wizard, Marvelous Land* (Bowling Green, Ohio: Bowling Green University Popular Press, 1974, p. 155). Baum is reiterating what a well-brought-up little girl Dorothy is.

was all that was left of the old woman, she cleaned and
dried it with a cloth, and put it on her foot again. Then,
being at last free to do as she chose, she ran out to the
court-yard to tell the Lion that the Wicked Witch of the
West had come to an end, and that they were no longer
prisoners in a strange land.

1. *The Rescue.* This chapter has two titles in the early editions of *The Wonderful Wizard of Oz* (1900) and *The New Wizard of Oz* (1903). While the table of contents lists it as "How the Four Were Reunited," this pictorial chapter title page reads "The Rescue." When Bobbs-Merrill reset the entire book in the 1920s, it dropped the chapter title pages and retained only "The Rescue" as the name of Chapter 12. Most subsequent editions use only this title.

Chapter XIII.
The Rescue

1.

This picture of the Scarecrow appeared on a flyer adver-
tising *Denslow's Scarecrow and the Tin-Man*
(New York: G. W. Dillingham, 1904).
Private collection.

The COWARDLY LION WAS much pleased to hear that the Wicked Witch had been melted by a bucket of water, and Dorothy at once unlocked the gate of his prison and set him free. They went in together to the castle, where Dorothy's first act was to call all the Winkies together and tell them that they were no longer slaves.

There was great rejoicing among the yellow Winkies, for they had been made to work hard during many years for the Wicked Witch, who had always treated them with great cruelty. They kept this day as a holiday, then and ever after, and spent the time in feasting and dancing.

"If our friends, the Scarecrow and the Tin Woodman,

were only with us," said the Lion, "I should be quite happy."

"Don't you suppose we could rescue them?" asked the girl, anxiously.

"We can try," answered the Lion.

So they called the yellow Winkies and asked them if they would help to rescue their friends, and the Winkies said that they would be delighted to do all in their power for Dorothy, who had set them free from bondage. So she chose a number of the Winkies who looked as if they knew the most, and they all started away. They travelled that day and part of the next until they came to the rocky plain where the Tin Woodman lay, all battered and bent. His axe was near him, but the blade was rusted and the handle broken off short.

The Winkies lifted him tenderly in their arms, and carried him back to the yellow castle again, Dorothy shedding a few tears by the way at the sad plight of her old friend, and the Lion looking sober and sorry. When they reached the castle Dorothy said to the Winkies,

"Are any of your people tinsmiths?"

"Oh, yes; some of us are very good tinsmiths," they told her.

"Then bring them to me," she said. And when the tinsmiths came, bringing with them all their tools in baskets, she enquired,

"Can you straighten out those dents in the Tin Woodman, and bend him back into shape again, and solder him together where he is broken?"

The tinsmiths looked the Woodman over carefully and then answered that they thought they could mend him so he would be as good as ever. So they set to work in one of the big yellow rooms of the castle and worked for three days and four nights, hammering and twisting and bending and soldering and polishing and pounding at the legs and body and head of the Tin Woodman, until at last he was straightened out into his old form, and his joints worked as well as ever. To be sure, there were several patches on him, but the tinsmiths did a good job, and as the Woodman was not a vain man he did not mind the patches at all.

When, at last, he walked into Dorothy's room and thanked her for rescuing him, he was so pleased that he wept tears of joy, and Dorothy had to wipe every tear carefully from his face with her apron, so his joints would not be rusted. At the same time her own tears fell thick and fast at the joy of meeting her old friend again, and these tears did not need to be wiped away. As for the Lion, he wiped his eyes so often with the tip of his tail that it became quite wet, and he was obliged to go out into the court-yard and hold it in the sun till it dried.

"If we only had the Scarecrow with us again," said the Tin Woodman, when Dorothy had finished telling him everything that had happened, "I should be quite happy."

"We must try to find him," said the girl.

So she called the Winkies to help her, and they walked all that day and part of the next until they came to the tall tree in the branches of which the Winged Monkeys had tossed the Scarecrow's clothes.

It was a very tall tree, and the trunk was so smooth that no one could climb it; but the Woodman said at once,

"I'll chop it down, and then we can get the Scarecrow's clothes."

2. Now while the tinsmiths had been at work mending the Woodman himself, another of the Winkies, who was a goldsmith, had made an axe-handle of solid gold and fitted it to the Woodman's axe, instead of the old broken handle. Others polished the blade until all the rust was removed and it glistened like burnished silver.

As soon as he had spoken, the Tin Woodman began to chop, and in a short time the tree fell over with a crash, when the Scarecrow's clothes fell out of the branches and rolled off on the ground.

3. Dorothy picked them up and had the Winkies carry them back to the castle, where they were stuffed with nice, clean straw; and, behold! here was the Scarecrow, as good as ever, thanking them over and over again for saving him.

Now they were reunited, Dorothy and her friends spent a few happy days at the Yellow Castle, where they found everything they needed to make them comfortable. But one day the girl thought of Aunt Em, and said,

2. *an axe-handle of solid gold.* Barry Moser noted on April 19, in *Forty-seven Days to Oz* (West Hadley, Mass.: Penny-royal Press, 1985), that this new handle "must also bear Winkie magic, for surely without magic such a handle would bend." But he was mistaken about the blade being replaced by precious metal: Baum says that it was polished until "it glistened like burnished silver."

3. *as good as ever.* Literally, the clothes make the man! But once he receives his brains from the Wizard, the Scarecrow forms a new definition of his identity. In *The Marvelous Land of Oz* (1904), he points out that even after he loses his straw again and is stuffed with other things, "my Brains are still composed of the same old material. And these are the possessions that always made me a person to be depended upon in an emergency" (p. 211).

This sketch appeared in an inscribed copy of the first edition that Denslow gave his physician, Dr. Omer C. Snyder, pictured taking the Tin Woodman's pulse.

Courtesy Justin G. Schiller.

"We must go back to Oz, and claim his promise."

"Yes," said the Woodman, "at last I shall get my heart."

"And I shall get my brains," added the Scarecrow, joyfully.

"And I shall get my courage," said the Lion, thoughtfully.

"And I shall get back to Kansas," cried Dorothy, clapping her hands. "Oh, let us start for the Emerald City to-morrow!"

This they decided to do. The next day they called the Winkies together and bade them good-bye. The Winkies were sorry to have them go, and they had grown so fond of the Tin Woodman that they begged him to stay and rule over them and the Yellow Land of the West. Finding they were determined to go, the Winkies gave Toto and the Lion each a golden collar; and to Dorothy they presented a beautiful bracelet, studded with diamonds;

4. *to stay and rule over them and the Yellow Land of the West.* By the time of the second Oz book, *The Marvelous Land of Oz* (1904), the Tin Woodman has bestowed upon himself the impressive title Emperor of the Winkies. When it is pointed out that an emperor rules an empire and the Land of the Winkies is only a kingdom, the Scarecrow warns, "Don't mention that to the Tin Woodman! You would hurt his feelings. He is a proud man, as he has every reason to be, and it pleases him to be termed Emperor rather than King" (p. 122). "Like a good many kings and emperors," the Tin Woodman later confesses in *The Tin Woodman of Oz* (1918), "I have a grand title, but very little real power, which allows me time to amuse myself in my own way" (p. 38).

5. *a beautiful bracelet, studded with diamonds.* Baum, like "all Americans—no, most Americans"—has "a fixation with gold, silver and precious jewels," observed artist Barry Moser on May 3, in *Forty-seven Days to Oz*. The bracelet must have been left behind in Oz, for "Dorothy never brought any jewels home with her" (*The Emerald City of Oz*, 1910, p. 23).

6. *silver oil-can*. This must be the same one described in *The Marvelous Land of Oz* (1904): "Upon a handsome center-table [in an antechamber of the Tin Woodman's Tin Palace in the Winkie Country] stood a large silver oil-can, richly engraved with scenes from the past adventures of the Tin Woodman, Dorothy, the Cowardly Lion and the Scarecrow: the lines of the engraving being traced upon the silver in yellow gold" (p. 124).

7. *it fitted her exactly*. Just like the Silver Shoes. See Chapter 3, Note 4. Now Dorothy possesses the marvelous talismans of both Wicked Witches. And in her innocence she does not know what extraordinary powers they contain or how to utilize them. Of course, magic itself is not evil, though the way in which it is used can be. The same may be said of modern technology or any other knowledge.

and to the Scarecrow they gave a gold-headed walking stick, to keep him from stumbling; and to the Tin Woodman they offered a silver oil-can, inlaid with gold and set with precious jewels.

6.

Every one of the travellers made the Winkies a pretty speech in return, and all shook hands with them until their arms ached.

Dorothy went to the Witch's cupboard to fill her basket with food for the journey, and there she saw the Golden Cap. She tried it on her own head and found that it fitted her exactly. She did not know anything about the charm of the Golden Cap, but she saw that it was pretty, so she made up her mind to wear it and carry her sunbonnet in the basket.

7.

Then, being prepared for the journey, they all started for the Emerald City; and the Winkies gave them three cheers and many good wishes to carry with them.

This sketch of the Scarecrow and the Cowardly Lion was drawn by W. W. Denslow for
the Chicago *Sunday Record-Herald*, August 3, 1902.
Courtesy the Billy Rose Theatre Collection, The New York Public Library,
Astor, Lenox and Tilden Foundations.

Chapter XIV.
The Winged Monkeys

1. *yellow.* These big fields of sweet-smelling buttercups and yellow daisies offer a pleasant contrast to the Deadly Poppy Field Dorothy encountered on her last visit to the Emerald City. But in most editions of *The Wizard of Oz*, the word "bright" replaces "yellow" here and the flowers and fields become "scarlet," although the locale is the Winkie Country, where yellow is the favorite color. The change first occurred in the 1903 Bobbs-Merrill edition of *The New Wizard of Oz* to conform the text with the new color scheme of the illustrations; it was not carried throughout the book. (The publishers also wanted to copyright these minor textual alterations along with Denslow's new pictures, but the Copyright Office said that that was unnecessary.) Elsewhere now, *The Bookseller* (December 1903) noted, "dear little girls in red dresses skip across the page down a red pathway" (although the colors in the text are blue and yellow). These typographic changes undercut Baum's original story, which speaks only of buttercups and yellow daisies, yellow flowers and yellow fields.

2. *we shall sometime come to some place.* Compare this logic with that in the following lines from the meeting of Alice and the Cheshire Cat in Chapter 6 of *Alice in Wonderland*:

> "Would you tell me, please, which way I ought to go from here?"
>
> "That depends a good deal on where you want to go to," said the Cat.
>
> "I don't care much where—" said Alice.
>
> "Then it doesn't matter which way you go," said the Cat.
>
> "—so long as I get somewhere," Alice added as an explanation.
>
> "Oh, you're sure to do that," said the Cat, "if you only walk long enough."

The reviewer in *The Dial* may have had this passage in mind when he compared *The Wizard of Oz* with Lewis Carroll's classic. As Baum himself suggests in his article on fairy tales (see Chapter 1, Note 1), his debt to the English don was slight. There are more obvious similarities between *A New Wonderland* (1900) and the Alice books, as Martin Gardner explained in his introduction to the 1968 Dover edition of *The Magical Monarch of Mo* (a revised version of *A New Wonderland*). This was the first children's book Baum ever wrote, and he modeled it in part on *Alice in Wonderland* and *Through the Looking-Glass*, but he had difficulty getting it published until R. H. Russell of New York took it in 1900. Gardner compared Baum and Carroll also in "A Child's Garden of Bewilderment" (*Saturday Review*, July 17, 1965).

3. *the little whistle.* This is the first mention of a whistle in the story. On page 157, the Queen of the Field Mice told Dorothy that should she ever need them again, she should only "come out into the field and call, and we shall hear you and come to your assistance." Perhaps Baum was thinking of the silver whistle with which the Wicked Witch of the West summoned her wolves, crows, and bees.

YOU WILL REMEMBER there was no road—not even a pathway—between the castle of the Wicked Witch and the Emerald City. When the four travellers went in search of the Witch she had seen them coming, and so sent the Winged Monkeys to bring them to her. It was much harder to find their way back through the big fields of buttercups and yellow daisies than it was being carried. They knew, of course, they must go straight east, toward the rising sun; and they started off in the right way. But at noon, when the sun was over their heads, they did not know which was east and which was west, and that was the reason they were lost in the great fields. They kept on walking, however,

1.

and at night the moon came out and shone brightly. So they lay down among the sweet smelling yellow flowers and slept soundly until morning—all but the Scarecrow and the Tin Woodman.

The next morning the sun was behind a cloud, but they started on, as if they were quite sure which way they were going.

"If we walk far enough," said Dorothy, "we shall sometime come to some place, I am sure."

But day by day passed away, and they still saw nothing before them but the yellow fields. The Scarecrow began to grumble a bit.

"We have surely lost our way," he said, "and unless we find it again in time to reach the Emerald City I shall never get my brains."

"Nor I my heart," declared the Tin Woodman. "It seems to me I can scarcely wait till I get to Oz, and you must admit this is a very long journey."

"You see," said the Cowardly Lion, with a whimper, "I haven't the courage to keep tramping forever, without getting anywhere at all."

Then Dorothy lost heart. She sat down on the grass and looked at her companions, and they sat down and looked at her, and Toto found that for the first time in his life he was too tired to chase a butterfly that flew past his head; so he put out his tongue and panted and looked at Dorothy as if to ask what they should do next.

"Suppose we call the Field Mice," she suggested. "They could probably tell us the way to the Emerald City."

"To be sure they could," cried the Scarecrow; "why didn't we think of that before?"

Dorothy blew the little whistle she had always carried about her neck since the Queen of the Mice had given it to her. In a few minutes they heard the pattering of tiny feet, and many of the small grey mice came running up to her. Among them was the Queen herself, who asked, in her squeaky little voice,

"What can I do for my friends?"

"We have lost our way," said Dorothy. "Can you tell us where the Emerald City is?"

"Certainly," answered the Queen; "but it is a great way off, for you have had it at your backs all this time." Then she noticed Dorothy's Golden Cap, and said, "Why don't you use

3.

the charm of the Cap, and call the Winged Monkeys to you? They will carry you to the City of Oz in less than an hour."

"I didn't know there was a charm," answered Dorothy, in surprise. "What is it?"

"It is written inside the Golden Cap," replied the Queen of the Mice; "but if you are going to call the Winged Monkeys we must run away, for they are full of mischief and think it great fun to plague us."

"Won't they hurt me?" asked the girl, anxiously.

"Oh, no; they must obey the wearer of the Cap. Good-bye!" And she scampered out of sight, with all the mice hurrying after her.

Dorothy looked inside the Golden Cap and saw some words written upon the lining. These, she thought, must be the charm, so she read the directions carefully and put the Cap upon her head.

"Ep-pe, pep-pe, kak-ke!" she said, standing on her left foot.

"What did you say?" asked the Scarecrow, who did not know what she was doing.

"Hil-lo, hol-lo, hel-lo!" Dorothy went on, standing this time on her right foot.

"Hello!" replied the Tin Woodman, calmly.

"Ziz-zy, zuz-zy, zik!" said Dorothy, who was now standing on both feet. This ended the saying of the charm, and they heard a great chattering and flapping of wings, as the band of Winged Monkeys flew up to them. The King bowed low before Dorothy, and asked,

"What is your command?"

"We wish to go to the Emerald City," said the child, "and we have lost our way."

"We will carry you," replied the King, and no sooner had he spoken than two of the Monkeys caught Dorothy in their arms and flew away with her. Others took the Scarecrow and the Woodman and the Lion, and one little Monkey seized Toto and flew after them, although the dog tried hard to bite him.

The Scarecrow and the Tin Woodman were rather frightened at first, for they remembered how badly the Winged Monkeys had treated them before; but they saw that no harm was intended, so they rode through the air quite cheerfully, and had a fine time looking at the pretty gardens and woods far below them.

Dorothy found herself riding easily between two of the biggest Monkeys, one of them the King himself. They had made a chair of their hands and were careful not to hurt her.

"Why do you have to obey the charm of the Golden Cap?" she asked.

"That is a long story," answered the King, with a laugh; "but as we have a long journey before us I will pass the time by telling you about it, if you wish."

"I shall be glad to hear it," she replied.

"Once," began the leader, "we were a free people, living happily in the great forest, flying from tree to tree, eating nuts and fruit, and doing just as we pleased without calling anybody master. Perhaps some of us were rather too full of mischief at times, flying down to pull the tails of the animals that had no wings, chasing birds, and throwing nuts at the people who walked in the forest. But we were careless and happy and full of fun, and enjoyed every minute of the day. This was many years ago, long before Oz came out of the clouds to rule over this land.

"There lived here then, away at the North, a beautiful princess, who was also a powerful sorceress. All her magic was used to help the people, and she was never known to hurt anyone who was good. Her name was Gayelette, and she lived in a handsome palace built from great blocks of ruby. Everyone loved her, but her greatest sorrow was that she could find no one to love in return, since all the men were much too stupid and ugly to mate with one so beautiful and wise. At last, however, she found a boy who was handsome and manly and wise beyond his years. Gayelette made up her mind that when he grew to be a man she would make him her husband, so she took him to her ruby palace and used all her magic powers to make him as strong and good and lovely as any woman could wish. When he grew to manhood, Quelala, as he was called, was said to be the best and wisest man in all the land, while his manly beauty was so great that

4. *ruby.* This is one of a couple of details in this chapter which suggest that Baum had not yet decided that the favorite color of the North was purple, as in *The Marvelous Land of Oz* (1904). Perhaps at this time he was considering it to be red, just as it is in the South of Oz.

5. *as any woman could wish.* Katharine Rogers suggested in "Liberation for Little Girls" (*Saturday Review*, June 15, 1972) that Gayelette is "a female version of Pygmalion, who creates a mate for herself because there isn't a man clever and good enough for her to love." Does the name Gayelette come from Galatea, the statue with whom Pygmalion falls in love?

Gayelette loved him dearly, and hastened to make everything ready for the wedding.

"My grandfather was at that time the King of the Winged Monkeys which lived in the forest near Gayalette's palace, and the old fellow loved a joke better than a good dinner.   One day, just before the wedding, my grandfather was flying out with his band when he saw Quelala walking beside the river.   He was dressed in a rich costume of pink silk and purple velvet, and my grandfather thought he would see what he could do.   At his word the band flew down and seized Quelala, carried him in their arms until they were over the middle of the river, and then dropped him into the water.

"'Swim out, my fine fellow,' cried my grandfather, 'and see if the water has spotted your clothes.'   Quelala was much too wise not to swim, and he was not in the least spoiled by all his good fortune.   He laughed, when he came to the top of the water, and swam in to shore. But when Gayelette came running out to him she found his silks and velvet all ruined by the river.

"The princess was very angry, and she knew, of course, who did it.   She had all the Winged Monkeys brought before her, and she said at first that their wings should be tied and they should be treated as they had treated Quelala, and dropped in the river.   But my grandfather pleaded hard, for he knew the Monkeys would drown in the river with their wings tied, and Quelala said a kind word for them also; so that Gayelette finally spared them, on condition that the Winged Monkeys should ever after do three times the bidding of the owner of the Golden Cap. This Cap had been made for a wedding present to Quelala, and it is said to have cost the princess half her kingdom. Of course my grandfather and all the other Monkeys at once agreed to the condition, and that is how it happens that we are three times the slaves of the owner of the Golden Cap, whomsoever he may be."

"And what became of them?" asked Dorothy, who had been greatly interested in the story.

"Quelala being the first owner of the Golden Cap," replied the Monkey, "he was the first to lay his wishes upon us. As his bride could not bear the sight of us, he called us all to him in the forest after he had married her and ordered us to always keep where she could never again set eyes on a Winged Monkey, which we were glad to do, for we were all afraid of her.

"This was all we ever had to do until the Golden Cap fell into the hands of the Wicked Witch of the West, who made us enslave the Winkies, and afterward drive Oz himself out of the Land of the West. Now the Golden Cap is yours, and three times you have the right to lay your wishes upon us."

As the Monkey King finished his story Dorothy looked down and saw the green, shining walls of the Emerald City before them. She wondered at the rapid

flight of the Monkeys, but was glad the journey was over.
The strange creatures set the travellers down carefully
before the gate of the City, the King bowed low to Dorothy, and then flew swiftly away, followed by all his band.

"That was a good ride," said the little girl.

"Yes, and a quick way out of our troubles," replied the
Lion. "How lucky it was you brought away that wonderful Cap!"

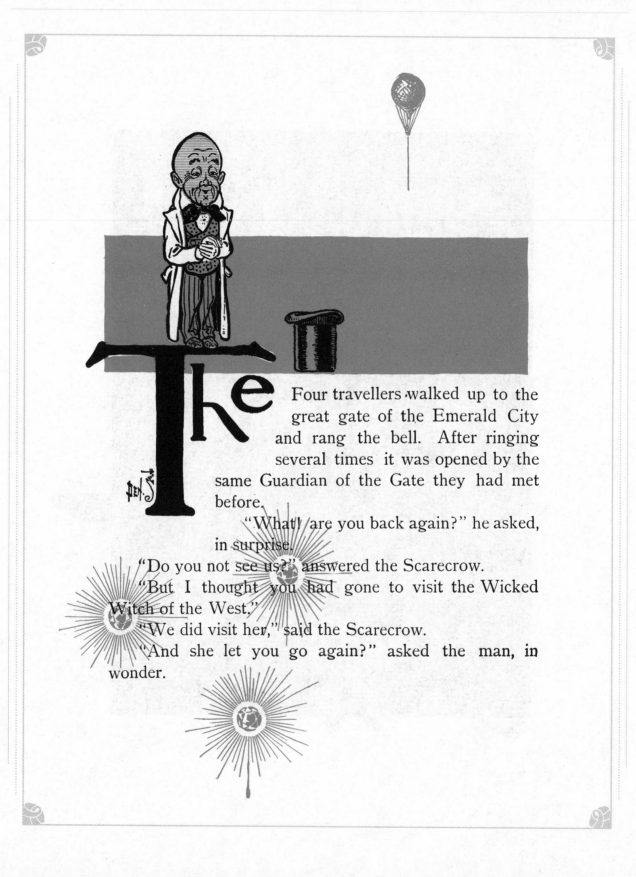

The Four travellers walked up to the great gate of the Emerald City and rang the bell. After ringing several times it was opened by the same Guardian of the Gate they had met before.

"What! are you back again?" he asked, in surprise.

"Do you not see us?" answered the Scarecrow.

"But I thought you had gone to visit the Wicked Witch of the West."

"We did visit her," said the Scarecrow.

"And she let you go again?" asked the man, in wonder.

"She could not help it, for she is melted," explained the Scarecrow.

"Melted! Well, that is good news, indeed," said the man. "Who melted her?"

"It was Dorothy," said the Lion, gravely.

"Good gracious!" exclaimed the man, and he bowed very low indeed before her.

Then he led them into his little room and locked the spectacles from the great box on all their eyes, just as he had done before. Afterward they passed on through the gate into the Emerald City, and when the people heard from the Guardian of the Gate that they had melted the Wicked Witch of the West they all gathered around the travellers and followed them in a great crowd to the Palace of Oz.

The soldier with the green whiskers was still on guard before the door, but he let them in at once and they were again met by the beautiful green girl, who showed each of them to their old rooms at once, so they might rest until the Great Oz was ready to receive them.

The soldier had the news carried straight to Oz that Dorothy and the other travellers had come back again, after destroying the Wicked Witch; but Oz made no reply. They thought the Great Wizard would send for them at once, but he did not. They had no word from him the next day, nor the next, nor the next. The waiting was tiresome and wearing, and at last they grew vexed that

Oz should treat them in so poor a fashion, after sending them to undergo hardships and slavery. So the Scarecrow at last asked the green girl to take another message to Oz, saying if he did not let them in to see him at once they would call the Winged Monkeys to help them, and find out whether he kept his promises or not. When the Wizard was given this message he was so frightened that he sent word for them to come to the Throne Room at four minutes after nine o'clock the next morning. He had once met the Winged Monkeys in the Land of the West, and he did not wish to meet them again.

1.

The four travellers passed a sleepless night, each thinking of the gift Oz had promised to bestow upon him. Dorothy fell asleep only once, and then she dreamed she was in Kansas, where Aunt Em was telling her how glad she was to have her little girl at home again.

Promptly at nine o'clock the next morning the green whiskered soldier came to them, and four minutes later they all went into the Throne Room of the Great Oz.

Of course each one of them expected to see the Wizard in the shape he had taken before, and all were greatly surprised when they looked about and saw no one at all in the room. They kept close to the door and closer to one another, for the stillness of the empty room was more dreadful than any of the forms they had seen Oz take.

Presently they heard a Voice, seeming to come

1. *four minutes after nine o'clock.* The absurd precision of this appointment recalls the ridiculous hours kept by another wizard, in *A New Wonderland* (1900). Over the entrance of his cave is written:

> A. WIZARD, Esq.
> Office hours:
> From 10:45 until
> a quarter to 11. (p. 101)

from somewhere near the top of the great dome, and it said, solemnly.

"I am Oz, the Great and Terrible. Why do you seek me?"

They looked again in every part of the room, and then, seeing no one, Dorothy asked,

"Where are you?"

"I am everywhere," answered the Voice, "but to the eyes of common mortals I am invisible. I will now seat myself upon my throne, that you may converse with me." Indeed, the Voice seemed just then to come straight from the throne itself; so they walked toward it and stood in a row while Dorothy said:

"We have come to claim our promise, O Oz."

"What promise?" asked Oz.

"You promised to send me back to Kansas when the Wicked Witch was destroyed," said the girl.

"And you promised to give me brains," said the Scarecrow.

"And you promised to give me a heart," said the Tin Woodman.

"And you promised to give me courage," said the Cowardly Lion.

"Is the Wicked Witch really destroyed?" asked the Voice, and Dorothy thought it trembled a little.

"Yes," she answered, "I melted her with a bucket of water."

"Dear me," said the Voice; "how sudden! Well, come to me to-morrow, for I must have time to think it over."

"You've had plenty of time already," said the Tin Woodman, angrily.

"We shan't wait a day longer," said the Scarecrow.

"You must keep your promises to us!" exclaimed Dorothy.

The Lion thought it might be as well to frighten the Wizard, so he gave a large, loud roar, which was so fierce and dreadful that Toto jumped away from him in alarm and tipped over the screen that stood in a corner. As it fell with a crash they looked that way, and the next moment all of them were filled with wonder. For they saw, standing in just the spot the screen had hidden, a little, old man, with a bald head and a wrinkled face, who seemed to be as much surprised as they were. The Tin Woodman, raising his axe, rushed toward the little man and cried out,

"Who are you?"

"I am Oz, the Great and Terrible," said the little man, in a trembling voice, "but don't strike me—please don't!—and I'll do anything you want me to."

2.

3.

2. *a bald head*. According to ancient tradition, a wizard's powers depend on the abundance of hair on his head. If that is true, then Oz can only be "a very good man, but a very bad wizard." However, James Hastings's *A Dictionary of the Bible* (New York: Charles Scribner's Sons, 1909) disclosed that Egyptian priests, to retain their supernatural powers, shaved their heads. Notice in the next picture of the Wizard in the basket on page 266 that he was not completely bald when he arrived in the Land of Oz. Apparently he aged after his arrival in Oz. See Note 13 below.

3. *I am Oz, the Great and Terrible*. My, how the mighty Oz has fallen, like Ozymandias in Shelley's poem:

> Two vast and trunkless legs of stone
> Stand in the desert. Near them, on the sand,
> Half sunk, a shattered visage lies. . . .
> Nothing beside remains. Round the decay
> Of that colossal wreck, boundless and bare,
> The lone and level sands stretch far away.

4. *a common man*. "Just like the rest of the wizards!" the Scarecrow slyly adds in Baum's first draft of *The Wizard of Oz* play.

5. *a humbug*. He is a flimflam man, a con artist, a huckster, a hustler, a snake-oil salesman, who indulges in all the chicanery of the carnival sideshow and dime museum. Justin G. Schiller observed in his afterword to the 1985 Pennyroyal edition of *The Wonderful Wizard of Oz* that "when the screen in the throne room of Oz fell, so did the 'persona' of Oz himself, and he is embarrassed over his own fallibility" (p. 265). The trickster is a stock character in American literature and folklore. Herman Melville observes in *The Confidence Man* (1857), "In new countries, where the wolves are killed off, the foxes increase." Probably the most famous of all these scam artists are the King and Duke of Mark Twain's *Adventures of Huckleberry Finn* (1884). The Wizard's position in Oz is reminiscent of Hank Morgan's in Camelot in Twain's *A Connecticut Yankee in King Arthur's Court* (1889). A little modern Yankee ingenuity works wonders in an uncivilized, superstitious nation. He is immediately appointed the new court magician, all the while knowing himself to be a fraud. Baum explored a similar theme in "The Forest Oracle," one of his "Animal Fairy Tales" (*The Delineator*, April 1905). Some of the creatures of the forest are much like human beings: "Not all the animals were agreed as to the value of the information thus conveyed through the Great Oracle. Some said the words of the Terrible Unknown were meaningless; but many declared that, if considered with care, one might always find just the advice he needed concealed somewhere in these wise utterances. These argued that not to understand the Oracle showed a great lack of intelligence." Then a little monkey discovers the secret of "the Terrible Unknown, the Mighty Oracle—the Fraud of the Forest." The exposed old monkey admits, "There are a good many ways to make an honest living; and although one may be born stupid, it is no bar to becoming a successful Oracle."

The Wizard is not really such a bad man. After all, his deception did keep the Wicked Witches of the East and West out of the part of the country where he built the Emerald City. He is a harmless scoundrel, like P. T. Barnum, "the Prince of Humbugs." After long experience with the American public, the circus impresario concluded that a sucker was born every minute. "Barnum was right when he declared that the American people liked to be deceived," Baum wrote in the Aberdeen (South Dakota) *Saturday Pioneer* (February 8, 1890). "At least they make no effort to defend themselves." Also could there be something in the humbug Wizard of Dr. William P. Phelon, the eccentric leader of the Ramayana Brotherhood, the Chicago branch of the Theosophical Society to which Frank and Maud Baum belonged? Other people have compared him with Thomas A. Edison, the Wizard of Menlo Park. Walter Gibson suggested in *The Master Magicians, Their Lives and Most Famous Tricks* (Garden City, N. Y.: Doubleday, 1966, p. 94) that the Wizard may have been inspired in part by Harry Kellar, the famous American magician of the late nineteenth century. Mild-mannered, baldheaded Kellar performed complex feats of "humbug" on stage as marvelous as anything devised by Oz, the Great and Terrible. Baum likely met Kellar many years later when both attended functions of the Uplifters' Club at the Los Angeles Athletic Club. Another of Baum's contemporaries whose life parallels that of the Great Oz was John A. Hamlin, the father of the producer of the *Wizard of Oz* musical extravaganza in 1902. The elder Hamlin earned fame and fortune from his cure-all "Wizard Oil." He traveled across the Midwest as a circus magician, giving demonstrations of the miracles achieved through the use of his marvelous concoction and promising that anyone else could be a wizard just by rubbing his hands with the wonderful oil at half a dollar a bottle. He promoted the product by doing everything from painting the name on rocks to producing traveling musical reviews. "The Wizard Oil remedies had their merits sung by slick-tongued comedians with banjos," recalled Chicago poet Carl Sandburg in *The American Songbag* (New York: Harcourt, Brace, 1927). "Flaring gasoline lamps lighted their faces as the throngs surged about listening to the promises made to the sick, lame, sore" (p. 52). He reprinted the show's theme song, to be sung "like a big city slicker." It included the following verse:

Our friends looked at him in surprise and dismay.

"I thought Oz was a great Head," said Dorothy.

"And I thought Oz was a lovely Lady," said the Scarecrow,

"And I thought Oz was a terrible Beast," said the Tin Woodman.

"And I thought Oz was a Ball of Fire," exclaimed the Lion.

"No; you are all wrong," said the little man, meekly. "I have been making believe."

"Making believe!" cried Dorothy. "Are you not a great Wizard?"

"Hush, my dear," he said; "don't speak so loud, or you will be overheard—and I should be ruined. I'm supposed to be a Great Wizard."

"And aren't you?" she asked.

"Not a bit of it, my dear; I'm just a common man."   4.

"You're more than that," said the Scarecrow, in a grieved tone; "you're a humbug."   5.

"Exactly so!" declared the little man, rubbing his hands together as if it pleased him; "I am a humbug."

"But this is terrible," said the Tin Woodman; "how shall I ever get my heart?"

"Or I my courage?" asked the Lion.

"Or I my brains?" wailed the Scarecrow, wiping the the tears from his eyes with his coat-sleeve.

"My dear friends," said Oz, "I pray you not to speak

Now, listen to what I'm going to say, and don't think I'm
  jesting
When I tell you for your aches and pains that Wizard Oil's
  the best thing.
It's healing and it's soothing, it's refreshing and it's thriving,
The proof of which, wherever it's sold the people all are
  thriving.
Chorus:
I'll take another bottle of Wizard Oil,
I'll take another bottle or two!
I'll take another bottle of Wizard Oil,
I'll take another bottle or two!

One of these Wizard Oil revues passed through Aberdeen, South Dakota, when Baum lived there, and he may well have taken in the show. According to Frank J. Baum and Russell P. MacFall's *To Please a Child* (p. 12), all Hamlin had to do was learn the title of Baum and Tietjens' musical play to decide to produce it. He probably thought that history might repeat itself and *The Wizard of Oz* would make as big a fortune for him as Wizard Oil had made for his father.

The role of the Wizard did not go over when John Slavin played him straight on opening night of the 1902 musical extravaganza in Chicago, so he turned him into a Dutch comedian. His successor, Bobby Gaylord, made Oz a wise-cracking Irishman. The Keystone Cops veteran Charles Murray, who knew Baum in the Uplifters, took the part in the dreadful 1925 Chadwick silent picture. W. C. Fields, who made a career of playing flimflam men, turned down the chance to portray the Wizard in the 1939 MGM movie. He was played instead by the delightfully bumbling Frank Morgan. André DeShields played him in the 1975 Broadway production of *The Wiz*, and Richard Pryor was the Wiz in the 1978 movie.

There is hardly a major twentieth-century political cartoonist who has not made reference to *The Wizard of Oz* in one way or another. W. A. Rogers caricatured newspaper publisher William Randolph Hearst, then the Democratic nominee for governor of New York, as "The Wizard of Ooze" in a series of editorial cartoons in *Harper's Weekly* (October 6 through November 3, 1906). (See illustration on page lxiii.) They helped crush any hope Hearst had for a political career. Pulitzer Prize–winning editorial cartoonist "Herblock" (Herbert Block) of the Washington *Post* has made use of Oz characters in his political caricatures ever since 1939, when the MGM picture came out. Predictably, Barry Moser in the 1985 Pennyroyal Press edition of *The Wonderful Wizard of Oz* depicted then-president Ronald Reagan as the Wizard (and his wife, Nancy, as the Wicked Witch of the West). Charles Santore had P. T. Barnum, Thomas Alva Edison, and W. C. Fields all in mind when he drew the Great and Terrible Humbug for the 1991 Jelly

Bean Press condensation. When Adlai Stevenson became the United States Representative to the United Nations in 1962, he wrote President John Kennedy about a curious letter he got from the Nobel laureate John Steinbeck. "I want to be Ambassador in Oz," Steinbeck informed Stevenson. "There is only one great danger that I can think of. In Oz they have a wizard who openly admits that he is a fake. Can you think what that principle would do to New York politics alone, if it should be spread, I mean?" (Quoted in Elaine Steinbeck and Robert Wallstein, *John Steinbeck, A Life in Letters,* New York: Viking Press, 1975, p. 692.) "Are the respected Wizards of our Emerald Cities really wizards," asked Gardner in his introduction to the 1961 Dover edition, "or just amiable circus humbugs who keep us supplied with colored glasses that make life greener than it really is?"

6. *make the eyes move and the mouth open*. Baum shared the Wizard's fascination with mechanical devices and stagecraft. Baum himself invented many of the special effects in his theatrical productions. His sister-in-law Helen Leslie Gage considered him "undoubtedly a genius. His talents are varied and many and he does well to whatever he puts his hand. . . . He intuitively knows how to repair the children's toys" ("L. Frank Baum: An Inside Introduction to the Public," *The Dakotan*, January–February–March 1903). He demonstrated in the technical treatise *The Art of Decorating Dry Goods Windows and Interiors* (1900) his knowledge of simple illusions and all sorts of mechanical gadgetry. As a form of relaxation, he took up woodworking and built all the oak furniture in the Baums' summer cottage, the Sign of the Goose, in Macatawa Park, Michigan. "Last of all, because all this had not yet rested his brain enough," recalled poet Eunice Tietjens, wife of the composer Paul Tietjens, in *The World at My Shoulder* (New York: Macmillan, 1938), Baum "had made an elaborate piano arrangement of Paul's music for *The Wizard of Oz*—though he was no musician it was pretty good—had then figured out the system by which a pianola records were made, and cut a full-length record of this arrangement out of wrapping paper! This seems to have done the trick, and he was presently back at work" (p. 15).

7. *a ventriloquist*. Throwing one's voice goes back to ancient times. Egyptian, Hebrew, and Greek priests were skillful at giving voice to sacred statues and oracles. By the nineteenth century, ventriloquism had become a parlor trick. Itinerant magicians tramped through Syracuse and other parts of central New York during Baum's boyhood, among them Donaldson, "Wizard of the East," who performed marvelous feats of necromancy and ventriloquism in October and December 1865.

of these little things.   Think of me, and the terrible trouble I'm in at being found out."

"Doesn't anyone else know you're a humbug?" asked Dorothy.

"No one knows it but you four—and myself," replied Oz. "I have fooled everyone so long that I thought I should never be found out. It was a great mistake my ever letting you into the Throne Room. Usually I will not see even my subjects, and so they believe I am something terrible."

"But, I don't understand," said Dorothy, in bewilderment. "How was it that you appeared to me as a great Head?"

"That was one of my tricks," answered Oz. "Step this way, please, and I will tell you all about it."

He led the way to a small chamber in the rear of the Throne Room, and they all followed him. He pointed to one corner, in which lay the Great Head, made out of many thicknesses of paper, and with a carefully painted face.

"This I hung from the ceiling by a wire," said Oz; "I stood behind the screen and pulled a thread, to make the eyes move and the mouth open."   6.

"But how about the voice?" she enquired.

"Oh, I am a ventriloquist," said the little man, "and I can throw the sound of my voice wherever I wish; so that you thought it was coming out of the Head. Here are   7.

8. *I was born in Omaha*. Perhaps too much has been made of the coincidence that the Democratic presidential candidate William Jennings Bryan also came from Omaha. There is nothing else remotely evident in the text that Baum was thinking of this politician and his famous "Cross of Gold" speech when writing *The Wizard of Oz* in 1899. In *Dorothy and the Wizard in Oz* (1908, p. 192), the little Wizard continues his history prior to his arrival in Oz. His father was a loquacious politician who named his boy Oscar Zoroaster Phadrig Isaac Norman Henkle Emmannuel Ambroise Diggs. Because that is such a long and difficult name to remember, the young man shortened it to Oz; the other letters spelled P-I-N-H-E-A-D, which he feared might be considered a reflection on his intelligence. He painted the new name on all his belongings and, when he joined the circus, on his balloon. When he descended from the clouds, the natives concluded that he must be their rightful ruler, for on the balloon was printed in large letters "O. Z." Oddly, Aleksandr Volkov named him James Goodwin in his 1939 Russian "translation."

the other things I used to deceive you." He showed the Scarecrow the dress and the mask he had worn when he seemed to be the lovely Lady; and the Tin Woodman saw that his Terrible Beast was nothing but a lot of skins, sewn together, with slats to keep their sides out. As for the Ball of Fire, the false Wizard had hung that also from the ceiling. It was really a ball of cotton, but when oil was poured upon it the ball burned fiercely.

"Really," said the Scarecrow, "you ought to be ashamed of yourself for being such a humbug."

"I am—I certainly am," answered the little man, sorrowfully; "but it was the only thing I could do. Sit down, please, there are plenty of chairs; and I will tell you my story."

So they sat down and listened while he told the following tale:

"I was born in Omaha—" 8.

"Why, that isn't very far from Kansas!" cried Dorothy.

"No; but it's farther from here," he said, shaking his head at her, sadly. "When I grew up I became a ventriloquist, and at that I was very well trained by a great master. I can imitate any kind of a bird or beast." Here he mewed so like a kitten that Toto pricked up his ears and looked everywhere to see where she was. "After a time," continued Oz, "I tired of that, and became a balloonist."

"What is that?" asked Dorothy.

"A man who goes up in a balloon on circus day, so all

9. to draw a crowd of people together and get them to pay to see the circus," he explained.

"Oh," she said; "I know."

"Well, one day I went up in a balloon and the ropes got twisted, so that I couldn't come down again. It went way up above the clouds, so far that a current of air struck it and carried it many, many miles away. For a day and a night I travelled through the air, and on the morning of the second day I awoke and found the balloon floating over a strange and beautiful country.

"It came down gradually, and I was not hurt a bit. But I found myself in the midst of a strange people, who, seeing me come from the clouds, thought I was a great Wizard. Of course I let them think so, because they were

10. afraid of me, and promised to do anything I wished them to.

"Just to amuse myself, and keep the good people busy,

11. I ordered them to build this City, and my palace; and they did it all willingly and well. Then I thought, as the coun-

12. try was so green and beautiful, I would call it the Emerald City, and to make the name fit better I put green spectacles on all the people, so that everything they saw was green."

"But isn't everything here green?" asked Dorothy.

"No more than in any other city," replied Oz; "but

9. *get them to pay to see the circus.* Balloon ascensions were popular attractions in central New York when Baum was growing up. On September 13, 1871, Professor C. C. Coe inflated his balloon *The New World* in Hanover Square right in front of Baum's father's place of business, the Second National Bank of Syracuse. P. T. Barnum's "Professor" Washington Harrison Donaldson, magician, ventriloquist, and balloonist, made an ascension near Chicago on July 15, 1875 and was never seen again. Balloons were a feature of the Brown County Fair in Aberdeen, South Dakota, when Baum lived there. Regular flights of a big yellow one were a feature of the 1893 World's Columbian Exposition in Chicago, and Baum noted in *The Art of Decorating Dry Goods Windows and Interiors* (1900, p. 154) how balloon ascensions were then in general use to advertise street fairs.

10. *anything I wished.* Edward Eager, an admirer of Baum's books, paraphrased the Wizard's history in his own "modernized" fairy tale *Seven-Day Magic* (1962), in which a group of children use a magic book to visit a magic land called Oswaldoland, accompanied by a stage magician named Oswaldo. Although he had grown up on the Oz books, Eager was ambivalent about their value as juvenile literature when he reread them aloud to his son. "I found the earliest volumes—*The Wizard of Oz, The Land of Oz, Ozma of Oz*—to have a certain homely American charm which in a way compensates for their lack of literary distinction," he said in "A Father's Minority Report" (*The Horn Book*, March 1948). "As L. Frank Baum continued to expand the series, his writing deteriorated, and some of his later books really typify all one doesn't like about the America of the World War One period." Even so, Eager learned considerably about writing fantasy from reading Baum's Oz books.

11. *I ordered them to build this City.* Just like the captains of industry who built the White City of the 1893 World's Columbian Exposition from the marshes along Lake Michigan. Frances Hodgson Burnett's description of the erecting of this ideal city in *Two Little Pilgrims' Progress* (1897) is reminiscent of the Wizard's recollection of the origins of his Emerald City:

> There was a great Magician who was the ruler of all the Genii in all the world. They were all powerful and rich and wonderful magicians, but he could make them obey him, and give him what they stored away. And he said: "I will build a splendid City, that all the world shall flock to and wonder at and remember forever. And in it some of all the things in the world shall be seen, so that the people who see it shall learn what the world is like—how huge it is, and what wisdom it has in it, and what wonders! And it will

make them know what they are like themselves, because the wonders will be made by hands and feet and brains just like their own. And so they will understand how strong they are—if they only knew it—and it will give them courage and fill them with thoughts." (p. 107)

Of course the magic of the White City of Chicago was all an illusion like that of the Emerald City of Oz.

12. *green spectacles.* Baum may be playing with the proverbial phrase "to wear rose-colored glasses," meaning to view the world as better than it really is. He made a similar point in his "Our Landlady" column, "She Discourses on Many Topics and tells how the Alley deals out the Corn" (Aberdeen *Saturday Pioneer*, May 3, 1890). A farmer who has lost his crops explains his unique way of trying to save his livestock: "I puts green goggles on my hosses an' feed 'em shavin's an' they think it's grass, but they ain't gittin' fat on it." Stuart Culver in "What Manikins Want" (*Representations*, Winter 1888) identified the likely source for this remark in Joseph Kirkland's obscure novel *Zury, the Meanest Man in Spring County* (1886). Russian critic Miron Petrovskii suggested in *Knigi neshego detsva* (Moscow: Kniga, 1986, p. 245) that Baum may have had in mind the German Romantic poet Heinrich von Kleist's famous response to Immanuel Kant's belief that one "superimposes" one's interior self on the real world, which only distorts its perception. "If everyone saw the world through green glasses," he wrote in 1801, "they would be forced to judge that everything they saw *was* green, and could never be sure whether their eyes saw things as they really are, or did not add something of their own to what they saw. And so it is with our intellect." This is another example of the conflict between the rational Enlightenment and the emotional Romantic Age referred to in Chapter 5, Note 22.

13.

14.

15.

when you wear green spectacles, why of course everything you see looks green to you. The Emerald City was built a great many years ago, for I was a young man when the balloon brought me here, and I am a very old man now. But my people have worn green glasses on their eyes so long that most of them think it really is an Emerald City, and it certainly is a beautiful place, abounding in jewels and precious metals, and every good thing that is needed to make one happy. I have been good to the people, and they like me; but ever since this Palace was built I have shut myself up and would not see any of them.

"One of my greatest fears was the Witches, for while I had no magical powers at all I soon found out that the Witches were really able to do wonderful things. There were four of them in this country, and they ruled the people who live in the North and South and East and West. Fortunately, the Witches of the North and South were good, and I knew they would do me no harm; but the Witches of the East and West were terribly wicked, and had they not thought I was more powerful than they themselves, they would surely have destroyed me. As it was, I lived in deadly fear of them for many years; so you can imagine how pleased I was when I heard your house had fallen on the Wicked Witch of the East. When you came to me I was willing to promise anything if you would only do away with the other Witch; but, now that you have melted her, I am ashamed to say that I cannot keep my promises."

13. *looks green to you.* As Janet Juhnke noted in "A Kansan's View" (in Gerald Peary and Roger Shatzkin, *The Classic American Novel and the Movies*, New York: Frederick Ungar, 1974, p. 168), that for all its beauty, there is nothing natural about the green of the Emerald City. The only plants ever mentioned there are the green flowers on the windowsill of Dorothy's room in the palace. Is Baum drawing a parallel between the illusion of the Emerald City and that of the White City of the 1893 Columbian World's Fair in Chicago? It too was not so magnificent as it appeared. The palaces and other beautiful buildings were finished to look like marble, but they were actually built of a mixture of plaster, cement, and fiber called "staff," a durable material lighter than wood. And they were not made to last. Although they were advertised as fireproof, some were destroyed in fires on the fairgrounds. They made magnificent ruins. Only one structure from the original fair still stands in Chicago today: the Fine Arts Building, which became Chicago's Museum of Science and Industry. "The Wizard is being over-modest and slightly untruthful," Gardner corrected him in Note 19 of *The Wizard of Oz and Who He Was.* "When he built the Emerald City he used more emeralds than any other special stone. The practice of wearing spectacles was never really necessary." Once General Jinjur's Army Revolt conquers the Emerald City in *The Marvelous Land of Oz* (1904), the use of green glasses is abolished.

14. *I am a very old man now.* This is questionable. It is unlikely that the Wizard could be much more than fifty years old. Although it had been a trading post since the eighteenth century, the city of Omaha did not receive its name until it was incorporated in 1854. The rest of the Wizard's history as well as his dress indicates that he came to Oz in the last half of the nineteenth century. Perhaps his stay in the Emerald City, avoiding all contact with others, has distorted his sense of time, so that he *thinks* he is an old man. "Old" is, of course, a relative term. In 1900, life expectancy in America was said to be forty-six years for men and forty-eight for women, for it factored in the high infant mortality rate. Still, one could hardly consider the Wizard "a very old man." In fact, the Wizard could not be much older than Baum himself.

The similarity in their ages as well as a few other details suggest that there is a good deal of Baum in the humbug Oz. For example, the writer shared the Wizard's interest in stage magic and his love of puns. "After half a lifetime stumbling through the Gilded Age and half the vocations a man could try," observed MacFall in *To Please a Child*, Baum "had found his fortune within himself, in the humble gift of story telling. Perhaps he even thought of himself as the Wizard, for as the saga of Oz extended itself through book after book, the Wizard of Oz who began as a Prince of Humbug became a genuine Wizard" (p. 131).

15. *shut myself up.* This is not entirely true. The Wizard made at least one journey to the Land of the Winkies, because the Wicked Witch used the Winged Monkeys to drive him from the West. Could this have been before he settled in the Emerald City? Or maybe the balloon landed in the Winkie Country, and he and his followers fled to where the capital now stands. Glinda the Good in Chapter 20 of *The Marvelous Land of Oz* (1904) reports that he made three visits to Mombi, during one of which he turned over the baby Ozma to the witch. (This information is based on a book compiled by Glinda's spies, who record two other curious things about the Wizard: He limps slightly on his left foot—the Scarecrow naturally thinks he suffers from corns—and he ate beans with a knife.) Yet when the Wizard and Princess Ozma meet in *Dorothy and the Wizard in Oz* (1908, pp. 191–92), there is no recognition on either side nor any animosity expressed. These three meetings with the witch may have occurred before the building of the Emerald City.

"I think you are a very bad man," said Dorothy.

"Oh, no, my dear; I'm really a very good man; but I'm a very bad Wizard, I must admit."

"Can't you give me brains?" asked the Scarecrow.

"You don't need them. You are learning something every day. A baby has brains, but it doesn't know much. Experience is the only thing that brings knowledge, and the longer you are on earth the more experience you are sure to get."

"That may all be true," said the Scarecrow, "but I shall be very unhappy unless you give me brains."

The false wizard looked at him carefully.

"Well," he said, with a sigh, "I'm not much of a magician, as I said; but if you will come to me to-morrow morning, I will stuff your head with brains. I cannot tell you how to use them, however; you must find that out for yourself."

"Oh, thank you—thank you!" cried the Scarecrow. "I'll find a way to use them, never fear!"

"But how about my courage?" asked the Lion, anxiously.

"You have plenty of courage, I am sure," answered Oz. "All you need is confidence in yourself. There is no living

16. *I'm a very bad Wizard.* The Wizard suffers from the psychological conflict between the Role, determined by society, and the Self, by the individual. According to "radical" psychologist R. D. Laing, the split between the two may result in schizophrenia—a rift he charges society with causing. Wizard is not yet delusional. He is perfectly aware that he is a very bad Wizard, but also a very good man. His people view him only in the role that they wish him to play; they do not even consider him a man. This presents another problem: They fear him, because they do not understand him. He is most dreadful and dreaded when he is not seen at all, when all that is present is the comprehension of his Role in society. When the screen falls, so too does the Role and he can be seen for his true Self, a little old humbug. When Dorothy asked in Chapter 2 if he was "a good man," she was told he was "a good Wizard." That is, of course, not the same thing at all. He disappoints her when she sees him for what he truly is. The Wizard stands exposed at the end of the nineteenth century. All the old beliefs seem stripped by revolutions, Darwin, Nietzsche. One must find for oneself and in oneself a new meaning in life at the start of a new century. Though one may be a wizard, one must also be a man.

17. *you must find that out for yourself.* The Scarecrow has already proved all along the Yellow Brick Road that he has the intelligence to use a brain properly. But because he has never actually had one, he has not had the opportunity yet to abuse it. Likewise, the Tin Woodman and Cowardly Lion have each shown they have the quality within themselves that they seek. These three individuals illustrate, as Gardner argued in *The Wizard of Oz and Who He Was*, "the human tendency to confuse a real virtue with its valueless outer symbol" (p. 25). The Wizard has already confessed that he knows no magic, but that is not good enough for them. They require something tangible to represent what they desire. A reversal of this situation occurs in *The Patchwork Girl of Oz* (1913): The Glass Cat has a red stone heart and pink brains for all the world to see, but she is vain and stupid. In his review of the 1939 MGM musical in the London *Spectator* (February 9, 1940), Graham Greene thought that, in this "American drummer's dream of escape," "the morality seems a little crude and the fancy material. . . . Once a drummer always a drummer, and the author of this fantasy remained the agile salesman, offering his customers the best material dreams—nothing irrational."

Self-reliance is a long-held American virtue. One immediately recalls Ralph Waldo Emerson's classic essay on the subject. It was also taught at the Ethical Culture Sunday School in Chicago, where the Baums sent their children. John Algeo in "Oz and Kansas: A Theosophical Quest" (in Susan R. Gannon and Ruth Anne Thompson's *Proceedings of the Thirteenth Annual Conference of the Children's Literature Association*, Kansas City: University of Missouri, 1988) identified it as an important tenet of Theosophy, as described in Mabel Collins's book of aphorisms *Light on the Path* (1885), which Baum may have known. "Desire only that which is within you," she advises. "For within you is the light of the world—the only light that can be shed upon the Path. If you are unable to perceive it within you, it is useless to look for it elsewhere." The Wizard could be paraphrasing her. Ray Bolger, however, recalled in "A Lesson from Oz" (*Guideposts*, March 1982) that his mother told him that the message of *The Wizard of Oz* came from the Bible: "The kingdom of God is within you" (Luke 17:21).

The value of their journey to the Great Oz does not lie in the gifts of a brain, a heart, and courage. The journey itself is more important than its conclusion, for it forced them to discover within themselves what they always possessed. They just had to test these virtues through experience. They learned how to use the gifts of the Great Oz, and in doing that they never really needed what he had to give them. Dorothy does not quite know the truth of what she is saying when she tells the Scarecrow in Chapter 3, "If Oz will not give you any brains you will be no worse off than you are now." He is better off now, for through testing his intelligence on the journey, he knows how to use a brain. The Wizard suggests that he has confused knowledge, the accumulation of facts, with intelligence, the ability to use that information once acquired. And only through experience can he gain knowledge with which to use his intellect.

thing that is not afraid when it faces danger. True courage is in facing danger when you are afraid, and that kind
of courage you have in plenty."

"Perhaps I have, but I'm scared just the same," said
the Lion. "I shall really be very unhappy unless you give
me the sort of courage that makes one forget he is afraid."

"Very well; I will give you that sort of courage to-
morrow," replied Oz.

"How about my heart?" asked the Tin Woodman.

"Why, as for that," answered Oz, "I think you are
wrong to want a heart. It makes most people unhappy.
If you only knew it, you are in luck not to have a heart."

"That must be a matter of opinion," said the Tin
Woodman. "For my part, I will bear all the unhappiness
without a murmur, if you will give me the heart."

"Very well," answered Oz, meekly. "Come
to me to-morrow and you shall have a heart. I
have played Wizard for so many years that I may
as well continue the part a little longer."

"And now," said Dorothy, "how
am I to get back to Kansas?"

"We shall have to think about that,"
replied the little man, "Give me two
or three days to consider the matter
and I'll try to find a way to carry you
over the desert. In the meantime you
shall all be treated as my guests, and

18. *that kind of courage you have in plenty*. Compare this remark to the moral of "The King of the Polar Bears" in *American Fairy Tales* (1901): "This story teaches us true dignity and courage depend not upon outward appearance, but come rather from within." Like the Scarecrow with a brain and the Tin Woodman with a heart, the Cowardly Lion must discover what he values, whether courage or confidence, within himself for a better understanding of himself. Baum realizes, according to Sheldon Kopp in "The Wizard Behind the Couch" (*Psychology Today*, March 1970), "the possibility of growth through coming to accept ourselves, with humor if need be, and of the central role of a loving relationship in solving our problems." Baum wrote "to express his dissatisfaction with Victorian ideas of building character through punishment, grave lectures, and inner struggle for self-control, sacrifice and self-denial." Baum explored the reality and worth of the Self, the Will. He was not concerned with those virtues promoted by Victorian juvenile literature, "the duties of industry, frugality, manly respect for the weak, and a sober Christian altruism," in the words of Mark Edmund Jones in *The Pursuit of Happiness* (Cambridge, Mass.: Harvard University Press, 1954). Baum introduced what Jones called "the *Wizard of Oz* formula," the pursuit of happiness, to American juvenile literature. Baum believed in the search for the individual's freedom, which lies only within the Self.

The Wizard of Oz is a subtle reflection on the fairy-tale tradition. A hero or heroine often seeks that one talisman that will cure an illness or misfortune, one that will make one whole. This sickness, according to M.-L. Franz in Carl Jung's *Man and His Symbols* (1964), is a feeling of emptiness and futility; the desired object will restore meaning to the afflicted person. And it is merely a reflection of the individual's Self. The Scarecrow, the Tin Woodman, and the Cowardly Lion all suffer from these feelings of inadequacy; each one must find that one special thing that will make him complete. But the talisman is only a symbol and has no value of its own; what it reflects within the Self is what is important. Now each of the three travelers realizes that what he has longed for has indeed always been within himself.

19. *without a murmur*. Another pun about heart ailments.

20. *agreed to say nothing*. Apparently someone did not keep his promise. Everyone in the second Oz book, *The Marvelous Land of Oz* (1904), knows that he is a humbug. Tip informs Jack Pumpkinhead that Oz "wasn't so much of a Wizard as he might have been" (p. 36).

while you live in the Palace my people will wait upon you and obey your slighest wish. There is only one thing I ask in return for my help—such as it is. You must keep my secret and tell no one I am a humbug."

20.   They agreed to say nothing of what they had learned, and went back to their rooms in high spirits. Even Dorothy had hope that "The Great and Terrible Humbug," as she called him, would find a way to send her back to Kansas, and if he did that she was willing to forgive him everything.

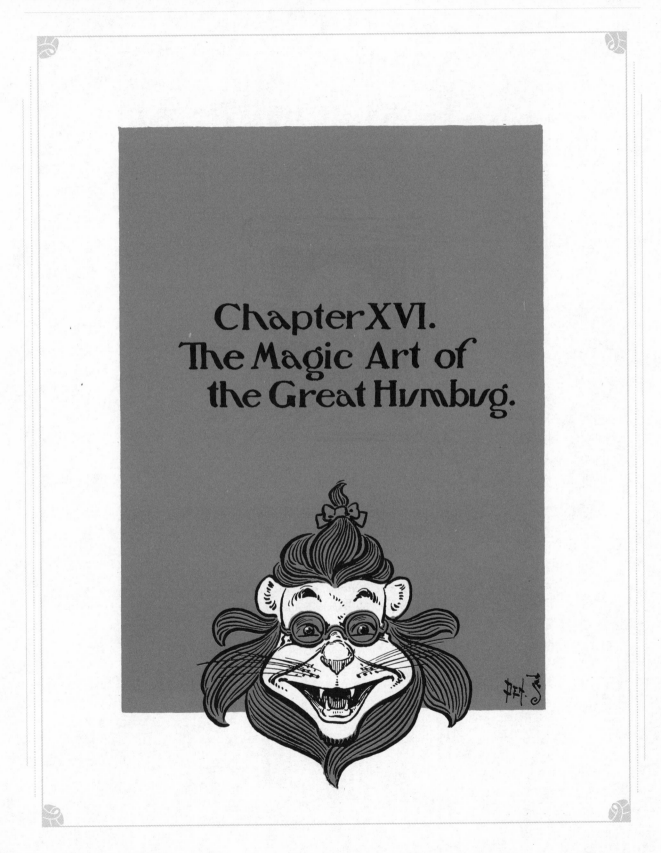

A previously unpublished sketch of the Scarecrow,
drawn by W. W. Denslow for Townsend Walsh,
publicity manager of the musical extravaganza
The Wizard of Oz, 1902.
Courtesy the Billy Rose Theatre Collection, The New York Public
Library for the Performing Arts, Astor,
Lenox and Tilden Foundations.

Next MORNING THE Scarecrow said to his friends:

"Congratulate me. I am going to Oz to get my brains at last. When I return I shall be as other men are."

"I have always liked you as you were," said Dorothy, simply.

"It is kind of you to like a Scarecrow," he replied. "But surely you will think more of me when you hear the splendid thoughts my new brain is going to turn out." Then he said good-bye to them all in a cheerful voice and went to the Throne Room, where he rapped upon the door.

"Come in," said Oz.

The Scarecrow went in and found the little man sitting down by the window, engaged in deep thought.

"I have come for my brains," remarked the Scarecrow, a little uneasily.

"Oh, yes; sit down in that chair, please," replied Oz. "You must excuse me for taking your head off, but I shall have to do it in order to put your brains in their proper place."

"That's all right," said the Scarecrow. "You are quite welcome to take my head off, as long as it will be a better one when you put it on again."

So the Wizard unfastened his head and emptied out the straw. Then he entered the back room and took up a measure of bran, which he mixed with a great many pins and needles. Having shaken them together thoroughly, he filled the top of the Scarecrow's head with the mixture and stuffed the rest of the space with straw, to hold it in place. When he had fastened the Scarecrow's head on his body again he said to him,

"Hereafter you will be a great man, for I have given you a lot of bran-new brains."

The Scarecrow was both pleased and proud at the fulfillment of his greatest wish, and having thanked Oz warmly he went back to his friends.

Dorothy looked at him curiously. His head was quite bulging out at the top with brains.

"How do you feel?" she asked.

1. *a measure of bran, which he mixed with a great many pins.* For his illustration in the 1985 Pennyroyal edition, Barry Moser came up with a curious equation: bran + pins = brains. He argued on May 11, in *Forty-seven Days to Oz*, "There is evidence since Baum obviously enjoyed such word/letter play (NY = OZ, e. g.) it seems entirely within reason that this might have been what he had in mind—not really 'bran-new' brains!" *The Tin Woodman of Oz* (1918) says that they were made of "mixed wheat-straw and bran" (p. 44).

"I feel wise, indeed," he answered, earnestly. "When I get used to my brains I shall know everything."

"Why are those needles and pins sticking out of your head?" asked the Tin Woodman.

"That is proof that he is sharp," remarked the Lion.

"Well, I must go to Oz and get my heart," said the Woodman. So he walked to the Throne Room and knocked at the door.

"Come in," called Oz, and the Woodman entered and said,

"I have come for my heart."

"Very well," answered the little man. "But I shall have to cut a hole in your breast, so I can put your heart in the right place. I hope it won't hurt you."

"Oh, no;" answered the Woodman. "I shall not feel it at all."

So Oz brought a pair of tinners' shears and cut a small, square hole in the left side of the Tin Woodman's breast. Then, going to a chest of drawers, he took out a pretty heart, made entirely of silk and stuffed with sawdust.

"Isn't it a beauty?" he asked.

"It is, indeed!" replied

the Woodman, who was greatly pleased. "But is it a kind heart?"

"Oh, very!" answered Oz. He put the heart in the Woodman's breast and then replaced the square of tin, soldering it neatly together where it had been cut.

2.

"There," said he; "now you have a heart that any man might be proud of. I'm sorry I had to put a patch on your breast, but it really couldn't be helped."

"Never mind the patch," exclaimed the happy Woodman. "I am very grateful to you, and shall never forget your kindness."

"Don t speak of it," replied Oz.

Then the Tin Woodman went back to his friends, who wished him every joy on account of his good fortune.

The Lion now walked to the Throne Room and knocked at the door.

"Come in," said Oz.

"I have come for my courage," announced the Lion, entering the room.

"Very well," answered the little man; "I will get it for you."

He went to a cupboard and reaching up to a high shelf took down a square green bottle, the contents of which

2. *He put the heart in the Woodman's breast.* It must have seemed like a great impossibility and only worthy of a fairy tale for the Wizard to give the Tin Woodman a heart back in 1900 when the book came out, but the first successful heart transplant was accomplished by Dr. Christiaan Barnard and his surgical team in South Africa in 1967. Dr. Norman Shumway and his staff were the first Americans to do it in 1968. The first artificial heart to be permanently implanted in a human being, on December 2, 1982, was created by the American inventor Dr. Robert K. Jarvik. It was made of plastic and aluminum rather than of silk and sawdust like the Wizard's. As yet no wizard has effectively given a scarecrow a brain.

3. *Full of courage.* "Courage" is colloquial for an alcoholic beverage. Raylyn Moore in *Wonderful Wizard, Marvelous Land* (Bowling Green, Ohio: Bowling Green University Popular Press, 1974, p. 87) identified the little green bottle of the Wizard's courage as similar to that which contained Dutch gin. Oz Club member C. Warren Hollister reported in *The Baum Bugle* (Spring 1966) his coming across a local brand of beer in England called "Courage"; he found another called "Brains" in Cardiff, Wales. Like that of booze, the effect of the Wizard's courage eventually wears off. When Dorothy asks the Cowardly Lion in *Ozma of Oz* (1907) how he has been, he replies, "As cowardly as ever. Every little thing scares me and makes my heart beat fast. . . . To others I may have seemed brave, at times, but I have never been in any danger that I was not afraid" (pp. 119, 122). As soldiers and prizefighters have attested, courage lies in how one deals with fear, not in the absence of it.

4. *do things that everybody knows can't be done.* Once a snake oil salesman, always a snake oil salesman! The Wizard can perform all sorts of miracles only because the gullible public believes them to be miracles. All is forgiven when the Wizard returns to the Emerald City in *Dorothy and the Wizard in Oz* (1908). After all, he is a very good man, even if he is a very bad Wizard. Fear and circumstance forced him previously to lie. Eventually he does become a very good Wizard, but only after long study and hard work under the wise tutoring of Glinda the Good. Dr. Sheldon Kopp reported in "The Wizard Behind the Couch" (*Psychology Today*, March 1970) that patients expected him too to perform miracles through psychoanalysis that everybody knows cannot be done. The Wizard treats Dorothy and her companions as if he were their therapist and they were his patients. No one can solve someone else's problems; he may give guidance, but the responsibility of change lies within the patient. The individual must believe within himself that he will be cured before he can be. Only then can miracles happen.

5. *It was easy.* How easy indeed! Because his head is stuffed with pins and needles, the Scarecrow thinks he is sharp-witted. Because his heart is silk-lined and filled with sawdust, the Tin Woodman feels he is tender-hearted. Because he has drunk some liquor of unknown content, the Lion boasts that he is full of courage. The Wizard, in effect, has provided each with a physical pun. Now the Scarecrow, the Tin Woodman, and the Cowardly Lion possess the concrete symbols, the tangible proof, of what they have always had within themselves.

he poured into a green-gold dish, beautifully carved. Placing this before the Cowardly Lion, who sniffed at it as if he did not like it, the Wizard said,

"Drink."

"What is it?" asked the Lion.

"Well," answered Oz, "if it were inside of you, it would be courage. You know, of course, that courage is always inside one; so that this really cannot be called courage until you have swallowed it. Therefore I advise you to drink it as soon as possible."

The Lion hesitated no longer, but drank till the dish was empty.

"How do you feel now?" asked Oz.

"Full of courage," replied the Lion, who went joyfully back to his friends to tell them of his good fortune.

3.

Oz, left to himself, smiled to think of his success in giving the Scarecrow and the Tin Woodman and the Lion exactly what they thought they wanted. "How can I help being a humbug," he said, "when all these people make me do things that everybody knows can't be done? It was easy to make the Scarecrow and the Lion and the Woodman happy, because they imagined I could do anything. But it will take more than imagination to carry Dorothy back to Kansas, and I'm sure I don't know how it can be done."

4., 5.

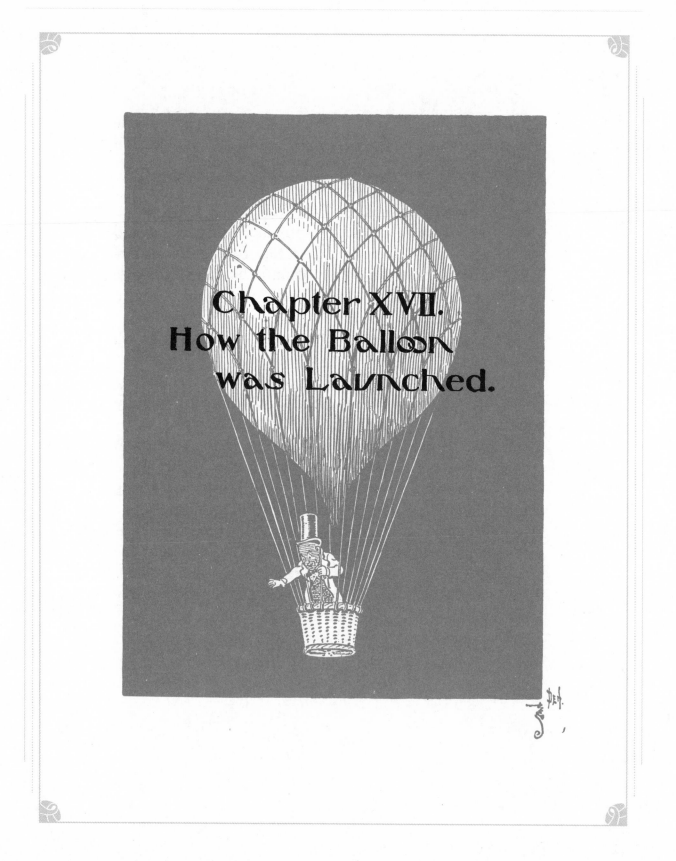

For Three days Dorothy heard nothing from Oz. These were sad days for the little girl, although her friends were all quite happy and contented. The Scarecrow told them there were wonderful thoughts in his head; but he would not say what they were because he knew no one could understand them but himself. When the Tin Woodman walked about he felt his heart rattling around in his breast; and he told Dorothy he had discovered it to be a kinder and more tender heart than the one he had owned when he was made of flesh. The Lion declared he was afraid of nothing on earth, and would gladly face an army of men or a dozen of the fierce Kalidahs.

1.

1. *no one could understand them but himself*. A regular pin-head! Compare this attitude with the Scarecrow's remark at the opening of the previous chapter that he will impress them with "the splendid thoughts my new brain is going to turn out." Again he confuses the meaningless outer symbol with the virtue it represents. Just because one has a brain does not mean one can think intelligently. The Scarecrow is just as foolish now as when he fell in the hole with no brain to guide him. Baum had no patience for pretension or pomposity of any kind. One of the funniest incidents in the Oz series is the interview between the Scarecrow and Jack Pumpkinhead in *The Marvelous Land of Oz* (1904). When Jack says that he cannot understand the King because he is a Munchkin and Jack is a Gillikin, the Scarecrow calls in an interpreter because he insists he cannot understand "the language of the pumpkinheads" (p. 74). Of course, everyone in Oz speaks the same language.

In the same book, Baum introduces one of his finest comic characters, Professor H. M. Woggle-Bug, T. E. He is even more pedantic than Scarecrow ever is. He was once just an ordinary insect when he crawled into a professor's classroom and began listening to the lectures. Soon he was "thoroughly educated." When the teacher caught him and projected him on a screen for study, he was now "highly magnified." With all his faults, the Woggle-Bug was one of Baum's favorite creations. Baum named his musical extravaganza based on *The Marvelous Land of Oz,* the second Oz book, *The Woggle Bug* and wrote a special picture book about him, *The Woggle-Bug Book* (1905). He became famous through the "What Did the Woggle-Bug Say?" contest which promoted the book. He also shared Baum's weakness for puns and founds the Royal College of Oz,

where students take learning pills so they can spend most of their time in sports instead of in courses (although the Woggle-Bug also invented meal pills, which can be taken in three courses). Not all educators have been amused by Professor Woggle-Bug; some have seen him as emblematic of Baum's anti-intellectualism.

2. *balloon*. "In keeping with his magical powers being composed of 'hot air,' " noted Justin G. Schiller in his afterword to the 1985 Pennyroyal Press edition, "the Wizard proposes to help Dorothy return to Kansas via hot-air balloon" (p. 266). This was not the first time that Baum employed this means to get a stranded visitor back to his far-off homeland. An astronomer in "The Man in the Moon" in *Mother Goose in Prose* (1897) mentions that "there's a big balloon in town which belongs to the circus that came here last summer, and was pawned for a bill board. We can inflate this balloon and send the Man out of the Moon home in it." But the people of Norwich succeed where Oz the humbug Wizard does not: "So the balloon was brought and inflated, and the Man got into the basket and gave the word to let go, and then the balloon mounted up into the sky in the direction of the moon . . . until finally the Man reached out and caught hold of the edge of the moon, and behold! the next minute he was the Man in the Moon again!" (pp. 115–16).

3. *made of silk*. Baum accurately describes an aeronautic balloon of the period. Silk was a common material for making one, and the glue was generally India rubber dissolved in oil of turpentine. Not until recently have other, more durable and less expensive materials been used.

Thus each of the little party was satisfied except Dorothy, who longed more than ever to get back to Kansas.

On the fourth day, to her great joy, Oz sent for her, and when she entered the Throne Room he said, pleasantly:

"Sit down, my dear; I think I have found the way to get you out of this country."

"And back to Kansas?" she asked, eagerly.

"Well, I'm not sure about Kansas," said Oz; "for I haven't the faintest notion which way it lies. But the first thing to do is to cross the desert, and then it should be easy to find your way home."

"How can I cross the desert?" she enquired.

"Well, I'll tell you what I think," said the little man. "You see, when I came to this country it was in a balloon. You also came through the air, being carried by a cyclone. So I believe the best way to get across the desert will be through the air. Now, it is quite beyond my powers to make a cyclone; but I've been thinking the matter over, and I believe I can make a balloon."

2.

"How?" asked Dorothy.

"A balloon," said Oz, "is made of silk, which is coated with glue to keep the gas in it. I have plenty of silk in the Palace, so it will be no trouble for us to make the balloon. But in all this country there is no gas to fill the balloon with, to make it float."

3.

4. *Hot air isn't as good as gas.* Air, although often referred to as a gas, is really a mixture of gases. The first successful balloon flight of the French brothers Joseph (1740–1810) and Jacques (1745–1799) Montgolfier, which occurred in June 1783, used hot air. The first pure gas to be used was hydrogen, isolated by the British chemist Henry Cavendish (1746–1823) in 1763. In 1783, the Frenchman J. A. C. Charles (1746–1823) was the first person to successfully use hydrogen, the standard gas for balloon flights in the nineteenth century. The Wizard is probably referring to it here; helium did not become practical until after World War I. Hydrogen is highly flammable, but a balloon filled with hot air will descend when the air cools, unlike a balloon filled with hydrogen.

"If it won't float," remarked Dorothy, "it will be of no use to us."

"True," answered Oz. "But there is another way to make it float, which is to fill it with hot air. Hot air isn't as good as gas, for if the air should get cold the balloon would come down in the desert, and we should be lost."

4.

"We!" exclaimed the girl; "are you going with me?"

"Yes, of course," replied Oz. I am tired of being such a humbug. If I should go out of this Palace my people would soon discover I am not a Wizard, and then they would be vexed with me for having deceived them. So I have to stay shut up in these rooms all day, and it gets tiresome. I'd much rather go back to Kansas with you and be in a circus again."

"I shall be glad to have your company," said Dorothy.

"Thank you," he answered. "Now, if you will help me sew the silk together, we will begin to work on our balloon."

So Dorothy took a needle and thread, and as fast as Oz cut the strips of silk into proper shape the girl sewed them neatly together. First there was a strip of light green silk, then a strip of dark green and then a strip of emerald green; for Oz had a fancy to make the balloon in different shades of the

color about them. It took three days to sew all the strips together, but when it was finished they had a big bag of green silk more than twenty feet long.

Then Oz painted it on the inside with a coat of thin glue, to make it air-tight, after which he announced that the balloon was ready.

"But we must have a basket to ride in," he said. So he sent the soldier with the green whiskers for a big clothes basket, which he fastened with many ropes to the bottom of the balloon.

When it was all ready, Oz sent word to his people that he was going to make a visit to a great brother Wizard who lived in the clouds. The news spread rapidly throughout the city and everyone came to see the wonderful sight.

Oz ordered the balloon carried out in front of the Palace, and the people gazed upon it with much curiosity. The Tin Woodman had chopped a big pile of wood, and now he made a fire of it, and Oz held the bottom of the balloon over the fire so that the hot air that arose from it would be caught in the silken bag. Gradually the balloon swelled out and rose into the air, until finally the basket just touched the ground.

Then Oz got into the basket and said to all the people in a loud voice:

"I am now going away to make a visit. While I am gone the Scarecrow will rule over you. I command you to obey him as you would me."

The balloon was by this time tugging hard at the rope that held it to the ground, for the air within it was hot, and this made it so much lighter in weight than the air without that it pulled hard to rise into the sky.

"Come, Dorothy!" cried the Wizard; "hurry up, or the balloon will fly away."

"I can't find Toto anywhere," replied Dorothy, who did not wish to leave her little dog behind. Toto had run into the crowd to bark at a kitten, and Dorothy at last found him. She picked him up and ran toward the balloon.

She was within a few steps of it, and Oz was holding out his hands to help her into the basket, when, crack! went the ropes, and the balloon rose into the air without her.

"Come back!" she screamed; "I want to go, too!"

"I can't come back, my dear," called Oz from the basket. "Good-bye!"

"Good-bye!" shouted everyone, and all eyes were turned upward to

5. *I can't come back.* There is good reason for this: The Wizard has failed in the balloon's construction to include some apparatus to control his flight. Neither the text nor the pictures suggest that he included a valve or guide rope. By pulling on the cord for a few seconds, the pilot allows air to slowly escape, and the balloon descends. The only way for it to come down without such a device is to wait for the air to cool. Denslow had sketched a guide rope in pencil on the drawing for the chapter title page, but perhaps Baum suggested that it be removed.

6. *the Wonderful Wizard.* He does return to the Emerald City in *Dorothy and the Wizard in Oz* (1908). He is invited to be the official Wizard of Oz again, and to live in his old room behind the Throne Room, no longer ruler, but soon no longer a humbug either.

7. *reached Omaha safely.* Oz Club member Ruth Berman suggested in the August 1961 *Baum Bugle* that the first indication that he did get back to America appears in *The Woggle-Bug Book* (1905). To escape a "bloodthirsty" laundryman, the Woggle-Bug jumps into the basket of a circus balloon and soars away, leaving his enraged antagonist and the real balloonist far below. Baum describes the circus performer only as "the Professor," but Ike Morgan draws him as an elderly bald man in tights and a top hat. This picture and the Midwestern locale suggest that "the Professor" is none other than Oz the Wizard. He reports in *Dorothy and the Wizard in Oz* (1908, p. 48) that when he returned to the United States he traveled around the Midwest as a balloonist with Bailum and Barney's Great Consolidated Shows.

8. *people remembered him lovingly.* But the way they speak of him in *The Marvelous Land of Oz* (1909) is anything but loving, once they learn he is a humbug.

where the Wizard was riding in the basket, rising every moment farther and farther into the sky.

And that was the last any of them ever saw of Oz, the Wonderful Wizard, though he may have reached 6., 7. Omaha safely, and be there now, for all we know. But the people remembered him lovingly, and said to one 8. another,

"Oz was always our friend. When he was here he built for us this beautiful Emerald City, and now he is gone he has left the Wise Scarecrow to rule over us,"

Still, for many days they grieved over the loss of the Wonderful Wizard, and would not be comforted.

Chapter XVIII.
Away to the
South.

Dorothy Wept bitterly at the passing of her hope to get home to Kansas again; but when she thought it all over she was glad she had not gone up in a balloon. And she also felt sorry at losing Oz, and so did her companions.

The Tin Woodman came to her and said, "Truly I should be ungrateful if I failed to mourn for the man who gave me my lovely heart. I should like to cry a little because Oz is gone, if you will kindly wipe away my tears, so that I shall not rust."

"With pleasure," she answered, and

brought a towel at once. Then the Tin Woodman wept for several minutes, and she watched the tears carefully and wiped them away with the towel. When he had finished he thanked her kindly and oiled himself thoroughly with his jewelled oil-can, to guard against mishap.

1.   The Scarecrow was now the ruler of the Emerald City, and although he was not a Wizard the people were proud of him. "For," they said, "there is not another city
2. in all the world that is ruled by a stuffed man." And, so far as they knew, they were quite right.

The morning after the balloon had gone up with Oz the four travellers met in the Throne Room and talked matters over. The Scarecrow sat in the big throne and the others stood respectfully before him.

"We are not so unlucky," said the new ruler; "for this Palace and the Emerald City belong to us, and we can do just as we please. When I remember that a short time ago I was up on a pole in a farmer's cornfield, and that I am now the ruler of this beautiful City, I am quite satisfied with my lot."

"I also," said the Tin Woodman, "am well pleased with my new heart; and, really, that was the only thing I wished in all the world."

"For my part, I am content in knowing I am as brave as any beast that ever lived, if not braver," said the Lion, modestly,

"If Dorothy would only be contented to live in the

1. *the ruler of the Emerald City.* Folk tales are full of simpletons, fools, and noodles who go out to seek their fortunes and become kings by the end of their adventures. The Scarecrow follows the proverbial American Dream of the country bumpkin who goes to the Big City to "make it." ("If I can make it there, I'd make it anywhere," Frank Sinatra sings in "New York New York.") One need only read Theodore Dreiser's *Sister Carrie,* published the same year as *The Wonderful Wizard of Oz,* to observe an ambitious contemporary woman clawing her way up by any means possible in Chicago and then New York to become a famous actress. Now the Scarecrow rules the city but will he be a better a monarch than the Wizard of Oz? Although Oz is not a democracy, it is now ruled by the Common Man, for nothing is more common than a Scarecrow even if he does have a brain. Other lands in Baum's fairy tales have unconventional governments. In the Pink Country of *Sky Island* (1912), the person with the lightest skin rules that part of the floating island, and lives in genteel poverty. "The Ruler is appointed to protect and serve the people," explains the Queen. "Therefore I am a mere agent to direct the laws, which are the Will of the People, and am only a public servant, obliged constantly to guard the welfare of my subjects. . . . No; our way is best. The Ruler, be it king or queen, has absolute power to rule, but no riches—no high station—no false adulation. The people have the wealth and honor, for it is their due" (pp. 142–43). In *Tik-Tok of Oz* (1914), Baum introduces a fairy realm full of kings and queens, but their one supreme Ruler is the Private Citizen.

2. *so far as they knew.* "The Royal Historian obviously implies that there may be a good many rulers outside of Oz who are stuffed figures," Gardner slyly observed in Note 22 of *The Wizard of Oz and Who He Was.*

3. *That cannot be done.* Evidently, there are limitations to Oz magic, for even an imaginary world must play by a set of rules. "His world once invented," argued George MacDonald in "The Fantastic Imagination" in *A Dish of Orts* (1893), "the highest law that comes next into play is, that there shall be harmony between the laws by which the new world has begun to exist; and in the process of his creation, the inventor must hold by those laws. The moment he forgets one of them, he makes the story, by its own postulates, incredible. To be able to live a moment in an imagined world, we must see the laws of its existence obeyed. Those broken, we fall out of it." Not everything can be done in Oz. When Dorothy in *Glinda of Oz* (1920) proposes that everyone in Oz should be able to wish for whatever he or she desires, Ozma not only defends the Puritan work ethic, but also proves that she is a fairly good judge of human nature:

> Instead of happiness your plan would bring weariness to the world. If every one could wave a wand and have his wants fulfilled there would be little to wish for. There would be no eager striving to obtain the difficult, for nothing would then be difficult, and the pleasure of earning something longed for, and only to be secured by hard work and careful thought, would be utterly lost. There would be nothing to do, you see, and no interest in life and in our fellow creatures. (p. 57)

There would be no drama in life, and no need for fairy tales. The Land of Oz too follows its own natural laws. The Golden Cap and the Silver Shoes have no power in Kansas. "Not everything can by done by magic [in Oz]," observed Donald Wollheim in his introduction to the 1965 Airmont edition of *The Wizard of Oz*; "only some things are possible and they must be found by experiment and thoughtful ingenuity. That is the basis of the scientific method, too, and perhaps this is one of the things that make Oz so credible to its young readers of this age of scientific marvels. It isn't too different from the science-oriented world of modern America." Matilda Joslyn Gage insisted in *Woman, Church, and State* (1893) that during the Inquisition, "The witch was in reality the profoundist thinker, the most advanced scientist of those ages. The persecution which for ages [was] waged against witches was in reality an attack upon science at the hands of the church" (p. 243). She argued that "magic" meant simply "superior science" or "knowledge of the effect of certain natural, but generally unknown laws; the secret operating of natural causes . . . consequences resulting from the control of the invisible powers of nature, such as are shown in the electrical appliances of the day, which a few centuries since would have been termed witchcraft" (p. 234). Aware of the healing

powers of herbs and other plants, women alone possessed the knowledge of medicine. They were the doctors and surgeons of their age.

Baum was profoundly aware of the connection between magic and the sciences. These disciplines have the identical aim: the understanding and control of Nature. Of course, modern physical science evolved from what is now called "magic." Chemistry came from alchemy, astronomy from astrology. Baum believed that fairy tales like his Oz books stimulated the imagination from which comes all scientific discovery, as explained in the introduction to *The Lost Princess of Oz* (1917):

> Imagination led Franklin to discover electricity. Imagination has given us the steam engine, the telephone, the talking-machine and the automobile, for these things had to be dreamed of before they became realities. So I believe that dreams—day dreams, you know, with your eyes wide open and your brain-matter whizzing—are likely to lead to the betterment of the world. The imaginative child will become the imaginative man or woman most apt to create, to invent, and therefore to foster civilization. A prominent educator tells me that fairy tales are of untold value in developing imagination in the young. I believe him.

In *The Patchwork Girl of Oz* (1914), the Shaggy recites, "I'll sing you a song of Ozland . . . where magic is a science." Although the fairies of Oz possess natural powers, others must be taught magic. After the Wizard returns to the Emerald City in *Dorothy and the Wizard in Oz* (1908, p. 197), Ozma appoints him the Official Wizard of Oz. Although the princess admits that a humbug "is the safest kind of a Wizard to have" (p. 198), he does eventually learn some real magic from Glinda the Good. "When the Good Glinda found that I was to live in the Emerald City always," he explained in *The Emerald City of Oz* (1910), "she promised to help me, because she said the Wizard of Oz ought really to be a clever Wizard, and not a humbug" (p. 153). They are the only two people in Oz allowed to practice magic, because, as Ozma explains in *The Patchwork Girl of Oz* (1913), they are the only ones she can trust "to use their arts only to benefit my people and to make them happier" (p. 230). In *Rinkitink of Oz* (1916, p. 278), the Wizard carries his black bag of magic tools just as a doctor in the olden days used to do on a house call with his bag of medicines. He explained in *The Lost Princess of Oz* (1917) that "a wizard without tools is as helpless as a carpenter without a hammer or saw" (p. 278). But Baum adds that "no thief, however skillful, can rob one of knowledge, and that is why knowledge is the best and safest treasure to acquire" (pp. 34–35). In *The Magic of Oz* (1919, p. 76), Dorothy visits him in his laboratory, where he carries out

Emerald City," continued the Scarecrow, "we might all be happy together."

"But I don't want to live here," cried Dorothy. "I want to go to Kansas, and live with Aunt Em and Uncle Henry."

"Well, then, what can be done?" enquired the Woodman.

The Scarecrow decided to think, and he thought so hard that the pins and needles began to stick out of his brains. Finally he said:

"Why not call the Winged Monkeys, and asked them to carry you over the desert?"

"I never thought of that!" said Dorothy, joyfully. "It's just the thing. I'll go at once for the Golden Cap."

When she brought it into the Throne Room she spoke the magic words, and soon the band of Winged Monkeys flew in through an open window and stood beside her.

"This is the second time you have called us," said the Monkey King, bowing before the little girl. "What do you wish?"

"I want you to fly with me to Kansas," said Dorothy.

But the Monkey King shook his head.

"That cannot be done," he said. "We belong to this country alone, and cannot leave it. There has never been a Winged Monkey in Kansas yet, and I suppose there never will be, for they don't belong there. We shall be glad to serve

3.

his magical experiments. Magic must be learned in Oz by
the scientific method of trial and error. "[Baum] has taught
American children to look for the element of wonder in the
life around them," explained Edward Wagenknecht in
Utopia Americana (Seattle: University of Washington Book
Store, 1929), "to realize that even smoke and machinery
may be transformed into fairy lore if only we have sufficient energy and vision to penetrate to their significance
and transform them to our use" (p. 29).

4. *while Oz was alive.* Is Baum suggesting that he was
killed during his balloon flight back to America? In
Dorothy and the Wizard in Oz (1908), the Wizard returns to
Oz alive and well.

you in any way in our power, but we cannot cross the desert.   Good-bye."

And with another bow the Monkey King spread his wings and flew away through the window, followed by all his band.

Dorothy was almost ready to cry with disappointment

"I have wasted the charm of the Golden Cap to no purpose," she said, "for the Winged Monkeys cannot help me."

"It is certainly too bad!" said the tender hearted Woodman.

The Scarecrow was thinking again, and his head bulged out so horribly that Dorothy feared it would burst.

"Let us call in the soldier with the green whiskers," he said, "and ask his advice."

So the soldier was summoned and entered the Throne Room timidly, for while Oz was alive he never was allowed to come further than the door.

"This little girl," said the Scarecrow to the soldier, "wishes to cross the desert.   How can she do so?"

"I cannot tell," answered the soldier; "for nobody has ever crossed the desert, unless it is Oz himself."

"Is there no one who can help me?" asked Dorothy, earnestly.

"Glinda might," he suggested.

"Who is Glinda?" enquired the Scarecrow.

5. "The Witch of the South. She is the most powerful of all the Witches, and rules over the Quadlings. Besides, her castle stands on the edge of the desert, so she may know a way to cross it."

"Glinda is a good Witch, isn't she?" asked the child.

"The Quadlings think she is good,' said the soldier,
6. "and she is kind to everyone. I have heard that Glinda is
7. a beautiful woman, who knows how to keep young in spite of the many years she has lived."

"How can I get to her castle?" asked Dorothy.

"The road is straight to the South," he answered, "but it is said to be full of dangers to travellers. There are wild beasts in the woods, and a race of queer men who do not like strangers to cross their country. For this reason none of the Quadlings ever come to the Emerald City."

The soldier then left them and the Scarecrow said,

"It seems, in spite of dangers, that the best thing Dorothy can do is to travel to the Land of the South and ask Glinda to help her. For, of course, if Dorothy stays here she will never get back to Kansas."

"You must have been thinking again," remarked the Tin Woodman.

5. *The Witch of the South.* MGM caused considerable confusion by combining the Good Witch of the North and Glinda, the Good Witch of the South, into one character: Glinda, the Good Witch of the North. But even Baum erred at least once. In *Tik-Tok of Oz* (1914), he states that Glinda's Castle is "far north of the Emerald City where Ozma holds her court" (p. 28).

6. *Glinda is a beautiful woman.* People brought up on Grimm and Andersen fairy tales tend to believe with Judy Garland in the 1939 MGM movie that "witches are old and ugly." But that was not always the case. "Uncommon beauty was as dangerous to a woman as possession of great wealth, which brought frequent accusations [of witchcraft] in order that the church might seize upon the witch's property for its own use," wrote Gage in *Woman, Church, and State* (pp. 231–32). "Old women for no other reason than that they were old, were held to be the most susceptible to the assaults of the devil, and the persons most especially endowed with supernatural powers for evil" (p. 270).

7. *how to keep young in spite of the many years she has lived.* Of course, not all witches even in European folklore are ugly. Think only of Circe and Medea of ancient times, rather than the hideous snake-haired Gorgon sisters. Baum explored this theme in greater depth in one of his best fairy tales, *Queen Zixi of Ix* (1905). The vain witch queen uses all her occult powers to appear young and beautiful to other eyes. The one thing she cannot fool is a common mirror, which reflects only her true self—a withered old hag. Although not by nature evil, Zixi is so obsessed with her appearance that she lies, cheats, and steals to gain her ends—all to no avail. Vanity of vanities, all is vanity!

"I have," said the Scarecrow.

"I shall go with Dorothy," declared the Lion, "for I am tired of your city and long for the woods and the country again. I am really a wild beast, you know. Besides, Dorothy will need someone to protect her."

"That is true," agreed the Woodman. "My axe may be of service to her; so I, also, will go with her to the Land of the South."

"When shall we start?" asked the Scarecrow.

"Are you going?" they asked, in surprise.

"Certainly. If it wasn't for Dorothy I should never have had brains. She lifted me from the pole in the cornfield and brought me to the Emerald City. So my good luck is all due to her, and I shall never leave her until she starts back to Kansas for good and all."

"Thank you," said Dorothy, gratefully. "You are all very kind to me. But I should like to start as soon as possible."

"We shall go to-morrow morning," returned the Scarecrow. "So now let us all get ready, for it will be a long journey."

Chapter XIX.
Attacked by the Fighting Trees.

1. *Attacked by the Fighting Trees.* Salman Rushdie noted in his monograph on the MGM movie that "all subplots . . . such as the visits to the Fighting Trees, the Dainty China Country and the Quadlings . . . come, in the novel, just after the dramatic high point of the Witch's destruction and fritter away the book's narrative drive" (p. 14). Actually much more happens between the melting of the Wicked Witch of the West and the encounter with the Fighting Trees—the unmasking of the Wizard of Oz, for example. Other readers have complained that the trip South is anticlimactic, but it does make sense within the context of the story. Each of Dorothy's friends now has what he has so long desired, but each must learn how to use it. And there is still the problem of getting Dorothy back to Kansas. She must go through one more stage of the classic heroic quest: Return. The MGM movie proved too pat: Glinda arrives like a good fairy to conveniently solve Dorothy's dilemma for her, whereas in the book she does it for herself. Volkov omitted Chapters 19 and 20 from his 1939 Russian "translation" of *The Wizard of Oz*, because he thought that they "slowed down the action and did not tie directly with the plot." He supplied two new ones, "The Flood" and "In Search of Friends."

The Next morning Dorothy kissed the pretty green girl good-bye, and they all shook hands with the soldier with the green whiskers, who had walked with them as far as the gate. When the Guardian of the Gate saw them again he wondered greatly that they could leave the beautiful City to get into new trouble. But he at once unlocked their spectacles, which he put back into the green box, and gave them many good wishes to carry with them.

"You are now our ruler," he said to the Scarecrow; "so you must come back to us as soon as possible."

"I certainly shall if I am able," the Scarecrow replied; "but I must help Dorothy to get home, first."

As Dorothy bade the good-natured Guardian a last farewell she said,

"I have been very kindly treated in your lovely City, and everyone has been good to me. I cannot tell you how grateful I am."

"Don't try, my dear," he answered. "We should like to keep you with us, but if it is your wish to return to Kansas I hope you will find a way." He then opened the gate of the outer wall and they walked forth and started upon their journey.

The sun shone brightly as our friends turned their faces toward the Land of the South. They were all in the best of spirits, and laughed and chatted together. Dorothy was once more filled with the hope of getting home, and the Scarecrow and the Tin Woodman were glad to be of use to her. As for the Lion, he sniffed the fresh air with delight and whisked his tail from side to side in pure joy at being in the country again, while Toto ran around them and chased the moths and butterflies, barking merrily all the time.

"City life does not agree with me at all," remarked the Lion, as they walked along at a brisk pace. "I have lost much flesh since I lived there, and now I am anxious for a chance to show the other beasts how courageous I have grown."

2. *how courageous I have grown.* To look for trouble would seem just as cowardly as to run from it. Just as the Scarecrow has grown conceited and the Tin Woodman self-absorbed, the Lion has become a bully. Each prizes the symbol above the virtue. They must now learn how to use the Wizard's gifts properly. Each has proved that he always had the quality that he sought; he just was not aware of it. Each had to test himself to see what he was capable of doing. Only experience can do that. Therefore, the three must accompany Dorothy on her trip to Glinda the Good to see if they can learn how to use their brain, heart, and courage.

They now turned and took a last look at the Emerald City. All they could see was a mass of towers and steeples behind the green walls, and high up above everything the spires and dome of the Palace of Oz.

"Oz was not such a bad Wizard, after all," said the Tin Woodman, as he felt his heart rattling around in his breast.

"He knew how to give me brains, and very good brains, too," said the Scarecrow.

"If Oz had taken a dose of the same courage he gave me," added the Lion, "he would have been a brave man."

Dorothy said nothing. Oz had not kept the promise he made her, but he had done his best, so she forgave him. As he said, he was a good man, even if he was a bad Wizard.

The first day's journey was through the green fields and bright flowers that stretched about the Emerald City on every side. They slept that night on the grass, with nothing but the stars over them; and they rested very well indeed.

In the morning they travelled on until they came to a thick wood. There was no way of going around it, for it seemed to extend to the right and left as far as they could see; and, besides, they did not dare change the direction of their journey for fear of getting lost. So they looked for the place where it would be easiest to get into the forest.

The Scarecrow, who was in the lead, finally discovered a big tree with such wide spreading branches that there was room for the party to pass underneath. So he walked forward to the tree, but just as he came under the first branches they bent down and twined around him, and the next minute he was raised from the ground and flung headlong among his fellow travellers.

This did not hurt the Scarecrow, but it surprised him, and he looked rather dizzy when Dorothy picked him up.

"Here is another space between the trees," called the Lion.

"Let me try it first," said the Scarecrow, "for it doesn't hurt me to get thrown about." He walked up to another tree, as he spoke, but its branches immediately seized him and tossed him back again.

"This is strange," exclaimed Dorothy; "what shall we do?"

"The trees seem to have made up their minds to fight us, and stop our journey," remarked the Lion.

"I believe I will try it myself," said the Woodman,

and shouldering his axe he marched up to the first tree that had handled the Scarecrow so roughly. When a big branch bent down to seize him the Woodman chopped at it so fiercely that he cut it in two. At once the tree began shaking all its branches as if in pain, and the Tin Woodman passed safely under it.

"Come on!" he shouted to the others; "be quick!"

They all ran forward and passed under the tree without injury, except Toto, who was caught by a small branch and shaken until he howled. But the Woodman promptly chopped off the branch and set the little dog free.

The other trees of the forest did nothing to keep them back, so they made up their minds that only the first row of trees could bend down their branches, and that probably these were the policemen of the forest, and given this wonderful power in order to keep strangers out of it.

The four travellers walked with ease through the trees until they came to the further edge of the wood. Then, to their surprise, they found before them a high wall, which seemed to be made of white china. It was smooth, like the surface of a dish, and higher than their heads.

"What shall we do now?" asked Dorothy.

"I will make a ladder," said the Tin Woodman, "for we certainly must climb over the wall."

3. *passed safely under it.* Enchanted forests of humanlike trees appear frequently in juvenile and other literature. These belligerent trees may have been suggested by the magic arbor in the Enchanted Ground of the Second Part of *The Pilgrim's Progress.* "The bushes," cries one of the children, "have got such fast hold on me, I think I cannot get away from them." The Island of Moving Trees in the North Atlantic got its name through a misconception: When sailors came upon it in the early seventeenth century, they thought they saw trees leaping from one bank to another; these "moving trees" were actually local barges decorated with thick, leafy branches. Ruth Plumly Thompson introduces two distinctive varieties in *Kabumpo in Oz* (1922) and *The Cowardly Lion of Oz* (1923). The forests of J. R. R. Tolkien's Middle Earth contain Old Man Willow, the Ents, and other fairy trees. The English artist Arthur Rackham filled his famous children's book illustrations with fantastic gnarled, elfin vegetation. Walt Disney paid homage to him in the first of the Technicolor "Silly Symphonies," *Flowers and Trees* (1932). In Canto XIII of Dante's *Inferno*, the Suicides are cast into a fruitless wood, where they are turned into trees and eternally tormented by Harpies gnawing at their limbs. They suffer the same excruciating pain that the Fighting Tree does when the Tin Woodman cuts off a limb.

4. *keep strangers out of it.* It is never explained exactly what they are protecting. This chapter could just as easily have ended here; the next few lines and the following chapter read like an afterthought. The other adventures in the Quadling Country serve to test the three companions' utilization of their new gifts, but the next chapter seems more like a pleasant interlude wedged between more intense activities. The action markedly slows down to a philosophical discussion. The Soldier with the Green Whiskers mentions the forests and the Hammer-Heads back in Chapter 18, but nothing about the China Country. This delicate, fragile kingdom seems foreign to the wild Quadling Country and may have been inspired by late developments in China. The next chapter reads like a stray episode from *Dot and Tot of Merryland* (1901), which Baum was probably working on at the time. Baum's method of composition was simple: He wrote the basic plot of a story and then went back to add new chapters with side excursions from the main thread of the narrative to pad out the book. "The Dainty China Country" was probably appended later to flesh out *The Wonderful Wizard of Oz*, requiring a little revision of the opening of Chapter 21. After conquering the Fighting Trees, the policemen of the forest, the four travelers are still in the woods. What are the Fighting Trees policing? The China Country already has a Great Wall to protect it. Perhaps in the original version, Dorothy and the others went on immediately to the meeting of Beasts. The China Country seems lost in this forest. Another indication that it was an afterthought is that the vocabulary differs significantly from that of the remainder of the book, as suggested by Howard P. Iker and Norman I. Harway's "A Computer Systems Approach Towards the Recognition and Analysis of Contents" (*Computer Studies in the Humanities and Verbal Behavior*, October 1968). When the authors used *The Wizard of Oz* to test a new computer system of programs (WORDS), they decided not to enter "The Dainty China Country," because it, unlike the other chapters, "added many different words for a very small increment in total data."

Some readers wish that Baum had tossed out the following chapter, but not so Neil Earle. "This episode in the Dainty China Country is so strikingly different in tone and mood that it stands as one of the most memorable scenes in *The Wonderful Wizard of Oz*," he argued in *The Wonderful Wizard of Oz in American Popular Culture* (Lewiston, N. Y.: Edwin Mellen Press, 1993). "The atmosphere of suspenseful anticipation, the mild reproof given to the four adventurers, the heavier moralizing—all of these subtle tonal vibrations conjure up a feeling that we have crossed the border into a different literary genre. Is this Baum's version of the Parable of the Good Samaritan in disguise? Is it a gently modulated paean of Brotherly Love presented through the pen of a former china salesman from the Midwest?" (p. 101). Perhaps Earle has read a bit too much into this minor episode in Dorothy's travels through Oz. Nothing much happens and it adds little to the plot, but it does resonate with themes introduced earlier in the story.

5. *a high wall . . . made of white china.* In Note 23 of *The Wizard of Oz and Who He Was*, Gardner suggests that Baum is referring to the Great Wall of China. The following chapter seems to echo recent antagonism in Asia, which led to the infamous Boxer Rebellion in the summer of 1900. The papers were full of xenophobic reports from China, and political cartoonists sometimes drew the Western powers scaling the Great Wall of China much as Denslow does Dorothy and her companions here. In November 1900, Denslow issued his own satire of the conflict as a color print titled "The Heathen Chinese," depicting three boys dressed for war, representing the Western powers, who threaten a small grinning Chinese doll. Tolerance for other peoples is the dominant theme of the visit to the dainty China Country. Dorothy learns the sad fate of any native of the China Country who is taken away from her homeland, which may reflect America's notorious immigration policy at the time. Dorothy too feels terribly disoriented in this fragile kingdom, something she does not seem to suffer in other parts of Oz however pleasant or terrible. If a political

theme must be drawn, it would have been influenced by
the country's growing anti-imperialism. Dorothy learns
from the breaking of a cow's leg and the smashing of a
church the great harm she and the others might cause
should they remain. This was a lesson the United States as
well as the other Western powers failed to heed, not only
in imperialist dealings with China, but elsewhere in the
world, notably in the Philippines, Puerto Rico, and other
colonial territories seized during the recent Spanish-
American War.

1. *While The Woodman*. The first printing of *The Wonderful Wizard of Oz* reads, "While Tin Woodman," but it was changed to "while The Woodman" in the second. Baum probably originally wrote, "While the Tin Woodman." Denslow repeated the printer's error in pencil on the pen-and-ink drawing for this headpiece, now in the Henry Goldsmith Collection, Prints and Drawings Division, the New York Public Library.

While The Woodman was making a ladder from wood which he found in the forest Dorothy lay down and slept, for she was tired by the long walk.

The Lion also curled himself up to sleep and Toto lay beside him.

The Scarecrow watched the Woodman while he worked, and said to him:

"I cannot think why this wall is here, nor what it is made of."

"Rest your brains and do not worry about the wall," replied the Woodman; "when we have climbed over it we shall know what is on the other side."

After a time the ladder was finished. It looked clumsy, but the Tin Woodman was sure it was strong and would answer their purpose. The Scarecrow waked Dorothy and the Lion and Toto, and told them that the ladder was ready. The Scarecrow climbed up the ladder first, but he was so awkward that Dorothy had to follow close behind and keep him from falling off. When he got his head over the top of the wall the Scarecrow said,

"Oh, my!"

"Go on," exclaimed Dorothy.

So the Scarecrow climbed further up and sat down on the top of the wall, and Dorothy put her head over and cried,

"Oh, my!" just as the Scarecrow had done.

Then Toto came up, and immediately began to bark, but Dorothy made him be still.

The Lion climbed the ladder next, and the Tin Woodman came last; but both of them cried, "Oh, my!" as soon as they looked over the wall. When they were all sitting in a row on the top of the wall they looked down and saw a strange sight.

Before them was a great stretch of country having a floor as smooth and shining and white as the bottom of a big platter. Scattered around were many houses made entirely of china and painted in the brightest colours. These houses were quite small, the biggest of them reaching only as high as Dorothy's waist. There were also pretty little barns, with china fences around them, and many cows and sheep and horses and pigs and chickens, all made of china, were standing about in groups.

But the strangest of all were the people who lived in this queer country. There were milk-maids and shepherd-esses, with bright-colored bodices and golden spots all over their gowns; and princesses with most gorgeous frocks of silver and gold and purple; and shepherds dressed in knee-breeches with pink and yellow and blue stripes down them, and golden buckles on their shoes; and princes with jewelled crowns upon their heads, wearing ermine robes and satin doublets; and funny clowns in ruffled gowns, with round red spots upon their cheeks and tall, pointed caps. And, strangest of all, these people were all made of china, even to their clothes, and were so small that the tallest of them was no higher than Dorothy's knee.

No one did so much as look at the travellers at first, except one little purple china dog with an extra-large head, which came to the wall and barked at them in a tiny voice, afterwards running away again.

"How shall we get down?" asked Dorothy.

They found the ladder so heavy they could not pull it up, so the Scarecrow fell off the wall and the others jumped down upon him so that the hard floor would not hurt their feet. Of course they took pains not to light on

2.

3.

4.

2. *milk-maids and shepherdesses.* Baum may well have been thinking of Meissen or Dresden porcelain. These brightly painted and exquisitely crafted figurines of amorous rustics are known as "Watteau scenes," after the French pastoral painter Antoine Watteau, and were first produced in Germany in the eighteenth century. Baum may have become familiar with this fine china when he was selling crockery and glassware on the road for Pitkin & Brooks of Chicago in the early 1890s.

3. *clowns.* If these figures are indeed Meissen china, then the clowns are likely Harlequins or Punchinellos from the *commedia dell'arte.* But Denslow draws Mr. Joker as a conventional American circus clown.

4. *one little purple china dog with an extra-large head.* Denslow depicts him as a little china pug. Could this possibly be a visual pun on the Chinese Boxers? Most Americans did not think the Boxers posed much of a threat to their interests until the rebels began killing missionaries at the close of 1899.

his head and get the pins in their feet. When all were safely down they picked up the Scarecrow, whose body was quite flattened out, and patted his straw into shape again.

"We must cross this strange place in order to get to the other side," said Dorothy; "for it would be unwise for us to go any other way except due South."

They began walking through the country of the china people, and the first thing they came to was a china milk-maid milking a china cow. As they drew near the cow suddenly gave a kick and kicked over the stool, the pail, and even the milk-maid herself, all falling on the china ground with a great clatter.

Dorothy was shocked to see that the cow had broken her leg short off, and that the pail was lying in several small pieces, while the poor milk-maid had a nick in her left elbow.

"There!" cried the milk-maid, angrily; "see what you have done! My cow has broken her leg, and I must take her to the mender's shop and have it glued on again. What do you mean by coming here and frightening my cow?"

"I'm very sorry," returned Dorothy; "please forgive us"

But the pretty milk-maid was much too vexed to make any answer. She picked up the leg sulkily and led her cow away, the poor animal limping on three legs. As she left them the milk-maid cast many reproachful glances over her shoulder at the clumsy strangers, holding **her** nicked elbow close to her side.

Dorothy was quite grieved at this mishap.

"We must be very careful here," said the kind-hearted Woodman, "or we may hurt these pretty little people so they will never get over it."

A little farther on Dorothy met a most beautiful dressed young princess, who stopped short as she saw the strangers and started to run away.

Dorothy wanted to see more of the Princess, so she ran after her; but the china girl cried out,

"Don't chase me! don't chase me!"

She had such a frightened little voice that Dorothy stopped and said,

"Why not?"

"Because," answered the princess, also stopping, a safe distance away, "if I run I may fall down and break myself."

"But couldn't you be mended?" asked the girl.

5.   "Oh, yes; but one is never so pretty after being mended, you know," replied the princess.

"I suppose not," said Dorothy.

5. *never so pretty*. Or so valuable on the open market, as Baum, the former china salesman, would have known. "The China Princess, fearful that a mended crack might mar her beauty," noted Nye in *The Wizard of Oz and Who He Was*, "lives a lonely, isolated life, avoiding all contact with those who might chip her perfection" (p. 6). These sentiments are similar to those of Chinese Empress Dowager T'zu Hsi, whose isolationist policies against foreign barbarians led to the cultural wars that culminated in the Boxer Rebellion in 1900. Baum, however, does not indicate any violence on the part of the natives; the only destruction results from the carelessness of the invaders. This episode is not as arbitrary as it may appear at first, for it reiterates one of the story's major themes, the importance of home. The fate of the little china princess is like that of Dorothy, who herself has been taken from her natural habitat and dropped into a strange foreign land. The figurine would look just as out of place on the mantel in Aunt Em and Uncle Henry's claim shanty in Kansas as the little girl does in the Dainty China Country.

6. *red and yellow and green*. Harlequin traditionally wears a costume of diamond shapes in all these colors. See Note 3 above.

7. *You'd eaten up a poker*. An obvious pun on the expression "poker face," meaning an expressionless stare. The phrase comes from the card game rather than from the long metal bar used for stirring fires. However, at least one of Lewis Carroll's contemporaries described the fussy old don as having the face of someone who had eaten up a poker. Baum would have been amused by Prof. Jack Zipes's suggestion in his notes to the 1998 Penguin Twentieth-Century Classics edition of *The Wonderful World of Oz* that "poker may refer to a species of liliaceous plants bearing spikes of scarlet or yellow flowers—known as the flame flower" (p. 376). And he would have found some of the assertions in *The Annotated Wizard of Oz* equally absurd!

8. *Well, that's respect, I expect*. Baum may have intended this line to be read as a couplet in keeping Mr. Joker in character as a mad individual like King Lear's Fool who speaks in rhyme. He changed this line in a revision of the chapter, "In Chinaland" in *L. Frank Baum's Juvenile Speaker* (1910), to "Well, I suspect, they expect no respect" (p. 133). The most famous example of these "village idiots" in the Oz books is Scraps, the zany verse-spouting Patchwork Girl who was made from an old crazy quilt.

"Now there is Mr. Joker, one of our clowns," continued the china lady, "who is always trying to stand upon his head. He has broken himself so often that he is mended in a hundred places, and doesn't look at all pretty. Here he comes now, so you can see for yourself."

Indeed, a jolly little Clown now came walking toward them, and Dorothy could see that in spite of his pretty clothes of red and yellow and green he was completely   6. covered with cracks, running every which way and showing plainly that he had been mended in many places.

The Clown put his hands in his pockets, and after puffing out his cheeks and nodding his head at them saucily he said,

> "My lady fair,
> Why do you stare
> At poor old Mr. Joker?
> You're quite as stiff
> And prim as if
> You'd eaten up a poker!"   7.

"Be quiet, sir!" said the princess; "can't you see these are strangers, and should be treated with respect?"

"Well, that's respect, I expect," declared the Clown,   8. and immediately stood upon his head.

"Don't mind Mr. Joker," said the princess to Dorothy; "he is considerably cracked in his head, and that makes him foolish."

"Oh, I don't mind him a bit," said Dorothy. "But you are so beautiful," she continued, "that I am sure I could love you dearly. Won't you let me carry you back to Kansas and stand you on Aunt Em's mantle-shelf? I could carry you in my basket."

"That would make me very un-happy," answered the china princess. "You see, here in our own country we live contentedly, and can talk and move around as we please. But

whenever any of us are taken away our joints at once 9.
stiffen, and we can only stand straight and look pretty.
Of course that is all that is expected of us when we are on
mantle-shelves and cabinets and drawing-room tables, but
our lives are much pleasanter here in our own country."

"I would not make you unhappy for all the world!"
exclaimed Dorothy; "so I'll just say good-bye."

"Good-bye," replied the princess.

They walked carefully through the china country.
The little animals and all the people scampered out of
their way, fearing the strangers would break them, and
after an hour or so the travellers reached the other side of
the country and came to another china wall.

It was not as high as the first, however, and by
standing upon the Lion's back they all managed to scram-
ble to the top. Then the Lion gathered his legs under
him and jumped on the wall; but just as he jumped he
upset a china church with his tail and smashed it all to 10.
pieces.

"That was too bad," said Dorothy, "but really I think
we were lucky in not doing these little people more harm
than breaking a cow's leg and a church. They are all so
brittle!"

"They are, indeed," said the Scarecrow, "and I am
thankful I am made of straw and cannot be easily damaged.
There are worse things in the world than being a Scarecrow."

9. *our joints at once stiffen.* Another example of how the natural laws of Oz do not coincide with those beyond its borders. This would also seem to be Baum's quiet plea for explorers, missionaries, and other foreigners to leave other cultures alone.

10. *a china church.* Or a Chinese church? Is Baum commenting on the recent conflict between the Chinese and foreign missionaries in China? As Gardner observed in Note 25 of *The Wizard of Oz and Who He Was*, this is the only mention in all of Baum's Royal History of a church in Oz. "The references to religion in the whole Baum authorship are extremely rare," observed March Laumer in his introduction to the 1969 Opium Press reprint of *Queen Zixi of Ix*; "offhand I recall only the china church which the Cowardly Lion accidentally knocks over in *The Wizard of Oz*. As far as I know it was the only church in Oz; the 'Church' never recovered from this fall!" Baum's fairies like the Elementals replace angels in their service to mortals; they are not as arbitrary as the gods and goddesses of Greek and Roman mythology. There is no church in Oz, for there is no religion nor need of it. Baum himself was not a churchgoer, and he and Maud allowed each son to take up whatever faith he wished once he was old enough to know what he was doing. They sent their sons to Ethical Culture Sunday school, which taught morality rather than religion. The Baums joined the Ramayan Theosophical Society in Chicago on September 4, 1892, but Theosophy was not an organized religion. Baum insisted in the Aberdeen *Saturday Pioneer* (January 25, 1890) that the Theosophists were simply "the seekers of Truth," that they "are the dissatisfied of the world, the dissenters from all creeds. . . . They admit the existence of a God—not necessarily a personal God. To them God is Nature and Nature God." Baum probably did not approve of what was then happening abroad. "In the name of religion," declared Matilda Joslyn Gage in *Woman, Church, and State*, "the worst crimes against humanity have ever been perpetrated"

(p. 263). Baum cared nothing for missionary work and selfish Christianity. His most cynical attack on religious hypocrisy is the poem "The Heretic" in *By the Candelabra's Glare* (1898), which includes the following verse:

> An' over at th' meetin'-house,
>   They took up a c'lection
> T' "spread th' Word" in Asia,
>   Or some other furrin section.
> They didn't care that layin' round
>   The city were a show
> O' heathens 'wuss ner Asia's—
>   'Twasn't Christianlike, ye know. (p. 50)

Fearing that these sentiments might offend his mother's conservative beliefs, Baum apologized in the copy of this book he gave Cynthia Stanton Baum, "You must remember, in reading 'The Heretic' that it is the heretic himself who is speaking, and that he only finds fault with *selfish* Christianity, which I am sure, dear, that *you* do not approve of."

Although instances are rare, Baum did make reference to the afterlife in his fairy tales. A school of "holy" mackerel in *The Sea Fairies* (1912) long to get caught and carried off to "glory." The Blues of *Sky Island* (1912) enter the Arch of Phinis when their allotted time is through. In *The Life and Adventures of Santa Claus* (1902), one of the Immortals addresses the evil Agwas: "You are a transient race, passing from life into nothingness. We, who live forever, pity but despise you. On earth you are scorned by all, and in Heaven you have no place! Even the mortals, after their earth life, enter another existence for all time, and so are your superiors" (pp. 110–11). Perhaps fearing the loss of his young audience over sectarian matters, Baum wisely avoided the subject of religion in his fairy tales. His own beliefs were unconventional, and he had the courtesy not to proselytize in his books. When he revised this chapter as "Chinaland" in *L. Frank Baum's Juvenile Speaker* (1910), Baum diplomatically deleted the incident about smashing the china church.

1. *a pleasanter home*. A common error in both literature and popular usage is that lions are beasts of the forests (as in Bert Lahr's "If I Were King of the Forest" in the 1939 MGM movie). They are creatures of the open countryside. Like Dorothy, the Lion believes that home is where the heart is, no matter how dismal it may appear to others.

2. *the animals were holding a meeting*. Animals of different species often meet in council in literature as do men in life. The lion, a symbol of both physical and temporal power, often serves as judge in the fables of Aesop and Reynard the Fox and elsewhere. King Gugu, a big yellow leopard, leads a delegation of animals in the Gillikin Country in *The Magic of Oz* (1919).

3. *The biggest of the tigers*. Denslow draws a bear here, although none is mentioned in the text. He also crowns the Lion even before he has killed the spider. Baum makes no reference to it in the story. A variation of this interview may be found in "The Story of Jaglon," the first of Baum's "Animal Fairy Tales" (*The Delineator*, January 1905); here the King of Beasts is a tiger, whom a lion challenges for the title. One of the most beloved of the Oz characters in the later books is the Hungry Tiger, hungry because he longs to eat fat babies, but his conscience will not allow it. He and the Cowardly Lion are the best of friends when the lion returns in *Ozma of Oz* (1907), but the tiger may have appeared earlier in the Royal History. Jack Snow suggested in *Who's Who in Oz* (1954, p. 99) that "the biggest of the tigers" mentioned here may be the Hungry Tiger himself.

4. *a great spider*. Other than its size, this creature is no different from any other spider. Hyperbole and carefully chosen similes make him sound terrible. Mythological monsters are often described with the same sort of exaggeration. Baum probably did not like spiders, for he makes them monsters again in *The Life and Adventures of Santa Claus* (1902) and *Glinda of Oz* (1920). There are others in literature, such as the spider in Edgar Allan Poe's story "The Sphinx" and Shelob in J. R. R. Tolkien's *The Lord of the Rings* (1954–1955).

After Climbing down from the china wall the travellers found themselves in a disagreeable country, full of bogs and marshes and covered with tall, rank grass. It was difficult to walk far without falling into muddy holes, for the grass was so thick that it hid them from sight. However, by carefully picking their way, they got safely along until they reached solid ground. But here the country seemed wilder than ever, and after a long and tiresome walk through the under-brush they entered another forest, where

the trees were bigger and older than any they had ever
seen.

"This forest is perfectly delightful," declared the Lion,
looking around him with joy; "never have I seen a more
beautiful place."

"It seems gloomy," said the Scarecrow.

"Not a bit of it," answered the Lion; "I should like
to live here all my life. See how soft the dried leaves are
under your feet and how rich and green the moss is that
clings to these old trees. Surely no wild beast could wish
1. a pleasanter home."

"Perhaps there are wild beasts in the forest now," said
Dorothy

"I suppose there are," returned the Lion; "but I do
not see any of them about."

They walked through the forest until it became too
dark to go any farther. Dorothy and Toto and the Lion
lay down to sleep, while the Woodman and the Scarecrow kept watch over them as usual.

When morning came they started again. Before
they had gone far they heard a low rumble, as of the growling of many wild animals. Toto whimpered a little but
none of the others was frightened and they kept along the
well-trodden path until they came to an opening in the
wood, in which were gathered hundreds of beasts of every
variety. There were tigers and elephants and bears and
wolves and foxes and all the others in the natural history,

and for a moment Dorothy was afraid. But the Lion explained that the animals were holding a meeting, and he judged by their snarling and growling that they were in great trouble.

2.

As he spoke several of the beasts caught sight of him, and at once the great assemblage hushed as if by magic. The biggest of the tigers came up to the Lion and bowed, saying,

3.

"Welcome, O King of Beasts! You have come in good time to fight our enemy and bring peace to all the animals of the forest once more."

"What is your trouble?" asked the Lion, quietly.

"We are all threatened," answered the tiger, "by a fierce enemy which has lately come into this forest. It is a most tremendous monster, like a

4. great spider, with a body as big as an elephant and legs as long as a

tree trunk. It has eight of these long legs, and as the monster crawls through the forest he seizes an animal with a leg and drags it to his mouth, where he eats it as a spider does a fly. Not one of us is safe while this fierce creature is alive, and we had called a meeting to decide how to take care of ourselves when you came among us."

The Lion thought for a moment.

"Are there any other lions in this forest?" he asked.

"No; there were some, but the monster has eaten them all. And, besides, they were none of them nearly so large and brave as you."

"If I put an end to your enemy will you bow down to me and obey me as King of the Forest?" enquired the Lion.

"We will do that gladly," returned the tiger; and all the other beasts roared with a mighty roar: "We will!"

"Where is this great spider of yours now?" asked the Lion.

"Yonder, among the oak trees," said the tiger, pointing with his fore-foot."

"Take good care of these friends of mine," said the Lion, "and I will go at once to fight the monster."

He bade his comrades good-bye and marched proudly away to do battle with the enemy.

The great spider was lying asleep when the Lion found him, and it looked so ugly that its foe turned up his nose in disgust. It's legs were quite as long as the tiger had said, and it's body covered with coarse black hair. It had a great mouth, with a row of sharp teeth a foot long; but its head was joined to the pudgy body by a neck as slender as a wasp's waist. This gave the Lion a hint of the best way to attack the creature, and as he knew it was easier to fight it asleep than awake, he gave a great spring and landed directly upon the monster's back. Then, with one blow of his heavy paw, all armed with sharp claws, he knocked the spider's head from its body. Jumping down, he watched it until the long legs stopped wiggling, when he knew it was quite dead.

The Lion went back to the opening where the beasts of the forest were waiting for him and said, proudly,

"You need fear your enemy no longer."

Then the beasts bowed down to the Lion as their King, and he promised to come back and rule over them as soon as Dorothy was safely on her way to Kansas.

The FOUR TRAVELLERS passed through the rest of the forest in safety, and when they came out from its gloom saw before them a steep hill, covered from top to bottom with great pieces of rock.

"That will be a hard climb," said the Scarecrow, "but we must get over the hill, nevertheless."

So he led the way and the others followed. They had nearly reached the first rock when they heard a rough voice cry out,

"Keep back!"

"Who are you?" asked the Scarecrow. Then a head

showed itself over the rock and the same voice said,

"This hill belongs to us, and we don't allow anyone to cross it."

"But we must cross it," said the Scarecrow. "We're going to the country of the Quadlings."

"But you shall not!" replied the voice, and there stepped from behind the rock the strangest man the travellers had ever seen.

He was quite short and stout and had a big head, which was flat at the top and supported by a thick neck full of wrinkles. But he had no arms at all, and, seeing this, the Scarecrow did not fear that so helpless a creature could prevent them from climbing the hill. So he said,

"I'm sorry not to do as you wish, but we must pass over your hill whether you like it or not," and he walked boldly forward.

As quick as lightning the man's head shot forward and his neck stretched out until the top of the head, where it was flat, struck the Scarecrow in the middle and sent him tumbling, over and over, down the hill. Almost as quickly as it came the head went back to the body, and the man laughed harshly as he said,

"It isn't as easy as you think!"

A chorus of boisterous laughter came from the other rocks, and Dorothy saw hundreds of the armless Hammer-Heads upon the hillside, one behind every rock.

1.

1. *Hammer-Heads*. "Hammerhead" is slang for a dullard, like "blockhead." But Baum recognizes the child's comprehension of words as "things." He often takes a common descriptive word, name, or phrase and looks at it through a child's eyes as if for the first time, transforming it literally into some unlikely creature. By doing so, he widens the vocabulary but also the young reader's awareness of the possibilities of the world; children often confront unfamiliar words in a concrete way by turning the commonplace into something quite extraordinary and poetic. It is the awakening imagination at work. By comparison, adults can be so prosaic. "Hammerheads [*sic*] are xenophobic, militaristic, and hide behind rocks," Barry Moser wrote on May 11, in *Forty-seven Days to Oz*, explaining why he depicted their leader as then–FBI director William Casey. "Their ability to extend their heads is for me suggestive of a phallic motif which I have only hinted at [in the picture]."

The Hammer-Heads are the first of Baum's whimsical tribes. He calls them "The Wild Men" in *The Emerald City of Oz* (1910, p. 32). The others include the Roly-Rogues in *Queen Zixi of Ix* (1905), the Wheelers in *Ozma of Oz* (1907), the Scoodlers in *The Road to Oz* (1909), the Hoppers and Horners in *The Patchwork Girl of Oz* (1913), the Loons of *The Tin Woodman of Oz* (1918), and the Flat-heads of *Glinda of Oz* (1920). Although each of these wild species may appear hostile and intimidating at first, each is easily overcome by some small flaw in their makeup. The Hammer-Heads resemble toy clowns with pop-up heads or jack-in-the-boxes. The release of a spring sends the head flying. These playthings may scare a child at first, but soon the child realizes they can do no harm and rather enjoys the trick. For his Russian "translation," Volkov transformed the Hammer-Heads into a band of mountaineers called Jumpers, with large heads, short necks, and big fists and the ability to leap to great heights.

The Lion became quite angry at the laughter caused by the Scarecrow's mishap, and giving a loud roar that echoed like thunder he dashed up the hill.

Again a head shot swiftly out, and the great Lion went rolling down the hill as if he had been struck by a cannon ball.

Dorothy ran down and helped the Scarecrow to his feet, and the Lion came up to her, feeling rather bruised and sore, and said,

"It is useless to fight people with shooting heads; no one can withstand them."

"What can we do, then?" she asked.

"Call the Winged Monkeys," suggested the Tin Woodman; "you have still the right to command them once more."

"Very well," she answered, and putting on the Golden Cap she uttered the magic words. The Monkeys were as prompt as ever, and in a few moments the entire band stood before her.

"What are your commands?" enquired the King of the Monkeys, bowing low.

"Carry us over the hill to the country of the Quadlings," answered the girl.

"It shall be done," said the King, and at once the Winged Monkeys caught the four travellers and Toto up in their arms and flew away with them. As they passed over the hill the Hammer-Heads yelled with vexation, and shot their heads high in the air; but they could not reach the Winged Monkeys, which carried Dorothy and her comrades safely over the hill and set them down in the beautiful country of the Quadlings.

2.

"This is the last time you can summon us," said the leader to Dorothy; "so good-bye and good luck to you."

"Good-bye, and thank you very much," returned the girl; and the Monkeys rose into the air and were out of sight in a twinkling.

The country of the Quadlings seemed rich and happy. There was field upon field of ripening grain, with well-paved roads running between, and pretty rippling brooks with strong bridges across them. The fences and houses and bridges were all painted bright red, just as they had been painted yellow in the country of the Winkies and blue in the country of the Munchkins. The Quadlings themselves, who were short and fat and looked chubby and good natured, were dressed all in red, which showed bright against the green grass and the yellowing grain.

3.

The Monkeys had set them down near a farm house, and the four travellers walked up to it and knocked at the door. It was opened by the farmer's wife, and when Dorothy asked for something to eat the woman gave them all a good dinner, with three kinds of cake and four kinds of cookies, and a bowl of milk for Toto.

4.

"How far is it to the Castle of Glinda?" asked the child.

2. *country of the Quadlings.* Although every map of the Land of Oz puts the area of the last four chapters through which Dorothy and her friends have just traveled in the Quadling Country, Baum unequivocally states that they do not reach Glinda's domain until they have crossed the Hill of the Hammer-Heads. As both the text and the pictures confirm, the countryside from the Forest of Fighting Trees to the farmlands of the Quadlings is brown and at this time probably not under Glinda's rule.

3. *the green grass and the yellowing grain.* As Gardner observed in Note 11 of *The Wizard of Oz and Who He Was*, this is one of several passages in the story where Baum had not yet decided to what extent the local flora and fauna take on the favorite color of that region. "Well, the grass is purple, and the trees are purple, and the houses and fences are purple," Tip describes this strange phenomenon in *The Marvelous Land of Oz* (1904). "Even the mud on the road is purple. But in the Emerald City everything is green that is purple here. And in the Country of the Munchkins, over at the East, everything is blue; and in the South country of the Quadlings everything is red; and in the West country of the Winkies . . . everything is yellow" (p. 35). Neill took this to an extreme in his own Oz books; even the air and the skin of the natives are the same color as the landscape where they live. Oz Club member Daniel P. Mannix speculated that Baum's confusion over the colors of the various countries of Oz may have been due to Denslow's different two-color illustrations in *The Wonderful Wizard of Oz*. Baum's text mentions only man-made objects like fences or houses being painted the favorite color of a particular region. Perhaps Baum hoped that the color scheme of the first Oz book might be carried over into the second. Unfortunately, the textual pictures in *The Marvelous Land of Oz* were printed in black and white only.

4. *three kinds of cake and four kinds of cookies.* These sweets indicate not only the affluence of the Quadlings but also why they are so chubby and good-natured. This highly caloric diet contrasts sharply with the more modest and better-balanced meal Dorothy is treated to at the farm-house outside the Emerald City in Chapter 10.

5. *three young girls.* All these troops of female soldiers who tramp through Baum's stories may have had their origin in the Aberdeen Guards, a group of South Dakota women who performed elaborate drills in 1890, dressed in blue jackets and red skirts and red caps trimmed with gold braid. "Well," Mrs. Bilkins, Baum's fictional landlady, reported in the *Saturday Pioneer* (May 31, 1890), "on comed the fierce an' furious warriors, their lances glitterin' an' their gum tucked temporarily under their tongues. Not one o' them thunk anything abut her back hair, not one paid any attention to the fit o' the coattails on the sodjer in front o' 'em! Every one was thinkin' of their country's enemies an' how they'd scratch their eyes out." Baum's amusement with the possibility of women soldiers reached its zenith with General Jinjur and her Army of Revolt in *The Marvelous Land of Oz* (1904), a gentle satire on militant suffragists.

6. *one of them.* In the original draft of *The Wizard of Oz* play that Baum submitted to Fred Hamlin, the Captain of Glinda's Guards turns out to be the Tin Woodman's lost love. "When the Wicked Witch [of the East] died," she informs him, "I was made queen of the Munchkins, and when we are married we will return to rule over our people." Since the Tin Woodman does not become Emperor of the Winkies in this version of the story, Baum here could conveniently tie up one of the loose ends left unresolved in his children's book. *The Tin Woodman of Oz* (1918), however, provides quite another history for the Munchkin girl. See Chapter 5, Note 9.

"It is not a great way," answered the farmer's wife. "Take the road to the South and you will soon reach it."

Thanking the good woman, they started afresh and walked by the fields and across the pretty bridges until they saw before them a very beautiful Castle. Before the gates were three young girls, dressed in handsome red uniforms trimmed with gold braid; and as Dorothy approached one of them said to her,

5.

6.

"Why have you come to the South Country?"

"To see the Good Witch who rules here," she answered. "Will you take me to her?"

"Let me have your name and I will ask Glinda if she will receive you." They told who they were, and the girl soldier went into the Castle. After a few moments she came back to say that Dorothy and the others were to be admitted at once.

DOROTHY

This picture of Dorothy appeared on
a trade card, c. 1910.
Private collection.

Chapter XXIII.
The Good Witch
Grants Dorothy's
Wish.

1. *Dorothy*. Denslow depicts Dorothy in this chapter dressed in the same simple frock she was wearing when she landed in Oz, not the one she has had on since her first visit to the Emerald City; Baum fails to mention any such change of clothing. Perhaps Glinda by her magic has returned the Kansas garment to her to avoid any embarrassment to Dorothy should the Oz gown suffer the same fate as the Silver Shoes.

2. *a throne of rubies*. This suggests an affinity between Glinda the Good Witch and Gayelette the sorceress of Chapter 14, who lives up North in a ruby palace.

3. *beautiful and young*. The prototype for Glinda the Good was Maetta the Sorceress of *A New Wonderland* (1900; later *The Magical Monarch of Mo*, 1903). Both wear white and live in the Southland; Baum describes Maetta as the most beautiful woman in the world, a title he grants Glinda in the later Oz books. Also in all of the stories (except the first), Glinda the Good Witch is known as Glinda the Good Sorceress. When Baum dramatized *The Marvelous Land of Oz* (1904) as *The Woggle-Bug* in 1905, Glinda became Maetta, who looked just like the Glinda in John R. Neill's illustrations in the second Oz book.

4. *pure white*. The witch color again, the same worn by the Good Witch of the North. Gretchen Ritter noticed in "Silver Slippers and a Golden Cap" (*Journal of American Studies*, 1997, p. 183) that Baum describes Glinda in the U.S. national colors: red (hair), white (dress), and blue (eyes). But Denslow does nothing with this color scheme in his illustrations.

5. *cannot afford it*. "Even the rites of death are a luxury in Kansas," noted Gretchen Ritter in "Silver Slippers and a Golden Cap" (*Journal of American Studies*, 1997, p. 177). Few modern readers realize the full meaning of Dorothy's concern. Nineteenth-century mourning practices were not only rigid but also expensive. They placed another unwanted burden on the poor. The Baum family had just suffered the agony of two funerals in one year when Matilda Joslyn Gage died in Chicago, on March 18, and their baby niece Dorothy Louise Gage on November 11, 1898, in Bloomington, Illinois.

(See Chapter 1, Note 1.) The undertaker's bill for Gage's funeral read as follows:

Black broadcloth casket	$65.00
Embalming	10.00
Floral door bouquet and ribbon	3.50
4 Carriages to Graceland [Cemetery]	20.00
Black funeral car	7.00
Cash paid 3 pall bearers	3.00
25 Funeral chairs and transportation	no charge
Services	no charge
4 Pairs gloves	1.00
	109.50
Rebate gloves	1.50
	108.00

This was a considerable amount at the time, one that no one in the family could easily afford. Custom demanded that Thomas Clarkson and Sophie Gage hire a big separate carriage to carry little Dorothy to the graveyard, but T. C. said that he could have brought the little coffin on his lap.

6. *well polished*. Not even the stately Glinda the Good is immune to Baum's weakness for puns.

Before

they went to see Glinda, however, they were taken to a room of the Castle, where Dorothy washed her face and combed her hair, and the Lion shook the dust out of his mane, and the Scarecrow patted himself into his best shape, and the Woodman polished his tin and oiled his joints.

When they were all quite presentable they followed the soldier girl into a big room where the Witch Glinda sat upon a throne of rubies.

1.

2.

3.   She was both beautiful and young to their eyes.   Her
hair was a rich red in color and fell in flowing ringlets over
4.   her shoulders. Her dress was pure white; but her eyes
were blue, and they looked kindly upon the little girl.

"What can I do for you, my child?" she asked.

Dorothy told the Witch all her story; how the cyclone
had brought her to the Land of Oz, how she had found
her companions, and of the wonderful adventures they had
met with.

"My greatest wish now," she added, "is to get back to
Kansas, for Aunt Em will surely think something dreadful
has happened to me, and that will make her put on mourning; and unless the crops are better this year than they
5.   were last I am sure Uncle Henry cannot afford it."

Glinda leaned forward and kissed the sweet, upturned
face of the loving little girl.

"Bless your dear heart," she said, "I am sure I can tell
you of a way to get back to Kansas."   Then she added:

"But, if I do, you must give me the Golden Cap."

"Willingly!" exclaimed Dorothy; "indeed, it is of no
use to me now, and when you have it you can command
the Winged Monkeys three times."

"And I think I shall need their service just those three
times," answered Glinda, smiling.

Dorothy then gave her the Golden Cap, and the
Witch said to the Scarecrow,

"What will you do when Dorothy has left us?"

"I will return to the Emerald City," he replied, "for Oz has made me its ruler and the people like me. The only thing that worries me is how to cross the hill of the Hammer-Heads."

"By means of the Golden Cap I shall command the Winged Monkeys to carry you to the gates of the Emerald City," said Glinda, "for it would be a shame to deprive the people of so wonderful a ruler."

"Am I really wonderful?" asked the Scarecrow.

"You are unusual," replied Glinda.

Turning to the Tin Woodman, she asked:

"What will become of you when Dorothy leaves this country?"

He leaned on his axe and thought a moment. Then he said,

"The Winkies were very kind to me, and wanted me to rule over them after the Wicked Witch died. I am fond of the Winkies, and if I could get back again to the country of the West I should like nothing better than to rule over them forever."

"My second command to the Winged Monkeys," said Glinda, "will be that they carry you safely to the land of the Winkies. Your brains may not be so large to look at as those of the Scarecrow, but you are really brighter than he is—when you are well polished—and I am sure you will rule the Winkies wisely and well."

Then the Witch looked at the big, shaggy Lion and asked,

6.

"When Dorothy has returned to her own home, what will become of you?"

"Over the hill of the Hammer-Heads," he answered, "lies a grand old forest, and all the beasts that live there have made me their King. If I could only get back to this forest I would pass my life very happily there."

"My third command to the Winged Monkeys," said Glinda, "shall be to carry you to your forest. Then, having used up the powers of the Golden Cap, I shall give it to the King of the Monkeys, that he and his band may thereafter be free for evermore."

The Scarecrow and the Tin Woodman and the Lion now thanked the Good Witch earnestly for her kindness, and Dorothy exclaimed,

"You are certainly as good as you are beautiful! But you have not yet told me how to get back to Kansas."

"Your Silver Shoes will carry you over the desert," replied Glinda. "If you had known their power you could have gone back to your Aunt Em the very first day you came to this country."   7.

"But then I should not have had my wonderful brains!" cried the Scarecrow. "I might have passed my whole life in the farmer's cornfield."

"And I should not have had my lovely heart," said the Tin Woodman. "I might have stood and rusted in the forest till the end of the world."

"And I should have lived a coward forever," declared the Lion, "and no beast in all the forest would have had a good word to say to me."

"This is all true," said Dorothy, " and I am glad I was of use to these good friends. But now that each of them has had what he most desired, and each is happy in having   8. a kingdom to rule beside, I think I should like to go back to Kansas."

"The Silver Shoes," said the Good Witch, "have wonderful powers. And one of the most curious things about them is that they can carry you to any place in the   9. world in three steps, and each step will be made in the wink of an eye. All you have to do is to knock the heels together three times and command the shoes to carry you wherever you wish to go."

7. *the very first day you came to this country.* Much like her three companions, Dorothy has always had the power to solve her problems within herself; she must realize for herself what powers she possesses. "What we want, [Baum] the moralist whispers, is within us," argued MacFall in *To Please a Child* (Chicago: Reilly & Lee, 1961); "we need only look for it to find it. What we strive for has been ours all the time" (p. 131). Perhaps the Scarecrow, the Tin Woodman, and the Cowardly Lion have always had the things they wanted, but they would never have discovered them if not for Dorothy.

This cultivation of the Self here may have a subtler significance. M.-L. Franz explained in Carl G. Jung's *Man and His Symbols* (1964) that it is often represented by a superior human being. For women, this being may appear as a wise and beautiful goddess (like the goddess Ceres or Demeter) or a helpful old woman (like the Woman-Learned-in-Magic in Hans Christian Andersen's "The Snow Queen" and the fairy godmother in George MacDonald's *The Princess and the Goblin*, 1871, and *The Princess and Curdie*, 1882). German fairy tales differ from the French in replacing the fairy godmother with the "wise woman" (sometimes translated "witch") as the guardian of the hero or heroine. Baum embraces both of them: The Good Witch of the North, in the role of the wise woman, presents Dorothy with the Silver Shoes; Glinda, as the fairy godmother, tells Dorothy how to use them. While Dorothy must seek what she desires, a way to get home, she finds her answer through the two Good Witches as extensions of her Self.

8. *having a kingdom to rule.* Fairy tales are full of characters of lowly origins who end up princes and tsars. This is also the American Dream of "getting on." Just like Horatio Alger's heroes, Dorothy's companions overcome their humble beginnings to find fame and fortune. The Scarecrow has become the ruler of the Emerald City, the Tin Woodman the leader of the Winkies, and the Cowardly Lion the King of the Forest.

9. *they can carry you to any place in the world in three steps.* Legend and literature often introduce magic shoes and boots for aerial transportation. There are the winged sandals of Mercury (Hermes), the god of trade. Ruth Plumly Thompson introduces a pair of Quick Sandals in *The Hungry Tiger of Oz* (1926). Odysseus too had his Shoes of Swiftness, and le Petit Poucet (or Hop o' my Thumb) as well as Jack the Giant Killer wear seven-league boots. Jack also has a Cap of Knowledge.

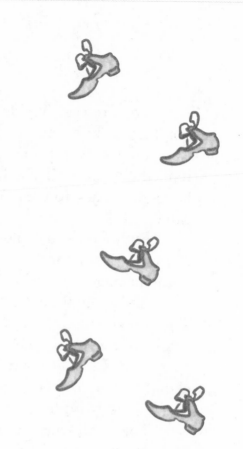

10. *"Take me home to Aunt Em!"* Those who would accuse *The Wizard of Oz* of being no more than "escapist" literature should recognize that Dorothy chooses not to stay in Oz but to return to reality. Not everyone has approved of her decision to go back to Kansas: According to Hugh Prestwood's song "Dorothy," performed by Judy Collins on her 1979 album *Hard Times for Lovers*, "Dorothy was a fool to leave, she had it made. . . ." When life proves to be too hard in Kansas in *The Emerald City of Oz* (1910), Dorothy *does* return to Oz to live and brings Aunt Em and Uncle Henry with her. "So Oz finally *became* home" Salman Rushdie observed in his monograph on the 1939 musical; "the imagined world became the actual world, as it does for all of us, because the truth is that once we have left our childhood places and started out to make up our lives, armed only with what we have and are, we understand that the real secret of the ruby slippers [in the movie] is not that 'there's no place like home,' but rather that there is no longer any such place *as* home: except, of course, for the home we make, or the homes that are made for us, in Oz: which is anywhere, and everywhere, except the place from which we began" (p. 57).

"If that is so," said the child, joyfully, "I will ask them to carry me back to Kansas at once."

She threw her arms around the Lion's neck and kissed him, patting his big head tenderly. Then she kissed the Tin Woodman, who was weeping in a way most dangerous to his joints. But she hugged the soft, stuffed body of the Scarecrow in her arms instead of kissing his painted face, and found she was crying herself at this sorrowful parting from her loving comrades.

Glinda the Good stepped down from her ruby throne to give the little girl a good-bye kiss, and Dorothy thanked her for all the kindness she had shown to her friends and herself.

Dorothy now took Toto up solemnly in her arms, and having said one last good-bye she clapped the heels of her shoes together three times, saying,

"Take me home to Aunt Em!"   10.

*   *   *   *   *

Instantly she was whirling through the air, so swiftly that all she could see or feel was the wind whistling past her ears.

The Silver Shoes took but three steps, and then she stopped so suddenly that she rolled over upon the grass several times before she knew where she was.

At length, however, she sat up and looked about her. "Good gracious!" she cried.

11.   For she was sitting on the broad Kansas prairie, and just before her was the new farm-house Uncle Henry built after the cyclone had carried away the old one. Uncle Henry was milking the cows in the barnyard, and Toto had jumped out of her arms and was running toward the barn, barking joyously.

12.   Dorothy stood up and found she was in her stocking-feet. For the Silver Shoes had fallen off in her flight through the air, and were lost forever in the desert.

11. *the new farm-house*. Baum reveals in *The Emerald City of Oz* (1910) that Uncle Henry "had to mortgage the farm to get the money to pay for the new house" (p. 21). He finally defaults on his loan, and the bank seizes the property. Throughout most of the nineteenth century, farmers feared nothing more than foreclosure. The threat of natural devastation or pestilence—drought, locusts, blight, even tornado—paled in comparison to the dread of the evil big-city banker who held the old homestead as collateral. Baum naturally sympathized with the farmers. After all, he had grown up on a farm that his parents were constantly mortgaging. Their luck finally ran out by 1880, and their creditors demanded that Rose Lawn be sold at public auction to meet their debt. Then on March 11, Frank Baum went up to the Onondaga County courthouse and bought back the property for his parents.

12. *the Silver Shoes had fallen off*. Again, Oz magic cannot work outside Oz. Here Baum again conforms to the pattern of the classical heroic quest. "At the return threshold," explained Joseph Campbell in *The Hero with a Thousand Faces* (Cleveland: World, 1956), "the transcendental powers must remain behind" (p. 246).

1. *covering her face with kisses*. This is the first sign of affection Aunt Em has shown the child in the story. The clinical psychologist Madonna Kohlbenschlag observed in *Lost in the Land of Oz* (New York: Crossroad, 1994) that on her return to Kansas, Dorothy "finds a new relationship to Aunt Em, symbol of her lost mothering. (Aunt Em no longer looks horrified at Dorothy, pressing her hand to her heart. She embraces Dorothy, covers her with kisses)" (p. 20). Aunt Em has changed remarkably in Dorothy's absence. She now knows how much Dorothy means to her and can finally express her deep love for her niece.

2. *gravely*. "Why did Baum choose the adverb *gravely* rather than, say, *happily?*" asked Janet Juhnke in "A Kansan's View" (in Gerald Peary and Roger Shatzkin, *The Classic American Novel and the Movies*, New York: Frederick Ungar, 1977). "Here is proof that, for Baum, Dorothy's adventures have constituted a kind of traumatic initiation. She has experienced terror and death, and she has felt disillusionment and sorrow, and has been forced to assume responsibility. She has begun to grow up—a sobering experience" (p. 170). Oz may be prettier and far more exciting than Kansas, but it lacks the security and safety of being back home with the people Dorothy loves.

3. *again*. "It's interesting to note," wrote Jack Snow in *Who's Who in Oz* (1954), "that the first word ever written in the very first Oz book was 'Dorothy.' The last word of the book is 'again.' And that is what young readers have said ever since those two words were written: 'We want to read about Dorothy again' " (p. 59).

Chapter XXIV.
Home Again.

AUNT EM HAD JUST COME out of the house to water the cabbages when she looked up and saw Dorothy running toward her.

"My darling child!" she cried, folding the little girl in her arms and covering her face with kisses; "where in the world did you come from?"

"From the Land of Oz," said Dorothy, gravely. "And here is Toto, too. And oh, Aunt Em! I'm so glad to be at home again!"

1.

2.

3.

The Denslow Appendix

AUM and Denslow jointly copyrighted all of their books and shared the royalties equally. This caused considerable confusion and dispute later on about exactly who owned what. It seemed logical at the time, since they equally paid the production costs of *Father Goose, His Book* and *The Wonderful Wizard of Oz,* that they should also reap equal rewards from their publication. But when they went their separate ways, each seemed to think that he was fully within his rights to exploit the characters as he saw fit without consulting the other. Of course, beginning with *The Marvelous Land of Oz* (1904), Baum produced a long line of Oz books without Denslow. And Denslow exploited the notoriety of the 1902 musical extravaganza of *The Wizard of Oz* and capitalized on the publication of *The Marvelous Land of Oz* by issuing several "Scarecrow and Tin-Man" projects all on his own.

As co-creator of *Father Goose, His Book,* Denslow readily reused the characters in various ways independent of Baum. He designed three different sets of "Father Goose" stationery, for Hill, for Baum, and for himself. The New York *World* invited him to draw two full-page color cartoons for the Sunday funnies, "Father Goose Shows the Children How to Run a Double-Ripper" (January 21, 1900) and "Father Goose at the Seashore" (June 22, 1900). (See color plate 2 in the Introduction.) Neither of these mentioned Baum as the author of the book on which they were based.

The Scarecrow and Tin Woodman appear in unexpected places in Denslow's work. Peering out of Santa Claus's bag in *Denslow's Night Before Christmas* (New York: G. W. Dillingham, 1902) is a tiny toy Tin Woodman from *The Wizard of Oz.* (See color plate 1.) And out in the cornfield in

Letter from Maud Gage Baum on the
George M. Hill Company "Father
Goose" stationery, 1899.
Private collection.

Letterhead of the George M. Hill
Company "Father Goose"
envelope, 1899.
Private collection.

Denslow's The House That Jack Built (New York: G. W. Dillingham, 1903) is the Scarecrow from the Land of Oz. (See color plate 2.) Both the Scarecrow and the Tin Woodman show up under letters "S" and "T" in *Denslow's A B C Book* (New York: G. W. Dillingham, 1903). (See color plate 3.)

When George W. Ogilvie & Co. took over the George M. Hill Company, the firm issued a little pamphlet made up of the original Hill color plates under the title *Pictures from The Wonderful Wizard of Oz.* It was obviously issued to capitalize on the play's reputation, for the lithographed wrappers show Montgomery and Stone in their Tin Woodman and Scarecrow costumes. (See color plate 9 in the Introduction.) Although Denslow's name is prominently displayed on the cover and title page, Baum's is nowhere to be found in the booklet. Ogilvie commissioned an entirely new story by Thomas H. Russell (1862–1944), "Adventures of the Scarecrow, the Tin Man, and the Little Girl," which was then printed on the versos of the plates. Neither the name Dorothy nor Oz appears in the text. The complete story is reproduced as a literary curiosity on pages 369–82.

Letterhead of "Father Goose" on L. Frank Baum's personal stationery, 1899.
Courtesy the Copyright Office.

The year *The Marvelous Land of Oz* was scheduled to come out, Denslow issued his own "Oz" book, *Denslow's Scarecrow and the Tin-Man* (New York: G. W. Dillingham, 1904). (See color plates 6–13.) He may have gotten the idea from the original title of Baum's story "The Further Adventures of the Scarecrow and the Tin Woodman," but his picture book, which he both wrote and illustrated, was not a sequel to *The Wizard of Oz.* Instead it told the misadventures of the actors off on a day's holiday from the theater. (It may have been inspired by an actual dispute Montgomery and Stone had with the management of the show.) It came out both as a single volume and collected with several other picture books in the series as *Denslow's Scarecrow and the Tin-Man and Other Stories* (1904). The Scarecrow also appeared on the handsome 1904 poster for "Denslow's New Series of Picture Books for Children." Denslow appropriately dedicated the book to "Little Freddie Stone."

When Baum's "Queer Visitors from the Marvelous Land of Oz" Sunday comic page began its syndication through the Philadelphia *North American* on November 28, 1904, Denslow decided to issue his own series. He

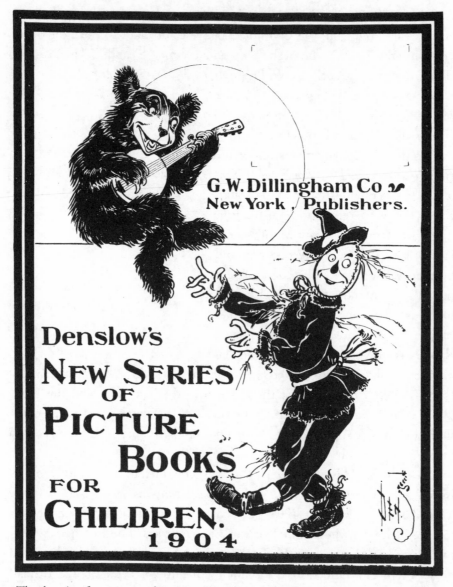

The drawing for a poster advertising "Denslow's New Series of Picture Books," 1904.
Courtesy Solton and Julia Engel Collection, Columbia University Libraries.

arranged with S. S. McClure to do a weekly "Denslow's Scarecrow and the Tin-Man" cartoon. (See color plate 20.) Following the same theme as Baum's page, it described the adventures of the Scarecrow, Tin Woodman, and Cowardly Lion in America. Only the first two episodes take place in the Land of Oz. It was a beautifully drawn page, but perhaps because of competition from Baum's feature, Denslow's series was poorly distributed. The Detroit *Free Press* printed only the first episode, "Dorothy's Christmas Tree," on December 18, 1904; the Minneapolis *Journal* ran it on Saturdays,

Drawing of "Denslow's Scarecrow and Tin-Man" comic page, March 12, 1905.

Private collection.

from December 10, 1904, until February 18, 1905. Two of the episodes ("About Town," December 31, 1904, and "Recaptured," January 7, 1905) reprinted the Dillingham picture book, *Denslow's Scarecrow and the Tin-Man.* Apparently only the Cleveland *Plain Dealer* published the complete series, on Sundays from December 11, 1904, through March 12, 1905. It had a surprisingly short run, only fourteen weeks compared to the twenty-seven weeks of Baum's series.

This self-caricature of W. W. Denslow with the Scarecrow was drawn for
Townsend Walsh, publicity manager of the musical
extravaganza *The Wizard of Oz*, 1902.
*Courtesy the Billy Rose Theatre Collection, The New York Public Library for the
Performing Arts, Astor, Lenox and Tilden Foundations.*

Toward the latter part of his career, Denslow issued an ambitious six-paneled decorative wall frieze based upon the old musical extravaganza. He only vaguely recalled the show, as suggested by the errors in the verses he wrote to accompany the illustrations. The date and the manufacturer of these lovely chromolithographs are unknown, but they were probably issued about 1910, when Denslow was designing advertising pamphlets for a Buffalo printing company. Some of the characters from these panels also graced a series of two-color trade cards.

Just as Baum did not mention Denslow in any of his later Oz projects, Baum's name never appeared in any of Denslow's "Scarecrow and Tin-Man" work. Each man wanted to establish his reputation independent of the other's, and the competition between the author and the illustrator was a major cause for the breakup of their partnership. There is no evidence that they ever spoke again after Denslow moved to New York in 1902. Each wanted sole credit for their collaboration. Denslow tended to exaggerate his contribution to the famous musical extravaganza. In a list of accomplishments prepared for Arthur Nicholas Hosking's *The Artist's Year Book* (Chicago: Fine Arts Building, 1905), now in the United States Military Academy Library at West Point, Denslow stated that he "designed costumes and color effects for stage production of *The Wizard of Oz* and originated the characters of Scarecrow and Tin Woodman in that play." He continued to receive royalties from their books even after Baum transferred his rights to Harrison H. Rountree during his bankruptcy proceedings. *The Wizard of Oz* would not have been the same without Baum or Denslow, but in the end neither man was willing to acknowledge the other's considerable contribution to their most important work.

PICTURES

FROM

The Wonderful Wizard of Oz

BY

W. W. DENSLOW

ILLUSTRATOR OF "FATHER GOOSE," DENSLOW'S "ONE RING CIRCUS," DENSLOW'S
"NIGHT BEFORE CHRISTMAS," ETC., ETC.

WITH A STORY TELLING THE

ADVENTURES OF THE SCARECROW
THE TIN MAN AND THE
LITTLE GIRL

BY

THOS. H. RUSSELL

GEORGE W. OGILVIE & CO., PUBLISHERS
181 MONROE STREET, CHICAGO, ILL.

CHAPTER I

HOW IT ALL BEGAN

THE morning was gray and the Little Girl was blue. Of course it was not the kind of blue that some of the people who lived a long time ago used to be when they painted their bodies blue to be in the fashion and keep out the cold. On the contrary, this Little Girl looked pink and rosy, as all little girls should, but she felt blue, as she had often heard her big sister say, when things did not go to suit her. And the morning being dull and gray did not suit the Little Girl at all, for you must know that she had promised a very nice friend of hers, a Boy, that on that very morning she would go with him to hunt gophers in a beautiful park that was The Boy's favorite playground. But here was a cloudy sky, threatening rain, and a dull day indoors, and so the Little Girl was blue.

Now, it is part of the nature of little girls to be quite like the clouds, which change their appearance often and quickly, and sometimes hide the smiling sun out of pure frolic. So nobody need feel surprised to learn that when a Boy's whistle was heard on the big porch just outside the Little Girl's house, all her blues were blown away, and she ran smilingly to the door. Here stood The Boy in all his vacation comfort of overalls and "barefeets."

"O," said the Little Girl, big-eyed with welcome, "isn't it a shame? We can't go to catch all those gophers, because it is going to rain."

"Aw, rain nothing!" replied The Boy, who attended a big public school, and who always tried to talk like the bigger boys. "What's a little rain? That won't hurt us. Besides, if it does rain I know a place where we can hide. I'll take care of you. Come on out and I'll show you how to catch 'em."

Of course that was just like a boy; it is part of his nature to try to lead little girls into danger and then rescue them at the risk of his life, for which they are supposed to love him ever after. So The Boy at once became a hero in the eyes of the Little Girl and away she skipped to find Nurse and kiss a permit from her for the great and risky expedition.

Just then a miracle happened, as miracles often do happen in this good old world to good little girls. The Rainman, a grumpy old fellow by the

name of Jupiter, had had his eye on the Little Girl ever since she tumbled out of her pink-and-white cot that morning, and he had been gloating over the prospect of spoiling her day. But he had been a boy himself once upon a time, and when he saw how glum The Boy looked as he stood in doubt on the Little Girl's porch, he took pity on him and pushed the clouds away, leaving all the sky bright and blue, with no possible excuse for Nurse to keep the Little Girl at home.

So then they started, The Boy and the Little Girl, for the big, wonderful playground that matter-of-fact, grown-up people called the park. Being city children, and knowing the ways of their elders, they did not go hand-in-hand, as children of all ages often do in the country, but better still they went heart-in-heart and were all in all to each other, as boys and girls have been at times since first the world was made.

How wonderful was the prospect that soon opened before them! Right in the heart of the busy city, and surrounded by its smoke and din, there were the cool, green shades, the splashing fountains, the spreading trees, the winding walks, the many-colored flower-beds, and the delightful little lakes of the famous park; and as the Little Girl and her proud young protector passed from the heated sidewalks into the shade of the big oaks and elm trees, they danced onto the nearest smooth lawn and clean forgot all such commonplace affairs as home and nurses, bath-tubs and books. How could any one remember such things when the roaring of the lions in the park zoo had replaced the rattle of the street-cars, and every step brought nearer new delights?

"I say, Boy," called out the Little Girl, as she ran away from him just for the pure pleasure of being caught again, "isn't this fine? Let's play this is fairyland."

"I'm with you," laughed The Boy, at her side in a moment. "You're a little fairy all right." You see, he was not so young that he didn't know little girls are not altogether displeased at being paid compliments by the proper person.

And then fairyland opened in earnest for the happy pair, though the Little Girl had no idea of the still more wonderful things in store for her before the day was done. The Boy became a giant and pretended to eat her at a single mouthful; then he transformed himself into Jack the Giant-killer and cut off his own head with one stroke of his trusty sword, though how he did it she never has been able to tell. He donned seven-league boots, and made believe to swoop down upon her from a great distance and carry her off to his castle in the air. He became a locomotive, and whistled and puffed under the strain of pulling the private car containing the Little Girl from

Chicago to New York in half a minute. He did so many remarkable things, and assumed the shape of so many strange men and animals under the magic wand of the fairy Little Girl, that it was a long, long time before she happened to remember that the main object of the expedition had not been attended to—that they had not yet captured a single gopher. So she mentioned the matter to The Boy.

"O, Boy," said she, "did you forget what we came here for? You know you promised to show me where the gophers live, and to catch some for me."

Then The Boy began to shine with even greater glory in the eyes of the Little Girl, for who but a boy could tell her all about the cunning little creatures that had been peeping timidly at her from their holes in the ground. He showed her how their houses were made with front and back doors, so that they could run into either one when danger threatened; and then, with wonderful patience for a boy, he waited for a chance to dart like lightning upon a gopher that ventured too far from home to pay a friendly visit to a neighbor. Soon the chance came, and like a flash The Boy pounced upon his prey and triumphantly bore the squirming animal to the Little Girl. What did he care for the bites of a gopher, anyway, as long as he had kept his promise, and his playmate had her prize? And how amply was he rewarded when he heard her say:

"I think you are just the nicest boy that ever lived, and when I grow up I am going to ask Nurse to let me marry you."

Then began the greatest gopher hunt of this or any other day. From one end of the great park to another ranged The Boy and his little lady fair. Never were eyes so sharp as his to spy out the little animals as they left their underground houses for a stroll in the bright sunshine; never were feet so swift to beat them in their race for home and safety. Gopher after gopher was cleverly caught and carried to the Little Girl to be admired and petted by her as it lay a prisoner in The Boy's well-bitten hands, and then released at her request to run back home and tell its fretting family of its strange adventures.

But, O, the miles they ran hither and thither, and the time it took to carry on this famous hunt! In quite another part of the big park an anxious Nurse was busily hunting the Little Girl, and the shadows were growing very long as the sun prepared to go to bed in the western sky, when at last she plumped herself down on the grass by the trunk of a big tree, and said, "Boy, I am tired! aren't you?"

Now, when a little girl admits that she is tired, and the evening shadows are falling, she is not far from the Land of Nod, where all good children

sleep; and almost before The Boy could say "Jack Robinson," if it had ever occurred to him to make that famous remark, the Little Girl was fast asleep, and he was face to face with the most tremendous responsibility of his short but busy life.

"Now, what shall I do!" he said to himself, as he gazed at the sleeping form. "I can't carry her home, and I guess I'd better run all the way to her house and get Nurse or somebody to come for her before it gets quite dark."

With that, The Boy started off as fast as his tired little legs would carry him, leaving the Little Girl fast asleep in a quiet nook where nobody was likely to pass, except, by chance, a gray park policeman, or maybe a gopher out for a midnight stroll.

CHAPTER II

THE SORCERER AND THE MAGIC LUNCH

"HELLO, Little Girl, how do you do this evening?"

At these words, uttered in a thin voice, with a foreign accent quite unlike anything she had ever heard before, the Little Girl looked up to see a little old gentleman with a very bald head and some curly white whiskers, who stood with a broad-brimmed hat in his hand, smiling down upon her. He was very strangely dressed in a green coat with big white buttons, which sparkled in the moonlight and shone like small electric lamps. Of course they were diamonds of the first water, but how was the Little Girl to know that on such short acquaintance? He certainly did not look like any of her father's friends and she was sure she had never seen him before. But then, he had called her by her name, and she was a very polite Little Girl, so in her very best society manner she replied:

"I am quite well, sir, thank you, and I hope you are the same. But, please, who are you?"

At that the strange gentleman laughed outright, and the Little Girl thought that his laugh sounded as if it had come through the funny phonograph her papa had at home.

"Why, Little Girl," he said, "you should be very glad to see me. I happen to be the Sorcerer of this particular park, and as I have just come on duty I shall be glad to show you a few things in my line if you have a little time to spare."

"Thank you very much, sir," said the Little Girl, who was rapidly getting over her first surprise. "But please, sir, will you tell me, sir, what is a park sorcerer? I have heard of park policemen and park phaetons, but I never did hear of a park sorcerer before."

"O my dear," said the little old gentleman, his sides shaking with laughter that made his diamond buttons twinkle like great stars, "I can assure you that every well-regulated park has its sorcerer nowadays. You see there are so many of us here that are hard at work all day long entertaining the public and can only play at night when the ordinary people have left the park. And, of course, there must be somebody official to regulate the doings of the Scarecrow and the rest of the boys. Well, that is the business of the park sorcerer, and here I am!"

"And please, sir, who is the Scarecrow?" asked the Little Girl.

"O I'll introduce him to you presently," replied the Sorcerer; "but first of all let me tell you something about the rest of the park folks. By the way, of course you have noticed the famous statues we have here?"

"O yes, sir," the Little Girl answered quickly. "Why, I know all their names by heart. And I think they are fine, all of them."

"Well, my dear," said the Sorcerer, "how would you like to be a statue, and stand up all day in one position for a crowd to stare at? It's bad enough to be sitting down all day in the same position, as Mr. Shakespeare over yonder does, but when you have to stand up and look pleasant all day long, like most of them, it is very trying to the nerves, and so they have to come down and get a little exercise and amusement after business hours, don't you see, when the public is gone?"

"Why, dear me, sir, that does seem reasonable," said the Little Girl, thoughtfully, "but I really never thought of it before."

"I know you haven't, Little Girl," said the Sorcerer, shaking his head almost sadly. "The public is very careless of its neighbors' comfort. But in this park we try to give our attractions a little amusement after their day's work. Now, how would you like to be an eagle, the bird of freedom, and be caged up inside iron bars all day long? Wouldn't you like to get out and fly high once in awhile? How would you like to be a polar bear and never see a piece of ice all summer? Answer me that!"

"Please, sir, I'd rather be the iceman," said the Little Girl, and then they both had a good laugh and began to feel like old friends.

"Well, my dear," said the Sorcerer, reaching down and taking the Little

Girl by the hand to help her to her feet, "if you will come along with me I will show you some of the sights the public never sees. But stay! you must be hungry, my dear, for it is long past your dinner-hour, so we will just whistle for a lunch."

With that the sorcerer lifted a little black wand which he had been carrying in his hand and gently blew into one end of it. Immediately there rose a sound that seemed to the Little Girl's ears like the faraway whistle of a great steamer. Before the sound had quite died away, a short, sharp bark was heard close at hand, and up ran a funny little black fuzzy dog with a strangely red head and carefully combed whiskers. In his mouth he carried a big lunch-basket, which he dropped at the Sorcerer's feet.

"Abracadabra," said the Sorcerer, and then you should have seen that wonderful dog spread a big white table-cloth on the dewy grass and lay out the daintiest lunch the Little Girl had ever seen. There seemed to be everything she had ever liked or wished for, and though her surprise almost took away her appetite, she soon recovered and ate as heartily as a hungry little girl can. Soon she was ready to accompany the Sorcerer, who stood smilingly waiting for her, and as they started off, hand in hand, the strange dog following close at their heels, she looked around at the remnants of her lunch and started with surprise, for table-cloth, dishes, lunch, and all had disappeared as completely as if they had never been.

"O, we are very careful to keep the park clean, my dear," said the Sorcerer. "We try to set a good example to the public, you see. But come along. Let's go and see the Scarecrow."

CHAPTER III

THE SCARECROW DOES THE HONORS

As the Sorcerer and the Little Girl left the quiet nook in which they had become acquainted so strangely, she could not help expressing a little curiosity about the Scarecrow whom she was so soon to meet. It was only natural, for curiosity has been common to little girls ever since the first little girl made a dolly and dressed it in leaves, long before men learned how to make silks and satins or thought of killing birds for ladies to wear on their hats while petting their pretty little pug dogs. So she said to the Sorcerer as she trotted along by his side:

"Please, Mr. Sorcerer, will you kindly tell me, before we meet Mr. Scarecrow, what kind of gentleman he is?"

"With pleasure, my dear," replied the Sorcerer, not to be outdone in politeness. "You know, of course, that we have a large and growing family of lions here, and also a very fine old family of gophers."

"O yes," said the Little Girl; "I had the pleasure of meeting some of the gophers to-day, and I have seen the lions as I passed along their street."

"Well," said the Sorcerer, "the Scarecrow's business is to keep the lions from eating the gophers when they are out at night, and I am bound to say that he earns his salary. He is not a very handsome gentleman, as you will soon see, but handsome is as handsome does, and he does his work well. We try to use him right, as the saying is, and I don't think he has any kick coming."

"O, now, Mr. Sorcerer," said the Little Girl, "you are talking just like a Boy I know, and I am beginning to like you ever so much."

The Sorcerer almost blushed.

"Thanks, my dear," he said, "we strive to please; but look, here is the Scarecrow!"

The Little Girl stopped and looked about her, but all that she could see was a big fence and the trunks of trees.

"Look up, my dear," said the Sorcerer.

So the Little Girl looked up, and there, in the moonlight, she saw a stolid gentleman sitting on the end of a pole, gazing at nothing in particular, and looking as if he had seen better days.

"He doesn't look comfortable," said the Little Girl.

"No, my dear; none of them do at this time of day," replied the Sorcerer. "I haven't called him off watch yet. He'll feel better when he quits work."

And then the Sorcerer once more lifted his magic wand and blew into it. This time the Little Girl felt sure she heard her Nurse singing in the distance a favorite song of hers, called "I've Worked Enough To-day," and looking again towards the Scarecrow, she saw that he had come down from his uncomfortable perch and was smiling broadly at her, like one relieved from arduous duty.

"Little Girl," said the Sorcerer, "permit me to present the Scarecrow."

"I am very glad to meet you, Mr. Scarecrow," said the Little Girl, graciously extending her hand to the new acquaintance. She noticed that his handshake was very cold and formal, not to say flabby, and immediately made up her mind that he must be a person of social importance.

"To what am I indebted for the honor of this visit?" asked the Scarecrow, in a husky voice, which sounded for all the world as if he had been eating straw.

"O, Mr. Scarecrow, I am just dying to know all about you and the rest of the boys Mr. Sorcerer speaks about," broke in the Little Girl, before the Sorcerer could say a word in explanation of her visit. "I want to know just what you do after you get through scaring the lions, and I want to meet all your friends."

"Tell her all you know, Scarecrow" said the Sorcerer; "it's the quickest way out of it."

"Well, madam," said the Scarecrow, who had scarcely seen the Little Girl at all, he was so busy looking straight ahead, but recognizing her as a lady by her voice, "my story is a sad one. The trouble with me is, that too many people take me for a man of straw, whereas I am in reality, a man of importance in this park, as you would understand if you were a gopher. My only pleasure in life is to come down from my perch, once in a while, when the Sorcerer says I may, and have a little fun with my friend the Tin Man, whom you will presently see. But, hold on, that is, don't hold onto me, for I am a little shaky on my pins, but wait a minute! Sometimes my good old friend the Stork does come around and take me out for an airing when I have been badly abused by some of the Rubberneck family that frequent the park. Then, I get a little sympathy at other times from a long-bearded policeman on the nightwatch, who once propped me up on the Diamond Chain, and gave me that beautiful millionaire feeling instead of the stuffy, tired feeling that stays with me all day long. So, perhaps, I shouldn't complain after all."

"I'm sure it's very nice if you to take such a cheerful view of things," said the Little Girl, who believed in scattering seeds of kindness. "But please tell me, didn't you come from a farm? I seem to see a few straws, or wisps of hay, or something, sticking out all over you."

"I don't care a straw what you see," replied the Scarecrow, sharply, "and you ought to know that ladies are not supposed to see everything. Besides, stuffing is very useful in its way, and it's quite the fashion, I'm sure. Ask any dude you know."

"The Boy is not a dude!" retorted the Little Girl, who always knew when her toes were trodden upon. "And if he were here, he'd make you take that back."

"Tut, tut, children!" said the Sorcerer, "no quarreling at this time of night! Leave that to the cats."

"O, Mr. Sorcerer," said the Little Girl, who was greatly interested in a certain Maltese Kitten at home, "what do you know about cats? Have you got any in your park?"

"Have we got any?" echoed the Sorcerer. "What do we keep the poor old Scarecrow here for, except to scare away cats? Aren't the lions big cats, and the tigers, and a lot of the rest of 'em that keep me awake nights? Don't the cats come in here and try to kill our birds? and don't I fix them when I catch them at it? Say, Little Girl, shall I tell you what I did with the last cat I caught with a bird in its mouth?"

"Please, Mr. Sorcerer," said the Little Girl, eagerly.

"Well, my dear, I was bound to stop the killing of birds somehow, so I thought I would make an example of that cat, and I threw it into the lake. Out it jumped, and I cut its head off. Ten minutes later it came trotting after me with its head in its mouth, and by that time I was so provoked that I took its head away from it and threw it square in its face. So, there now, that's what I know about cats!"

The Little Girl looked surprised; then sad.

"Mr. Sorcerer," said she.

"Well, my dear," said the Sorcerer.

"I think you're a wonder," said the Little Girl.

"Not at all, my dear," replied the Sorcerer. "Wait until you meet the Tin Man."

CHAPTER IV

THE TIN MAN AND HIS FRIENDS

THE Sorcerer had no sooner mentioned the Tin Man to the Little Girl than a faint tinkling sound was heard near by, and the wonderful dog that had been quietly listening to the conversation with the Scarecrow began to yelp.

"He doesn't like that style of music," said the Sorcerer.

"Why not?" asked the Little Girl. "I'm sure," said she, "it's as good as any music our next-door neighbor's girl can play."

Now, wasn't that a spiteful remark for a nice little girl to make? And wouldn't we be surprised at it if we didn't know that little girls will make spiteful remarks about the neighbors once in a great while?

"O fie, my dear," said the Sorcerer, "you shouldn't make comparisons.

But come along and meet the Tin Man. He's in the doctor's hands. Come on, Scarecrow."

Then the Sorcerer placed one hand under the arm of the Scarecrow, who seemed to move with difficulty, and taking hold of the Little Girl with the other, he led them carefully between the trees in the direction of the tinkling noise. Pretty soon a curious scene appeared before them, and it was some minutes before the astonished eyes of the Little Girl could take it all in.

Seated on the stump of a tree, in the center of an open space which seemed almost as light as day, there was a merry gentleman who looked very much like an old-fashioned stove, and all around him were busy little men in leather aprons and spectacles. Each little man had a hammer in his hand, except one, who seemed to be burning out the merry gentleman's eyes with a red-hot iron. At this sight the Little Girl closed her eyes and almost screamed with fright, but the Sorcerer patted her on the head and said:

"Don't mind a little thing like that, my dear. It is only the Tin Man taking a treatment."

"I'll be with you in a minute, Little Girl," said the merry gentleman on the stump, just as if he had been introduced in correct style.

Then the Little Girl looked again, and saw that the busy little men were hammering away at the Tin Man's arms and legs, which they had kindly removed for the purpose, and not knowing what to make of such strange proceedings, she held her peace like a wise little girl and waited until she was spoken to.

"Well, my dear," said the Sorcerer, after awhile, "what do you think of it?"

"I don't know what to think," said the Little Girl. "This is the strangest thing I've ever seen. What does it all mean?"

"Wait until the doctors are through with the Tin Man, and he'll tell you all about it," replied the Sorcerer. So the Little Girl was forced to wait.

Just then she noticed, for the first time, that close behind the busy little men whom the Sorcerer called the doctors there stood an immense yellow lion watching the scene with wide-open eyes. Suddenly, as the Little Girl gazed at him in affright, the lion uttered a shrill cry, like that of a lady in distress, and springing straight up in the air, disappeared among the tree-tops.

"Whatever does that mean?" asked the Little Girl, staring up to were the lion had vanished like her lunch.

The Sorcerer laughed. "O, that's just our friend the Lion," he said. "I

Illustration from *Denslow's Night Before Christmas* (New York: G. W. Dillingham, 1902).
Private collection.

Illustration from *Denslow's The House That Jack Built* (New York: G. W. Dillingham, 1903).
Private collection.

The Scarecrow and the Tin Woodman in *Denslow's A B C Book* (New York: G. W. Dillingham, 1903).
Private collection.

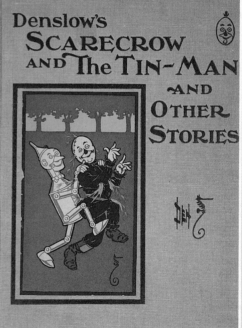

Cover of *Denslow's Scarecrow and the Tin-Man and Other Stories* (New York: G. W. Dillingham, 1904).
Private collection.

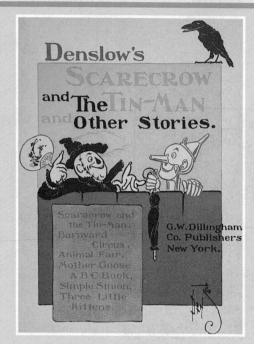

Title page of *Denslow's Scarecrow and the Tin-Man and Other Stories* (New York: G. W. Dillingham, 1904). *Private collection.*

The complete text and pictures of *Denslow's Scarecrow and the Tin-Man* (New York: G. W. Dillingham, 1904). *Private collection.*

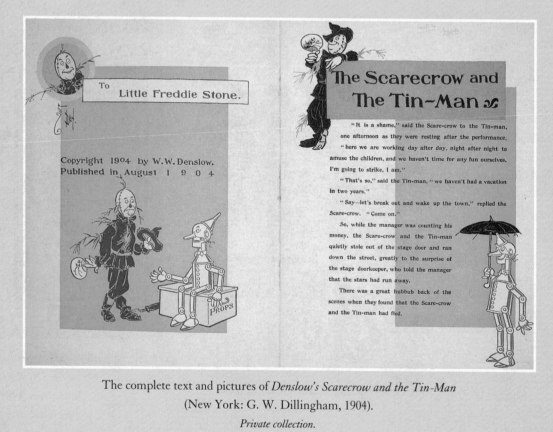

The complete text and pictures of *Denslow's Scarecrow and the Tin-Man* (New York: G. W. Dillingham, 1904). *Private collection.*

The police were notified and searchers were sent everywhere to catch the truants, for the evening performance could not go on without them.

Meanwhile the runaway pair were having a wild, jolly time in the old town.

They ran until they thought they were safe from pursuit, and then jumped on a street car to get as far from the theater as they could in a short time.

"Fare," said the conductor.

"What's that?" asked the Scare-crow.

"Pay your money or get off!" said the conductor.

The Scare-crow and the Tin-man laughed at the idea of anyone wanting money from them.

"We haven't any," said the Tin-man.

"Then off you go!" and the conductor tossed the two from the car.

"That Tin-man had a hard face," said an old lady near the door.

Bang! went the Tin-man and the Scare-crow into a banana and apple stand kept by an Italian on the corner, as they came off the car in a hurry.

Down went the stand, fruit and the two friends into the gutter.

Of course the banana man was angry, and talked loudly in broken English.

Away the two friends flew down the street with the angry banana man after them, calling loudly for his pay for the spoiled fruit.

"Everybody seems to want money," said the Scare-crow, as he jumped into an automobile that was standing by the curb. In tumbled the Tin-man, and away they dashed, leaving the Italian waving his arms wildly on the corner.

"This is great," said the Scare-crow.

"It beats the theater all to pieces," replied the Tin-man, as they fairly flew over the avenue at a reckless pace.

"Hi! Stop there," shouted a bicycle policeman. "You are going too fast."

But they only waved him a tra-la as they sped along.

The policeman blew a loud blast on his whistle, and the auto was hemmed in and surrounded by policemen just as the Scare-crow steered the machine into a mortar bed in front of a new building.

The automobile turned a complete somersault, scattering mortar, brick and sand in all directions over the policemen and the crowd that was collecting.

At this stage the auto commenced to sizzle and suddenly blew up sending our friends high in the air.

One of the policemen turned in an alarm, and the fire-engines were soon on the spot to put out the fire on the auto, and taking

The complete text and pictures of *Denslow's Scarecrow and the Tin-Man*
(New York: G. W. Dillingham, 1904).
Private collection.

advantage of the confusion the two friends dodged down an alley, out on another street and were soon far away.

By and by they found themselves in Madison Square near the fountain, when a man carelessly threw a lighted match directly into the straw that was sticking out of the Scare-crow's chest and set him in a blaze.

The Tin-man seeing this danger, with rare presence of mind caught up his friend and dumped him into the fountain, but in doing so he stumbled and fell in himself.

Now, what was good for the Scare-crow was not good for the Tin-man, and after they had crawled out of the water he began to rust, and as he had left his

The complete text and pictures of *Denslow's Scarecrow and the Tin-Man*
(New York: G. W. Dillingham, 1904).
Private collection.

oil-can at the theater, he was soon stiff in all his joints, so that the Scare-crow had to help him along.

Just then they heard a voice behind them say, "There they are; arrest them."

It was the voice of the manager who was hunting them with a squad of policemen.

There was no escape, as the Tin-man was so rusty by this time that he could scarcely move, and the happy pair were soon hustled into a patrol wag-on and given a ride to the station.

When they came before the judge, and he had heard the com-plaint of the man-ager, he sentenced the Scare-crow and the Tin-man to another year in the theater to make fun for the children.

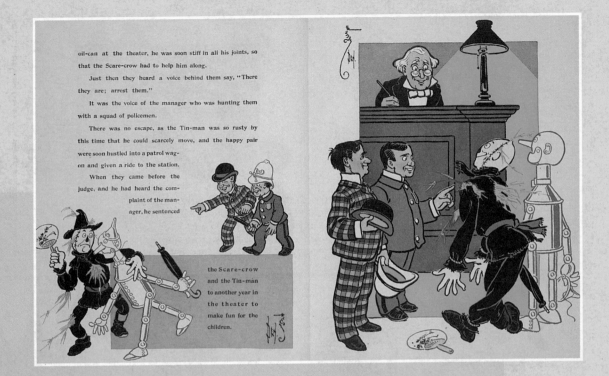

"That's all right," said the Scare-crow. "We have had our little fun and it's all right. We go back with pleasure."

The Scare-crow oiled up the Tin-man so that he was as good as ever, and got some new straw to swell out his own chest, and the two friends shone with new luster at the evening performance that night. The children laughed as they had never laughed before at the droll antics of the Scare-crow and the Tin-man.

The complete text and pictures of *Denslow's Scarecrow and the Tin-Man*
(New York: G. W. Dillingham, 1904).
Private collection.

FROM·KANSAS·LITTLE·DOROTHY·TO·OZ·WAS·BLOWN·AWAY;
WHERE·FIRST·SHE·MET·THE·GAY·SCARECROW·THE·MAN·ALL·STUFFED·WITH·HAY.
IMOGENE·THE·SPOTTED·CALF·WAS·GLAD·TO·SEE·HIM·TOO,
AND·TRIED·AT·ONCE·TO·EAT·HIM·UP·WHICH·SCARED·HIM·THROUGH·AND·THROUGH.

THE·TIN·MAN·IN·A·SHOWER·OF·RAIN·GOT·RUST·IN·EVERY·JOINT,
SO·HE·MUST·CARRY·AN·OIL·CAN·HIS·ELBOWS·TO·ANOINT
NEXT·CAME·A·LION·COWARDLY·AS·TIMID·AS·A·BIRD;
YET·IF·SOME·DANGER·THREATENED·DOT·HIS·MIGHTY·ROAR·WAS·HEARD.

THE·LION·WISHED·THAT·HE·WERE·BRAVE;·THE·SCARECROW·WANTED·BRAINS,
THE·TIN·MAN·CRAVED·A·LOVING·HEART·WITH·ALL·ITS·JOYS·AND·PAINS
FAIR·DOROTHY·WOULD·FAIN·GO·BACK·TO·KANSAS·AND·HER·FOLKS·
ALTHOUGH·SHE·LIKED·THE·TIN·MAN·AND·THE·SCARECROW'S·JOLLY·JOKES.

Lithographed wallpaper frieze of characters from the musical extravaganza
The Wizard of Oz, drawn by W. W. Denslow, c. 1910.
Courtesy Willard Carroll Collection.

Lithographed wallpaper frieze of characters from the musical extravaganza
The Wizard of Oz, drawn by W. W. Denslow, c. 1910.
Courtesy Willard Carroll Collection.

"Dorothy's Christmas Tree," one of "Denslow's Scarecrow and the Tin-Man"
comic pages, Minneapolis *Journal,* December 10, 1904.

Courtesy Jay Scarfone/William Stillman Collection.

guess a gopher tickled his toes, and he always goes up in the air when he's tickled."

The Little Girl could not help thinking this was rather strange conduct for a lion, even when the Sorcerer was around, but the Tin Man's arms and legs were replaced by this time, and he was hopping towards her on one leg, holding out a hand that looked like the elbow-joint of a stovepipe.

"How do, Little Girl?" said he. "I'm glad to see you again."

"I think there is some mistake, sir," replied the Little Girl, who was at all times extremely proper. "I do not remember ever having met you before, and I am sure we have not been introduced this evening."

"O, that's all right, all right," said the merry Tin Man. "You'll know me when I tell you who I am. Why, I'm the statue you stood looking at so long the other day. I was a famous statesman once, and you know all about me. But I get off my pedestal once in awhile, you know, to have a little fun with my old friend, the Scarecrow here, and we're out for a good time tonight all right."

"Excuse me, sir, but I'm sure you do not talk at all like a statesman," said the Little Girl, "and besides, I thought all statues were made of everlasting bronze, while you seem to be have come from a tinshop." Even little girls get suspicious of merry gentlemen sometimes, you see.

"O, that's all right, little one," said the Tin Man, with a laugh. "Didn't I tell you this was my night off? You see I get so rheumaticky standing up there on that pedestal in all sorts of weather that I am glad to have a red-hot-iron treatment once in awhile, and of course I have to disguise myself in this outing-suit of tin for the sake of my reputation. You wouldn't have a famous statesman caught out upon a lark at midnight in bronze clothes he wears before the public in the daytime, would you?"

The Little Girl admitted that there was something in that, and in fact began to sympathize very deeply with the Tin Man. So then he told her that she was welcome to the reserved seat upon the stump which he had just left, and that he would call in a few friends to meet her. "I am tired of being on the stump, anyway," he said, when the Little Girl protested that he was old and famous and ought to take the only seat in sight. Then the Little Girl climbed up on the Tin Man's seat, and the wonderful things that followed she will never forget—no, not if she lives to be as old as Methusaleh.

CHAPTER V

THE SORCERER AND THE ANIMALS

As soon as the Little Girl was fairly seated in the Tin Man's place, the Sorcerer stepped before her, and waving his magic wand, transformed the scene into one of brilliant beauty. Instead of an old oak stump the Little Girl's seat became a throne studded with diamonds, the light from which made even the big brilliants on the Sorcerer's coat look like tallow candles. Little boys and girls, the very images of her own playmates, but oh, so beautifully dressed, danced before her; music that surpassed any she had ever heard played by the big bands in the park filled the air, and it all seemed to come from a single strange instrument played by a young gentleman who looked like The Boy, but was dressed like a fairy prince. Strawberry ice-cream, peaches, and angel cake were served to all within the magic circle by good-looking little colored boys, who seemed to have no feet, but wings, and never waited for a tip. The Scarecrow and the Tin Man did a cake-walk and seemed to have forgotten all their pains and sorrows, until a big oak tree, that had been laughing fit to split its trunk, took the Scarecrow in its arms, and nearly squeezed the straw stuffing out of him. The Lion-Afraid-of-a-Gopher came down out of the clouds and said he had only been up for an airing, and could whip any gopher alive or dead, and all was going as merrily as a marriage-bell when a great whizzing and whirring of wings was heard, and down from the treetops there flew the most wonderful lot of monkeys that ever was seen. There were monkeys with feet like ducks and wings like eagles; monkeys that could talk every language under the sun, and a few more besides; monkeys that thought no more of throwing the Lion on his back and tying him up than they would of eating a peanut; monkeys that finally, at the Sorcerer's command, caught up the Little Girl and her friend the Tin Man and gave them the fastest ride that ever was made in the air, and then brought them back to the scene of this wonderful midnight circus, as gently as if they had never gone at all. And then, when the Little Girl started to climb back into her big, bediamonded throne there was an immense Face without a body staring at her, as if to say, "What a good time you are having, to be sure," and pretty soon there was a big parade of all hands around the arena, with the Little Girl riding in state on the Lion's back and a wonderfully funny park policeman leading the

way. The Tin Man followed close behind with an ax, watching for a chance to chop off the policeman's whiskers, while the Scarecrow flirted most outrageously with a spectator who looked strangely like Nurse. Then, at a wave of the Sorcerer's wand, some wonderful creatures, which the Scarecrow called Metazoans, half-tiger and half-bear, bounded into the arena and saluted the Little Girl with mighty roars as queen of the circus, until a big tree fell on them and knocked them into a hole in the ground that opened suddenly and had no bottom.

And the Sorcerer kept waving his magic wand and changing the scenes so rapidly that in less time than it takes to read about it the Little Girl had been to a picnic party on an island with the Scarecrow and the Dog that was so handy at getting up a lunch; she had breakfasted with the Lion and scared him half to death by telling him there was a mouse under the table; she had taken an oil-can and doctored the Tin Man for his rheumatism, and cured him of it entirely; and she had received friendly visits from all the witches and wizards that dwelt in those parts. Then came the Fairy Queen with all her attendant fairies, and the Little Girl received them in state and introduced them to the Lion, who was decorated for the occasion with a golden crown, because the cap of liberty wouldn't fit him. And all the gophers in the park came out and shook hands with her, calling the Little Girl their great and good friend, and asking her to drop in any time she was near their holes. And then she went up in an airship as big as a barn and caught the wonderful waiter-dog winking at another little girl, for which she never forgave him, though she had the satisfaction of pinching his ear and dropping him back to earth. And last, but by no means least, she caught the great Sorcerer himself in the act of telling the Tin Man and the Scarecrow what a very nice Little Girl she was, and that being about as much as she could stand in one short evening she missed all the rest of the wonderful things that certainly must have happened while the park people were at play.

CHAPTER VI

AWAKE AT LAST

"HERE she is now! Asleep under that tree!"

The voice was the voice of Nurse, and there were tears in it, for not only Nurse, but the Little Girl's father and mother and sisters and brothers, and

all the friends they could find, had been searching for her all over the big park for four hours or more. The Boy, of course, was fast asleep at home.

"Where's the Scarecrow?" demanded the Little Girl, as she was ruthlessly awakened to find herself surrounded by a tearful circle of familiar faces. "And where's the Tin Man? And the Sorcerer, where is he?"

"Why, darling, whatever do you mean? You must have been dreaming!"

"O, I don't know," said the Little Girl, sleepily, "but if I was, it was perfectly lovely, and I'd just like to dream it all over again. Where's The Boy?"

THE END

Bibliography

Books

Baum's Complete Stamp Dealers Directory, containing a complete list of all dealers in the United States, together with the principal ones of Europe, and a list of philatelic publications. Compiled and published by Baum, Norris & Co. Syracuse: Hitchcock & Tucker, 1873. Preface by L. Frank Baum, William Norris, and Henry Clay Baum.

The Book of the Hamburgs, a brief treatise upon the mating, rearing, and management of the different varieties of Hamburgs. Hartford, Conn.: H. H. Stoddard, 1886.

Mother Goose in Prose. Illustrated by Maxfield Parrish. Chicago: Way & Williams, 1897.

By the Candelabra's Glare: Some Verse. Illustrated by W. W. Denslow and others. Chicago: Privately printed, 1898.
This edition of 99 copies was printed and bound by Baum. Many of the selections first appeared in the Aberdeen *Saturday Pioneer* and the Chicago *Sunday Times-Herald*. Several verses were reprinted in *Father Goose, His Book*.

Father Goose, His Book. Illustrated by W. W. Denslow. Chicago: George M. Hill, 1899.
The pages of verse were hand-lettered by Ralph Fletcher Seymour, assisted by Charles J. Costello.

The Army Alphabet. Illustrated by Harry Kennedy. Chicago and New York: George M. Hill, 1900.
The pages of verse were hand-lettered by Charles J. Costello.

The Art of Decorating Dry Goods Windows and Interiors. Chicago: Show Window Publishing, 1900.

The Navy Alphabet. Illustrated by Harry Kennedy. Chicago and New York: George M. Hill, 1900.
The pages of verse were hand-lettered by Ralph Fletcher Seymour, assisted by Charles J. Costello.

A New Wonderland, being the first account ever printed of the Beautiful Valley, and the wonderful adventures of its inhabitants. Illustrated by Frank Ver Beck. New York: R. H. Russell, 1900.

The Wonderful Wizard of Oz. Illustrated by W. W. Denslow. Chicago and New York: George M. Hill, 1900.
Baum had expected the first edition of 10,000 copies to be ready for presentation by May 1 and the official publication date to be May 15, his forty-fourth birthday. Publication was postponed until August 1, but copies were not in the stores until mid-September. The book was unavailable in 1902 when Hill went bankrupt and not available again until 1903 when Bobbs-Merrill reissued it as *The New Wizard of Oz*.

American Fairy Tales. Illustrated by Harry Kennedy, Ike Morgan, and N. P. Hall. Chicago and New York: George M. Hill, 1901.
Cover, title page, and decorative borders designed by Ralph Fletcher Seymour. These stories were serialized in the Chicago *Chronicle* and other newspapers, March 3 through May 19, 1901. "The Magic Bon-Bons" was republished in *Today's Magazine*, July 15, 1912.

Dot and Tot of Merryland. Illustrated by W. W. Denslow. Chicago and New York: George M. Hill, 1901.

The Master Key; An Electrical Fairy Tale, founded upon the Mysteries of Electricity and the Optimism of its Devotees. . . . Illustrated by Fanny Y. Cory. Indianapolis: Bowen-Merrill, 1901.

The Life and Adventures of Santa Claus. Illustrated by Mary Cowles Clark. Indianapolis: Bowen-Merrill, 1902.

The Enchanted Island of Yew Whereon Prince Marvel Encountered the Hi Ki of Twi and Other Surprising People. Illustrated by Fanny Y. Cory. Indianapolis: Bowen-Merrill, 1903.

The Maid of Athens. . . . [Chicago]: Privately printed, 1903.
  The scenario for an unproduced musical comedy by
  L. Frank Baum and Emerson Hough.

Prince Silverwings. [Chicago]: A. C. McClurg, 1903.
  The scenario for an unproduced "musical fairy spectacle in
  three acts and eight scenes" by L. Frank Baum and Edith
  Ogden Harrison, based upon her children's book of the
  same name, published in 1902.

*The Surprising Adventures of the Magical Monarch of Mo
  and His People.* Illustrated by Frank Ver Beck. Indianapolis: Bobbs-Merrill, 1903.
  A slightly revised version of *A New Wonderland*, with
  some new marginal illustrations. An entirely new edition
  illustrated by Evelyn Copelman appeared in 1947.

*The Marvelous Land of Oz being an account of the Further
  Adventures of the Scarecrow and Tin Woodman. . . .*
  Illustrated by John R. Neill. Chicago: Reilly & Brit-
  ton, 1904.

Queen Zixi of Ix; or the Story of the Magic Cloak. Illustrated
  by Frederick Richardson. New York: Century, 1905.
  Originally serialized in *St. Nicholas*, November 1904
  through October 1905.

The Woggle-Bug Book. Illustrated by Ike Morgan. Chicago: Reilly & Britton, 1905.

John Dough and the Cherub. Illustrated by John R. Neill.
  Chicago: Reilly & Britton, 1906.
  Serialized in the Washington *Star* and other newspapers
  October 14 through December 30, 1906.

*Father Goose's Year Book: Quaint Quacks and Feathered
  Shafts for Mature Children.* Illustrated by Walter J.
  Enright. Chicago: Reilly & Britton, 1907.
  Baum planned one other Father Goose book, "Father
  Goose's Party," but it was never published.

Ozma of Oz. . . . Illustrated by John R. Neill. Chicago:
  Reilly & Britton, 1907.

*Baum's American Fairy Tales; Stories of Astonishing Adven-
  tures of American Boys and Girls with the Fairies of
  their Native Land.* Illustrated by George Kerr. Indianapolis: Bobbs-Merrill, 1908.
  A rearranged and enlarged version of the 1901 edition
  with three new stories: "The Witchcraft of Mary-Marie,"
  "The Adventures of an Egg" (appeared in the Chicago
  Daily Tribune, March 30, 1902), and "The Ryl."

Dorothy and the Wizard in Oz. Illustrated by John R. Neill.
  Chicago: Reilly & Britton, 1908.
  The running title is *Little Dorothy and the Wizard in Oz*.

The Road to Oz. Illustrated by John R. Neill. Chicago:
  Reilly & Britton, 1909.

The Emerald City of Oz. Illustrated by John R. Neill.
  Chicago: Reilly & Britton, 1910.

*L. Frank Baum's Juvenile Speaker; Readings and Recitations
  in Prose and Verse, Humorous and Otherwise.* Illustrated by John R. Neill and Maginel Wright Enright.
  Chicago: Reilly & Britton, 1910.
  This collection of stories, poems, and illustrations from
  earlier books as well as some previously unpublished selections includes the play "Prince Marvel," which originally
  appeared in *Entertaining* (December 1909); this children's
  play was adapted from *The Enchanted Island of Yew* and
  written in the manner of the English toy theater. (One
  poem, "Mr. Doodle," was reprinted in the Los Angeles
  Daily Times, July 5, 1918.)

*Baum's Own Book for Children; Stories and Verse from the
  Famous Oz Books, Father Goose, His Book, Etc., Etc.
  With Many Hitherto Unpublished Selections.* Illustrat-
  ed by John R. Neill and Maginel Wright Enright.
  Chicago: Reilly & Britton, 1911.
  A reissue of *L. Frank Baum's Juvenile Speaker* with a new
  introduction.

The Daring Twins: A Story for Young Folk. Illustrated by
  Pauline M. Batchelder. Chicago: Reilly & Britton, 1911.

The Sea Fairies. Illustrated by John R. Neill. Chicago:
  Reilly & Britton, 1911.

Phoebe Daring: A Story for Young Folk. Illustrated by Joseph
  Pierre Nuyttens. Chicago: Reilly & Britton, 1912.
  Baum planned to continue the series and even began
  another addition to be called either "Phil Daring's Experiment" or "The Daring Experiment," but he and the publishers lost interest.

*Sky Island; being the Further Adventures of Trot and Cap'n
  Bill after Their Visit to the Sea Fairies.* Illustrated by
  John R. Neill. Chicago: Reilly & Britton, 1912.

The Little Wizard Series, six small volumes (*Jack Pumpkinhead and the Sawhorse, Little Dorothy and Toto, Ozma
  and the Little Wizard, The Cowardly Lion and the
  Hungry Tiger, The Scarecrow and the Tin Woodman*,
  and *Tiktok and the Nome King*). Illustrated by John
  R. Neill. Chicago: Reilly & Britton, 1913.

The Patchwork Girl of Oz. Illustrated by John R. Neill.
  Chicago: Reilly & Britton, 1913.

The Little Wizard Stories of Oz. Illustrated by John R.
  Neill. Chicago: Reilly & Britton, 1914.
  A reissue of *The Little Wizard Series* in one volume.

Tik-Tok of Oz. Illustrated by John R. Neill. Chicago: Reilly & Britton, 1914.
  This book was based on Baum's musical extravaganza of
  the previous year, *The Tik-Tok Man of Oz*.

The Scarecrow of Oz. Illustrated by John R. Neill. Chicago:
  Reilly & Britton, 1915.
  This book was based in part on the 1914 Oz Film Manufacturing Company motion picture *His Majesty, the Scarecrow of Oz* (released in 1915 as *The New Wizard of Oz*).

Reilly & Britton also issued in 1915 *The Oz-Toy Book*, with cutouts of the Oz characters by John R. Neill but no text.

Rinkitink in Oz. Illustrated by John R. Neill. Chicago: Reilly & Britton, 1916.

To keep his promise of an Oz book a year, Baum rewrote this non-Oz fairy tale by adding Oz characters and changing its title from *King Rinkitink* to *Rinkitink in Oz*; the original manuscript was written as early as 1905 but had not been published.

The Snuggle Tales, six small volumes (*Little Bun Rabbit*, *Once upon a Time*, *The Yellow Hen*, *The Magic Cloak*, *The Ginger-Bread Man*, and *Jack Pumpkinhead*). Illustrated by John R. Neill and Maginel Wright Enright. Chicago: Reilly & Britton, 1916 and 1917.

The first four volumes (from material in *L. Frank Baum's Juvenile Speaker*) came out in 1916, the last two in 1917. Reilly & Lee reissued the series as *Oz-Man Tales* in 1920.

Babes in Birdland. Illustrated by Maginel Wright Enright. Chicago: Reilly & Britton, 1917.

A reissue of the 1911 edition by "Laura Bancroft" but with Baum's name on the title page and cover and with a new introduction signed by him.

The Lost Princess of Oz. Illustrated by John R. Neill. Chicago: Reilly & Britton, 1917.

The Tin Woodman of Oz. . . . Illustrated by John R. Neill. Chicago: Reilly & Lee, 1918.

The Magic of Oz. . . . Illustrated by John R. Neill. Chicago: Reilly & Lee, 1919.

Glinda of Oz. . . . Illustrated by John R. Neill. Chicago: Reilly & Lee, 1920.

The next Oz book, *The Royal Book of Oz* (1921), is credited to Baum but was entirely the work of Ruth Plumly Thompson.

Our Landlady. Mitchell, S. D.: Friends of the Middle Border, 1941.

A selection of Baum's columns from the Aberdeen *Saturday Pioneer* (1890–1891).

Jaglon and the Tiger Fairies. Illustrated by Dale Ulrey. Chicago: Reilly & Lee, 1953.

A revision by Jack Snow of "The Story of Jaglon," the first of Baum's "Animal Fairy Tales" (*The Delineator*, January 1905). This was the first and only published volume in a projected series of book reprints of these stories.

The Musical Fantasies of L. Frank Baum. Illustrated by Dick Martin. Chicago: Wizard Press, 1958.

A collection of three projected but never produced plays by Baum with Emerson Hough ("The Maid of Athens" and "The King of Gee-Whiz") and with George Scarborough ("The Pipes o' Pan"). Also includes a monograph on Baum's theatrical ventures and checklist of his work compiled by Alla T. Ford and Dick Martin.

The Visitors from Oz. . . . Illustrated by Dick Martin. Chicago: Reilly & Lee, 1960.

Selection of stories from Baum's 1904–1905 "Queer Visitors from the Marvelous Land of Oz" comic page, heavily revised by Jean Kellogg.

The Uplift of Lucifer. . . . Los Angeles: Privately printed, 1963.

Compiled with an introduction by Manuel Weltman. Contains "The Uplift of Lucifer, or Raising Hell," a play written for the Uplifters in 1915; and "The Corrugated Giant," a monologue adapted from *Prince Mud-Turtle* by "Laura Bancroft." Illustrated with photographs and contemporary cartoons.

Animal Fairy Tales. Illustrated by Dick Martin. Chicago: International Wizard of Oz Club, 1969.

Introduction by Russell P. MacFall. Collection of all nine "Animal Fairy Tales" that originally appeared in *The Delineator* (January through September 1905), with illustrations by Charles Livingston Bull.

A Kidnapped Santa Claus. Illustrated by Richard Rosenblum. Indianapolis and New York: Bobbs-Merrill, 1969.

Introduction by Martin Williams. First separate book publication of a story which originally appeared in *The Delineator* (December 1904), with pictures by Frederick Richardson.

The Third Book of Oz. Edited by Martin Williams. Illustrated by Eric Shanower. Savannah, Ga.: Armstrong State College Press, 1986.

The first unabridged collection of the twenty-seven stories of the "Queer Visitors from the Marvelous Land of Oz" comic page (1904–1905), plus the text of *The Woggle-Bug Book* (1905).

Our Landlady. Lincoln and London: University of Nebraska Press, 1996.

Edited and annotated with an introduction by Nancy Tystad Koupal. First complete collection of the "Our Landlady" columns from the Aberdeen *Saturday Pioneer* (1890–1891). Illustrated with photographs.

"Johnson," "Molly Oodle," and "The Mystery of Bonita." Three unpublished novels, the manuscripts of which are now lost.

Anonymous and Pseudonymous Books

ANONYMOUS

The Last Egyptian; a Romance of the Nile. Illustrated by Francis P. Wightman. Philadelphia: Edward Stern, 1908.

FLOYD AKERS

The Boy Fortune Hunters in Alaska. Illustrated by Howard Heath. Chicago: Reilly & Britton, 1908.
> A reissue of *Sam Steele's Adventures on Land and Sea* by "Capt. Hugh Fitzgerald" (1906).

The Boy Fortune Hunters in Egypt. Illustrated by Emile A. Nelson. Chicago: Reilly & Britton, 1908.

The Boy Fortune Hunters in Panama. Illustrated by Howard Heath. Chicago: Reilly & Britton, 1908.
> A reissue of *Sam Steele's Adventures in Panama* by "Capt. Hugh Fitzgerald" (1907).

The Boy Fortune Hunters in China. Frontispiece by Emile A. Nelson. Chicago: Reilly & Britton, 1909.

The Boy Fortune Hunters in Yucatan. Frontispiece by George A. Rieman. Chicago: Reilly & Britton, 1910.

The Boy Fortune Hunters in the South Seas. Frontispiece by Emile A. Nelson. Chicago: Reilly & Britton, 1911.

LAURA BANCROFT

The Twinkle Tales, six small volumes (*Bandit Jim Crow*, *Mr. Woodchuck*, *Prairie-Dog Town*, *Prince Mud-Turtle*, *Sugar-Loaf Mountain*, and *Twinkle's Enchantment*). Illustrated by Maginel Wright Enright. Chicago: Reilly & Britton, 1906.

Policeman Bluejay. Illustrated by Maginel Wright Enright. Chicago: Reilly & Britton, 1907.
> Reissued as *Babes in Birdland* in 1911 and 1917, the last with a new introduction and Baum's name on the cover and title page.

Twinkle and Chubbins; Their Astonishing Adventures in Nature-Fairyland. Illustrated by Maginel Wright Enright. Chicago: Reilly & Britton, 1911.
> Reissue of *The Twinkle Tales* in one volume.

JOHN ESTES COOKE

Tamawaca Folks, Summer Comedy. [Chicago]: Tamawaca Press, 1907.
> "Tamawaca" is an anagram of Macatawa, where the Baums spent their summers. The pseudonym comes from John Esten Cooke, a popular Virginian novelist and historian.

CAPT. HUGH FITZGERALD

Sam Steele's Adventures on Land and Sea. Illustrated by Howard Heath. Chicago: Reilly & Britton, 1906.

Sam Steele's Adventures in Panama. Illustrated by Howard Heath. Chicago: Reilly & Britton, 1907.

SUZANNE METCALF

Annabel, A Novel for Young Folks. Illustrated by H. Putnam Hall. Chicago: Reilly & Britton, 1906.
> A second edition with a new frontispiece by Joseph Pierre Nuyttens appeared in 1912.

SCHUYLER STAUNTON

The Fate of a Crown. Illustrated by Glen C. Sheffer. Chicago: Reilly & Britton, 1905.
> The Philadelphia *North American* syndicated this adult novel with illustrations by John R. Neill, June 4 through August 6, 1905. The pseudonym came from Baum's deceased uncle Schuyler Stanton. Reissued in 1912 with a new frontispiece by Hazel Roberts.

Daughters of Destiny. Illustrated by Thomas Mitchell Peirce and Harold DeLay. Chicago: Reilly & Britton, 1906.
> Reissued in 1912 with a new frontispiece by Joseph Pierre Nuyttens.

EDITH VAN DYNE

Aunt Jane's Nieces. Illustrated by Emile A. Nelson. Chicago: Reilly & Britton, 1906.

Aunt Jane's Nieces Abroad. Illustrated by Emile A. Nelson. Chicago: Reilly & Britton, 1907.

Aunt Jane's Nieces at Millville. Frontispiece by Emile A. Nelson. Chicago: Reilly & Britton, 1908.

Aunt Jane's Nieces at Work. Frontispiece by Emile A. Nelson. Chicago: Reilly & Britton, 1909.

Aunt Jane's Nieces in Society. Frontispiece by Emile A. Nelson. Chicago: Reilly & Britton, 1910.

Aunt Jane's Nieces and Uncle John. Frontispiece by Emile A. Nelson. Chicago: Reilly & Britton, 1911.

The Flying Girl. Illustrated by Joseph Pierre Nuyttens. Chicago: Reilly & Britton, 1911.

Aunt Jane's Nieces on Vacation. Frontispiece by Emile A. Nelson. Chicago: Reilly & Britton, 1912.

The Flying Girl and Her Chum. Illustrated by Joseph Pierre Nuyttens. Chicago: Reilly & Britton, 1912.
> Baum began another addition to this series, "The Flying Girl's Brave Venture," for 1913, but it was never completed and never published.

Aunt Jane's Nieces on the Ranch. Unsigned frontispiece. Chicago: Reilly & Britton, 1913.

Aunt Jane's Nieces Out West. Frontispiece by James McCracken. Chicago: Reilly & Britton, 1914.

Aunt Jane's Nieces in the Red Cross. Frontispiece by Norman P. Hall. Chicago: Reilly & Britton, 1915.
> Reissued in 1918 with four additional chapters to reflect recent developments in World War I.

Mary Louise. Frontispiece by J. Allen St. John. Chicago: Reilly & Britton, 1916.

> Named for Baum's sister Mary Louise Brewster. At his publishers' suggestion, Baum abandoned the original story and wrote an entirely new one, which was published.

Mary Louise in the Country. Frontispiece by J. Allen St. John. Chicago: Reilly & Britton, 1916.

Mary Louise Solves a Mystery. Frontispiece by Anna B. Mueller. Chicago: Reilly & Britton, 1917.

Mary Louise and the Liberty Girls. Frontispiece by Alice Carsey. Chicago: Reilly & Britton, 1918.

> Reilly & Lee issued one other title in this series, *Mary Louise Adopts a Soldier* (1919), which Baum did not write; it may have been the work of his son Harry Neal Baum. The publishers hired Emma Speed Sampson to write three more *Mary Louise* books as "Edith Van Dyne" after Baum's death in 1919. She also did two *Josie O'Gorman* books for them, again as "Edith Van Dyne."

Published Songs

Louis F. Baum's Popular Songs as Sung with Immense Success in His Great 5 Act Irish Drama, Maid of Arran. New York: J. G. Hyde, 1882.

> A pamphlet containing lyrics and music (both by Baum) of six songs: "Waiting for the Tide to Turn," "Oona's Gift," "When O'Mara Is King Once Again," "A Rollicking Irish Boy," "A Pair of Blue Eyes," and "The Legend of Castle Arran."

The Wizard of Oz, a book of selections and ten pieces of sheet music published separately ("Poppy Song," "When We Get What's A'Comin' to Us," "The Traveler and the Pie," "The Scarecrow," "The Guardian of the Gate," "Love Is Love," "Just a Simple Girl from the Prairie," "When You Love, Love, Love," "It Happens Everyday," and "The Different Ways of Making Love"). Lyrics by Baum. Music by Paul Tietjens. New York and Chicago: M. Witmark & Sons, 1902.

> Nathaniel D. Mann composed the music for the last two songs. Another number, "Niccolo's Piccolo," is now attributed to Baum and Tietjens and published by Green Tiger Press, San Diego, 1999.

Down Among the Marshes: The Alligator Song. Words and music by Baum. New York and Chicago: M. Witmark & Sons, 1903.

> Originally written for one of Baum's annual vaudeville nights at Macatawa Park, Michigan, this song was also intended to be interpolated into the unproduced musical extravaganza *Prince Silverwings*, 1903.

What Did the Woggle-Bug Say? Lyrics by Baum. Music by Paul Tietjens. Chicago: Reilly & Britton, 1904.

The Woggle-Bug, a book of selections and twelve pieces of sheet music published separately ("The Sandman Is Near," "Hobgoblins," "The Doll and the Jumping Jack," "There's a Lady Bug A'Waitin' for Me," "Patty Cake, Patty Cake, Baker's Man," "Equine Paradox," "Sweet Matilda," "Soldiers," "To the Victor Belongs the Spoils," "The Household Brigade," "My Little Maid of Oz," and "H. M. Woggle-Bug, T. E."). Lyrics by Baum. Music by Frederic Chapin. New York and Chicago: M. Witmark & Sons, 1905.

> "Patty Cake, Patty Cake, Baker's Man" was originally written for the unproduced musical extravaganza *Prince Silverwings*, 1903; the words for "Soldiers" were actually written by Chapin and those for "Sweet Matilda" by Arthur Gillespie, both of which songs having been first published in 1901.

The Tik-Tok Man of Oz, a book of selections and fourteen pieces of sheet music published separately ("The Magnet of Love," "When in Trouble Come to Papa," "The Waltz Scream," "Dear Old Hank," "So Do I," "The Clockwork Man," "Oh My Bow," "Ask the Flowers to Tell You," "Rainbow Bride," "Just for Fun," "The Army of Oogaboo," "Work, Lads, Work," "An Apple's the Cause of It All," and "Folly"). Lyrics by Baum. Music by Louis F. Gottschalk. New York and Detroit: Jerome H. Remick, 1913.

> "When in Trouble Come to Papa" was originally written for *The Girl from Oz*, 1909. In 1914, M. Witmark & Sons published Gottschalk's "Gloria's Dream Waltz," a musical number (without lyrics) from the original score for the Oz Film Manufacturing Company motion picture *The Patchwork Girl of Oz*.

Susan Doozan. Lyrics by Baum. Music by Byron Gay. Los Angeles: Cooper's Melody Shop, 1920.

> Originally written for *The Uplifters' Minstrels*, 1916.

Produced and Projected Plays

The Mackrummins (a comedy-drama in three acts) by "Louis F. Baum," never produced and possibly never completed, copyrighted Richburg, New York, February 11, 1882.

The Maid of Arran (an Irish idyll in five acts), written with music and lyrics by "Louis F. Baum," opened at Weiting Opera House, Syracuse, New York, May 15, 1882.

Matches (a comedy in three acts) by "Louis F. Baum," performed at Brown's Opera House, Richburg, New York, June 1, 1882.

Kilmourne, or O'Connor's Dream (an Irish drama), written by "Louis F. Baum," performed by the Young Men's Dramatic Club at the Weiting Opera House, Syracuse, New York, April 4, 1883.

The Queen of Killarney (an Irish drama), never produced and possibly never completed, c. 1885.

King Midas (a comic opera), book and lyrics by Baum, music by Paul Tietjens, never produced and possibly never completed, 1901.

The Octopus; or the Title Trust (a comic opera), book and lyrics by Baum, music by Paul Tietjens, never produced and possibly never completed, 1901.

Two numbers ("Love Is Love" and "The Traveler and the Pie") written for this play were later interpolated into the 1902 *Wizard of Oz* musical extravaganza.

The Wonderful Wizard of Oz, book and lyrics by Baum, music by Paul Tietjens, September 18, 1901.

The Wizard of Oz (a musical extravaganza), book and lyrics by Baum, music by Paul Tietjens, staged by Julian Mitchell, opened at the Grand Opera House, Chicago, June 16, 1902.

Baum wrote two versions of this libretto, based upon a scenario provided by Mitchell. Glen Macdonough worked on the final script.

Montezuma (a comic opera in three acts), book and lyrics by Baum and Emerson Hough, music by Nathaniel D. Mann, never produced and possibly never completed, November 1902.

The Maid of Athens (a musical comedy in three acts), a musical scenario by Baum and Emerson Hough, never produced, November 1903.

Reprinted in Alla T. Ford and Dick Martin, *The Musical Fantasies of L. Frank Baum* (1958). Also known as *Spartacus*.

Prince Silverwings (a three-act musical fairy tale), scenario by Baum and Edith Ogden Harrison, music by Paul Tietjens, never produced, October 1903.

Based upon Mrs. Harrison's book *Prince Silverwings* (1902). "Down Among the Marshes," a song with lyrics and music by Baum, was to be part of the score. In 1909, it was announced that the first production of a projected Children's Theatre in New York was to be *Prince Silverwings*; as late as 1916, Mrs. Harrison was trying to secure a production of this play, as either a musical written by Dr. Hugo Felix or a motion picture by the Essanay Film Manufacturing Company.

King Jonah XIII (a comic opera in two acts), book and lyrics by Baum, music by Nathaniel D. Mann, never produced, September 1903.

The Whatnexters, book and lyrics by Baum and Isadore Witmark, never completed, c. 1903.

Father Goose, book and lyrics by Baum, music by Paul Tietjens, never completed, August 1904.

Baum suggested that some *Father Goose* jingles be interpolated into his script of *The Wonderful Wizard of Oz* (1901).

The Pagan Potentate, book and lyrics by Baum, music by Paul Tietjens, never completed, c. 1904.

The King of Gee-Whiz (a musical extravaganza in three acts), a scenario and general synopsis by Baum and Emerson Hough, never completed, 1905.

Reprinted in Alla T. Ford and Dick Martin, *The Musical Fantasies of L. Frank Baum* (1958). Hough cobbled together elements from this scenario for a children's book of the same name published by Bobbs-Merrill in 1906.

The Son of the Sun (a musical extravaganza in three acts), book and lyrics by Baum and Emerson Hough, music by Nathaniel D. Mann, never produced, 1905.

A revision of *Montezuma*.

The Woggle-Bug (a musical extravaganza in three acts), book and lyrics by Baum, music by Frederic Chapin, staged by Frank Smithson, opened at the Garrick Theater, Chicago, June 19, 1905.

A dramatization of *The Marvelous Land of Oz* (1904).

(Untitled musical play set in Egypt), never produced and possibly never completed, January 1906.

Montgomery and Stone suggested this play to Baum just as he was heading for Egypt and Europe.

Down Missouri Way, never produced and possibly never completed, c. 1907.

Our Mary, never produced and possibly never completed, c. 1907.

The Fairylogue and Radio-Plays (a slide and motion picture lecture), written, produced, and performed by Baum, music by Nathaniel D. Mann, filmed at the Selig Studios, Chicago, opened at St. Cecilia Hall, Grand Rapids, Michigan, September 24, 1908.

Selig produced four one-reelers based on Baum's books: *The Wonderful Wizard of Oz*, released March 24, 1910; *Dorothy and the Scarecrow in Oz*, April 14, 1910; *The Land of Oz*, May 19, 1910; and *John Dough and the Cherub*, December 19, 1910. Baum did not write the scenarios for these silent movies.

The Koran of the Prophet (a musical extravaganza in two acts), never produced and possibly never completed, February 23, 1909.

The Rainbow's Daughter; Or The Magnet of Love (a musical extravaganza in two acts), a scenario, music by Manuel Klein, scenic effects by Arthur Voetglin, February 23, 1909.

Ozma of Oz (a musical extravaganza in two acts), a scenario by L. Frank Baum and Manuel Klein, music by Manuel Klein, scenic effects by Arthur Voetglin, never produced, c. March 1909.

A revision of *The Rainbow's Daughter* (1909).

Ozma of Oz (a musical extravaganza in two acts), book and lyrics by L. Frank Baum, music by Manuel Klein, scenic effects by Arthur Voetglin, never produced, April 15, 1909.

Peter and Paul (an opera), book and lyrics by Baum, music by Arthur Pryor, never produced and possibly never completed, 1909.

The Pipes o' Pan (a musical comedy in three acts), book and lyrics by Baum and George Scarborough, music by Paul Tietjens, never produced and possibly never completed, March 31, 1909.

Probably based on *King Midas* (1901) and *The Pagan Potentate* (c. 1904). Only the first act was copyrighted and then reprinted in Alla T. Ford and Dick Martin's *The Musical Fantasies of L. Frank Baum* (1958).

Mortal for an Hour (a children's play), benefit performance for Fresh Air Fund of Chicago Commons, Macatawa, Michigan, 1908.

Reprinted as "The Fairy Prince" in *Entertaining* (December 1908) and as "Prince Marvel" in *L. Frank Baum's Juvenile Speaker* (1910).

The Girl from Oz (a musical comedy in two acts), never produced, 1909.

Years later Frank Joslyn Baum rewrote this play as a radio operetta.

The Pea-Green Poodle, never produced, c. 1910.

Based on the "Animal Fairy Tale" (*The Delineator*, 1905) of the same name.

The Clock Shop, never produced, c. 1910.

The Girl of Tomorrow (a musical comedy), never produced and possibly never completed, 1912.

Possibly a reworking of *The Girl from Oz* (1909).

The Tik-Tok Man of Oz (a fairyland extravaganza in three acts), book and lyrics by Baum, music by Louis F. Gottschalk, staged by Frank Stammers, opened at the Majestic Theatre, Los Angeles, March 31, 1913.

The produced version of *Ozma of Oz* (1909).

The Patchwork Girl of Oz (a musical play for children), scenario by Baum, music by Louis F. Gottschalk, 1913.

King Bud of Noland, or The Magic Cloak (a musical play for children), scenario by Baum, music by Louis F. Gottschalk, 1913.

Stagecraft, or the Adventures of a Strictly Moral Man, book and lyrics by Baum, music by Louis F. Gottschalk, produced by the Uplifters at the Los Angeles Athletic Club, January 14, 1914.

The Patchwork Girl of Oz, a motion picture scenario by Baum, music by Louis F. Gottschalk, produced and filmed by the Oz Film Manufacturing Company, released by Paramount Pictures, September 28, 1914.

The Magic Cloak of Oz, a motion picture scenario by Baum, produced and filmed by the Oz Film Manufacturing Company, 1914.

Based on *Queen Zixi of Ix* (1905). Released by the National Film Corporation August 1917, and American Pictures Corporation issued a shortened version, c. 1920.

High Jinks, book and lyrics by Baum, music by Louis F. Gottschalk, produced by the Uplifters for their first annual outing, Del Mar, California, October 24, 1914.

The Last Egyptian, a motion picture scenario by Baum, music by Louis F. Gottschalk, produced and filmed by the Oz Film Manufacturing Company, released by Paramount Pictures, December 7, 1914.

Based upon Baum's 1908 anonymous novel of the same name.

His Majesty, the Scarecrow of Oz (released as *The New Wizard of Oz*), a motion picture scenario by Baum, produced and filmed by the Oz Film Manufacturing Company, released by Alliance Film Company, March 1915.

Violet's Dreams: four one-reel comedies: *The Box of Robbers* (released as *The Box of Bandits*), *A Country Circus*, *The Magic Bon-Bons*, and *The Jungle* (released as *In Dreamy Jungleland*), produced and filmed by the Oz Film Manufacturing Company, 1914.

The first three released by Universal Victor and the last by Universal Rex on respectively August 27, September 10, and October 22, 1915, and February 1, 1916.

The Uplift of Lucifer, or Raising Hell ("an allegorical squazosh"), book and lyrics by Baum, music by Louis F. Gottschalk, staged by Dave Hartford, produced by the Uplifters for their second annual outing, Santa Barbara, California, October 23, 1915.

Revived on "L. Frank Baum Night," staged by Max Polluck, with Hal Roach as Demon Rum, January 27, 1920.

The Birth of the New Year (holiday skit), staged by George Towle, Los Angeles Athletic Club, December 31, 1915, to January 1, 1916.

Blackbird Cottages (an original blackface comedy), book and lyrics by Baum, music by Louis F. Gottschalk, staged by Willis Marks, produced by the Uplifters for their third annual outing, Del Mar, California, October 28, 1916.

Snow White (a musical comedy), book and lyrics by Baum, never completed, December 1916.

Based on a London Christmas "pantomime," with sets and costumes to be designed by Maxfield Parrish.

The Orpheus Road Show ("a paraphrastic compendium of mirth"), book and lyrics by Baum, music and staged by Louis F. Gottschalk, produced by the Uplifters for their fourth annual outing, Coronado Beach, California, October 27, 1917.

Introductions and Other Contributions

"Every Man his own Printer." New York: Adams Press, 1873.

A brochure advertising the Young American Printing Press and containing a letter by Baum to Joseph Watson, a sales agent in Boston, dated February 4, 1873.

Holton, M. Adelaide, ed. *The Holton Primer.* "Lights of Literature Series." Chicago: Rand McNally, 1901.

Cover and endpapers designed by Ralph Fletcher Seymour. Reprints the poem "Where Do the Chickens Go at Night?" from *Father Goose, His Book* (1899). The editor was the supervisor of the primary school of Minneapolis.

The Christmas Stocking Series, six small volumes of nursery rhymes and stories (*The Night Before Christmas, Cinderella and Sleeping Beauty, Animal A. B. C.—A Child's Visit to the Zoo, The Story of Little Black Sambo, Fairy Tales from Grimm,* and *Fairy Tales from Andersen*). Illustrated anonymously. Chicago: Reilly & Britton, 1905–1906.

Each book contains the same introduction by Baum. In 1911, *The Story [sic] of Peter Rabbit,* illustrated by John R. Neill after Beatrix Potter, replaced *Animal A. B. C.—a Child's Visit to the Zoo.*

Baum, Maud Gage. *In Other Lands Than Ours.* Chicago: Privately printed, 1907.

With preface and photographs by Baum; he also edited the text.

Madison, Janet, ed. *Sweethearts Always.* Illustrated by Fred Manning. Chicago: Reilly & Britton, 1907.

Box and jacket designed by John R. Neill. Reprints Baum's poem "Her Answer" from *By the Candelabra's Glare* (1898).

Nesbitt, Wilbur D., ed. *The Loving Cup.* Chicago: P. F. Volland, 1909.

Contains Baum's poem "Smile."

Lefferts, Sara T., ed. *Land of Play.* Illustrated by M. L. Kirk and Florence England Nosworthy. New York: Cupples & Leon, 1911.

Reprints Baum's introduction (slightly abridged) to *The Christmas Stocking Series* (1905–1906). An abridged version of this book was reprinted as *The House of Play.*

Rice, Wallace and Frances, eds. *The Humbler Poets (Second Series); A Collection of Newspaper and Periodical Verse—1885–1910.* Chicago: A. C. McClurg, 1911.

Reprints Baum's poems "Father Goose" and "Captain Bing" from *Father Goose, His Book* (1899).

The University Society and the After School Club of America, eds. *Famous Tales and Laughter Stories.* Vol. 1. New York: University Society, 1912.

Reprints Baum's short story "Juggerjook" (*St. Nicholas,* December 1910). In 1911, the University Society reprinted this anthology as part of its nine-volume *Boy's and Girl's Bookshelf* and listed Baum's name on the title page as one of its editors.

Skinner, Ada M., ed. *Little Folks' Christmas Stories and Plays.* Chicago: Rand McNally, 1915.

Reprints Baum's short story "Kidnapping Santa Claus" (originally "A Kidnapped Santa Claus," *The Delineator,* December 1904).

The Uplifters. *Uplifters Hymnal.* Los Angeles: Privately printed, 1915.

Includes "So Do I" from *The Tik-Tok Man of Oz* (1913).

The Uplifters. *Songs of Spring.* Los Angeles: Privately printed, 1917.

Edited by Baum. A pamphlet of poems originally delivered at "The Uplifters' Spring Poets' Dinner," 1914, 1915, and 1916, containing an introduction and five poems by Baum: "The Massacre," "The Orchestra," "Safety First," "Claudius Raymond," and "An Uplifter's Song of the Shirt." There are several references to Baum in other contributions as well as "A Toast to L. Frank Baum" by Harry Crouch.

The Uplifters. *The Uplifter's Hymnal.* "Silver Anniversary Edition." Los Angeles: Privately printed, 1938.

Contains several songs by Baum from various Uplifters and other theatrical productions. A selection of these songs ("Never Strike Your Father, Boy," "We're Having a Hell of a Time," "Susan Doozan," and "Apple Pie") and Baum's "Uplifters' Platform" were reprinted by Alla T. Ford in the pamphlet *The High-Jinks of L. Frank Baum. . . .* Chicago: Wizard Press, 1959.

Magazine and Newspaper Work

Editor, *The Rose Lawn Home Journal,* October 20? and November 20, 1870; July 1, August 1, and September 1, 1871.

Editor, *The Stamp Collector,* March?, June?, September 1872 and January 1873.

Editor, with Thomas G. Alford Jr., *The Empire,* 1873?

"Another Reply to C. B" (letter), *The Cultivator & Country Gentleman*, June 26, 1879.

Editor, *The Poultry Record*, March through December 1880.

"The Poultry Yard" (column), *New York Farmer and Dairyman*, January through April 1881.

"Hamburgs" (article), *The Poultry World*, July through November 1882.

 Reprinted as *The Book of the Hamburgs* (Hartford, Conn.: H. H. Stoddard, 1886).

"Mr. Baum Replies to Mr. Rutledge" (letter), *The New York Dramatic Mirror*, July 22, 1882.

"The Descent of Mann" (poem), unidentified Syracuse newspaper, 1880s.

"A Russian Wedding" (article), Aberdeen (S.D.) *Daily News*, July 24, 1889.

 Reprinted in *Dakota Ruralist*, July 27, 1889.

"Why?" (poem), Aberdeen (S.D.) *Daily News*, July 25, 1889.

"The Kids and the Goose Eggs" (poem), Aberdeen (S.D.) *Daily News*, July 26, 1889.

"How Shall We Vote?" (letter), Aberdeen (S.D.) *Daily News*, September 12, 1889.

"A Last Appeal" (letter), Aberdeen (S.D.) *Daily News*, October 1, 1889.

"Big Bargains in Every Style of Hanging Lamps!" (poem), Aberdeen (S.D.) *Daily News*, October 28, 1889.

 Advertisement for Baum's Bazaar. It may be assumed that Baum wrote all of the advertisements for this store that appeared in the Aberdeen *Daily News*, *Republican*, and other local newspapers between September 22, 1888 and December 31, 1889.

Editor, Aberdeen (S.D.) *Saturday Pioneer*, January 25, 1890, through April 4, 1891.

Editor, *The Western Investor*, August through November 1890.

"They Played a New Hamlet," Chicago *Sunday Times-Herald*, April 28, 1895.

"A Cold Day on the Railroad," Chicago *Sunday Times-Herald*, May 26, 1895.

"La Reine est Mort [*sic*]—Vive La Reine" (poem), Chicago *Sunday Times-Herald*, June 23, 1895.

 Reprinted in *By the Candelabra's Glare* (Chicago: Privately printed, 1898).

"Farmer Benson on the Motocycle" (poem), Chicago *Sunday Times-Herald*, August 4, 1895.

 Reprinted in *By the Candelabra's Glare* (1898).

"Who Called 'Perry'?," Chicago *Sunday Times-Herald*, January 19, 1896.

"Yesterday at the Exposition," Chicago *Sunday Times-Herald*, February 2, 1896.

"How History Is Made" (poem), Chicago *Sunday Times-Herald*, May 17, 1896.

"Two Pictures" (poem), Chicago *Sunday Times-Herald*, May 17, 1896.

"The Latest in Magic" (poem), Chicago *Sunday Times-Herald*, May 31, 1896.

"Right at Last" (poem), Chicago *Sunday Times-Herald*, June 14, 1896.

 Reprinted in *By the Candelabra's Glare* (1898).

"When McKinley Gets the Chair " (poem), Chicago *Sunday Times-Herald*, July 12, 1896.

"My Ruby Wedding Ring," copyrighted by the Bacheller Syndicate, October 12, 1896.

 Recopyrighted by the American Press Association, January 16, 1903.

"A Sonnet to My Lady's Eye" (poem), Chicago *Sunday Times-Herald*, October 25, 1896.

 Reprinted in *By the Candelabra's Glare* (1898).

"The Extravagance of Dan," *The National Magazine*, May 1897.

"How Scroggins Won the Reward," copyrighted by the Bacheller Syndicate, May 5, 1897.

 It is not known whether this story was ever published.

"The Return of Dick Weemins," *The National Magazine*, July 1897.

"The Suicide of Kiaros," *The White Elephant*, September 1897.

Editor, *The Show Window*, November 1897 through October 1900.

"A Shadow Cast Before," *The Philosopher*, December 1897.

"The Mating Day," *Short Stories*, September 1898.

"Aunt Hulda's Good Time," *The Youth's Companion*, October 26, 1899.

"Some Commercial Drawings and a Sketch of Charles Costello Designer" (article), *Arts for America*, November 1899.

"Dear Den . . . " (poem), Syarcuse *Sunday Herald*, November 19, 1899.

"The Loveridge Burglary," *Short Stories*, January 1900.

"The Real 'Mr. Dooley' " (article), *The Home Magazine* (of New York), January 1900.

"To the Grand Army of the Republic, August 1900" (poem), Chicago *Sunday Times-Herald*, August 26, 1900.

"The Bad Man," *The Home Magazine* (of New York), February 1901.

"American Fairy Tales," Serialized in the *Chicago Chronicle* and other newspapers, March 3 through May 19, 1901.

"Little Cripples Royally Feasted" (article), Chicago *American*, November 29, 1901.

"An Easter Egg," *The Sunny South*, supplement to the Atlanta *Constitution*, March 29, 1902.

> An abridgment of this story appeared as "The Strange Adventures of an Easter Egg" (Chicago *Tribune*, March 30, 1902). It was reprinted in *Baum's American Fairy Tales* (1908).

"Mr. Baum on Song Records" (letter), Chicago *Sunday Record-Herald*, May 31, 1902.

"What Children Want" (article), Chicago *Evening Post*, November 29, 1902.

"Frank Baum on Father Goose" (verse), Quincy (Ill.) *Herald*, December 3, 1902.

Letter to James O'Donnell Bennett, "Music and the Drama" (column), Chicago *Record-Herald,* February 3, 1903.

"Mr. Baum to the Public" (letter), Chicago *Tribune*, June 26, 1904.

"Queer Visitors from the Marvelous Land of Oz," syndicated by the Philadelphia *North American*, August 28, 1904, through February 26, 1905.

> A selection of these stories was considerably revised by Jean Kellogg and published as *The Visitors from Oz* (Chicago: Reilly & Lee, 1961); the stories as written by Baum along with *The Woggle-Book* (1905) appeared as *The Third Book of Oz* (Savannah, Ga.: Armstrong State College Press, 1986).

"Queen Zixi of Ix, or The Story of the Magic Cloak," *St. Nicholas*, November 1904 through October 1905.

> Reprinted in book form, New York: Century, 1905.

"A Kidnapped Santa Claus," *The Delineator,* December 1904.

> Reprinted in book form, Indianapolis: Bobbs-Merrill, 1969.

"Animal Fairy Tales," *The Delineator*, January through September 1905.

> Reprinted in book form, Escanaba, Mich.: International Wizard of Oz Club, 1969.

"In Memoriam" (poem), San Diego *Union and Daily Bee*, February 15, 1905.

"Coronado: The Queen of Fairyland" (poem), San Diego *Union and Daily Bee*, March 5, 1905.

> Reprinted in *The* (San Diego High School) *Russ*, June 1905.

"Nelebel's Fairyland," *The* (San Diego High School) *Russ*, June 1905.

"Fairy Tales on the Stage" (article), Chicago *Sunday Record-Herald*, June 18, 1905.

"Jack Burgitt's Honor," copyright by the American Press Association, August 1, 1905.

> It is not known whether this story was ever published.

"L. Frank Baum's Witty Presentation Speech," San Diego *Union and Daily Bee*, February 10, 1907.

"To Macatawa, a Rhapsody" (poem), Grand Rapids (Mich.) *Sunday Herald*, September 1, 1907.

"Well, Come!" (poem), San Diego *Union and Daily Bee*, April 16, 1908.

"Famous Author Once Lived Here" (letter), Aberdeen (S. D.) *Daily American*, June 22, 1909.

"Modern Fairy Tales" (article), *The Advance*, August 19, 1909.

"The Fairy Prince" (play), *Entertaining*, December 1909.

> Reprinted as "Prince Marvel" in *L. Frank Baum's Juvenile Speaker* (1910).

"Juggerjook," *St. Nicholas*, December 1910.

"The Man Fairy," *The Ladies' World*, December 1910.

"The Tramp and the Baby," *The Ladies' World*, October 1911.

"Bessie's Fairy Tale," *The Ladies' World*, December 1911.

"Boys' and Girls' Paper," Sunday newspaper supplement syndicated by the Philadelphia *North American*, August 11, 1912, through January 3, 1915.

> Reprinted books by "Floyd Akers," "Suzanne Metcalf," and "Edith Van Dyne" as well as *The Daring Twins* (1911).

"Aunt 'Phroney's Boy," *St. Nicholas*, December 1912.

> Revised version of "Aunt Hulda's Good Time" (*The Youth's Companion*, October 26, 1899).

"Lived Here Now Famous" (letter), Aberdeen (S.D.) *Daily American*, June 15, 1913.

"Still in Moving Picture Business" (letter), Hollywood *Citizen*, January 22, 1915.

["My Hobby"] (poem), *The* (Los Angeles Athletic Club) *Mercury*, July 1, 1915.

" 'Our Hollywood'—" (article), Hollywood *Citizen*, December 31, 1915.

" 'Julius Caesar,' An Appreciation of the Hollywood Production" (article), *The* (Los Angeles Athletic Club) *Mercury*, June 14, 1916.

"This Is Paradise of Flower Lovers," Los Angeles *Daily Times*, November 7, 1916.

> Reprinted slightly condensed as "Secret of Prize Blossoms" in the Los Angeles *Times*, "Annual Midwinter Number," January 1, 1917.

"Suggested by Frank Baum" (letter), *The* (Los Angeles Athletic Club) *Mercury*, April 15, 1917.

"What Are We Goin' To Do With 'Em" (poem), *The* (Los Angeles Athletic Club) *Mercury,* September 6, 1917.

"Genealogical Gleanings" (article), *The* (Los Angeles Athletic Club) *Mercury*, January 3, 1918.

"The Yellow Ryl," *A Child's Garden*, August and September 1926.

"My dear Mrs. Boothe . . ." (poem), *The Baum Bugle*, October 1957.

"The Tiger's Eye," *The American Book Collector*, December 1962.

"The Runaway Shadows," *The Baum Bugle*, April 1962.

"The King Who Changed His Mind," *The Baum Bugle*, Spring 1963.

"Our Den once made a picture . . ." (poem), *The Baum Bugle*, Spring 1964.

"Christmas Comin'!" (poem), *The Baum Bugle*, Christmas 1972.

"The Man with the Red Shirt," *The Baum Bugle*, Spring 1973.

"The Littlest Giant, an 'Oz' Story," *The Baum Bugle*, Spring 1975.

"Gee, there's been a lot of fuss . . ." (poem), *The Baum Bugle*, Summer 1981.

"The Diamondback," *The Baum Bugle*, Spring 1982.

"To the Littlefield Baby" (poem), *The Baum Bugle*, Spring 1989.

About L. Frank Baum

Algeo, John. "A Notable Theosophist: L. Frank Baum." *The American Theosophist*, August–September 1986.

The American Book Collector, December 1962.
    Special L. Frank Baum number.

Baughman Roland. "L. Frank Baum and the 'Oz Books.'" *Columbia Library Columns*, May 1955.

Baum, Frank J. "The Oz Film Co." *Films in Review*, August–September 1956.

Baum, Frank Joslyn, and Russell P. MacFall. *To Please a Child*. Chicago: Reilly & Lee, 1961.

The Baum Bugle, June 1957–current. Published by International Wizard of Oz Club.

Carpenter, Angelica Shirley and Jean Shirley. *L. Frank Baum: The Royal Historian of Oz*. Minneapolis: Lerner, 1992.

Cech, John, ed. *Dictionary of Literary Biography: American Writers for Children, 1900–1960*. Vol. 22. Detroit: Gale Research, 1983.

Gage, Helen Leslie. "L. Frank Baum: An Inside Introduction to the Public." *The Dakotan*, January, February, March 1903.

Gardner, Martin. "The Royal Historian of Oz." *Fantasy and Science Fiction*, January and February 1955.

Hampsten, Elizabeth, ed. *To All Enquiring Friends: Letters, Diaries and Essays in North Dakota 1880–1910*. Grand Forks, N.D.: University of North Dakota, 1979.

"How the Wizard of Oz Spends His Vacation." Grand Rapids (Mich.) *Sunday Herald*, August 18, 1907.

Jones, Vernon H. "The Oz Parade." *New Orleans Review*, Fall 1973.

Kelly, Fred C. "Royal Historian of Oz." *Michigan Alumnus Quarterly Review*, May 23, 1953.

Kessler, D. E. "L. Frank Baum and His New Plays." *Theatre Magazine*, August 1909.

"L. Frank Baum Is 'Broke,' He Says." New York *Morning Telegraph*, June 5, 1911.

MacDougall, Walt. "L. Frank Baum Studied by MacDougall." St. Louis *Dispatch*, July 30, 1904.

Mannix, Daniel P. "The Father of the Wizard of Oz." *American Heritage*, December 1964.

Potter, Jeanne O. "The Man Who Invented Oz." *Los Angeles Times Sunday Magazine*, August 13, 1939.

Seymour, Ralph Fletcher. *Some Went This Way*. Chicago: Privately printed, 1945.

Snow, Jack. *Who's Who in Oz*. Chicago: Reilly & Lee, 1954.

Tietjens, Eunice. *The World at My Shoulder*. New York: Macmillan, 1938.

Torrey, Edwin C. *Early Days in Dakota*. Minneapolis: Parnham Printing & Stationery, 1925.

Vidal, Gore. "The Wizard of the 'Wizard.'" *The New York Review of Books*, September 29, 1977.

Wing, W. E. "From 'Oz,' the Magic City." *New York Dramatic Mirror*, October 7, 1914.

Worthington, J. E. "Mac-a-ta-wa, the Idyllic." Grand Rapids (Mich.) *Sunday Herald*, September 1, 1907.

About Baum's Work

Abrahm, Paul M., and Stuart Kenter. "Tik-Tok and the Three Laws of Robotics." *Science Fiction Studies*, March 1978.

Algeo, John. "*The Wizard of Oz*: The Perilous Journey." *The American Theosophist*, October 1986.
    A slightly revised version of this article appeared in *The Quest*, Summer 1993.

Attebery, Brian. *The Fantasy Tradition in American Literature*. Bloomington: Indiana University Press, 1980.

Averell, Thomas Fox. "Oz and Kansas Culture." *Kansas History*, Spring 1989.

Barasch, Marc. "The Healing Road to Oz." *Yoga Journal*, November/December 1991.

Baum, Frank J. "Why the Wizard of Oz Keeps On Selling." *Writer's Digest*, December 1952.

The Baum Bugle, June 1957–current. Published by International Wizard of Oz Club.

Beckwith, Osmond. "The Oddness of Oz." *Kulchur*, Fall 1961.

Bewley, Marius. "Oz Country." *The New York Review of Books*, December 3, 1964.
    A revision of this study, "The Land of Oz: America's

Great Good Place," appears in Bewley's *Masks and Mirrors* (New York: Atheneum, 1970).

Bingham, Jane, ed. *Writers for Children*. New York: Scribner's, 1988.

Bolger, Ray. "A Lesson from Oz." *Guideposts*, March 1982.

Bradbury, Ray. "Two Baumy Promenades Along the Yellow Brick Road." *Los Angeles Times Book Review*, October 9, 1977.

Brink, Carol Ryrie. "Some Forgotten Children's Books." *South Dakota Library Bulletin*, April–June 1948.

Brotman, Jordan. "A Late Wanderer in Oz." *Chicago Review*, December 1965.
　Reprinted in *Only Connect*, edited by Sheila Egoff and others (New York: Oxford University Press, 1965).

Butts, Dennis, ed. *Stories and Society*. New York: St. Martin's Press, 1992.
　Includes Mark I. West's "The Dorothys of Oz: A Heroine's Unmaking."

Callary, Edward, ed. *From Oz to the Onion Patch*. DeKalb, Ill.: North Central Name Society, 1986.

Cath, Stanley H., and Claire Cath. "On the Other Side of Oz: Psychoanalytic Aspects of Fairy Tales." *Psychoanalytic Study of the Child,* Vol. 33 (1978).

Culver, Stuart. "Growing Up in Oz." *American Literary History*, Winter 1992.

———. "What Mannikins Want: *The Wonderful Wizard of Oz* and *The Art of Decorating Dry Goods Windows and Interiors*." *Representations*, Winter 1988.

Dervin, Daniel. "Over the Rainbow and Under the Twister: A Drama of the Girl's Passage Through the Phallic Phase." *Bulletin of the Menninger Clinic*, January 1978.

Devlin, Mary, "The Great Cosmic Fairy Tale." *Gnosis Magazine,* Fall 1996.

Downing, David C. "Waiting for Godoz: A Post-Nasal Deconstruction of *The Wizard of Oz*." *Christianity & Literature*, Winter 1984.

Eager, Edward. "A Father's Minority Report." *The Horn Book*, March 1948.

Erisman, Fred. "L. Frank Baum and the Progressive Dilemma." *American Quarterly*, Fall 1968.

Eyles, Allen. *The World of Oz*. Tucson: HPBooks, 1985.

Field, Hana S., "Triumph and Tragedy on the Yellow Brick Road: Censorship of *The Wizard of Oz* in America," *The Concord Review*, Fall 1999.

Franson, J. Karl. "From Vanity Fair to Emerald City: Baum's Debt to Bunyan." *Children's Literature*, Vol. 23 (1995).

Gannon, Susan R., and Ruth Anne Thompson, eds. *Proceedings of the Thirteenth Conference of the Children's*

Literature Association. Kansas City: University of Missouri, 1988.

Gardner, Martin. "A Child's Garden of Bewilderment." *Saturday Review,* July 17, 1965.
　Reprinted in *Only Connect*, edited by Sheila Egoff and others (New York: Oxford University Press, 1965).

———. "The Librarians in Oz." *Saturday Review*, April 11, 1959.

Gardner, Martin, and Russel B. Nye. *The Wizard of Oz and Who He Was*. East Lansing: Michigan State University Press, 1957.

Gold, Lee B. "A Psychoanalytic Walk Down the Yellow Brick Road." *Journal of the Philadelphia Association for Psychoanalysis*, 1980.

Greene, David L., and Peter E. Hanff. *Bibliographia Oziana*. Kinderhook, Ill.: International Wizard of Oz Club, 1976.

Greene, David L., and Dick Martin. *The Oz Scrapbook*. New York: Random House, 1977.

Greene, Graham. Review of *The Wizard of Oz*. London *Spectator*, February 9, 1940.

Hamilton, Margaret. "There's No Place Like Oz." *Children's Literature*, Vol. 10 (1982).

Hearn, Michael Patrick. *The Annotated Wizard of Oz*. New York: Clarkson N. Potter, 1973.

Hearn, Michael Patrick, ed. *The Critical Heritage Series: The Wizard of Oz*. New York: Schocken Books, 1983.

Herbert, Stephen G. "The Metaphysical Wizard of Oz." *The Journal of Religion and Psychical Research*, January 1991.

Hudlin, Edward W. "The Mythology of Oz: An Interpretation." *Papers on Language and Literature*, Fall 1989.

Jackson, Shirley. "The Lost Kingdom of Oz." *The Reporter*, December 10, 1959.

Kopp, Shelden. "The Wizard Behind the Couch." *Psychology Today*, March 1970.

La Cassagnère, Christien. *Visages de l'angoisse*. Paris: Université Blaise-Pascal, 1989.
　Includes Alain Montandon's "Visages de l'angoisse dans l'univers de Frank Baum."

Lanes, Selma G. *Down the Rabbit Hole*. New York: Atheneum, 1971.

Leach, William. *Land of Dreams: Merchants, Power, and the Rise of a New American Culture*. New York: Pantheon Books, 1993.

L. Frank Baum—The Wonderful Wizard of Oz. New York: Columbia University Libraries, 1956.
　Exhibition catalogue, with an introduction by Roland Baughman and descriptive notes by Baughman and Joan Baum.

Littlefield, Henry M. "The Wizard of Oz: Parable on Populism." *American Quarterly*, Spring 1964.

A slightly expanded version of this article appeared in *The American Culture*, edited by Hennig Cohen (Boston: Houghton Mifflin, 1968).

Luers, Robert B. "L. Frank Baum and the Land of Oz: A Children's Author as Social Critic." *Nineteenth Century*, Fall 1980.

McMaster, Juliet. "The Trinity Archetype in *The Jungle Book* and *The Wizard of Oz*." *Children's Literature*, Vol. 20 (1992).

McReynolds, Douglas J., and Barbara J. Lips. "A Girl in the Game: *The Wizard of Oz* as Analog for the Female Experience in America." *North Dakota Quarterly*, Winter 1986.

Magder, David. "*The Wizard of Oz*: A Parable of Brief Psychotherapy." *Canadian Journal of Psychiatry*, November 1980.

Marling, Karal Ann. *Civil Rights in Oz; Images of Kansas in American Popular Culture*. Lawrence, Kans.: University of Kansas, 1997.

Matthews, Gareth B. *Philosophy and the Child*. Cambridge, Mass.: Harvard University Press, 1980.

Mitrokhina, Xenia. "The Land of Oz in the Land of the Soviets." *Children's Literature Association Quarterly*, Winter 1996–1997, pp. 183–88.

Moore, Raylyn. *Wonderful Wizard, Marvelous Land*. Bowling Green, Ohio: Bowling Green University Popular Press, 1974.

Morena, Gita Dorothy. *The Wisdom of Oz*. San Diego: Inner Connections Press, 1998.

Moser, Barry. *Forty-seven Days to Oz*. West Hatfield, Mass.: Pennyroyal Press, 1985.

Nathanson, Paul. *Over the Rainbow: The Wizard of Oz as a Secular Myth of America*. Albany: State University of New York Press, 1991.

Papanikolas, Zeese. *Trickster in the Land of Dreams*. Lincoln and London: University of Nebraska Press, 1995.

Pattrick, Robert R. *Unexplored Territory in Oz*. Kinderhook, Ill.: International Wizard of Oz Club, 1963.

Payne, David. "*The Wizard of Oz*: Therapeutic Rhetoric in Contemporary Media Ritual." *Quarterly Journal of Speech*, February 1989.

Peary, Gerald, and Roger Shatzkin, eds. *The Classic American Novel and the Movies*. New York: Frederick Ungar, 1974.
Includes Janet Juhnke's "A Kansan's View."

Petrovskii, Miron. *Knigi nashego detstva*. Moscow: Kniga, 1986.

Prentiss, Ann E. "Have You Been to See the Wizard?" *The Top of the News*, November 1, 1970.

Rahn, Suzanne. *The Wizard of Oz: Shaping an Imaginary World*. New York: Twayne Publishers, 1998.

Reckford, Kenneth J. *Aristophanes' Old-and-New Comedy*. Vol. 1. Chapel Hill and London: University of North Carolina Press, 1987.

Riley, Michael O. *Oz and Beyond*. Lawrence: University Press of Kansas, 1997.

Ritter, Gretchen. "Silver Slippers and a Golden Cap: L. Frank Baum's *The Wonderful Wizard of Oz* and Historical Memory in American Politics." *Journal of American Studies*, Vol. 31 (1997).

Robb, Stewart. "The Red Wizard of Oz." *New Masses*, October 4, 1938.

Rockoff, Hugo. "The 'Wizard of Oz' as a Monetary Allegory." *Journal of Political Economy*, August 1990.

Rogers, Katharine. "Liberation for Little Girls." *Saturday Review*, June 17, 1972.

Rushdie, Salman. *The Wizard of Oz*. London: BFI, 1992.

Rushmore, Howard. " 'Wizard of Oz' Excellent Film for Young and Old." *The Daily Worker,* August 18, 1939.

Sackett, S. J. "The Utopia of Oz." *The Georgia Review*, Fall 1961.

St. John, Thom. "L. Frank Baum: Looking Back at the Promised Land." *Western Humanities Review*, Winter 1982.

Sale, Roger. "L. Frank Baum and Oz." *Hudson Review*, Winter 1972–1973.
Revised and reprinted in *Fairy Tales and After* (Cambridge, Mass.: Harvard University Press, 1978).

Schreiber, Sandford. "A Filmed Fairy Tale as a Screen Memory." *The Psychoanalytic Study of the Child*, Vol. 29, (1974).

Schuman, Samuel. "Out of the Fryeing Pan and into the Pyre: Comedy, Mirth and *The Wizard of Oz*." *Journal of Popular Culture*, Fall 1972.

Starrett, Vincent. "The Wizard of Oz." *Chicago Sunday Tribune Magazine*, May 2, 1954.
Reprinted in *Best Loved Books of the Twentieth Century* (New York: Bantam, 1955).

Street, Douglas. "The Wonderful Wiz That Was: The Curious Transformation of *The Wizard of Oz*." *Kansas Quarterly*, Summer 1984.

Thurber, James. "The Wizard of Chit[t]enango." *The New Republic*, December 12, 1934.

Tuerk, Richard. "Dorothy's Timeless Quest." *Mythlore*, Autumn 1990.

Vidal, Gore. "On Rereading the Oz Books." *The New York Review of Books*, October 13, 1977.

Wagenknecht, Edward. *As Far as Yesterday*. Norman: University of Oklahoma Press, 1968.

———. *Utopia Americana*. Seattle: University of Washington Book Store, 1929.

Watt, Lois Belfield. "L. Frank Baum: The Widening

World of Oz." *The Imprint of the Stanford Libraries Associates*, October 1979.

About W. W. Denslow

The American Book Collector, December 1964.
Most of the material of this special Denslow number originally appeared in *The Baum Bugle* (Autumn and Christmas 1963 and Spring 1964).

Armstrong, Leroy. "W. W. Denslow, Illustrator." *The Home Magazine* (of New York), October 1898.

The Baum Bugle, Autumn 1963, Autumn 1972, and Autumn 1992.

Bowles, J. M. "Children's Books for Children." *Brush and Pencil*, September 1903.

"Chronicle and Comment" (column). *The Bookman*, October 1909.

Crissey, Forrest. "William Wallace Denslow." *Carter's Monthly*, March 1898.

Decker, Harrison. "An Artist Outdoors." *Outdoors*, September 1904.

"Denslow: Denver Artist, Originator of Scarecrow and Tin Man." Denver *Republican*, September 4, 1904.

"Denver Artist Rules an Island." Denver *Republican*, January 17, 1904.

Gangloff, Deborah. *The Artist, the Book, and the Child*. Lockport: Illinois State Museum, Lockport Gallery, 1989.

Goudy, Frederic W. *A Half-Century of a Type Design, 1895–1946*. New York: Typophiles, 1946.

Greene, Douglas G. "W. W. Denslow: The Rock-Strewn Yellow Brick Road." *The Imprint of the Stanford Libraries Associates*, October 1979.

———. "W. W. Denslow Illustrator." *Journal of Popular Culture*, Summer 1973.

Greene, Douglas G., and Michael Patrick Hearn. *W. W. Denslow*. Mount Pleasant: Central Michigan University, Clarke Historical Library, 1976.

Hearn, Michael Patrick. "An American Illustrator and His Posters." *American Book Collector*, May–June 1982.

———. "W. W. Denslow, the Forgotten Illustrator." *American Artist*, May 1973.

———. *W. W. Denslow, The Other Wizard of Oz*. Chadds Ford, Pa.: Brandywine River Museum, 1996.

Lane, Albert. *Elbert Hubbard and His Work*. Worcester, Mass.: Blanchard Press, 1901.

"A Lover of Children Who Knows How to Make Them Laugh." Detroit *News*, September 13, 1903.

"Our Own Time" (column). *The Reader*, April 1907.

Penn, F. "Newspaper Illustrators: W. W. Denslow." *The Inland Printer*, January 1894.

Shay, Felix. *Elbert Hubbard of East Aurora*. New York: William H. Wise, 1926.

Snow, Jack. *Who's Who in Oz*. Chicago: Reilly & Lee, 1954.

Waldren, Charles W. "At Dinner with Denslow." Lewiston (Me.) *Saturday Journal Illustrated Magazine*, February 18, 1905.

———. "Mother Goose in a New Gown." Lewiston (Me.) *Saturday Journal Illustrated Magazine*, October 26, 1901.

———. "A Peep into Bohemia." Lewiston (Me.) *Saturday Journal Illustrated Magazine*, February 21–26, 1903.

Who Was Who in America, 1897–1942.